P9-CFP-152

Praise for
Reluctant Smuggler

"Devotees of classic romantic suspense will love Jill Elizabeth Nelson's *Reluctant Smuggler*. Lots of bad guys, a handsome fiancé, a cool chick who's not afraid to hunt for the truth, stolen artifacts, danger and delight, wedding plans and gangster schemes, it's all here. Desiree and Tony are expertly developed characters who are only larger than life when duty requires it. The rest of the time, they are just like the rest of us, and that makes them supremely likeable—and very deserving of this book's very satisfying ending."

—SUSAN MEISSNER, author of *Widows and Orphans*

"Author Jill Elizabeth Nelson delivers the goods in *Reluctant Smuggler*. Desiree Jacobs and Tony Lucano are daring, endearing protagonists portrayed in a lively and distinctive style sure to delight readers."

—KACY BARNETT-GRÁMCKOW, author of *The Genesis Trilogy*

"Jill Elizabeth Nelson's *Reluctant Smuggler* will steal your attention with its fast-paced action and your heart with its south-of-the-border romance. A real page-turner from a master writer."

—DIANN MILLS, author of *When the Nile Runs Red*

"Sassy security expert Desiree Jacobs faces her toughest challenge yet in *Reluctant Smuggler*. Not only is someone out to wreck Desi's business, she seems to have upset some very powerful bad guys whose influence reaches all the way from the Mexican underworld to her home in Boston. Jill Elizabeth Nelson delivers a fast-paced tale of danger, political intrigue, and a breathtaking dash through the jungles of Mexico. Blend all that with a satisfying touch of romance and the result is one terrific read."

—VIRGINIA SMITH, author of *Stuck in the Middle*,
Book 1 of the Sister-to-Sister Series

"Jill Elizabeth Nelson has crafted an amazing tale of international intrigue, pulse-pounding drama, and sacrificial love, as well as one exceptional story line. *Reluctant Smuggler* is a great read and highly recommended!"

—MARK MYNHEIR, homicide detective and author of
The Void

"*Reluctant Smuggler* is a must-read from romantic suspense author Jill Elizabeth Nelson! Security expert Desiree Jacobs will be sure to 'steal' your heart—all while she tries to track down art thieves in the exotic jungles of Mexico's Yucatan Peninsula. *Reluctant Smuggler* takes readers on the ultimate adventure—in love, in faith, and in danger! It's just my kind of book."

—CHRISTY BARRITT, author of the Squeaky Clean
Mystery Series

"What a ride! *Reluctant Smuggler* has everything—intrigue, adventure, exotic locations, wonderful characters, and through it all, the knowledge that God's grace is sufficient. Jill Elizabeth Nelson has just become one of my very favorite authors."

—DEANNA JULIE DODSON, author of *In Honor Bound*

"Take one exotic location, add a beautiful woman, a dedicated FBI agent, a few missing artifacts, and mix at high speed and you have one nonstop thrill ride that will have you flipping the pages late into the night. Just when you think it couldn't possibly get any worse, Jill Nelson manages to turn the heat up on her wonderful characters. You'll find yourself gasping more than once and quickly turning the page to see how it turns out."

—WANDA DYSON, critically acclaimed author of
The Shefford-Johnson Case Files

RELUCTANT
SMUGGLER

TO CATCH A THIEF / BOOK THREE

JILL ELIZABETH NELSON

MULTNOMAH
BOOKS

RELUCTANT SMUGGLER
PUBLISHED BY MULTNOMAH BOOKS
12265 Oracle Boulevard, Suite 200
Colorado Springs, Colorado 80921
A division of Random House Inc.

The characters and events in this book are fictional, and any resemblance to actual persons or events is coincidental.

ISBN: 978-1-59052-688-0

Copyright © 2008 by Jill Elizabeth Nelson

All rights reserved. No part of this book may be reproduced or transmitted in any form or by any means, electronic or mechanical, including photocopying and recording, or by any information storage and retrieval system, without permission in writing from the publisher.

MULTNOMAH is a trademark of Multnomah Books, and is registered in the U.S. Patent and Trademark Office. The colophon is a trademark of Multnomah Books.

Library of Congress Cataloging-in-Publication Data
Nelson, Jill Elizabeth.
    Reluctant smuggler : a novel / Jill Elizabeth Nelson. — 1st ed.
        p. cm.— (To catch a thief ; bk. 3)
    ISBN 978-1-59052-688-0
1. Art thefts—Fiction. I. Title.
    PS3614.E44585R46 2008
    813'.6—dc22
                        2007034049

Printed in the United States of America
2008—First Edition

10 9 8 7 6 5 4 3 2 1

To the International Justice Mission (IJM)
and other ministries that work tirelessly
to fight enslavement and abuse
of the vulnerable throughout the world.

ACKNOWLEDGMENTS

*L*ove and gratitude to my dear husband, Doug, whose steadfast encouragement supplies the wind beneath my wings.

And heartfelt thanks to my delightful crit buds: Donita K. Paul, Sharon Hinck, Linda Wichman, and Virginia Smith, who hold my feet to the fire.

Special thank-yous to experts who offered their unique knowledge to supply and verify details for this novel: Larry Grong, MD; Ronda Wells, MD; Karen Tilbury, Dietary Supervisor; Rod Martin, Technology Expert; world traveler Virginia Smith; and indispensable language advisors Jim and Paulette Harris, Lee Carver, Ruth Axtell Morren, Gina Conroy, and Paul Hawley. Any errors or absurdities are mine.

Many hugs to my children and extended family of parents, siblings, and their families, and my church family, who form an enthusiastic cheering section.

Highest honor and respect go to my excellent editors, Lisa Ham and Julee Schwarzburg, who provide the polish to my prose. Grateful thanks to Liz Johnson, Multnomah publicist, who impresses me constantly with her faithfulness and service.

And to my Lord Jesus Christ, whom I adore and wish only to serve with my writing or any other way He inspires.

AUTHOR'S NOTE

While I am aware that security companies do not normally make a business practice of staging thefts, the notion makes for fun fiction. Chichén Itzá is one of many fascinating ancient ruins in Mexico; however, the cenote scenario is pure fabrication. Do not bring your snorkeling gear! I snuck in a bit of literary license at the Temple of Kukulcan. I believe tourists are no longer allowed to climb the steps due to liability issues, but I could hardly ditch the opportunity for a great scene full of pathos, humor, and romance! The Museo de Arte Mejicana is a fictitious representation of the variety of fine museums in Mexico City. The Fraternidad de la Garra (Brotherhood of the Claw) is my invention, but it's based on a very real, ultravicious, and widespread international gang, the Mara Salvatrucha (also known as the MS-13).

One

*D*esiree Jacobs deadpanned a steady look below the eye of a security camera in the world-famous Museo de Arte Mejicana, an ornate building embedded in the heart of Mexico's capital city. Her gaze held on the Alfredo Ramos Martínez painting in front of her, a colorful rural scene depicting native women carrying sacks of produce on their backs. *That's it, Señor Camera. Take a good film of this browsing* turista, *because mousy Myra is all you'll see.*

"*Señores* and *señoras*, we will move on to the work of Francisco Goitia," the tour guide said. "Not as well known as others, he was still one of the great Mexican painters of the last century. Goitia reflected the heart of his people with great love and passion."

The guide went on with her spiel, and Desi trailed the group like an obedient tourist. Her flat-footed, slump-shouldered gait helped her fall farther and farther behind. The group disappeared around a corner, and Desi stopped beside a custodial closet.

Heart rate quickening, she glanced both ways. All clear. She pulled a pin from beneath her gray wig and worked the lock. A moment later, she stepped into the closet and shut the door. Standing in the dark, she smiled. No one in the tour group would miss the dowdy little nobody who never said a word and avoided eye contact.

Desi shrugged out of her backpack, a big no-no for a visitor to haul around in a museum. But a ruckus in the foyer, caused by a street person only too willing to earn a fistful of pesos, had helped her melt into the tour group before anyone could demand she check her bag at the desk. Not even the tour guide had given mousy Myra a second glance since. Hopefully the hungry-looking begger she hired had made good his escape from the irate museum staff so he could enjoy his well-gotten gains.

Grinning, Desi got to work removing her frumpy clothes, wig, and blue contact lenses.

If she and Max had miscalculated on the smallest detail, those dirty, rotten Greybecks would score big again. Her jaw clenched. That couldn't happen. Her future—and the futures of those who trusted her—depended on success.

Dad, I won't let you down. He wasn't alive to defend himself. She was his legacy. His hope. Tonight's heist, and the aftermath, would redeem his reputation.

Desi pulled her knees up to her chest and rested her chin on them. What would Daddy have done while biding his time in the dark? She knew.

Pray.

—⁓—

At midnight, snug inside the ventilation duct, Desiree peered from the vent through night-vision goggles that bathed the darkened museum showroom in a surreal greenish glow. Her gaze focused on a display case containing the golden headdress of Pakal, mightiest of the ancient Mayan kings. This single item, dating from a few centuries after Christ, was the pride and joy of the Museo de Arte Mejicana.

Not for long.

"You are *mine*, Your Majesty," Desi murmured in south-of-the-border Spanish.

Behind the mask over her mouth, the words echoed hollowly. She'd practiced for hours to breathe right without the need to think about it—inhaling through her nose and exhaling through her mouth. Tubes from her mask trailed over her shoulders and sent the lung-warmed air down the shaft, away from the vent opening.

In the showroom, the SmartSensor hunted for an infrared heat signature larger than a mouse. She might be small, but a mouse she wasn't. Her breathing apparatus allowed her to move close enough to shut the system down.

Desi checked her watch. A few more seconds and… Okay, time. The first of a series of stink bombs should have gone off elsewhere in the museum, drawing the security guard from the control room to check out the smell. Now she had ten, maybe fifteen minutes, while he chased the elusive scent from one site to the next, like an odorous animal scampering ahead of him.

Elbows clamped to her sides in the enclosed space, she wiggled a thin box out of the breast pocket of her jumpsuit. Max's Miracle, Desi had dubbed the gadget, brainchild of the best accomplice a thief could ever have. Clayton Greybeck, the electronics expert for Greybeck and Sons Security Company, might consider himself a techno-god and the Casanova of geekdom, but Desi knew a West Texas ranch girl named Maxine Webb who could think rings around him. Too bad Max had to sit this caper out. A sick kid and urgent damage-control projects had kept her home in Boston. Desi was solo on this one, but their plan was foolproof.

Maybe. She swallowed. It had to be.

She flipped the gadget on and pointed the lighted end at the dual-action motion detector/heat sensor on the other side of the room. The pinprick of light danced around the unit. Man, it was hard to aim in the cramped conditions. Desi's breathing rasped, and a drop of sweat filmed her vision. She set the gadget down, lifted her goggles, and wiped her eyes with the back of her sleeve.

"You've got one chance to hit the target spot-on," Max had said. *"Then the lithium battery's dry, and you're toast."*

Well, she'd be toast anyway if she fooled around any longer. She scooped up the gadget, pointed, and blasted. A pop and a little puff of smoke came from the sensor box. No more heat or motion detector. Desi grinned. Amazing what a pulse of electromagnetic energy could do.

Desi tugged on a rope attached to her waist, and a cordless hot knife slid into her fingers. She fired up the knife and sliced through the bolts holding the vent cover in place. The grill clattered to the marble floor, and Desi's heart kabumped. *Easy now, girl.* The guard should be out of earshot, chasing smells at the other end of the building. A museum ought to have two night guards, but the board of directors liked to pinch pesos. Good deal for her tonight. Hard to say whether that would hold true tomorrow.

She lowered a nylon rope through the opening. A yank proved the line held fast on a joint inside the duct. Desi squirmed onto her back, pulled her torso out, and slapped a pair of short-handled suction cups onto the wall on either side of the vent. She hauled the rest of her body out of the duct, and then released the cup handles. Her feet met the floor, impact flowing through her body, familiar as a routine dismount from the parallel bars.

A security camera in the corner watched every move, transmitting it to the empty control room. Desi waved at the electronic eye. No one would watch the footage until the theft was discovered, and with her mask and goggles on, they couldn't make identification.

A tug on another line brought her pack out of the vent. She removed two wooden sticks an inch thick and eighteen inches long, one of them fitted with a lever, and screwed them together. Next she took out a square of plastic framed with cord, unfolded it to its full three-foot by three-foot size, and attached it to the handle. The resulting object resembled an oversized butterfly net, using plastic instead of gauze, and with a cord and hollow tube sticking out at the spot where the plastic joined the handle. But this was no insect catcher. It was a history-maker.

Smiling behind her mask, Desi took her net and her backpack and stepped up to the case that displayed the bust of a dusky-skinned Mayan. A skull piece of beaten gold hugged the statue's head, and above it arched a golden cornhusk encrusted with jewels—a tribute to the nourishing golden grain the Mayans had worshiped more than the metal. Magnificent!

Desi itched to step up and grab, but that would be a fatal mistake. Four tiny red eyes guarded the case—wireless heat sensors. If a gawker got too close, alarms went off. Desi tugged on neoprene gloves, and then pulled a metal canister like a mini fire extinguisher from her pack. She attached the nozzle to the tube on the net.

From a safe distance, she lowered the plastic over the case and pulled the lever on the handle. The net snicked shut like a noose over the case. Desi turned a knob on the metal canister and released gas at a temperature of ninety degrees below zero. The glass instantly iced over. So did the heat sensors. They'd be out of commission for just long enough.

Moving quickly now, Desi released the lever, loosened the suction, and pulled the plastic net off the case. She worked her pick in the lock, and a click signaled release. The gloves protected her hands as she took the cover from the pedestal. Pulse throbbing, she lifted the headdress from the model Mayan.

Heavens! The mighty Pakal would have needed mighty neck muscles to support his crown. Hugging the headdress with one arm, she took a padded bag from her pack and eased the antiquity inside. She put the bag into her pack on top of her Myra disguise.

From the looted case, the bare head of the Mayan pouted at her with thick lips and cold eyes. A shiver darted down her spine.

"Sorry, buddy," she whispered. "Let's see if we can fix you up."

She took a chip from her pocket, placed it on his head, and pressed a button. The crown of Pakal appeared on the model's head. Desi pulled her hand back through the hologram. Quickly she fitted the cover on the pedestal and retreated. Exhilaration sang in her veins.

The headdress was hers!

Not if she didn't skedaddle pronto. Was the guard still chasing stink? She checked her watch, and her heart stuttered. He could be headed back to the control room right now.

Desi shoved her equipment and backpack into a corner out of sight of the security camera, which was trained on the Pakal case. She slung the heavy sack containing the crown onto her shoulders and shinnied up the rope to the vent opening. Grunting, she stuffed the pack into the hole and followed it fast.

She plunged into the pitch darkness of the ductwork. Here, even her night-vision goggles were nearly blind. Smooth metal passed beneath her stomach, punctuated by seam bands.

Her nose tickled. *Ah-choo!* The sound echoed, and she froze. *Please, God, don't let the guard hear that.* Clenching her jaw, she crawled on.

Where was that left turn? She passed her hand along the duct wall. She was supposed to come to it before she reached the vent in the custodial closet where she'd waited. If she missed the turn, she'd have to push backward and find it. Not fun in this cracker box. Good thing she wasn't claustrophobic.

Her hand passed into air.

Desi stuffed the crown into the opening, and it jammed tight. Great! She tugged the bag, but it didn't budge. Double great! The duct she was supposed to follow out of the building must be smaller than the one she was in. The schematic she and Max had used to plan the caper had shown it as older, but the drawing hadn't mentioned that the older ductwork was also narrower. Even if she got the crown loose, she wouldn't fit into the opening herself. Triple great!

Plan B. Desi closed her eyes and concentrated on recalling the building plans. If she continued down this passage, where would she end up?

Her thoughts scurried like mice in a maze. What was the matter with her? A sound like a rushing wind filled her head, and the atmosphere closed in. Heavy. Dark. She could die here. Never see light again.

Sucking air through her nose, her mind cleared. She ripped the mask off and flung it away, along with the useless goggles. No wonder she couldn't think. After that sneeze, she'd started breathing in through her mouth, getting mostly her own exhaled carbon dioxide from the tubes down her back. She could have killed herself without realizing what she was doing.

Buckle down, woman. First order of business—get the crown unstuck, and that would take old-fashioned elbow grease. Desi jerked and tugged. How had she jammed the antiquity so tightly into the small space? Poor judgment—no doubt a side effect of her near asphyxiation. She gave a mighty yank. With a crack and a rip, the pack sprang free. Her mouth went dry. She'd better not have damaged the headdress.

No time to speculate. Now that her mind was clear, she knew this duct would take her to the elevator shaft, where she could climb to the roof and then leave the building via the fire escape. Not as clear-cut as a short crawl to the rear workroom where she could disable a simple alarm and walk out the back door, pretty as you please, but it would have to do.

Thirty minutes later, Desi's feet left the last rung of the fire escape and touched the packed dirt of a deserted alley outside the museum building. Mexico City's cool January air refreshed her lungs. Stillness enfolded her as she gazed toward the velvet blackness of a sky populated with fading stars. This was the magic time before dawn, when even the cantina music had fallen silent.

Tension melted from her muscles. She was a walking dust bunny and could stand under a hot shower for a week, but she'd done it—beaten the Greybeck security system and grabbed the greatest prize of her career.

But had she damaged the piece during her exit? Her heart hit her toes. She pulled the padded bag from her pack and ran her hands over the crown's outline. No obvious deformities. Maybe she should get back to her hotel and check.

No, this couldn't wait. She was as private here as anywhere. Desi placed the bag on a crate where a shaft of light from a street lamp reached into the alley. Her fingers trembled on the drawstring, and her pulse throbbed.

If she'd harmed the headdress, she'd run shrieking into the street. She'd turn herself in at the nearest police station. She'd sell her home to pay for the repairs. She'd bow and kiss Clayton Greybeck's feet. *Blech!* She'd step down as head of HJ Securities. She'd…

Desi gaped at the flakes and chunks that slipped from the bag along with the headdress, minus the tip of one cornhusk leaf. Her jaw snapped shut. Flakes? She picked one up and tasted it. Paint! Chunks? She cradled one in her palm and examined it. Lead!

She gave a strangled cry. Those double-dealing, dastardly cowards. She'd spent days of planning and a sleepless, nerve-racking night to pilfer a piece of junk. Not to mention just about having heart failure when she thought she'd damaged a priceless antiquity.

Those Greybecks…no, wait. Not them—the museum board of directors. A tight smile stretched her lips. The stuffed shirts suspected she might get away with it, and they'd hedged their bets by making sure she wouldn't lay her hands on the real deal. A backhanded compliment if she ever heard of one. Worse, Greybeck and Sons must have been informed she was coming—a violation of the provisional contract with HJ Securities.

Desi stuffed the leaden fake into the bag, then swept the chunks and flakes into her palm and put them in the pocket of her jumpsuit opposite the one that held Max's miracle gadget. Let's see what the august gentlemen of the board had to say for themselves tomorrow—er, today. She glanced at her watch. A few hours remained to plan a suitable response, and—

"There she is!" a man grated in Spanish. "Get her!"

Desi whipped around to find three large shapes charging toward her up the alley. The menacing rhythm of booted feet sent her heart into overdrive.

"Run!" Did she holler that out loud? Yes, but it got her moving.

She grabbed the bag and backpack and tore up the alley. The leaden crown weighted her steps. Why not fling it at them? The worthless thing might do good damage. She clutched the bag. Too stubborn for her own good. A slingshot swing would work better if they got closer.

Desi burst onto the deserted street. To her right, voices shouted from the other end of the museum, followed by more galloping feet. She took off in the opposite direction. Canopied adobe buildings flashed past.

"Don't let her get away!"

Desi made out the words from the garble of frenzied Spanish behind her. What did these thugs want? Did they think she had the real headdress? Well, duh! Her blood chilled. Men would kill for the crown of Pakal.

She glanced over her shoulder. Five of them—and gaining on her. Desi's lungs burned. Bother this altitude! She wasn't used to 7,000-plus feet above sea level, and she couldn't run much longer. Correction. She couldn't run *any* longer.

Wheezing, Desi stopped and turned. The man in the lead faltered, and the others passed him. Smart fellow. She whirled the bag by the drawstring…faster…faster.

Her pursuers slowed. Streetlights bathed their looming figures, but she couldn't make out faces beneath dark clothing and ski masks. One of the men put up his hands—big hands, spatulate, with index fingers longer than the middle fingers. "Be careful, *señorita*."

She breathed in air heavy with spicy cooking scents from the closed restaurant beside her. "You want it? Go get it." She let go of the string, and the bag flipped end over end to land above their heads in the striped canopy over the entrance.

A collective groan came from her pursuers. They stared at the canopy.

Desi took off. Without the crown's weight, she could do the few hundred feet to her car. But only if they didn't chase her. Her energy meter had plunged into the wimp zone.

She dashed around a corner into an alley, leaped over the huddled form of a street beggar, and reached a private lot behind a building. Her breath caught. Where was her rental VW Bug? She'd paid good money to the manager for overnight parking. It better be…

There! Somebody had parked a hulking Mercedes beside it, blocking her view. She opened the Bug, threw her pack inside, and collapsed behind the wheel, pulse off the Richter scale.

Desi peeled out of the lot with nary a glimpse of her pursuers. Fine! She'd left them holding the bag. It was their own fault if they ended up with a two-ton sack of nothing.

Laughter bubbled up…until the tears came. All she had for all she'd done was a whole lot of nothing too.

Two

At five minutes to nine, Desi walked into the Museo de Arte Mejicana. The cavernous building extended a cold greeting—stiff marble columns, remote vaulted ceiling—and her low-heeled pumps echoed
on the tiled floors. The hint of a malodorous scent touched her nostrils.

She straightened her suit jacket and approached the reception desk.
After a crisp exchange, a frowning guard escorted Desi into a private
section of the museum. A grandfather clock chimed the hour as she
stepped into the meeting of the board of directors. The dozen men
around the conference table rose as one.

Squaring her shoulders, she met each pair of eyes in turn, finding
puzzlement here, resentment there, and amusement on one aquiline
face—the single person in the room she had assumed would offer her a
fair shake, Presidential Aide Esteban Corona. The aide looked away,
smoothing his salt-and-pepper mustache.

Jaw tight, Desi nodded to Fernando Vidal, the chairman of the
board, who stood at the head of the long oak table. Vidal's thick gray
hair put him on the upper side of fifty, but handsome with a sturdy
build and strong, even features. Smoky gaze cold and steady, the chairman nodded back, no smile, and waved toward the empty chair at the
opposite end.

Setting her briefcase on the floor, Desi assumed her seat, folded her
hands in front of her, and went still. The others in the room settled in,

and long seconds ticked past. Clothes rustled, throats cleared, and a pen tapped.

Chairman Vidal twisted the thick ring on his finger. "I understand congratulations are in order." His English carried a strong accent.

"Spanish, *por favor.* I am fluent."

"Very well." He consulted a piece of paper. "Early this morning our night guard discovered that the headdress of Pakal was gone." The chairman's eyes narrowed to slivers. "We demand the immediate return of our priceless antiquity."

Desi shook her head. "I don't have it, as you are aware."

Several board members leaped to their feet, and the room filled with a babble of voices.

Desi's spine stiffened. Didn't they know the headdress was a fake? But she no longer had the leaden lump of junk in order to prove it. HJ Securities could get blamed for losing a national treasure that wasn't real to begin with.

"Silence!" The chairman rose, glaring at her. "It was not you who took the artifact?"

"I took what was in the display case, but it wasn't the headdress of Pakal." Thankfully, her voice came out steadier than her insides.

Blank faces stared. Esteban Corona studied the table.

She pulled an envelope from her briefcase. "The headdress was made of this." She stood and dumped the envelope's contents into an empty ashtray. "Lead covered in gold paint. I assumed you substituted the forgery to prevent me from taking the real thing."

"You have the crown, and you plan to keep it," a shrill voice spat. "You're trying to trick us with those sprinkles of rubbish." The man's pointed goatee quivered. "The Greybecks warned us your father was involved in shady dealings. Like father, like daughter."

Furious voices rumbled around the table.

Hostility pounded her like mortar fire. Desi sank into her chair. Those awful rumors about her father. They cropped up like weeds planted by whispers from the Greybecks. She nipped one in the bud, then a dozen sprang up elsewhere—and she couldn't say the words that would chop them off for good. No one could ever know what had really happened eight months ago.

Desi pressed her fingers to the sides of her nose. This whole scenario had been a trap to destroy HJ Securities. A trap set by that conniving Randolph Greybeck and his double-dealing offspring Wilson and Clayton. Like father, like sons. Oh yes! And she'd walked into the snare, led by pride and thirst for revenge.

God, forgive me. God, save me. Somehow.

"Gentlemen, your attention please." A voice of calm rose above the angry tide. Heads turned toward Señor Corona. "Your outrage is understandable, but misplaced. If you wish to castigate anyone, it must be me...or perhaps our nation's president."

Indrawn breath hissed through many throats.

Corona arched a pale brow. "When the headdress was placed in this museum four years ago, *El Presidente* became concerned about its attraction for thieves. He authorized the display of a forgery, and the real crown was stored in the palace vault."

Relief bubbled in Desi's veins.

"You have condemned an innocent woman," the aide continued, "when you should affirm your chairman's too brief word of congratulations."

Vidal planted fists on the table. "Our first concern had to be the return of the crown."

"Our first concern must be the safety of every piece of national heritage in our care. That is why it is in our best interests to engage the most capable security company. Wasn't that the point of this exercise?"

Gazes dropped away. One examined his fingernails, another rubbed his chin.

Corona frowned. "Where is our administrator? Doesn't he attend our meetings?"

Vidal let out a heavy sigh, fingers unclenching. "I asked him to wait in another room with a representative of Greybeck and Sons."

Desi rose. Many things suddenly made sense. "May I inject a word here?"

Corona nodded. Vidal's nostrils flared. The other board members gaped at her as though she'd materialized from thin air.

Desi allowed herself a chilly smile. "Last night after I left the museum, five masked men chased me through the streets. Aware that the item I carried was worthless, I abandoned it, and they let me go. By the time I reached my hotel room, I had figured out who took the piece."

She gazed at the chairman. "Am I correct, Señor Vidal, that at your word, Administrator Ramírez and one or more of the Greybecks will step in, eager to return the crown of Pakal and reap the thanks of a grateful board?" She tapped her upper lip with her forefinger. "Oh, and prove the unfortunate carelessness of HJ Securities?"

The chairman's face went ruddy as excited comments flew around the room.

Corona clapped his hands, and the board members quieted. "Let us proceed with the next act. Call for your players, Vidal, but give them no cues. We wish to see how well they ad-lib."

Vidal and Corona exchanged glares. Then the chairman stalked to the door. He spoke in a low voice to the guard outside and returned to his seat, stiff shoulders radiating fury.

The clock ticked thirty seconds, and the door opened. A lean Hispanic man with a sharp profile entered, followed by a stocky, white-haired Anglo and his younger, white-blond clone, who carried a cloth bag. Administrator Ramírez, Randolph Greybeck, Clayton Greybeck, and the pseudo–Pakal headdress. All present and accounted for, except the weasely bean counter Wilson Greybeck. Maybe they had left him in the States. Just as well. That high-pitched snicker of his would drive Desi right over the edge today.

Clayton slanted Desi a look as he walked by. Did the louse wink at her? Her blood pressure spiked a fresh peak.

Ramírez murmured a greeting to the board and took a seat to the right of Chairman Vidal. The elder Greybeck shook hands with the chairman, and then settled in an empty chair near the middle of the table. A cigar peeked from his jacket pocket. Clayton grabbed a spot across from his father and set his bundle in front of him. The Greybecks smiled at Desi.

Placing her elbows on the table, she raised her forearms, rested her chin on the twined fingers of her hands, and twinkled back at them. Clayton's blond eyebrows lifted. *That's right, get a clue something's up.* But he probably wouldn't. Too sure they'd had the last laugh.

Chairman Vidal cleared his throat. "Ms. Jacobs succeeded in stealing the headdress on display in our showroom." He spoke in accented English to accommodate the Greybecks. "However, she did not succeed in keeping it." He nodded toward the bag. "Have I summarized correctly?" The chairman directed his question toward the elder Greybeck.

Randolph lifted a square chin, and the dimple in the middle flexed. "That is correct, if rather brief. Immediately after Ms. Jacobs exited the museum, a band of street thugs stole the priceless antiquity from her. In fact—" he glowered at her like a headmaster at an unruly student— "our witness claims she abandoned the piece to save herself."

A small titter greeted his remark, and Greybeck's thick lips spread in a smile. "Thanks to the vigilance of the night perimeter patrol we hired last week, the bandits never got the precious artifact in their hands before they were chased off by a warning gunshot. The patrolman came to our hotel and turned the piece over to me for safekeeping until this morning. And now—" he motioned toward the bag—"we have brought the crown home." He folded blunt-fingered hands across his paunch and gazed around like a lawyer resting his case with the jury.

"Intriguing tale." Señor Corona nodded. "But I believe there is a saying in America. It is time for *the rest of the story.*"

Vidal's cheeks sucked in like he'd bitten an unripe persimmon. "Proceed."

Corona studied the elder Greybeck. "We would like to see what you have returned to us."

"Wait!" Desi leaned forward. "May I ask a question?"

Board members nodded, faces bronzed with anticipation. Desi had sat through enough meetings to know when a group scented blood and didn't care whose it was as long as proceedings took an interesting turn. Evidently, Randolph Greybeck knew those kinds of meetings too. His gaze brooded on the padded sack.

"Ask away." Clayton grinned at Desi. "Unless you're wondering whether we checked to see that the crown is in here; then don't ask. We did."

Close, but he could forget about winning his daddy's cigar. "Did you take the crown out and examine it?"

"A peek inside the sack was sufficient."

"I don't think so." A slow burn filtered through her. The Greybecks didn't care about the heritage they protected, or they couldn't have slept until they examined the headdress.

Clayton worked the knot on the sack. In a few moments, the headdress gleamed golden on the table—except for the tip of one leaf, broken off and showing a dull pewter color.

Randolph lunged to his feet. "You Jezebel! You switched the crowns!"

A Bible analogy? Oh, that's right, the Greybecks took vocal pride in being fine, upstanding pew-warmers in the most prestigious church in New York.

Desi shook her head. "I can't accept that much credit, though I did know the crown was a forgery. Why else do you think I tossed it away for your hired thugs to go after instead of me?"

Clayton's steel-blue eyes widened, and then he laughed. "You and whose army was going to keep the *street bandits* from taking it away from you?"

"You'll just have to wonder about that." She clamped her jaw shut. Not totally gormless of him to sidestep her verbal trap.

The elder Greybeck crossed his arms. "Where is the headdress of Pakal?"

"Safe." Señor Corona ran a finger along his mustache. "Kindly sit down, sir. Ms. Jacobs fulfilled her commission, and your firm failed to stop her. That is the bottom line. This morning's posturing is mere theatrics."

Nods and mutters of assent traveled around the table but ended at Chairman Vidal, who studied the tabletop. The senior Greybeck spluttered and sank down. He pulled out his cigar, popped it in his mouth, took it out, and then twiddled it between his fingers like the classic comedian W. C. Fields, but minus the sense of humor.

Desi bottled a grin. She'd have to repent later for gloating. *But Lord, this does feel good.*

"Well, then." Vidal grimaced and sat tall. "I suggest that the security company representatives withdraw from the meeting so we might discuss this important decision."

"Agreed," said the man with the pointed goatee who had spoken harshly to Desi earlier. Now he offered a muted smile in her direction. "Who protects the priceless objects under our care is one of the gravest choices this board faces."

A bittersweet heaviness filled Desi. She lifted a hand. "If I may speak, Mr. Chairman?"

"So recognized." He jerked his chin.

She stood and surveyed the board. Many, but not all, returned her look with receptive eyes. "I gave this matter much thought between the wee hours of the morning and the time I stepped into this meeting. And I believe that it's in the best interests of all concerned that HJ Securities withdraw its bid for security services at the Museo de Arte Mejicana."

Señor Corona frowned. The corners of Señor Vidal's mouth tipped upward. Clayton's eyes bugged, and the senior Greybeck dropped his cigar into his lap. Too bad it wasn't lit.

"In the delicate matter of antiquities protection," Desi continued, "trust between museum management and the security company is vital. That element has been lacking from the start and was further eroded by the events of last night."

Administrator Ramírez sat forward. "Are you suggesting this museum didn't act in good faith?"

"What you make of my comment is between you and your conscience. But I remind you that informing the rival security company about your agreement with HJ Securities is a violation of the provisional contract."

The administrator sank back.

Desi hefted her briefcase. "It's obvious that your consideration of my firm for security services has thrown this board into disharmony. Not a profitable situation for any of us. Good day, gentlemen." She left them with their mouths open.

—⁂—

"Hey, sweetheart." Desi yawned into the receiver. Seated on the edge of the hotel bed, she glanced at the clock. Three hours under the covers, one of them trying to make her thoughts wind down and two of them actually sleeping, and then her cell phone rings. Good thing she wanted to hear from the person on the other end—her fiancé, Tony Lucano.

"Hey yourself, beautiful. I'm dogging it up the freeway through six inches of snow. Are you snoozing in the tropical sun? You sound on the shady side of asleep."

Desi grinned. "In the mountains around Mexico City, it doesn't get over seventy degrees Fahrenheit by the crack of noon this time of year, so I'm snoozing inside, thank you very much."

"Beats ten below."

She wandered to the window and parted the curtain on a sun-drenched day. "I've been sleeping off a successful night in the trenches, followed by a tense morning in the boardroom."

"Congratulations on the heist." Tony laughed. "Strange thing for an FBI agent to say, but you must've gotten the contract if you got the crown."

"Wouldn't sign on the dotted line for love nor money."

"They didn't treat you right? Who should I punch out for you, babe?"

"My hero!" A memory flickered—Tony's solid form slamming a kick into the chest of a motorcycle outlaw with bad intentions. Her agent-man was kidding now, but he'd done it for real a few months ago. No wonder he made her feel safe. "The list of deserving recipients is too long, starting with those rotten Greybecks. They pulled some shenanigans again but splattered more egg on their faces than mine. I wish I could have found ammunition to shoot down their smear campaign against HJ Securities, but I'm lucky to get out of here with no more damage done."

Tony snorted. "The Greybecks need to watch their step. Low business tactics have a way of turning around to bite the hand that deals them. I see it all the time."

"Reap what you sow. I'm counting on it, but it can't happen soon enough for me. Right now, I need to come home and collect a few comfort kisses."

"I'm the man for the job. When should I pick you up at Logan International?"

Desi's fingers itched to muss his black hair. She loved those coarse waves he hated. "My flight leaves in three hours. I've got a layover in Detroit, so I won't land in Boston until around ten tonight. Too late for you to pick me up?"

"Woman, nothing short of my pager could stop me, not even the weather. Hate to tell you, but this sky looks ready to dump another load."

Desi groaned. "Beantown in January. Let's hope my flight isn't delayed."

"Yeah, it's been too long already."

Three weeks and two days since she'd last seen the laugh lines crinkle around a pair of brown eyes that could x-ray straight through the crown of Pakal, but who was counting? Desi bit her lip against another protest about the extra committee duty that had taken Tony to Washington for a whole week. She was one to talk; the day he came home, urgent business had whisked her off to Pakistan, and now she'd wasted days in Mexico.

"Sore subject?" Tony prompted.

Desi let out a long breath. "There's a lot that needs to be worked out. I don't know…" She rubbed the back of her neck. Call her an idiot. The most magnificent male on earth wanted her for his wife, and she obsessed on issues she didn't have answers for.

"Getting cold feet about marrying me?" His tone weighed as much as the Boston sky.

"I can't wait to marry you! Besides, you're the one in wintry Massachusetts. My tootsies are warm in Mexico." He didn't laugh at her lame joke. She didn't blame him.

"Okay, here's the deal." Desi left the window and began pacing the carpet. "We want to be together, but it seems like we never are." She stopped at the wardrobe mirror and stared at her funky brunette bed-head, all knotty clumps and out-of-control spikes. Nice visual on the way her life was going right now. "We both love our jobs, but where do we draw the line so we can make a marriage? You just turned thirty-six, and I'm not that far behind. When are we going to put family first?"

"You're referring to my commitment to the Joint Terrorism Reorganization Committee. That assignment ends in two months. There's a difference between short term and never ending."

Youch! Desi plunked down in front of the desk and picked up an antique medallion attached to a thick chain. Emeralds dotted the large disk that filled her palm, the weight solid gold, not a speck of lead.

Solid gold—like Tony. "The bureau knows when it's got a good thing. Don't worry. There'll be a next project for Supervisory Special Agent Anthony Lucano. And you need to finish your thesis for your master's degree." She caught a low-voiced mutter at the other end. Something about an inability to say no herself. "Don't get your tie in a knot, handsome. My schedule is part of the problem. You think I should give up some of my responsibilities, but—"

"Not 'give up,' darlin'. Delegate. You're wearing yourself out."

"It's not only the job." She laid the medallion on the desk. "This wedding has me going in a bazillion directions, and we haven't even set a date."

Long sigh. "Where does that leave us?"

"Conflicted, but madly in love. Right now, I just want you to hold me."

"Ah, what diabolical torture. Bring it on."

"Torture?"

"You know what I mean."

"I do."

"Those're the words I want to hear from you, the sooner the better."

Desi laughed. "I promise we'll set a date and do this thing ASAP, even if it causes an international incident."

"A what?"

"You do know that Indians—and I mean India Indians—and Pakistanis can't stand each other. Well, while I was securing the safety of the crown jewels, the Pakistani prime minister, who I've known for years, decided that since I'm now an orphan I should be treated like a daughter to him and—"

"Invited himself to the wedding."

"Exactly."

"And the Maharaja Chakra Singh is coming out of gratitude for securing his pet archaeological dig. Didn't you say an Israeli government official and an Iraqi cultural affairs rep are on the list too?"

"Check."

"What a nightmare!"

"Y'know, for a G-man you're passably bright. Is it any wonder the seating arrangement keeps me up nights?" An odd series of snorts came back at her. "Tony, are you laughing?"

"Heaven forbid." *Snort.* "Say, I'm coming up on the Big Dig tunnel, and we're going to get cut off."

"Don't you dare pull a duck and run on me. You need to take this seriously. I—"

"…always take you seriously…hang in there…may have…solution…" The connection trailed away into dead air.

Desi scowled at her cell phone. She'd like to hear his grand wedding solution. Elope? Hah! The all-purpose male avoidance mechanism for tuxedos and reception lines. Forget it, buster! She wanted a church wedding with all the bells and whistles—well, lace and flowers.

And she wanted to wear satin and pearls and a flowing gossamer veil and glide up the aisle to the traditional wedding march. But most of all she wanted something she could never, ever have. Desi sank down on the edge of the bed.

Daddy, you were supposed to…

An ache blossomed under her breastbone. Her lower lip trembled, but she sucked it in and leaped to her feet. Time for a shower. No time for bawling like a baby, because that's what would happen if she let the dam break.

—⁓—

An hour later, clean and dressed in a Spanish skirt and blouse, Desi plunked the last of her clothes into a suitcase. The taxi should arrive in about five minutes. Three measured raps sounded on the door. Hotel staff to say her taxi was here early? No, they'd use the phone.

She opened the door to the end of its chain and peeked out. Tall, blond, and husky, Clayton Greybeck grinned at her. His orange polo shirt hugged weightlifter's hills and valleys like it was painted on. A musclebound geek. What was this world coming to?

"Aren't you going to invite me in?" Clayton's grin dimmed by the smallest degree.

"No."

He glanced up and down the hall. A chatting couple meandered past. "You might not want passersby to hear our conversation."

Desi slammed the door, undid the chain, and flung the door wide. "Keep it brief."

She held on to the doorknob while he sauntered around the room, gaze wandering. Not much to see since she was packed, except…oh, bother, the medallion sat out in plain sight. She'd hoped for a call from an antiquities dealer before she left. Hadn't happened. Another disappointment from a fruitless trip.

Desi cleared her throat. "You had a purpose in coming here?"

Clayton leaned a hip against the desk. "Waiting for you to close the door."

She checked her watch. "My taxi will be here in two minutes, so talk or leave."

"How did you guess about the guys who took back the Pakal—er, the fake headdress?"

"Pu-lease! A Mercedes parked next to my VW Bug? Had to be Greybecks around."

"You're the best cat burglar in the world. I mean it." He crossed his arms, and his biceps rippled. Was she supposed to be impressed? "Couldn't say that in front of Dad, though. He would've had my hide. What's left of it after you almost got away with the headdress."

"Should I feel sorry for you?"

"You're a hard woman, Desiree Jacobs." His gaze fastened on the medallion.

"Don't touch and don't ask."

Clayton stalked toward her, and her stomach clenched.

He stopped inches from her. The Kirk Douglas chin dimple flexed. "How come you never gave us a chance? We could be working with each other instead of against."

"HJ Securities has never worked *against* Greybeck and Sons. We compete with your firm for bids, but we leave the dirty tricks department to you. As far as you and me on a personal level?" She held the door wider. "I'm ashamed to admit it took me three whole dates to figure out that if I ever let you charm me to the altar, I'd be an acquisition, not a partner."

The jerk smiled like the Cheshire cat. "You think I'm charming? There's hope!"

"Oh, good grief, Clayton, you missed the point, as usual. Plus I'm engaged to an FBI agent who'd be delighted to kick your arrogant tail to Antarctica." She flashed her ring at him. "Be content with keeping your contract at the Museo de Arte Mejicana."

His smile crumpled. "They gave us the boot. Went with some local company. Who knew there was a third bidder? So I guess the U.S. is out of the security business in Mexico City, and the greasers stick together." He laughed.

Desi's free hand fisted. Why had she ever gone on one date with this guy, let alone three?

He shook his head. "Sheesh, Des! Lighten up. It was a joke."

In a pig's eye, like Max would say. "I'm leaving for the airport."

"I'm gone." Clayton stepped into the hallway, and she shut the door.

Almost. He stuck his foot in the gap and poked his head inside. "Engaged isn't married." He winked and pulled his foot away.

Desi slammed the door and squealed. She should have punched the creep in the nose when she had the chance. Marching over to the bed, she grabbed her suitcase and snatched up her carry-on. Almost to the exit, she halted. The medallion! She tucked it in her skirt pocket.

A knock sounded.

That idiot Greybeck! She blew through her nostrils and yanked open the door. "Clayton, you crumb... Oh." She blinked into the wide-eyed face of Señor Corona.

The presidential aide tendered a small bow. "We realize the inconvenience of the request, señorita, but President Fernando Montoya would be grateful if you would accept his invitation to meet with him. A limousine awaits your response."

Desi's jaw flopped open. How could she refuse a summons from the president of a sovereign nation? She couldn't. But oh, she didn't want to go anywhere except home.

With the sense of stepping into darkness when she should be running toward the light, she followed Señor Corona out of the hotel.

Three

*D*esi's tongue burned to ask why the president wanted to see her, but small talk dominated the short drive through noisy city streets. The limo glided into Chapultepec Park. Families and couples strolled paths between sculpted hedgerows and fountains.

They came to a high stone wall, and the guarded gate swung wide. Soon a massive building loomed. The red, white, and green Mexican flag flew from a flat roof. Los Pinos, residence of the presidents since 1938. The car slid past the imposing structure.

Señor Corona smiled. "For the sake of confidentiality, El Presidente would prefer to meet with you in one of the cottages."

The limo whispered to a halt in front of an ornate rancho-style building. The single-story structure must cover half an acre, agleam with windows and capped with a red-tiled roof. Some cottage! Why did the president of Mexico want to keep their meeting a secret? If this were the movies, she could be Debbie Reynolds to the mustachioed Ricardo Montalban look-alike next to her. And this would be a convent, like in the classic 1960s movie *The Singing Nun*. Too bad this was real life, and she was headed into a den of political intrigue.

Desi followed Señor Corona through a wrought-iron gate into a courtyard, where they entered the house through an arched doorway. The aide led her down a carpeted corridor into a room flooded with light from a generous window. A Salvador Dalí sculpture of an angel blowing a trumpet stood on a side table, and a Jose Velasco painting hung on the wall above a settee.

The aide gestured toward the settee. "Please, be comfortable. El Presidente will be with you in a few minutes."

Desi perched on the edge of the cushion. "May I know what this is about?"

"Mutual interests. More than that, I cannot say." Corona bowed and then left.

Desi walked to the window and looked out on a cement patio. The sun was at its zenith, the sky a clear blue. She should be ready to fly into that limitless expanse. Instead, she was grounded on a murky errand far from friendly faces and a familiar environment. Sadness draped her shoulders like an invisible mantilla.

What was the matter with her? Setbacks and challenges used to exhilarate her. Maybe she was just exhausted from the stress of an impending wedding and hostile business competitors.

Her hand brushed her skirt and found the lump of the ancient necklace. She pulled it out. The emeralds glinted in the sunlight, especially the large one in the upper right quadrant. Not a woman's ornament, yet it had been found near a weathered female skull.

A throat cleared, and she turned to find a compact man gazing at her with fierce dark eyes. Thick white hair capped a square face. He stood little more than five and a half feet tall, but his husky frame filled out a pair of pale chinos and a print shirt, creating an illusion of size. Or maybe the illusion came from innate dignity. Fernando Montoya, elected head of the United Mexican States.

Desi slipped the medallion into her pocket and stepped forward, hand extended. "*Buenas tardes*, Señor Presidente."

Montoya gripped the offered hand. "Welcome to Mexico, Señorita Jacobs. Has anyone spoken those words to you yet?"

Desi shook her head.

"Pity." The president frowned. "We are a warm people." He guided them toward the furniture and took a seat in a stuffed chair. Desi resumed her place on the settee.

"A lovely place to visit for a holiday…or perhaps a honeymoon?" He nodded toward her left hand.

Desi let out a grudging laugh. "I've been to Mexico a number of times. During college, I toured archaeological sites for a whole summer. Many wonderful memories."

The president beamed. "I love my country, señorita, and for this reason you are here today." His smile faded. "I knew your father. Hiram Jacobs impressed me with his integrity and attention to detail."

Her breathing quickened. "When did you meet Dad?"

"He designed the security system for Los Pinos, this building, and the grounds."

She did some mental calculations. "That was seven years ago. You weren't the president."

"True, but I was on the committee that hired your company for design-only services at the palace and the presidential home. I was also on the board of directors of the Museo de Arte Mejicana the year we contracted with Greybeck and Sons. A regrettable choice that went against my arguments, but the rest of the board saw the lower bid and not the better reputation."

"The Greybecks are doing their best to undermine that reputation."

"Of this I am aware." He pulled a folded sheet of paper from his shirt pocket.

She took the paper and opened it. "A copy of an e-mail sent this morning from Randolph Greybeck to Ed Bayne, his publicity director in New York. How did you get this?"

Montoya's expression flattened.

"No matter." Desi lifted a hand. "It's useful to have my suspicions confirmed that e-mail sent from a hotel connection may be monitored." Her gaze returned to the message, and her jaw tightened.

Ed, reword this into something appropriate for an interoffice memo to high-level Greybeck staff, but omit the quote from me. Then use the usual channels to leak the memo to the press, along with the quote, as if the source overheard a private conversation between Wilson and me.

Media manipulation. No surprise there.

Desi scanned the title of the memo. "Pakal Headdress Recovered from Bungled Theft." Her teeth ground together. *Unethical* didn't begin to describe these bottom feeders. She moved on into the body of the message.

We did it! The attempted theft of the priceless headdress of the Mayan King Pakal from the Museo de Arte Mejicana in Mexico City, Mexico, ended in triumph for the home team. Due to foresight and precautions taken by our staff, the would-be thief scampered off empty-handed, and I was able to personally restore the museum's property to the thanks of the Mexican government. Once again, we've proven ourselves the premier security company in the world.

A growl escaped Desi's throat. "Scampered! I'll scamper all over this pack of lies. Did the man attend the same meeting I did?"

Montoya grimaced. "I often ask myself that question in the course of my duties."

Desi absorbed the next words.

Greybeck and Sons' performance assured that the covert bidding tactics of HJ Securities would not steal the contract with the Museo de Arte Mejicana. Desiree Jacobs flew home from Mexico with nothing to show for large amounts of effort and expense. Keep up the good work.

Now here's the quote, Ed: "I have a bad feeling about the bottom line of HJ Securities under Ms. Jacobs's direction. In the eight months since her father's death, I've noticed changes in policy and approach that may run her firm into the ground."

Desi surged to her feet, crinkling the paper in her fist. "This is personal. The Greybecks have spread rumors and half-truths about HJ Securities, but they've never directed a personal attack. They're desperate. The rumor mill hasn't been doing the job fast enough. Now they're flying just under the radar of a libel suit." She tapped her upper lip. "I wonder what's going on behind the scenes at Greybeck and Sons to cause such panic."

The president bellowed a laugh. "What an extraordinary young woman. Despite high emotion, you see into the heart of matters. I believe I have made the right choice."

"What choice, Señor Presidente? You didn't bring me here to share information you could have faxed to my office or ignored. What does rivalry between security companies mean to you?" She held up the piece of trash in her hand. "You could refute this to the public."

Montoya shook his head. "I'm sorry, señorita. I cannot risk the people becoming aware that a national treasure is a fake. It would call into question all of our antiquities on display."

"But you have the genuine article in the palace vault. Surely, such a reassurance would satisfy your countrymen."

The president gave a small shake of the head.

"Do you mean you don't want to tell people the real treasure sits in the palace vault? Or do you mean you don't have it at all?"

"The latter. Unfortunately."

Desi's breath hitched. "What happened to the headdress?"

"That is what I need you to find out. And when you do, HJ Securities will receive the thanks of a grateful Mexican government...publicly."

"But what? How? Why me?" A rumble from her middle ruined the gravity of her questions, and her face warmed.

The president chuckled. "I have been a terrible host. Come, we will eat. Esteban is waiting for us, and all of your questions will be answered."

He led the way into a small dining room. A mahogany table held a variety of cheeses, cold meats, sauces, fruit, and bread. A spicy scent drifted from a brown kettle on a buffet. Señor Corona rose from his seat at the table. A nod passed between the two men. Desi's skin prickled.

"My housekeeper makes the best fresh-squeezed lemonade." The president gestured toward a sweating glass pitcher. "Esteban, would you do the honors?"

Corona poured pale liquid into crystal glasses, while Montoya held Desi's chair and seated her like a grand lady. Too bad she felt more like the helpless pigeon. Corona set a glass in front of her.

The president took a sip and sighed. Desi reached for her glass, thankful for anything to wet her dry throat. Lemon sparkled on her tongue.

"You're right." She nodded. "This is the best I've ever tasted."

Señor Corona served steaming bowls of tortilla soup, and Desi accepted slices of bread, meat, and cheese as the plates were passed. Spreading her linen napkin on her lap, she watched the two men construct North American-style sandwiches thick enough to choke a moose. The simple male activity brought on a pang. *Tony.*

Whatever President Montoya wanted, she'd have to disappoint him.

The men dug into their food. Desi nibbled, but then hunger took over, and she devoured the sandwich and soup. The men laughed and passed her more fixings, as well as the bowl of fruit. Conversation revolved around the weather (wonderful), the health of Señor Corona's wife (poor), and complications with new construction in Mexico City. Desi fielded questions about the weather in Massachusetts (poor), the health of her fiancé (wonderful), and troubles with the Big Dig tunnel near downtown Boston.

She finished her lemonade, wiped her mouth, and laid her folded napkin on the table. "HJ Securities isn't an investigative firm. We're about protection, not recovery. The latter is the function of law enforcement, as my FBI agent fiancé is quick to remind me."

Montoya leaned forward. "Was he displeased when you helped the Iraqi government recover items stolen from their Baghdad museum during the overthrow of Saddam Hussein?"

"That was different. In setting up a security system for them, I came across clues that pointed me in the right direction. I referred my knowledge to appropriate authorities, and they made the recovery."

Corona bobbed his head. "That is all we ask."

"Help us, Ms. Jacobs," said the president. "We want our national treasures back. Our archaeological sites are being looted. Point us in the right direction. We will make the arrests and bring our heritage home."

Desi blinked at the two men. "Other items are missing?"

They gazed back at her like a pair of sad-faced basset hounds.

Her stomach went hollow. Ancient marvels disappeared each year all over the world, like heritage sucked into a black hole. She pushed back against her seat, as if a few inches of extra distance could remove her from the pull of their request. "Thank you for your confidence, but—"

"I myself—" the president drew himself up—"will issue a statement to the press that Greybeck and Sons no longer provides security services for the Museo de Arte Mejicana. Such an announcement should blunt the edge of their boasts in the newspapers."

Desi glanced from one man to the other. Their faces beamed hope. She couldn't say no. She wanted to, but she couldn't.

—◇◇◇—

Tony's landline phone rang. He set a sheaf of papers on his desk and checked the caller ID. Desi. She should be flying toward her layover in Detroit. Blast! He'd have to tell her there was no way she'd land in Boston tonight. Disappointment tasted rank on his tongue.

"Hey, darlin'." His chair creaked as he leaned back. "Are you on your way?"

Telltale pause. He stiffened.

"Still in Mexico. I just finished lunch with President Montoya and his senior aide."

"If anybody else had said that, I'd figure they were joking."

Desi laughed, but it ended on a sour note. "Wish I were. Lunches with government honchos complicate life."

"Don't tell me they've invited themselves to the wedding too."

This time her laugh was genuine. "No, thank goodness. The Mexican government has hired me to do a hush-hush investigation into missing antiquities."

"Des…"

"No running around after bad guys, Mr. Protective. They want me to evaluate data, interview people, and give an opinion. Their wording of the assignment was 'point them in the right direction.' I'll leave the raids and arrests to the law enforcement types."

"Hmm."

"Hold the skepticism, hon." She sighed. "It doesn't look like I'll be home for another few days." Her voice broke, and a sob came over the line. "Oh, Tony, I can hardly stand it. I'm so homesick. What's the matter with me?"

"Aw, sweetheart, don't cry." His insides melted. "If it makes you feel better, I wouldn't have been able to pick you up at the airport anyway. The squad and I are pulling an all-nighter."

Soft sniffle. "Big case?"

"Big blizzard. The city's at a standstill. Nobody can get home, and the airport's closed. You would've been stuck in Detroit. At least you can hang out in the sunshine a little longer. Everybody here is going to envy you."

"Wish I envied me. I'll call you later. President Montoya had to return to his office, but Señor Corona wants to go over the assignment with me. I may end up jogging all over the country, so who knows where you'll hear from me next."

"I'll be right here in the land of snow and ice. Promise me you'll be careful."

"Didn't you once call me the Queen of Careful?"

"My tongue was in my cheek at the time."

"Oh, har-de-har-har. Got to go. Señor Corona's waiting."

Tony hung up and stared at the paperwork piled on his desk, seeing nothing. What was wrong with Des? Could those long hours on the job be a cover-up for what was really bugging her? The woman needed a friendly face and a firm hand to rein her in long enough to figure it out. He couldn't get away so soon after being gone a week on his special assignment to Washington, but he knew someone who might go in a flash. He punched in a phone number.

"Webb residence," a boy's voice answered.

"Hey, Luke, how's the man of the house today?"

"Hi, Uncle Tony. Grandpa Steve's at the store with Grandma Lana, picking up milk and stuff. They took the Yukon. Grandpa says that monster sled can beat up on anything a Boston winter can dish out."

"Sounds like Steve." Tony chuckled. Interesting that Max Webb's seven-year-old considered Tony's ex-partner the man of the house. Must be because Stevo spent so much time over at Max's house acting as unofficial grandpa. He was the last guy Tony would've pegged to turn into family-man-of-the-year since starting to date Max's mother, Lana. Might not be long and the honorary title of Grandpa would be official. Desi'd have a fit. Tony grinned. "Is your mom around?"

"Mom!"

Tony shook his head. Good thing for his ear the kid hadn't yelled into the receiver.

"Hello?" Max's voice came on.

"Tony here. Is Emily over her bronchitis yet?"

"She was a pretty sick little cookie for a while, but now she's up and at 'em and giving her big brother a run for his money. Thanks for asking."

"Good. Then how about a Mexican vacation as soon as this storm clears?"

"Vacation? I've got deadlines on two projects, and no room for error. Both accounts are iffy, thanks to the hogwash those Greybecks keep spreadin' around like peanut butter on dry toast. I'm workin' out of my home office today." She stopped and huffed. "So I'm babblin'. What's up? You were jokin', right?"

"Des has some special project going for the Mexican government."

"Like she needs somethin' more on her plate. Tell you what, I'll call—"

A door slammed in the background, followed by a loud male voice mixed with a breathless female voice.

"Oh, my goodness." Max's tone went up an octave. "My mom and Steve were in an accident. I'll get back to you."

The line went dead. Tony stood and jammed his hands into his pants pockets. What a day to be stuck in the office. He couldn't get a handle on what was going on in the same city, much less another country.

He stalked over to the glass wall that looked out into the field agent bull pen. His squad was at work, along with most of the day shift and any of the night people that had dashed in early to beat the weather. None of them were going home.

In the middle of the chaos, stocky Hajimoto had a finger in one ear and the other ear stuck to a telephone receiver. Dark-haired Polanski pecked at her computer. Slidell patted his comb-over and studied a report. Tony glimpsed the crown of the new guy's carrot-topped head poking over the far side of a work station. Who knew what the kid was doing? Maybe he should check. Bergstrom sure wasn't Erickson, even if they were both Scandinavian. Who would have thought they could lose a sharp agent so fast on a routine questioning mission?

Gunshots echoed in Tony's head, and a picture flashed—blood pooling beneath the sprawled body of a tall man with blond hair.

Tony sucked in a breath and turned away from the window. Maybe he should plow through more paperwork. The stuff piled up worse than a Boston snowbank.

—〰—

"Here is the list of missing antiquities." Señor Corona handed Desi a stack of printed paper.

She rifled through it. "So many!"

"Indeed." He handed her a portfolio. "In here, you will find the incident reports, including pictures. Our *policía* has been unable to formulate a consistent modus operandi, except that the thefts are professional quality and sometimes not discovered for days."

"Puzzling." Desi glanced through the list. "Mexico is hardly unique with this problem. Many countries, especially those in turmoil like Iraq, have lost artifacts of incalculable value."

"Do you think ours have been dispersed through the black market, or is a private collector behind the looting?"

"I'll know more after I study the information, but don't expect anything except an educated opinion. Catching criminals must be left with your law enforcement personnel." Desi's gaze dropped to her skirt pocket, and she bit her lip.

"Understood." Corona tilted his head. "Why do I sense that you have a request?"

"The monetary compensation is satisfactory, but if I carve time out of my busy schedule to do this, I would like your help on a personal matter."

Desi pulled out the medallion and handed it to him.

"Where did you get this?" He studied the necklace.

"Do you recognize it?"

He smoothed his mustache. "I have never seen this before."

"I found the piece stuffed into a crevice in a blind canyon in New Mexico. A skull was discovered nearby. Forensic examination showed it to be the remains of a woman. Both the medallion and the skull appear to be from the time of the Spanish occupation."

"Intriguing." Corona ran a finger over the random scattering of emeralds.

"The work is typical seventeenth-century Spanish," Desi continued, "and the emeralds are poor quality. It looks like an heirloom. For my own satisfaction, and to give the woman's remains closure, I'd like to find out the provenance—where it came from and who owned it. I've made inquiries since coming to Mexico. Antiquities dealers want to buy it from me and become angry when I won't sell, but they don't offer information. Either it's because I'm an Anglo, or they have knowledge they prefer not to share. I'd appreciate help from your government."

"That you shall have." His hand closed over the medallion. "May I show it around?"

"I'll keep it, but I have photographs in my luggage that I'll give you before I leave."

Frowning, Corona handed the necklace back. Desi tucked it into her pocket. Was she wrong in the impression that she'd almost had to fight Señor Corona to reclaim her property?

"Maybe I should start at Palenque, the ancient Mayan city where the crown of Pakal disappeared." She smiled at Corona. "Did you know I had the privilege of examining Pakal's tomb when I was college age?"

The aide smiled back. "A treat afforded a rare few, but then, the Jacobs name opens doors in the antiquities world. Did you enjoy your tour?"

"A fascinating place but…oppressive. I guess that's the word I'd use." She returned to the list of stolen artifacts. "Interesting that the looters consistently strike at public attractions."

Corona shrugged. "Too many tourists to monitor everyone's movements. The thieves could have posed as one of them. Tourists provide a healthy share of Mexico's income, but they also create endless problems."

Desi laughed. "People create problems, but I'm afraid we're stuck with each other."

The aide chuckled. "A wise perspective. But I recommend that you start not at Palenque—the trail is cold there—but on the Yucatán Peninsula. The most recent thefts have occurred at the Mayan ruins of Uxmal, Sayil, and Ek Balam."

"What about Chichén Itzá? That would be a logical target."

Corona shook his head. "No reports of missing items there, but perhaps you should stop at Chichén and observe security measures? Helpful tips would be appreciated."

"Who provides protection at the site?"

"Since the thefts have started, the *Policía Judicial Estatal* from each region cooperates with the *Policía Federal Preventiva*."

"The state *and* federal police?" She'd pay good money to be excluded from any situation where law enforcement agencies vied for kudos. Too late now. And neither the *judiciales* nor the *federales* would appreciate helpful tips from a *gringa*.

The aide grinned understanding. "Forward your recommendations to me. Changes in procedure will reach them from the highest level. And to ensure that you have no trouble, a government aide will accompany you at all times." He handed Desi a business card. "Señor Ramon Sanchez is the head of cultural affairs in the Yucatán. He will see to it that one of his people looks after you."

"Very good." Desi tucked the card inside the portfolio. "I'd best get started."

A short time later she was on her way to the airport in a taxi. She stared out the window at the passing city. Modern skyscrapers vied with mom-and-pop businesses. Executives in suits rubbed elbows with ragged laborers. Elegant señoras in haute couture shared the sidewalks with women in traditional bright-colored skirts and serapes.

Desi dug out her cell and called her Boston headquarters to give them her new itinerary. Next she called Tony to let him know her destination. Then she began to study the information Corona had given her. No pattern to the thefts jumped out at her, but there had to be a common factor, something no one had recognized. And how did the looters get away with the goods? Someone had a first-class smuggling scheme going.

Desi pulled the Spanish medallion from her pocket. Why wouldn't anyone speak to her about this ancient necklace? Some dealers had been downright hostile, especially when she wouldn't sell. If she had no answers yet for the Mexican government, at least she might leave Mexico City with a little personal satisfaction. Only the hand of God could have led her to discover the medallion and the skull in a remote desert location that had seen no human being in centuries. He must want her to solve the mystery.

But that meant hazarding her last resort. Her mouth went dry. Should she beard an old family enemy in his den?

She checked her watch. A half hour to spare if she shaved it close to flight time. Her presidential VIP pass should zoom her right through security. Leaning forward, she tapped the driver on the shoulder. "Take me here." She handed him a slip of paper with an address scribbled in her father's hand. She'd found the scrap among his things not long ago. One of many memory-jolting items she kept running across in the house that they both used to call home. "Extra tip if we get there in five minutes," she added.

Desi hung on as the cabbie earned his gratuity, tires squealing and horn honking. The cab entered a business neighborhood past its prime. Traces of gentility remained in a flower box here and there, but the sidewalks were cracked, and some businesses were boarded up.

"Wait for me." She handed the driver the promised pesos and got out in front of a squat brick building huddled between a pair of taller sweatshop factories. *Guerrera,* the sign said on the front. Her heart rate quickened. No other markings to indicate the type of establishment.

Albon Guerrera only dealt with those who knew what he did without the need to advertise. Most thought secret equaled exclusive. Desi knew better. Only a handful of people shared that knowledge.

Did she dare step inside? She looked at the medallion and moved forward.

A bell jingled as she passed through the door. Cool dimness enfolded her. The air smelled as old as some of the ancient treasures displayed on wooden shelves. Like stepping into Pakal's tomb. Desi shivered. She shouldn't have come here and risked awakening dormant hostilities. Her father had spoken of Guererra with a shudder, and the man's violent temper may not have gentled with the passing of years. She turned away.

"Desiree Jacobs."

She froze at the guttural hiss behind her.

Four

*D*esi faced the old man who stood behind a glass counter. "Señor Guerrera."

He stared at her from a face dark and wizened like a raisin. Hunched shoulders led to a hump on his back, but the proud set of his head, the thick shock of white hair, and the fierce beak of a nose gave him the look of an ancient eagle. He planted age-spotted hands on the countertop. "To what do I owe the honor of a visit from the daughter of my old nemesis?" He addressed her in English.

Desi tore her gaze away from Guerrera's hands. No way had this octogenarian chased her through the streets last night, index finger longer than the middle finger or not. "I've come in search of your expertise."

"No small talk? No reminiscing?" His words came out measured and sibilant, like some Hispanic version of Bela Lugosi in his famed Dracula role.

Desi swallowed. "My father admired your genius as much as he deplored your using it to take what wasn't yours. That was twenty years ago. I was a child. You and I have no history. If you wish to live in the past, then I've come to the wrong place." She headed for the door.

"A medallion on a chain, is it not?"

She halted and turned. "Ah, so the dealers' network is talking. That's how you know who I am, though we've never met."

Guerrera inclined his head. "I am curious." He held out his palm.

Desi went back to the counter and gave him the necklace. "We can speak Spanish."

"*Gracias.* The stroke while in prison did strange things to me. My native tongue comes more easily." He fitted a jeweler's loupe over his head and examined the medallion.

Desi waited in heavy silence intruded upon by muffled traffic noises.

Guerrera lifted his head, blinking. "Three thousand dollars. No more. The gold is good, but the emeralds are so-so. And I need to make a little something when I resell."

"The piece isn't for sale. I want to know who owned it."

He handed her the medallion. "The pattern of the gems is unusual."

"I don't see a pattern."

"Precisely. You don't see. You must gaze upward in the darkness."

"What are you trying to tell me?"

He backed away. "Good day, Ms. Jacobs. Take care."

Another runaround. "Thank you for your time." She started to turn, then stopped. "If you were going to sell the medallion to someone, who would it be?"

"That, my dear, is an excellent question." Guerrera sneered with yellowed teeth and then hobbled off through a curtain into the back room.

Desi stalked out to the cab. Rude man. No more helpful than the others. Or was he? What did the ex–art thief mean by a pattern she couldn't see? And why wouldn't he tell her who might be interested in buying the medallion and yet hint that the question was important?

She squeezed the pocket with the necklace inside. Maybe she should toss the thing out the window and let someone else deal with the aggravation. Sighing, she slumped against the seat. Maybe she should quit stressing and let God lead her to the answers. Yes, that would work…if she didn't have such a horrible case of chronic impatience.

At the airport, she put the medallion in her carry-on and boarded a plane to Mérida, hub city of the Yucatán Peninsula. Once in the air, she closed her eyes to sneak in a few z's, but the lanky man next to her snored and had strange body odor, as if he were sweating jalapeños. With a sigh, she pulled the portfolio from her laptop case and studied the list of missing objects. The items were cataloged in chronological order of theft date. On her laptop, Desi made lists according to types of antiquities.

Many shady dealers specialized in certain objects, and unscrupulous collectors had particular tastes. She'd pinpointed the Iraqi antiquities by playing match the missing item with the most likely suspect. Should she consider Señor Guerrera among them? She'd suspect one of his offspring of being among the thugs who chased her in the street, if the man had any. But Dad had told her he was childless. So she was left with a useless similarity in physical characteristics.

Desi returned to her lists and worked in silent concentration. Some time later, the smelly scarecrow next to her stirred and scratched his narrow nose. Desi put her work away. Her seatmate with the digital camera around his neck probably wouldn't know an antiquity if it bit him, but El Presidente had made it clear her task was to remain top secret. She had a plan for that—one even Tony might approve if it didn't mean she had to ditch her government escort.

A thrill shot through her. Why did she so enjoy going incognito? She was a head case, all right. But at least she didn't plan to do anything more dangerous than pose as one of those tourists Señor Corona bemoaned.

Smiling, Desi leaned her head against the window and watched the rain forest pass beneath the plane's belly. If she couldn't go home, at least she could revisit some of the most intriguing archaeological sites in the world. She'd loved Chichén Itzá as a college student. Now she could explore the ancient mysteries again and get paid for her enjoyment.

"Business or pleasure?" The words came out in queen's English.

"What?"

The man showed rabbity teeth in a smile. "Business, I'm guessing, since you brought your laptop and some sort of prospectus. American too. Jolly Brit here." He held out a bony hand. She took it and came away damp. "Pleasure for me," he continued. "Though you could say I'm combining the two." He honked a laugh. "Professor of world history at Cambridge. Never miss an opportunity to visit a place I'm required to teach about. Going to see the Chicken."

"The chicken?"

"Chichén Itzá. A little educator joke there. Ha-ha! Some of my students mispronounce the name on first glance. You should take a break from the boardroom and come along. Raise your consciousness, et cetera."

At least the fellow said Chee-chen Eetzah this time, emphasis on second syllables. She was about to doubt his professor credentials. "I've been to the site, Mr....ummm..." Desi heard herself and groaned on the inside. Politeness could be a curse sometimes. She wanted to know this man's name like she craved a hole in the head.

"Preston Standish, Esquire, at your service."

How did she keep from introducing herself? "Esquire. You're *Sir* Preston?"

"Technically. But who wants to go about flaunting a title?" The rabbit smile again.

"Understandable." *And that's why Sir Jalapeño made sure to throw* Esquire *in there.* "This is your first visit to the—er—Chicken? What's the occasion?"

Standish folded his hands over his concave tummy and launched into a detailed account of a "well-earned sabbatical" and a world tour that, by his account, rivaled Phileas Fogg's fabled *Around the World in Eighty Days.* Desi half tuned him out and nearly wept with gratitude when the plane taxied to a stop at the terminal.

She collected her laptop from under the seat, while Standish hopped up and rummaged in the overhead compartment.

"Here you are, m'dear." He handed down her wheelie.

She awarded him a tight smile and took him up on his offer to let her go up the aisle ahead of him. The heavenly scents of hot tarmac and jet fuel greeted her as she emerged into the tropical sunshine at the top of the airplane stairs. She entered the terminal building and scurried ahead of Sir Jalapeño to the baggage claim area. A single seat remained on a bench not far from the carousel, and she grabbed it. Next to her a Mexican family laughed and joked.

Standish nodded as he went by and then stood with his back to her in front of the carousel. Desi expelled a long breath and rubbed the bridge of her nose. A stale donut had more get-up-and-go than she did. She yawned. Better head to the hotel for a decent snooze before she tackled anything more complex than pulling down the sheets.

Thankfully, the professor's bags were among the first to arrive. He wandered off, and Desi got up to wait for her suitcase. A large, black hard-shell slid down the chute, one among many similar, but the bright red and yellow ribbons on the handle identified it as hers. She loaded her carry-on atop the larger case and headed for the exit, laptop bag weighing a million pounds on her shoulder. Thank goodness, the hotel shuttle should be here any minute.

Halfway out the door, she halted. Clayton Greybeck, big as life in a Panama hat, stood beside a hatchback Audi. Alarm speared her insides. He must not spot her.

—᱑᱑᱑—

Tony wandered into the break room, drawn by the smell of coffee. He poured himself a cup and sipped. Stale and scorched as usual, but java nonetheless.

Several members of another squad lounged around a scarred table. They nodded to him and returned to their banter. All but one, who hunched over a newspaper, sections scattered across the table. A headline on the back of the section in the guy's hands caught Tony's eye. Caffeine sludge stalled on his tongue, and he swallowed with an effort.

"You through with that?" He lifted his cup toward the paper.

"Just a sec. Let me finish an article."

Tony choked down a rock-hard Danish, then nabbed the section. "Thanks."

"Welcome." The guy disappeared behind the sports pages.

Tony took his prize to a corner table. "Boston Women Disappear in Mexico." The headline socked him between the eyes.

With great excitement, sisters Rosa Garza and Martina López, ages twenty-two and twenty, planned their trip to visit cousins in a small village on the Yucatán Peninsula of Mexico. Rosa and Martina left for the Yucatán thirty days ago, but they never arrived at their destination, and they never came home.

Their parents, naturalized U.S. citizens, thought they had little reason for concern about the journey. The much-publicized kidnapping and murder of women seemed isolated to border communities such as Ciudad Juárez and Chihuahua. What could happen to their daughters in the highly policed tourist center on the Atlantic coast?

Authorities in Mexico remain baffled as the FBI works with them in the investigation. Drug cartel involvement has not been ruled out. A reliable source told the *Boston Globe* that the Yucatán has seen increased use as a shipping port for drugs and young women destined for prostitution in the United States. Rumors of significant Fraternidad de la Garra gang presence in the jungles of this vacation paradise are growing.

On the U.S.–Mexico border, where infighting between drug cartels has taken a bloody toll, women often disappear. Sometimes their raped and tortured bodies are discovered in an isolated location.

Tony swallowed as the words urged him onward.

No such violence has occurred in the Yucatán as yet, though Mexican police have noted an increase in reports of missing women. They are quick to note that the kidnappers prey only on Hispanic females. No reports of missing tourists have been lodged.

A full breath returned to Tony's lungs.

"If the cartels or a gang are involved, they would not be eager to draw pressure on the Mexican government from other countries," a source said. "In the case of Garza and López, the abductors may have been unaware that these women are United States citizens."

Thank God, no one would mistake Desi for anything but an Anglo. He needed to call her about this anyway. He pulled out his phone and flipped it open. Blast this storm! His service bars showed blank. That Corona fellow better have arranged adequate security for his fiancée, or Tony would make himself a one-man international incident.

—◊◊◊—

Desiree back-pedaled into the terminal. "Excuse me." She offered the breathless apology to a rotund woman she nearly bowled over.

Why was Clayton Greybeck in Mérida? Following her, or did he have his own agenda?

Desi moaned and headed for the ladies room. She hadn't wanted to pull the presto chango yet. And now she'd have to switch hotels, not to mention postpone her bedtime. Bother! But she couldn't let Clayton catch a whiff of her whereabouts. Sticking his nose in her business would be a priority with him if he knew she was here.

The rest room was small but clean, and by some miracle, the backmost stall was empty. Desi muscled her bags into the cubicle. Hardly room enough to stand, but she got busy.

Twenty minutes later, a middle-aged woman shuffled out of the cubicle with a crick in her back from the quick-change contortions. Desi checked herself in the mirror. The eyes that stared back at her were blue, not her natural hazel, and her mouse-colored hair was cropped close to her head, nothing like her own thick sable locks that reached below her shoulder blades. She scratched behind her ear. Stupid wig itched already.

Desi smoothed makeup on her face, neck, and forearms—the perfect paper-pale office-worker look. Lines around her mouth and eyes made her half again her age. She did up another button on the frowzy print blouse she wore over khaki slacks. Then she grabbed her cases and left the bathroom, her gait flatfooted and tired. The tired part was no act.

A few feet up the hall she stopped. Sleep-deprived half-wit! She pulled her cases to an empty bench and removed the labels identifying her as Desiree Jacobs. Uh-oh. She stared at her engagement ring. This was going to hurt. Dowdy, introverted Myra wouldn't have a fiancé. The ring had to go. Desi slipped the band from her finger. She cradled the symbol of promise in her palm, and then unzipped a side pouch on her carry-on and tucked the labels and the ring inside.

Hold it! Her heart seized. She opened the pouch again and groped inside. Airline tags. Her ring. Oxygen rushed from her lungs. No medallion!

Desi leaped up, head whipping in all directions. People paused to stare. *Cool it, girl.* What had she expected to see? A figure dressed in black slipping away in the crowd?

The medallion was missing before she stepped into the bathroom to change persona. It had been in her carry-on when she put it in the overhead bin on the plane, but when she left the plane she hadn't checked. Too eager to get away from her obnoxious seatmate. A picture of his lanky form rummaging in the overhead compartment returned to her.

But how had the "jolly Brit" known what was in her carry-on? Albon Guerrera wanted the piece. Maybe he had arranged... No, not enough time to set up a snatch. Esteban Corona had wanted to keep the medallion. Maybe... Desi shook herself. There went her wild imagination again, formulating conspiracy theories. Besides, she liked Corona. Probably Preston Standish, Esquire, had been in a nearby security line when the airline agent examined the necklace. Standish saw what he wanted and took it when the opportunity presented.

Going to see the Chicken? To help himself to more goodies? Had she run afoul of the mysterious antiquities looter? The hairs under her wig prickled. An operation that complex and widespread couldn't be handled by one man, but maybe she'd found a puzzle piece.

At the cost of an article she treasured.

Desi hefted her laptop over a squared shoulder. Then she grabbed her cases and strode for the doors. Sir Jalapeño wouldn't see the businesswoman he'd met on the plane, but he'd soon discover mousy little Myra was a force to be reckoned with. Er, he might if she remembered to stay in character. She slowed and let her figure droop as she pushed out into the tropical warmth of Mérida.

Palm trees waved at her, but no lurking Greybecks. Hopefully, Clayton's business would remove him from the area. His presence probably had nothing to do with her anyway. Who knows? Maybe he was vacationing to take the edge off his disappointment over Mexico City.

First task? Find modest accommodations in keeping with an hourly worker's paycheck. At this time of year, almost as tricky as catching a nest of crooks.

Desi moved up the sidewalk, hunting for a taxi. The driver might know a good place to—

A small figure darted from a doorway and rammed into her. Desi staggered. Losing her grip on her bags, she tripped over the larger one and sprawled backward onto the cement. Her head spun, while her right elbow and her tailbone screamed in unison.

She glimpsed the pinched face of a dirty urchin. A grown-up male voice shouted in Spanish. The skinny boy grabbed the handle of her carry-on and took off across the busy road. Tires screeched, horns honked, and a uniformed security guard dashed in the little thief's wake.

A slender woman in an airline suit bent over Desi. "Are you all right, señora?" She spoke decent English.

"I'm fine. Just let me...ow!...get up." Desi stayed with her native tongue as she struggled to her feet with the woman's assistance.

The urchin and the security guard had disappeared.

The woman tugged her arm. "We should get you to the first-aid station. You are bleeding." She pointed to Desi's elbow.

A red trail crept down her arm. "It's just a scrape."

"Which must not become infected. Come with me."

"But my case." Desi stared in the direction it had gone. *My engagement ring! Oh, Tony, how could this happen?*

"When the guard catches the little *ladrón,* he will bring your bag back here."

Fighting tears, Desi retrieved her belongings and trudged into the terminal. Her benefactress said "when," not "if" the carry-on was recovered, but that was diplomacy speaking. How could she have been so careless? Robbed twice within an hour. The medallion. Her ring! Gone.

But the child sure had appeared hungry. Those black eyes were almost bigger than the kid's face. Couldn't have been much older than Luke Webb. Desi's heart softened. Her hand curled around the strap of her laptop case. She'd trade this for the carry-on. Her money, credit cards, and cell phone were in here—safe. The child could have them for her ring back.

The woman led her through a door marked with a red cross and left her with a nurse who disinfected and bandaged Desi's elbow.

A knock sounded, and the nurse opened the door as Desi gathered her things. A frowning man in a suit stepped inside. Some airport official by the insignia on his lapel.

"Señora." The man spread his hands toward Desi. "Humble apologies for the rude welcome to Mérida."

"Señorita." Staring at her scuffed loafers, Desi corrected his mode of address in a small voice. She was Myra now, all-around underdog.

"Señorita, may we offer you assistance getting to your destination?"

She looked up. "If you could help me find a place to stay. Not too expensive."

The man pursed his lips. "You have no reservation?"

She shook her head.

He scratched his brow and then snapped his fingers. "I know of just the place. A home where they take in a guest now and then."

Desi smiled inside. Probably this guy's aunt or some other relative. That was the way things worked in Mexico. "Yes, please."

"*Bueno*. I will get you into a taxi and make sure you are taken straight there, no charge. The room rate will be most reasonable, I assure you. And we will know where to find you when your bag is recovered."

Desi quirked her lips and trailed the airport official. If she'd been Desiree Jacobs, prosperous businesswoman, she'd be on her way to a five-star hotel, and the charge would be compliments of the city of Mérida. But that was the way things worked all over the world.

A few minutes later, she sat in the rear of a taxi, darting at breakneck speed through dense traffic. The driver laid on the horn as they narrowly missed another collision. Desi paid little attention. She'd been through this drill before. Myra would be gripping the seat in white-knuckled terror, but for a few minutes, she needed to be herself and think.

Her disguise might be superfluous anyway. Two thieves making a play for her carry-on? Hardly a coincidence. If someone had targeted her, using that little street beggar, they knew what she looked like as her alter ego. That possibility was scarier than the oncoming truck that nearly swiped the mirror off the taxi.

Could more than one person be after the medallion? One had succeeded, and the other one only thought they had. But why would the ancient necklace inspire so much attention?

Clayton Greybeck had to be a factor in this incomplete equation. He wasn't in Mérida by chance. Was he after the medallion, or did his mission involve her assignment for the Mexican government? Neither thought made sense.

And where did Preston Standish, Esquire, fit? Fair bet he wasn't who he said he was. A good research job for Tony.

The taxi slowed in a neighborhood of run-down adobe houses with dirt yards. Children scattered off the packed-earth street. The driver pulled up in front of a house better kept than others around it. He turned, arm across the back of the seat. "This is the place, señorita."

She blinked like she didn't understand his Spanish words. He sighed and got out. She went with him to the rear of the taxi, where he pulled her case from the trunk. His hand went out again. She gave him a few coins that would have been on the edge of insult ten years ago. He scowled, rolled his eyes, hopped into his vehicle, and roared off in a trail of dust.

"Sorry, pal." She couldn't afford to have him mark her as a target fare. Given recent events, it wasn't wise to have anyone interested in her location or where she might go next.

Lugging her laptop, Desi pulled her suitcase up the dirt track to the house, aware of many children's gazes studying her progress. Probably some adults too, peeking out their windows. Before she reached the cracked steps, the door swung open, and a plump woman came out, smile as bright as her skirt and blouse. The smile didn't reach her small black eyes. Counting her pesos then, not genuine welcome.

Desi smiled back. "You have a room?"

"*Sí, sí.*" The woman motioned her inside. "I am Zapopa."

"Myra." Desi stepped over the threshold.

The smell of grease greeted Desi's nose. Her hostess led her through a shabby front room into a kitchen where the back door stood wide and mottled chickens pecked in the weed-grown yard. The woman opened a warped door and rubbed her hands together while Desi peeked inside.

The room was cramped and dark, but not as dirty as she'd feared. A quilt-covered bed filled most of the space. A rough-hewn table and chair stood in the corner, and a dresser supported a white wash basin and pitcher. Talk about early last century. But give her one night's rest in this little hovel away from home, and she'd be out of here. She nodded to the woman, who smiled while Desi counted coins into her palm.

Zapopa made eating motions. Desi shook her head and pantomimed laying her head on her hands. The woman nodded and turned away.

Desi went into the room, closed the door, and released a long breath. She grabbed a straight-backed chair from beside a small table and propped it under the doorknob. Then she concealed her laptop in the spot she always used when she was in a strange place. An intruder would have to get through her to get to it.

She pulled back the shutters and stared at an adobe wall a few feet away. She closed the shutters, got out her cell phone, and checked the reception. Not bad. Hadn't she even seen satellite dishes on several houses on the block? She shook her head. People would do without a lot of things these days, but not their television or telephone.

She punched in the number for Señor Corona.

He answered on the third ring. "Ah, Señorita Jacobs, I trust the accommodations are satisfactory. We wished you to have the best."

Desi wrinkled her nose. A swirling hot tub would have been heavenly right now. "Your arrangements were most generous, but I've had a change of plans."

"Oh?"

"I have no clue of my current address. It's a rented room in a private home, but you can reach me on my cell."

"Has there been trouble?" The man's voice sharpened.

"I've had a run-in with thieves."

Corona gasped. "Outrageous! We never guessed our assignment would place you in danger. You must return to Mexico City at once. I will tell El Presidente—"

"Unnecessary. I have no reason to believe the incidents had anything to do with my mission for your government. My medallion was the target." *And my ring was a casualty.*

Heavy silence. "Is the item safe?" The words came out breathless.

Not, "Are you all right?" Desi measured her next statement. "No harm has come to the antiquity." She could be reasonably certain she was telling the truth. Standish would need the piece in pristine condition if he wanted the best price.

A long sigh answered her. "You are unharmed then?"

"Shook up, but not knocked out of the game." She touched the bandage on her elbow and sat on the edge of the bed, thankful for the softness on her bruised behind. "I've taken different lodging to throw off further interest from medallion-nappers."

Corona cleared his throat. "And what of the escort who was to accompany you to Chichén Itzá?"

"It might be best if I simply join one of the usual tour buses and play dull tourist. Less intimidating when striking up conversations."

"Dull? Not a term I would apply to you, Ms. Jacobs."

"You haven't seen me on vacation." *Or as Myra.*

The aide chuckled. "Stay in touch, would you? El Presidente awaits word of your progress."

"I'll do that, but remind him to be patient. I plan to move carefully." In a literal sense. She shifted to a more comfortable position on the lumpy mattress.

"Sí. Exercise the utmost caution."

Desi closed the connection, then entered Tony's cell number but got a hiss of static. Great! If the blizzard was as bad as Tony had said, towers might be out. She punched in Tony's landline number but stopped before the last digit. Tony already knew she'd gone to Mérida. He'd just worry for nothing about her change of approach to Chichén Itzá. She could return to the airport tomorrow and log into their Wi-Fi connection so she could e-mail him her little assignment on Sir Jalapeño. If she talked to him tonight, she'd probably just bawl in his ear about the engagement ring.

Hugging herself, Desi battled useless tears into submission. Limbs leaden, she poured water from the pitcher into the basin and removed her makeup. Then she put on a soft sleep shirt and crawled between crisp, air-dried sheets. No one and nothing had better disturb her tonight.

—⁂—

Desi was finally dozing off when a bass roar jerked her awake. Her eyes popped wide. What? That sounded like an explosion. She sat up.

"*¡Fuego! ¡Fuego!*"

The shouts came again, and her chest constricted. Outside, voices screamed a Latino chorus of "fire."

Five

*D*esi sucked in a breath and tasted a hint of smoke. She went to the door and touched the knob. It was cool. Getting on her knees, she sniffed the crack under the door. Clear. The explosion had sounded nearby, but not immediate.

She darted to the window and opened the shutters on the narrow lane between her room and the wall next door. Smoke obscured the stars. More shouts rang outside, and then sirens joined the din. Desi's heart pounded. Something had blown up and fire had struck the neighborhood. Not this home, but close.

Desi threw on clothes and then covered her American attire with a poncho she'd bought in Mexico City. She climbed out the window, slunk along the wall, and peered into the street. Clusters of people stood in their yards. Others hurried toward the flames that leaped above the rooftops a block away. Desi trailed along, keeping her eyes averted. No one glanced at her. Too absorbed in the disaster up ahead.

She rounded a corner and gasped. Ah, these poor people. Living hand to mouth, and now a half-dozen homes were engulfed in flames—many more in peril. Three City of Mérida fire engines pumped water at the conflagration. Another one wet down neighboring houses. Some of the crowd members were clearly gawkers. Others stood in family groups, wrapped in blankets and hugging each other, gazes stricken. Thick smoke strangled the air.

Above the roar of fire, the hiss of water, and the cries of dismayed people, a woman's shriek rose. "*¡Mi bebé!* My baby!"

Heart in her throat, Desi sank to the ground beneath a tree. Not everyone had escaped. What caused an explosion on this clear, still night?

A trio of onlookers stopped near her.

"…this is the work of the Fraternidad de la Garra…"

Brotherhood of the Claw? A chill wafted through her. She focused on the three men, but they paid her no attention. Perhaps they didn't see her hunkered on the ground in the shadows.

"I told Juan," said one of them, "if he didn't deliver, something bad would happen."

Desi went cold in the balmy air. The fire was set on purpose?

"Sí," agreed another. "*El Jaguar* is not fond of disappointment."

The third man crossed himself. "If he asks me to get one of those shiny baubles in exchange for my shipment, I will do it. I would rather risk getting caught by the federales than this." He lifted his hands toward the fire.

The men drifted away into the flickering darkness.

Desi pressed her hand against the rough tree bark and stood. Her knees trembled. Shiny baubles? As in golden antiquities like the crown of Pakal? Or had she misunderstood the conversation? She went back to Zapopa's house.

Raised voices carried from inside, a man and a woman. Desi halted and listened but could make out no words. She sneaked up the narrow passage to her window and crawled inside. Sinking onto the lumpy mattress, she buried her head in her hands.

The angry voices had stilled, but she couldn't silence the voices in her head. What kind of rabbit hole had she tumbled down? At least two different parties after her medallion, Clayton Greybeck in the same city, and now a fire set by a drug lord named El Jaguar who liked shiny baubles. A breath stuck in Desi's throat. Could that reference be connected to her medallion and not the antiquities thefts? No, that conclusion didn't square with the mention of federales. The Mexican federal police could not care less about her antique necklace.

A faint ruddy pall from the fire cast a dim glow in her room. Something wasn't right. Desi rose and padded to the light switch. She winced at the stark brilliance and then gasped. Someone had rifled through her things.

She'd perched her hard-sided case on the rickety table. The lid, which she'd closed and latched before she went to bed, was unlatched, and though it was still closed, bits of clothing stuck out the sides. She hurried over and flung the case open. Careless fingers had made a stew of her pants and shirts and underthings. Fury heated her pulse. They'd ripped out the quilted lining of the case and added that to the mix. The emergency hundred-dollar bill and credit card that she had tucked into the lining were gone.

She whirled toward the scuffed dresser by the bed. Her toiletries bag lay on its side. Cosmetics, shampoo, and toothpaste littered the top of the dresser and the floor. The cell phone she'd laid beside the bag after her attempt to call Tony was missing.

Her laptop! She crept to the bed on the side where she hadn't been sleeping and lifted the edge a little. Then a little more. Air gushed from her lungs, and she snatched the case.

Hugging her laptop, her gaze followed the trail of mayhem around the room. A rush job. Too quick for a thorough search. This was her third robbery in less than twenty-four hours, and that was three too many.

She checked the door. Yes, her chair remained wedged under the doorknob. The thief must have come in through the window after she went out. But that meant someone was watching her movements. She caught her breath.

Someone still after the medallion? Antiquities robbers searching for information on her assignment for the government? That miserable Clayton Gr—no, that was seriously reaching.

There was another possibility. The memory of angry male/female voices ran through her mind. Maybe the woman and her male accomplice had been watching the exits to see if she left the room? And maybe they fought because they hadn't found enough loot to satisfy them?

Footsteps sounded in the kitchen.

Heart thudding, Desi took a step toward the window, an escape route if necessary—and if accomplice number two wasn't lying in wait outside. She hefted the laptop by its strap. Heavy enough to pack almost as good a wallop as the leaden crown she took from the Museo de Arte Mejicana. A fist hammered on the door panel, and the knob rattled.

—∿∿—

A knock sounded on Tony's doorjamb. "It's open." He signed off on the file in front of him and looked up. His eyebrows climbed. Stevo? At midnight in the middle of a raging blizzard? He waved the man in.

Steve Crane lumbered into the room, damp and cold emanating from the unzipped parka that hugged his burly shoulders. He plopped into Tony's guest chair.

Tony tapped his pen against his fingertips. "You lost or out practicing for the Iditarod?"

Crane scowled. "Women! They can get you to do the dumbest things."

"I thought Lana reformed your misogynistic tendencies?"

The other man's craggy face colored—like a rock blushing. "Yeah, well, she's special."

"No argument there. Anyone who can get you to give up gum-chewing without going back to cigarettes qualifies for sainthood in my book."

Crane shot him a thin smile. "Don't give up the day job. A comedian you're not."

"If you felt the need to insult me, why didn't you pick up a phone?"

"Service is out in our area. A skidding semi sideswiped a major relay station. I'm surprised you've still got a connection."

Tony picked up his landline phone. Silence. "No dial tone. And cell service is next to nil. Hard for people to get emergency services." Boston had just become Nightmare City. "Why hasn't anybody around here no—"

"Hey, boss!" A freckled face topped by carrot hair poked through the doorway. "Phones are dead as a doornail."

"I know, Bergstrom."

"Oh." The eager puppy look fell away. "Guess I'll get back at it then."

"Back at what?"

"Huh?"

"What are you doing?"

Bright spots appeared on the kid's cheeks. "Well, actually, I was—uh." Bergstrom jingled the change in his pocket. "I was helping the night maintenance guy fix a floor scrubber. I'm pretty good at that sort of thing, and I—"

"Did you get the machine fixed?"

"Almost. He's putting it back together now."

Tony frowned, too much bad coffee swishing through his veins. "You're not paid to repair floor scrubbers. Get your case paperwork up to date."

"Done."

"Then collect the squad's expense slips for the month and enter them in the computer."

Bergstrom's shoulders drooped. "Right." He hustled away.

Crane shook his head. "First-station newbies." He jerked a nod at Tony. "The kid reminds me of you."

"You'd better have a good reason for that remark."

"Hands in the pockets when he's jittery."

Tony snorted. "We're all about stir-crazy around here tonight. Too many of us crammed into limited floor space and nowhere to go but in each other's hair."

"Think positive. Close quarters is giving you a chance to get the cranky boss thing down pat. I could give you a few pointers on your scowl, though. A little more with the teeth. Eyes narrower."

"Let's get back to business. Are you here to tell me about the phones, or is something else bugging you?"

"You're not going to believe this, but Max practically tossed me out into the snow."

"I know you too well to doubt that statement. I only have two questions: Why didn't she do it sooner, and why didn't you go home?"

Crane groaned and rubbed his face with a meaty hand. "She's got some bee under her bonnet that Desi's in trouble."

Tony's gut clenched. "How does she know?"

"A feeling. That's it. And she won't lay off about it, so here I am."

Emotions warred in Tony's chest. Amusement at Stevo's walleyed stare. Frustration at lack of specifics. Alarm for Desi. How seriously should he take Max's feeling?

Very. The knowledge came full-blown and certain. "Only one thing to do in a case like this. We're going to pray."

Crane shifted like he was perched on an egg. "I was afraid you'd say that. Better leave me out of the deal. The Big Guy won't have time for me." He eased to his feet.

"Sit down and follow along."

The ex-agent subsided into his seat, thick fingers fidgeting with his jacket zipper.

"Relax, Stevo. No lightning bolt's going to zap you from above."

"Let's get this over with."

Tony closed his eyes and shoved fear into a dark corner of his mind. "Lord, there's no situation that takes You by surprise—whether it's phones that don't work or loved ones alone in a tight spot. I'm not the best at trusting You with Desiree, and You keep putting me in positions where I have to do it. I ask You to defend her with Your strong arm. Give her wisdom to temper that reckless courage. And thank You that You've given Your children authority in Your Son's name. In the name of Jesus, I bind the plans of the enemy against Desiree and command those operations to cease."

Tony fell silent and waited for assurance to come over him. He got a blank as murky as the blizzard. He could practically hear the hiss of white noise. What was going on?

"You figure that helped?" Crane's whisper was worthy of a cathedral.

Tony opened his eyes. "You figure it didn't?" *Wish I knew.*

"Sounded…good. Real nice. Guess I can go now." He stood.

"What did you drive? Your little nut-bucket wouldn't cut through this weather, and I thought you had an accident in Max's Yukon."

"Fender bender. At least as far as that monster SUV was concerned. The joker who slid into our rear end should never have been out in this weather in that tin can. Nobody hurt, though." He nodded at Tony and tromped out.

Tony rose and stretched, but a weight stuck to his shoulders. Good thing Crane didn't hang around for the rest of the praying, if that little dab threw him for a loop. Something was going on with his Des, and she couldn't contact him. He glared at the inoperative phone.

Scowling, he went to the door and started to close it, but something was in the way. "Stevo? I thought you left."

His ex-partner barged in, shut the door, and leaned against it.

Now what? Tony had business to conduct with the only One who could help Desi.

Crane stared at the carpet. "You gonna do some more of that praying?"

"Figured I might."

"I'd take it as a personal favor if you'd mention I plan to pop the question to a certain lady. If there's anything He can do to make her say yes, I'd be grateful. I mean, if He's inclined to help out a poor chump with no more brains than to tie the knot again. I'll be real good to her, if she'll have me."

What a loaded request. How could he turn Stevo down and hold out hope at the same time? "I know you'll be good to Lana, and she's good for you too."

"You got that right. She's saved this old buzzard."

Tony shook his head. "She's a gift to you from Someone who cares more than any earthly person, but God doesn't make people do things. Lana will have to choose for herself. I think you'll improve your chances if she sees you're the sort of man who does his own praying."

"You're telling me I have to join your club in order to be good enough?" His voice rose. "You can take a flying leap if you think I'm going to play the religion game to get a woman."

"You're off base, Stevo. I—"

"Forget it!" He yanked the door open. "Don't do me any favors, okay?" He stormed up the hall, nearly ramming Bergstrom, who did a wide-eyed dodge-step.

The kid stared after Crane, turned and blinked at Tony, and then dove into the bull pen.

Cranky boss? Was he too hard on the new guy? Maybe. A certain amount of hazing followed a first-station agent, but Tony always thought he'd be better than that, especially when he was the one with the power. His face heated. But Bergstrom wasn't Erickson.

Tony closed his office door and settled behind his desk. He slid his fingers through his hair. He'd alienated Stevo. Surprise! Surprise! Trying to help that guy was like sticking a hand into a wolf's cage.

And Desi needed backup. Not the kind that could charge in, guns blazing. Or maybe she did, and he couldn't be there.

—∞—

"Señorita, may I speak with you?" Zapopa's heavily accented voice carried through the closed door. "Is important."

The hairs on the back of Desi's neck prickled. "A few minutes, please."

"I wait out here."

Desi closed and locked the window shutters. Long practice streamlined her makeup and clothes change into the Myra persona. Not a good idea to walk into Zapopa's kitchen as someone the woman had never met—even if Desi was reality and Myra a handy fiction.

Hand on the knob, Desi hesitated. She had to step out of this room sometime. Clutching her laptop case, she opened the door.

Dressed in a baggy white nightdress, Zapopa stood by the kitchen table. Her eyes were red, face puffy. The woman pointed to the table-top.

A hundred-dollar bill, a credit card, and a cell phone.

Desi's eyes widened. "You're returning them?"

The dark head bobbed. "I did not take." She shook her head, and a strand loosened from the braid that hung down her front to her thick waist. "You went to see fire. Someone came. He take. I took back."

Zapopa drew herself up, gaze fierce despite a fresh tear that coursed down her mottled cheek.

Desi ventured a step forward. "This thief didn't hurt you?"

The woman closed her eyes and bowed her head, a hand on her chest. "In here only."

The thief was someone this woman loved. Husband? Son? Other relative? "You are an honest woman, Zapopa."

Her eyes popped open. "Sí."

Desi's heart softened at the statement, so simple, so proud, spoken through tears. She set her laptop on the table and wrapped the ample figure in her arms. Total impulse. Powerful response. The woman clutched Desi. Ribs creaking, Desi breathed in scents of corn flour and sweat that permeated the woman's nightdress.

Zapopa plopped into a chair, and a great sigh heaved from the large bosom. "You are kind. Please." Her black stare bored into Desi. "You will not report this?"

Desi took a chair across from her hostess. "You are protecting someone."

"You do not report, and I do not tell that Myra uses a credit card of Desiree Jacobs."

Desi picked up her card and money and tucked them into a pouch on her laptop case. She studied Zapopa, a woman of contrasts. Eager for gain, yet particular about how she came by it. Protective of her guest, yet equally protective of the one who preyed upon a defenseless gringa. "You let me use your phone for an international call—I'll pay with my credit card—and then I'll call a taxi to take me to a hotel."

The woman's lips pursed. "Best you go. Maybe you make your out-of-country call from the hotel, eh?" Zapopa's gaze darted to the back door, closed now but offering flimsy defense against a determined intruder.

Desi stiffened. "The thief may return?"

Zapopa's cheeks went the color of paste. "Others who do not listen to me." She leaned toward Desi. "This was a safe *barrio,* but then he came with the drugs. Our young people are sucked in. Some sell. Easy money, they think. Some use. Fun, they think." Her upper lip curled. "My grandson is good boy. I am long time a widow, but I raise him from a child. Manuel will soon see the way of the *pandillas* is not the right one."

"Pandillas?"

"You call them in United States gangs. With the fire, the pandillas have come out."

Desi swallowed a hard lump. "Let me call a taxi."

"Sí." Zapopa heaved to her feet. "The phone is—"

A crash and splinter of breaking wood sounded from Desi's bedroom. Zapopa squealed. Desi snatched her laptop and dashed for the front room. She spotted the phone on a table next to a threadbare sofa. Grabbing the handset, she slid the laptop behind the sofa. The dial tone buzzed in her ear. What should she punch in? Nine-one-one didn't work in Mexico.

The front door burst open. Three shaggy-haired young men trooped inside, dressed in dirty short-sleeved shirts and filthy jeans. Desi's gaze fixed on the objects in their hands. One thick length of chain. One crowbar. One gun that looked more homemade than manufactured.

No matter. Any of the weapons could kill.

Six

*G*et out of my house!" Zapopa screeched a few descriptive terms for the home invaders.

Chain Man rattled the links. "Shut up, old woman. Nobody gets hurt if that one gives us her money and credit cards." He shook the chain at Desi.

Crowbar Dude smacked the length of metal against his palm.

If Desi shivered as hard on the outside as she did on the inside, she'd shake the house.

"Gringa, your money." Chain Man spoke in English, while Gun Guy lifted his weapon.

Desi moistened her lips. How should she answer? Tony would say give them whatever they wanted to make them leave. Her laptop case was hidden behind the end of the sofa. If these punks saw it, they'd snatch it to pawn for drug money. The case contained secrets worth more to the Mexican government than a few dollars and cancelable credit cards. What would Señor Corona want her to do? Did it matter? Her life was at stake.

She shot a look at her hostess. The woman was staring at Desi's empty hands. Empty. Yes! Desi held out those hands toward the intruders. "You're too late. I've already been robbed."

Chain Man glared at Zapopa. "This is true?" He reverted to Spanish.

"¡Sí!" Her eyes spat fire. "You pandillas think you can go where you want, take what you want, but you destroy your own barrio. The place you should protect."

Gun Guy stepped forward, teeth bared, his pupils dilated chunks of midnight. Chain Man barked a rebuke, and Gun Guy halted, muscles twitching.

"We take care of our own." The spokesman wrapped his chain around his fist. "The gringa is not one of us."

"She is my guest. You have forgotten the old ways of hospitality."

Chain Man snorted. "She is a turista. You want her money, as we do. Give us half of what she gave you, and we will go. If you run a guesthouse, you must pay the tax for protection."

"Half! You take only fifteen percent from the shops and the buses."

The spokesman shrugged. "You did not ask permission before you took in the gringa."

"¡Ay-yeee!" The woman clutched the sides of her head. "And who has put himself in charge now? You? Or should I go to El Jaguar? He would not even know your name. You are not the Fraternidad. Just little boys playing at being tough."

What was this spooky Brotherhood? The comparison drew a snarl from Gun Guy. He lifted his weapon, and thunder clapped. Zapopa cried out and crumpled forward.

Desi smacked a palm over her mouth, absorbing a scream.

"¡Abuela!" The cry of "grandmother" came from a male voice in the kitchen. A skinny young man with a fuzzy goatee raced into the room and knelt by Zapopa, who sprawled facedown and still. Manuel, no doubt. He must be the person who crashed into Desi's guest room at the same time his buddies burst through the front door. The young man glared at the gang members and unleashed a torrent of filthy language.

"Shut up!" Chain Man barked.

A feral growl came from Gun Guy, who stepped forward, gun muzzle descending. Chain Man and Crowbar pulled him toward the door. The shooter struggled, and then let his friends shove him into the night.

Desi stepped toward her downed hostess and the slimy grandson. A red stain crept from under the woman's head. "Is she breathing?" Desi spoke in Spanish.

The wild-eyed youth looked up at her. "Sí."

"Get a rag and press it to the wound. I'll call for help."

The grandson's attention flew toward the open door.

Desi put her hands on her hips. "Do you want your grandmother to live?"

Manuel's mouth hardened. He darted into the kitchen.

Desi retreated to the phone, her palm clammy around the handset. She dialed the operator and asked to be put through to the policía. A brief conversation elicited a promise of help, but not how soon it would come. Mouth dry, stomach sour, Desi returned to the pair of figures on the floor. Manuel held his abuela's head in his lap, pressing a semiclean rag to the side of her head.

"Still alive?"

"Sí." His hoarse tone hinted at leashed tears. "So much blood."

"Head wounds are like that. Maybe it's just a crease."

His gaze met hers, a spark of hope in muddy brown eyes. Then his stare flattened. "This was not supposed to happen. She should do as she is told. Stubborn woman. And you! This is your fault." The youth rocked his grandmother in his arms.

"Zapopa is right. The pandillas hurt the ones they should help. They are no good. She stood up against them for your sake, not mine."

Manuel hung his head. A siren sounded in the distance. *Thank You, God.* "They're coming, and I will leave with them."

The grandson shifted, glancing at the door. "You hold her. I need to go."

Desi stabbed a finger at him. "You will stay until help arrives, and you will take care of your grandmother when she returns from the hospital." *Please, God, heal Zapopa, so that her grandson can find a reason to live an honorable life.*

The young man squeezed his eyes shut, chest heaving.

Desi held her breath. Would he defy her and run off? Or would her impulsive words reach him?

His chin bobbed, but he didn't make eye contact. "Sí."

Desi grabbed her laptop and went to her room. She scooped her cosmetics into her travel kit then threw it into her large bag.

A knock sounded at the front door. Manuel yelled for them to come in. "*¡Apúrate!*" Calm, professional voices filled the front room. Desi grabbed her things. While the rescue workers prepared his grandmother for transport, the young man leaned against the wall, blood staining his ragged T-shirt and jeans. He stared at his red-streaked hands.

Desi approached a uniformed officer who had come in with the emergency personnel. "Por favor, I would like to ride with you to your station and use your telephone."

The man examined her, flat-eyed. "We need to take your statement. And this *pandillero*—" he pointed to the young man, who paled a shade whiter—"will give an account." He reached for the cuffs on his belt.

"Not necessary, officer." Desi lifted a hand. Forget staying in character. Right now, she was Desiree Jacobs in a Myra wig and makeup. "This is the woman's grandson. He came to save her from the armed pandillas who invaded this home. I will describe them for you."

Manuel eyes widened, and then he looked down, rubbing his hands on his pants.

The officer shrugged Hulk Hogan shoulders. "When we get to the station, we will see who has done what."

Stretcher rattling, the ambulance workers pulled Zapopa out the door. Her eyes were closed, the top of her head swathed in bandages. Desi winced. She'd seen better color on the face of a corpse.

The officer shoved Manuel outside. Desi followed, tugging her case, laptop slung over her shoulder. Emergency lights flickered. A miniature version of the fire-gazing crowd stood around. Voices murmured, and words carried to her—"pandillas," "El Jaguar," and "Fraternidad."

There was that Brotherhood again. What was it?

The officer stuffed Zapopa's grandson into the rear of his vehicle. Then he popped his trunk and stowed Desi's suitcase. Desi nodded her thanks, and the officer cracked a smile as he opened his passenger door for her. A little bit of macho gallantry. A whole lot of don't offend the turista. This government worker knew which side of the tortilla held the filling. Unfortunately, the inside of his vehicle stank like stale cigarette smoke.

Siren off but lights whirling, the police car dashed through traffic. Cantina lights blazed, music blared, and knots of people took up the sidewalks and parts of the streets. Typical Mérida in festival. The partiers scattered for the police car.

Desi prayed silently for wisdom for the medical team and for Zapopa's recovery. The woman's grandson sat sullen in the back. That young man needed a good shake, maybe a slap or two, to knock some sense into him.

Quit being a punk.

You don't have to like the authorities, but you do need to respect them.

Tell only what you saw when you invaded your grandmother's house the second time.

His first foray into Zapopa's house didn't pertain to the shooting incident, but the kid must be shaking in his sandals in fear that she would expose his theft of her money and credit card.

She ought to. The juvenile thief had a little justice coming. Still, Zapopa would need someone to look after her—that's if Manuel had enough decency left in him. Desi gritted her teeth as they took another Mario Andretti corner.

Tony, I need you now!

She should never have taken this commission for the Mexican government. Failure stared her in the face. Worse, she didn't care if she flopped. What was the matter with her? Desiree Jacobs never accepted defeat as an option.

—⁓—

What was the matter with him? Tony jiggled his computer mouse to bring up the screen. Maybe Desi couldn't phone, but she might have sent an e-mail. The hotel in Mérida should have Wi-Fi.

He opened his account and scanned his messages. Not many—nothing important and nothing from Desi. He blew a sharp breath. What's up, woman? You need to contact me soon, or I'm going to…do what?

Leaning back in his chair, he closed his eyes. Time for that heart-to-heart with—

"Lucano!"

Tony's eyes popped open. Bernard Cooke, the assistant special agent in charge, filled his doorway. Tony came to his feet.

The bulky black man stomped in. "I understand the need for a little shut-eye in this zoo, but Immigration just radioed with breaking news on that human contraband case. A small freighter belonging to Jagre Shipping docked in Boston harbor just before this weather hit. An informant claims they're going to unload the women tonight."

"Are they crazy?"

"Crazy like a fox. But we're the hounds, and we've got 'em treed. SWAT is going in first to eliminate any sentries on deck—water approach. Then your squad will join them—land approach. Everything's got to run like a Swiss watch. We need to wait until the transport truck shows up so we can nab those guys, as well as the slavers aboard ship. But then we've got to charge in before they start shooting the sick ones and dumping the bodies overboard."

Tony came around his desk. "Any chance we can use the satellite imaging truck? Eyeball surveillance isn't going to work in this mess. We'll need heat signatures to tell us when the truck arrives and the smugglers board the ship."

Cooke smirked. "It's all set up. We lucked out. The CIA is testing one of their infrared satellites smack dab over this handy-dandy blizzard we've got going on. They decided to play nice and let us use it for a few hours tonight…unless, of coure, they yank it away at any given moment. So get cracking. Time's awasting." He walked to the doorway, then turned and jabbed a finger at Tony. "If there's any drugs aboard the ship, find the stash before the DEA decides to join the party. We can give 'em a late Christmas present and have one up."

Tony rubbed the bridge of his nose. The ASAC made interagency rivalry an art form. He headed into the bull pen to gather the troops. *Sorry, Des.* Praying would have to wait, because those poor women on that ship couldn't.

—⁊⁊⁊—

How did a simple plan to duck out of sight turn into a three-ring circus? Even a decade ago, when Desi was last here, the poorer barrios hadn't been so drug infested. Thanks for nothing to that airport official who directed her to poor Zapopa. Desi bit her lip and watched the night duty sergeant at the police precinct.

The porcine man across the desk stared at her photo ID and passport taken from the luggage and laptop case. He shook his head, chins waggling. "So you claim you are Desiree Jacobs, even though you do not look like her." He leaned across the desk. "I think you are a not-so-clever imposter. What have you done with Señorita Jacobs?"

Desi rubbed her forehead. A dull ache throbbed between her eyebrows. Outside the sergeant's cubicle, the chaos of a Mérida night reigned. Curses and whimpers of prisoners. Barks of harried officers. The tramp of feet. The smells of sweat and fear. Desi's skin itched to leave the depressing place. "Allow me to change in the bathroom."

The man snorted. "You will try to escape. You have already caused much trouble." His scowl would have made a real Myra-type quiver in her tourist flip-flops.

Desi stripped bobby pins from beneath her wig. "And what makes it my fault that young people have so little hope for their future that they turn to drugs and gangs as a way of life?" She tore off the wig, ripping out a stray pin and some real hair. Scalp stinging, she flung the hairpiece on the sergeant's desk.

The man's wheeled chair grumbled backward, and he stared at the wig like she'd tossed him a rat. He squinted at her. "But your face. It is not—"

"I'm good with makeup, okay? And my eyes are hazel beneath these contact lenses. I suggest you call the number on the card you found in my laptop case. You will reach Señor Ramon Sanchez, the government agent assigned to me by Presidential Aide Esteban Corona."

The sergeant eyed his phone like it might bite him. "But we will wake him up."

"Would you rather disturb an aide to President Montoya?"

The chins jiggled from a visible swallow. "We will wait until morning, and then—"

"Fine. I can sit in your office all night. Or better yet, you can stash me in a cell with the group of prostitutes that just came through. I'm sure Señor Sanchez will thank you for endangering his guest in order to guard his sleep."

"But—"

"What would I gain except extra jail time by lying about something like this if I'm the thief you think I am? And what will you gain but a demotion if you don't believe me?"

The sergeant cleared his throat. Frowning, he tapped in the number with a pudgy finger. They waited. At last, someone picked up, and the sergeant began a skeptical and apologetic explanation. A voice blasted, and the man held the handset away from his ear. He flushed red. "At once, señor. Sí, it shall be done. Señorita Jacobs is safe with me." Sucking in air, he cradled the phone. "A car is coming to pick you up, Señorita Jacobs."

"May I have my belongings now?"

"Sí, it shall be done."

Amazing how a low-echelon bully started repeating himself as soon as a bigger kid on the playground barked an order. "And the young man brought in with me needs to be released and taken to the hospital where his grandmother is being treated."

"Sí, it shall—"

"I know."

Twenty minutes later, Desi had removed her makeup, changed clothes, and given her statement. Now she stood in the foyer with an officer, waiting for her government car. After a night like this, if Clayton Greybeck picked up her trail, she'd just give him a black eye and be done with it.

The inner set of glass doors opened, and Manuel slouched through them. He glanced at her and the armed officer, and his gaze slid away.

"Young man." Desi stepped forward.

Zapopa's grandson peered at her, no recognition in his eyes.

"Do what is right." She handed him a thousand pesos.

His fist closed around the bills.

"Go to your grandmother," Desi said

Manuel stared at the money and licked his lips. Desi could practically hear his thoughts. A thousand pesos could buy some good drugs. Why waste it on taxi fare and taking care of an old lady? A huge dilemma for a youth barreling down the wrong road.

Desi sensed the officer's gaze jab between her shoulder blades. He knew that lesson all too well. Was she acting the fool to trust this kid, or would the Hispanic reverence for family ties override the powerful undertow of rebellion?

The young man's shoulders squared. "I will honor my abuela."

Desi nodded, and Manuel hustled out the door. The officer uttered a foul word.

A limousine pulled up, and the officer hefted her suitcase. Laptop on her shoulder, she followed him into the gentle warmth of the Mérida night. Salsa smell spiced the air from a street vendor kiosk, closed until daylight brought tourists. The limo driver opened the passenger door. She slid onto the supple leather seat, let her case slip to the floor, and closed her eyes.

Desi felt the limo slide away from the curb and laid her head back. What next and where was she being taken? The answers didn't matter as consciousness faded.

A lurch jerked her body and brought her eyes open. Through the clear plastic partition that separated her from the driver, she watched him lower his window. A deep voice growled a command to get out, followed by a sharp click.

Desi's neck hair stood on end. That sounded like—

The snout of a gun poked through the open window.

Seven

*T*he limo driver got out, hands climbing upward. A dim streetlight revealed they'd been accosted near a park, deserted except for scattered trees and an empty bench. The back door jerked open, and a ski-masked head popped inside. Desi's heart did a tap dance.

"Where is he?" The masked man's voice crackled with cold authority.

Desi swallowed. "Where's who?"

The intruder slid in beside her. "Are you his *sancha*?" His silky tone conveyed intimate insult.

Desi's fingers clawed into the leather seat. "I have never met the owner of this limo—making it rather difficult for me to be his kept woman."

"Then you will give him a message." The man leaned close, and her nostrils filled with the smell of cheap cigars. He gripped her chin in merciless fingers.

Desi bit her tongue against a cry. Great! A bruised face and a sore mouth to add to a scraped elbow and tender bottom.

He smiled with all the warmth of a crocodile. "Tell him how easy it was to stop this vehicle and get to the passenger. He will understand the point." The man released her and slithered out of the car as if he were part snake. Not a bad analogy.

The vehicle jiggled, and the driver resumed his place behind the wheel. Snake Man slammed her door, and the limo leaped forward with a screech of tires, leaving the pit of her stomach somewhere on the pavement. They drove for another ten minutes at ridiculous speeds.

Finally, the car slowed in front of a barred gate that barely swung out of the way fast enough to admit them to a horseshoe drive in front of a large brick home. The portico light glowed between a pair of entry columns. Hope of safe haven quickened Desi's breathing.

She rubbed her sore chin. Maybe this local government poobah could tell her why she'd been robbed, accosted, and assaulted from the moment she arrived in Mérida, a city that trumpeted its low crime rate in the glossy brochures. This last incident was directed right at Mr. Poobah. What was going on? Corruption? Not much of a shocker. Or something more sinister?

The driver opened her door, and Desi climbed out. His scowl could have soured milk.

She went up the stairs toward the front door. A dog growled, joined by another, both animals hidden in the shadows. Ant feet crawled across Desi's skin. The driver issued a sharp command, and the growls ceased.

Then a smiling, bobbing Hispanic woman in a long housecoat filled the doorway and beckoned Desi inside. Friendly face much appreciated, thank you very much. Desi staggered more than walked into the foyer.

To her left, dimly lit stairs swooped upward in a graceful curve. To her right and ahead lay darkened rooms. She checked her watch. Three a.m.? Oh, brother, no wonder she was tired. About two hours of sleep in as many days, and precious little before that in the planning stages of her caper in Mexico City. The Pakal fiasco seemed long ago and far away.

Housecoat Woman led her toward the stairs, high cheekbones and broad nose denoting a citizen of Mayan extraction. Desi went up the carpeted stairs on the woman's heels. The chauffeur tromped behind with Desi's bag. At the top of the stairs, they stopped at a white door. The woman pushed it open and stood aside. Desi stepped into a spacious bedroom. Her feet sank into smooth carpeting, and a large, canopied bed drew her with a silent siren song.

She turned to thank her escorts, but the hall was empty. Her bag sat by the door. Silence cloaked the house. Strange that no one had spoken a word to her. She shrugged. Was the woman the housekeeper or mistress of the home? Desi guessed the former.

Her jaw creaked around a yawn. She glanced at the bed, but an open door invited her into a bathroom fitted with every convenience known to man—or woman. Should she shower or bathe her face and fall onto the mattress? The face-splash won. A shower sounded like too much effort.

She threw off her outer clothes, clicked off the light, and crawled between sheets so sleek and crisp they had to have been ironed. The pillow cradled her head in blessed softness.

Oh, crumb! She stiffened. She forgot to try calling Tony. Sighing, she clicked on the bedside lamp and dug out her cell phone. Aack! The battery was dead, and her charger had been in her carry-on. She needed to find a house phone, but it wasn't a good idea for a stranger to go prowling around in the dark. Oh, well, morning was almost here.

She rolled onto her side. What was the big lug up to? Her eyes drifted shut. Probably twiddling his thumbs in his sixteenth-floor office, watching snowflakes fall. She smiled. At least one of them was enjoying an uneventful night.

—~~~—

Inside the satellite imaging van, Tony passed out cups of hot coffee to his squad. Outside, the storm shrieked, but it barely rattled the FBI vehicle sheltered between a pair of warehouses on the pier. "Enjoy the java now, kiddies. When that transport truck arrives, no more lounging in the warmth. Dell will stay with the van, but the rest of us'll have at least a block to cover on foot."

Slidell didn't stir at the mention of his name. His gaze stayed glued to the satellite screen. Typical. Tony sat down and scratched inside his thermal boot. Hot as blazes now, but he'd be glad of the footwear once his team stepped outside.

"Walk in the park, right?" Polanski nudged Hajimoto.

"Speak for yourself." He grimaced. "I hate winter. Who would have guessed this far north in the middle of January would be a hotbed of the South American slave trade?"

"Jagre Shipping has an office in Quebec too," Slidell said, staring at his screen. "Technically, we are not the farthest north, though I believe Quebec is enjoying better weather."

"Thanks for the report, Dell." Polanski snickered. "If we wanted to do an arrest in nice weather, we should have boarded this boat in Miami or Charleston. Jagre's got presence there too. Anybody up for a transfer?"

"What about that name?" Bergstrom spoke up.

All eyes turned toward the new agent…except Dell's.

Haj sat forward, elbows on his knees. "What name are you talking about?"

The kid flushed but didn't turn away. "Jagre. Seems like it should mean something, but we haven't found anybody named Jagre on the ownership papers for the corporation, just a bunch of foreign directors who may or may not exist."

Intelligent observation. Tony eyed the new agent. Maybe he'd work out. "Hopefully, we'll arrest somebody tonight who can give us the answer. We do know that the Fraternidad gang has its finger in this pie, but they needed someone with business expertise, not just street smarts to set it up. I'd say we're dealing with a dangerous hybrid—a white collar–gang mix—and the quicker we shut it down, the better."

Silence fell, except for the slurping of coffee and the roar of the storm. Tony cradled his foam cup between his palms, absorbing warmth. They'd better perform on the cutting edge of excellent tonight, or they could wind up a bunch of empty-handed Popsicles. And those people in the cargo hold would be dead or worse than dead.

"Incoming." Dell leaned toward his screen. "Good-sized vehicle. Heated end for end."

Haj snorted. "At least they don't plan on freezing the ladies from here to wherever they stash them."

"Suit up, children." Tony grabbed his jacket. "And be careful out there when we get close to the water. I don't want to have to fish any-body out of the drink."

"The truck stopped," Dell said. "Two warm bodies just got out. Moving. Moving." He fell silent, watching the screen. "Okay, they've disap-peared onto the boat. No other human heat signatures in the truck cab."

"Good break for us. Bergstrom can secure the vehicle while we con-duct shipboard business." Tony adjusted his radio headset. "Stay close together. Once we're away from the buildings, visibility will be nil. Dell will let us know if we go astray."

He pulled up his parka hood and took a deep breath of warm air. Then he gripped the handle and opened the rear of the van. A white world swirled into his face. He hopped out and held the door for the others, and then muscled it closed as a wind gust fought him.

He passed down the side of the van, the others on his heels. He stepped into driving snow and turned right, blazing a path through a three-foot snowbank parallel to the dark blob of a warehouse nearly obscured by drifts. Frozen pellets stung exposed parts of his face and lodged in his eyelashes. He scrubbed his eyes with the back of his glove. Labored grunts behind him indicated that his squad followed.

"You're on track. Keep going," Dell reported in his ear. Tony didn't answer, saving his breath for his next step.

The transport truck wasn't half a block away, but he couldn't see it. Only the ship's light bobbing on the swells. A few more steps, and headlights poked out of the haze not far ahead.

"SWAT reports a go on their end." Dell's voice came through.

So far so good. Tony reached the side of the truck, turned his back on the wind, and leaned against the solid bulk. Great to breathe without inhaling ice. The rumble of the motor barely registered over the howl of the wind.

Who figured this as a golden opportunity bust anyway? Suicide was a closer approximation. But then, the slavers probably figured no cop in their right mind would be out in this. But a bunch of crazy feds? They were here, weren't they? Guess that answered the question.

A thud sounded, followed by a feminine grunt. The truck panel rippled.

Tony made out a form that came up to his chin. "Polanski, that you?"

"It's not the Easter Bunny."

Tony chuckled. "More like the Abominable Snow Agent."

"Anybody ever tell you you're not that funny?"

Yeah, humor used to be Erickson's department. A door slammed, and the truck jiggled. "Bergstrom made his post."

"Lucky dog. He'll be warm inside that cab."

"Bored pooch. Just sit tight and make sure nobody tries to make a getaway."

"Bored is good for a first-station agent." Hajimoto's voice drifted to them. His stocky bulk made a dark splotch in the white.

Tony shivered, not entirely from cold. Eerie not to be able to make out people's faces. "Glad you could join the party. We're cleared to board."

He led the way past the truck and focused on spotting the gangplank. The ship loomed ahead. He pressed on, and his boot struck a hard object. The bottom of the gangplank. Grasping the cables on both sides of the plank, Tony surged upward. The plank twisted and groaned beneath his feet. And the slavers thought they'd get a bunch of frightened women down this flimsy thing without someone falling in? Not likely.

The side of the ship came within arm's reach. From the deck, a figure waved him onward. SWAT. One of their own.

Tony put a foot forward, but it slid back on a slick spot. He lurched, grabbing at the side of the ship, but his feet went out from under him, and he toppled against the gangplank line. His breath hitched as the cable sagged, and the surging Atlantic slammed the freighter, sucking him toward the greedy waves. His heart ping-ponged around his chest cavity. Then a gloved hand grabbed his arm and yanked him onto the deck.

"Welcome aboard, Lucano." A familiar voice spoke in his ear.

"McCluskey?" Tony shouted over the storm. He'd worked with this guy eight months ago when they rescued Desi from a terrorist.

"Guilty as charged." The man stood, legs splayed, dressed in a neoprene dry suit that made swimming in forty-degree water the walk in the park Polanski had mentioned. The SWAT leader cradled an automatic weapon in the crook of one arm.

"I had no idea you and your guys were scuba-trained."

"Your all-around elite team." McCluskey grinned as Haj and Polanski joined them. "Bagged a couple of sentries on the bridge and one in a passageway. No hitches. No alarms. My guys are in place to take the hold, so if you'll follow me." The Irishman became a blob in the white as he headed up the deck.

McCluskey swung a hatch wide. "You ready to get out of the wind?"

"Lead on!" Tony stepped through the door and onto a broad landing at the top of steep stairs. Overhead, a single light bulb glowed behind wire mesh. The air warmed. Not a lot, but enough to feel like the tropics to his chilled body.

Haj crowded inside, then Polanski, who shut the door on the storm's howl. Trailing the SWAT leader, Tony and his squad members went down the stairs and into a cracker-box room that smelled like sweaty socks.

"Leave your coats," McCluskey said. "Boots too. Those things make too much noise."

Tony started tugging off his snow gear. "This is not an optimal situation for any of us. No hesitation on deadly force to keep a hostage situation from developing."

McCluskey jerked a nod. "We'll neutralize the firepower and let you handle the arrests."

Tony pulled out his Glock handgun and checked the load. The piece was warm in his frigid hands. It had been cradled against his body under the parka. "We're good to go, then?"

McCluskey flashed a shark grin. "Let's do it."

The SWAT leader led out. Tony waved his people ahead and took up the rear. They went through a deserted mess hall and a bunk area. At the top of another set of stairs, McCluskey motioned for quiet. They crept down and stopped on a narrow walkway. The barred railing on one side overlooked a laundry area.

A stench wafted upward—a combination of feces and vomit. Conditions below had to be hideous.

Tony assessed their location. To the right, the walkway led to an open hatch and a dimly lit passage. To the left, it went toward another drop-off that was probably more stairs. McCluskey led left, toward another guy in a neoprene suit who hunkered on his knees, watching through the bars. He glanced their way and stood as they joined him.

The SWAT leader and the sentry started a low-voiced conversation. As the caboose of the train, Tony glanced back and caught a movement in the passage beyond the walkway. His spine went stiff. Could McCluskey's team have missed a sentry? He jabbed Haj in the ribs.

"Huh?" The stocky Japanese looked at him.

"Cover me. We may have unfriendly company." Tony flattened himself against the wall.

Haj knelt, gun brandished. Tony edged toward the passageway, Glock hugged to his body, muzzle pointed upward.

One sidestep. Another. His movement gained the rest of the group's attention. Out of the corner of his eye, Tony saw them turn and lift weapons. A burst of automatic fire exploded in the passageway. The shots weren't aimed at them. Probably a warning to the others down below.

Tony hustled forward, Haj and Polanski on his heels.

"We're blown!" McCluskey shouted. "My team'll secure control of the lower hold."

"We'll get the shooter." Tony plunged through the hatch door, lowered gun tracing an arc. The door to the room on his right stood open. Empty. He turned toward the closed door.

"I'm on it," Haj said.

Tony moved on, Polanski trailing. More empty rooms.

"Clear!" Haj caught up to them.

Gunfire and shouts sounded below. Tony kept his gaze ahead. The passage dead-ended into one perpendicular. He hugged the wall. "FBI. Drop your weapon and show yourself."

Someone giggled. Giggled?

"Come and get me, señor." Her voice gave sultry new meaning. "I promise you warm welcome."

More shots from below, then silence. Tony counted a long ten seconds. All remained still. Had to be McClusky's triumph. No way did a few lowlifes take out a whole SWAT team in a few rounds of shots. "The battle's over. Give it up."

No answer, but no sound of movement either.

"Secure below!" the SWAT leader bellowed up the passageway.

"You heard that." Tony edged toward the corner. "Your friends are either dead or captured. Lay down your weapon, and come out with your hands on your head."

"My friends?" Frigid contempt flowed from the words. An automatic delivered a burst, and then came the sound of running feet. The footfalls became a hollow clatter against metal stairs.

Tony peeked around the corner to see small boot-clad feet disappear onto the level above. He motioned for his squad to follow and hustled after. He clambered up the stairs until his head came even with the floor. A quick clearance check, then he lunged upward and raced after the fading sound. In a few paces, the passage branched. Which way?

"We'll take right." Haj nudged his shoulder.

Tony nodded. "Polanski, go with him."

"Gotcha." The two darted off.

Tony moved down the left passage, listening. The wind was louder this close to the top deck. He commanded his heart rate to slow, muting the internal thunder. Feet pattered on stairs. "This way!" he shouted over his shoulder.

"Coming!" Polanski's words came back faint as Tony plunged forward through a bunk area, then ahead full toward the stairs. He was not going to lose this larcenous Lolita. Especially since Bergstrom was all that stood between her and escape.

On the next deck, another set of stairs began at a right angle to the ones Tony had just left. From an open door at the top, dawn's light brought illumination but not warmth. Freezing air slapped his cheeks. Was she waiting for him above?

Tony went up in a cautious crouch and then flattened himself beside the door. He leaped out into the teeth of the storm, Glock ready.

The deck lay empty. What was strange about this picture? He blinked. No snow. The wind howled, but the snow had stopped and dawn paled the air.

Teeth chattering, deck an ice cube beneath his stocking-clad feet, Tony glanced around. He was in the forecastle, facing the harbor buildings. He darted to the rail. There she was, an undainty figure swathed in parka, jeans, and boots lumbering down the gangplank. She clutched a bundle that wasn't a gun.

He brought his weapon up, fighting shivers. "Stop right there." The wind ate his words, and she didn't react.

Tony took aim at a spot on the snow-piled quay below her and squeezed the trigger. The gangplank line parted and whipped against the hull. Crack shot—if he'd been aiming for the cable.

But it got her attention. She clutched her bundle in one hand and lifted her gun in the other. Tony got off another shot and missed again. He ducked as her automatic rattled, and Polanski shouted a warning in the same heartbeat. Bullets spanged off the ship's rail near where his heart should have been. If he wasn't a crack shot in the cold, she sure was.

Another gun barked. Different caliber. A woman screamed, followed by a splash.

Tony stared over the rail. Bergstrom stood in shooter's stance, gun leveled at the spot where the woman had been. A body bobbed on the waves between the quay bumpers and the pier. Tony's mouth fell open, but he snapped it shut. Why should he be surprised? The kid was trained at Quantico. He'd heard firing, gotten out of the truck, and taken care of business.

Tony headed toward the gangplank, Haj and Polanski flanking him. "Tough break Bergstrom had to cut his teeth on a kill shot against a woman. Hope it doesn't ruin him."

"Makes that much difference?" Polanski shot him a look.

"You bet." Haj holstered his gun. "A guy always feels worse if he shoots a female."

Polanski hugged herself. "We should get below and put on our snow gear."

"You and Haj go," Tony said. "Check on status in the lower hold, and make sure any deserving p-parties are treated to their Miranda rights and the c-cuffs. It's just as close for m-me to trot down there, climb in that warm t-truck cab, and have a chat with Bergstrom. We'll c-call in some fresh faces to clean up this m-mess." He halted at the top of the plank.

On the quay, Bergstrom leaned against the side of the truck, gun arm limp at his side. Wind-tossed snow swished up at his lanky form from a drift at his feet. The kid was in the numb disbelief phase, but he needed to snap out of it and get on with the job. It was the best thing.

"Watch that slick spot, boss." Haj waved as he and Polanski left the rail.

Tony gripped the remaining gangplank line and watched where he planted the feet he could no longer feel. A sharp smack against the hull reminded him that the other cable waved loose at the mercy of the gale. Better get off this thing pronto and tell the others to find a safer way to leave the ship.

The wind shrieked and grabbed at his hair. From the corner of his eye, he saw the free line whip toward him, and he jerked his arm up. The cable struck his ribs, and pain splintered through him. His scream meshed with the wind's as he tumbled end over end from the plank.

Tony hit the water feet first. An arctic vise squeezed his bones. Excruciating ache shot from his legs straight through the top of his head. Momentum plunged him toward the bottom. He flailed. At least, he thought he did.

He reached toward the pale sheet overhead. Must be daylight. Air. Icicles sank razor teeth into his marrow. The brightness grew closer, and then receded—like something kept pulling him back. An undertow? He gave a mighty kick and hit a wall. The ship? The quay? Precious breath left his lungs as he caromed off the hard object into liquid oblivion. The light was gone.

His head bumped something solid but soft. What? Oh, yes, the woman's body. He grabbed and missed. The ocean breathed around him, pushing out, sucking in. He couldn't feel himself anymore.

No! Not like this, God!

Desi's face filled his inner vision. He'd never marry her now. Despair stole the last of his breath as consciousness winked out.

Eight

*D*esi drifted awake. What delicious cloud was she floating on? She sighed and opened her eyes to an unfamiliar room painted a buttery yellow. Light trickled through vertical blinds. What? Where? She stiffened. Oh, yes, the home of Ramon Sanchez, cultural affairs honcho for the state of Yucatán, Mexico. He'd be at work by now, but she'd hunt him down at his office. An overabundance of nasty events needed serious attention.

She sat up and winced. That was one awkward landing on the pavement when the kid stole her carry-on. Her stomach tightened. Her ring! Her medallion! Tony! Find a house phone and a new charger for her cell. She shook her head and slumped. Maybe she should drop him an e-mail. If the weather had broken in Boston, he'd probably be home catching some shut-eye.

How could she tell him she'd lost her engagement ring? Did she want to do that over the phone from thousands of miles away? But, oh, she needed to hear the deep timbre of his voice.

Time to go home.

She'd give the powers-that-be her tidbit about the drug lord interested in "shiny baubles," and they could take it from there. She wasn't a private investigator, and she sure wasn't a DEA agent. Maybe Ramon Sanchez could have Preston Standish picked up, and she'd get her medallion back. If she could book a flight to Boston, she wasn't going to stick around to find out.

She swung her legs out of bed. Youch! The sore rear didn't want to get in gear today. She probed the insides of her cheeks with her tongue. Hamburger, thanks to last night's limo invader with the pincher fingers. A tremor rippled through her. *Get a grip! The guy wasn't even after you.* But why was he after Señor Sanchez?

And what about Zapopa? Had the woman made it through the night?

What kind of a terrible person was she that the wounded grandmother took last place on her list? She shook her head. Too many questions before she'd even hit the shower.

A half-hour later, dressed in a peasant skirt and blouse, she left her room. In the hallway, heavenly scents greeted her nostrils. She'd missed breakfast, but maybe she was in time for lunch. Her nose led her down polished hardwood stairs and into a dining room adjacent to the foyer. She halted on the threshold of a white room accented in midnight blue. A woman, a teenager, and a man sat around a table covered in a linen cloth.

"Buenos días," Desi said.

The woman's sharp nose pinched, and the teenager scowled.

Desi's face heated. *"Permiso."*

The white-haired man who sat at the head of the table rose, napkin in hand. Golden-brown eyes gazed at her from a strong, square face. Shadows beneath the eyelids and a droop of the mouth betrayed weariness. Señor Sanchez?

He smiled, but a second too late to be wholehearted. "Señorita Jacobs. Please join us. We trust you slept well."

"Thank you. I was quite comfortable."

Sanchez waved toward an empty seat beside the teenager. "Carlos!"

The man's bark brought the teen to his feet. Eyes hooded by thick lashes, the youth pulled back Desi's chair.

She glanced up into his sulky face as she sat. "Gracias."

"De nada." He resumed his place and attacked his food like it might bite him if he didn't get it first.

The plump housekeeper Desi had met last night came in through a different entrance, sandals slapping on the parquet floor. She set a plate, napkin, and silverware in front of Desi, and then poured water from a Perrier bottle into a cut-crystal glass and added the glass to the place setting.

"Gracias." Desi smiled up at her.

The housekeeper's cheeks went pink, and she bobbed a little bow, then rushed out.

"Señorita Jacobs." Sanchez resettled his napkin on his lap. "Allow me to introduce my wife, Pilar, and my son, Carlos. I am Ramon. We are honored to entertain an American businesswoman."

"Please call me Desiree. I'm thankful to be here." *You have no idea. Or maybe you do.* She studied him.

Ramon pursed his lips and turned his attention to his food.

A smile split Pilar's ruby-red lips. She folded her hands together, manicured nails as bright as her mouth. "We are happy to have you in our home. The clothes fooled me for a moment. You *norteamericanos* love the native dress. We will shop this afternoon. Sí?"

So that's what brought on the woman's nose-pinch when Desi appeared in her doorway. Wonder what the lady of the house would have thought if she'd appeared as Myra?

Desi dished Spanish rice onto her plate. "I appreciate your kindness, señora."

"Pilar, please."

Desi helped herself to an enchilada in creamy white sauce. The entrée smelled like it had some kind of seafood filling. "I must conduct business today, Pilar, but perhaps another time we can browse the shops." Or maybe never.

"Have some salsa." Ramon passed a brightly painted Talavera bowl, a smile straining his flushed face. He launched into a tourist-friendly description of city festivals.

Desi ate and nodded. Pilar's eyes glazed over. Carlos mumbled something about getting ready for football practice and bolted from the table. Why wasn't the teenager in school? And why was a busy government executive home in the middle of the day?

Her fork halted halfway to her mouth. It was Saturday. Good grief, her world was so inside out, she didn't know the day of the week.

"Would it be possible to visit with you after lunch, Ramon? And, por favor, use a landline phone? My cell is dead."

"Most certainly. And do you require a wireless Internet connection?"

"That would be most helpful."

The rest of the meal passed in small talk, and then her host pushed back his chair. "I am at your disposal." He nodded to Desi. "Shall we retire to the patio?"

Pilar fluttered languid fingers as they left the room.

Ramon led the way through a sunken living room and out French doors onto a shaded patio. The air was warm, but not heavy, and scented with the exotic breath of white gardenias. Multihued beds of flowers adorned the lush green lawn that spread to a line of trees half the length of a soccer field away. To her left and down a set of stone stairs a swimming pool sparkled. To her right sat a round, glass-topped table flanked by wicker chairs.

Ramon pulled one out for her, then took a seat opposite. "I understand from Luis that you had an unfortunate encounter on your way here last night."

"A series of unfortunate encounters that began on the plane to Mérida."

Her host's brows knotted. "Enlighten me."

"We can start with last night and work backward. I assume Luis is your chauffeur, and that he told you we were waylaid by a group of armed men."

Ramon nodded, gaze veiled by dark lashes.

"One of the thugs got into the car," Desi went on, "and said he was demonstrating how easily they could access the passenger. He expected to find you in that seat. Do you often drive around the city in the middle of the night?"

He flushed. "I was told you were astute. Most would have demanded to know who accosted them and what I was going to do about it."

"I'm getting to that."

Ramon grimaced. "Very well. You are owed an explanation. Yes, the midnight hour too often finds me on the streets." He paused and sighed. "Looking for Carlos. He has become involved with bad people. I have been using all my power to remove this evil, but the gang wants me to stop interfering in their business. Last night was only another threat among many. My apologies that you found yourself in its path."

A picture began to form in Desi's mind, and not a pretty one. She tapped her upper lip. "Would these 'bad people' be in the employ of a gang leader who calls himself El Jaguar?"

Ramon's eyes widened. "Where did you hear of this man? This parasite!"

Desi clasped her hands in front of her. "There was an explosion and fire last night in a poor barrio not far from the airport. I was lodging with a woman there—"

"You were not at the hotel downtown?"

"Señor Corona must not have called you to explain my change of plans."

Ramon frowned. "It seems there has been a lack of communication, but Señor Corona's schedule is not often his own."

"Of course. But he didn't try to call you this morning, either?"

The cultural affairs director lifted his hands. "I have no explanation, but I will request one. Please continue with your story about last night."

Desi filled him in on the conversation she'd heard at the scene of the fire.

Ramon got up and paced the length of the patio. "So these men believe the fire was ordered by El Jaguar because one of his dealers did not deliver some trinket?"

"Probably more than a trinket. Does this gang leader collect antiquities? Perhaps he is behind the rash of cultural-heritage thefts."

Ramon stopped by his chair. "We have heard the rumor that he is a collector, but we—"

Desi's voice rose. "You knew, and your government sent me into this situation anyway?"

"El Jaguar collects antique Spanish jewelry. He is *loco* for it."

"Antique jewelry?" Desi subsided against her chair. No wonder dealers had been eager to buy her medallion and angry when she refused to sell. Albon Guerrera could have warned her, but then, why spare the daughter of his enemy from the attention of a dangerous man?

"On the flight to Mérida, I was robbed of an antique medallion by an Englishman who introduced himself as Preston Standish. He claimed to be a history professor on holiday. Could he be working for El Jaguar or planning to sell him the medallion?"

Ramon shook his head. "A foolish move for a foreign professor. El Jaguar despises Anglos. He would shoot him, take the medallion, and call it a day well spent."

"Who is the gang leader? His real name, not the cartoon persona."

Ramon demonstrated the elaborate Latino shrug. "This we would like to know. His headquarters lie in the Yucatán jungle, but we have not found the location." He resumed his seat. "You must finish your story about last night. How did you end up at the police station?"

Desi told him about her stolen luggage, the confrontation with the three pandilleros, the shooting, and the grandson who promised to honor his abuela. She skipped the part about her Myra disguise. No need to confuse an already complicated situation.

Ramon sat back with a long exhale. "I am mortified that you were subjected to such behavior in my country—my city." His fingertips beat a tattoo on the tabletop. "The pandillas are pale imitations of the real thing—the Fraternidad de la Garra or simply the Fraternidad. This gang is popping up all over the United States and South America. Here, El Jaguar is their leader."

Desi's scalp prickled. If Zapopa had been shot by a wannabe gangster, what must the genuine be like? She knew. Like the man who slithered in and out of the limo last night. He'd done nothing but pinch her face and speak words of menace, but he made the drugged, jittery pandilleros look like mama's boys.

"The Fraternidad is organized," Ramon continued. "They are focused. Their violence is not random, and they have no conscience or fear of the authorities."

"This bullyboy's got a private army. No wonder he's tough to root out."

Ramon inclined his head. "You have said it."

"Will you check on Zapopa?"

"Most certainly. And call Señor Corona." Ramon's face hardened. "Also, if Señor Standish is still in the Yucatán, he will be found. It is not acceptable that you have been treated so ill. I wish you to know Mexico's friendly face. There is much to see, to do—"

"Mexico is beautiful. I've been here before and plan to return."

"Ah." His gaze brightened. "You have a special someone to bring along, perhaps?"

Desi laughed. "Another thing I love about Mexico. You are all romantics at heart."

"It is so." Ramon pressed a hand to his chest.

"I'm engaged. Unfortunately, my ring was in the bag that was stolen."

"¡Ay, chihuahua! I will call the airport to see if your property was recovered. I am disturbed that the official sent you into a dangerous area for lodging. Inexcusable." He motioned toward the pool. "Take a refreshing dip, por favor, while you wait for my report. Ask our house-keeper, Juanita, for anything you need." He looked at his watch. "My son has gone to practice, and Pilar will be out for the afternoon with her friends. You are not disappointed about the shopping trip?"

Desi laughed. "Muchas gracias for your kindness. But if you have a second extension, I must call my fiancé and my office."

"Very well. When you are done with the telephone, the password cinco blanca will let you onto our wireless network." Her host stood. "Come with me."

She followed him down a hall, and they came to a small room decorated in high-end Spanish froufrou. In the midst of pink and yellow tasseled lamps, overstuffed chairs, and a pillow-drowned settee, a dainty filigree desk cowered beneath a load of statuettes and flower vases. The dark eyes of the woman in the sophisticated Frida Kahlo painting on the wall seemed to stare down in horror. A laugh started to escape, but Desi pressed her lips together.

Ramon's teeth flashed. "Pilar's study. The phone is somewhere in here."

"I'll find it." She headed for the desk then stopped. "Señor Sanchez."

He turned in the hallway. "Ramon, por favor."

"This question is too serious for informality. You say you have received threats from the Fraternidad. Aren't you afraid for yourself and your family?"

His face darkened. "Fear attacks me every moment, but I cannot allow it to paralyze me. My family can never be safe as long as this gang is free to seduce our youth and attack our citizens."

"You are a man of vision and courage, Ramon Sanchez."

One side of his mouth lifted. "Or perhaps an idealistic fool, as Pilar sometimes says. But a man must be willing to lay down his life for something, sí?"

A prickly sensation came over Desi's skin. Not an unpleasant feeling, just…urgent. A God-moment. "Sí." She licked her lips. "How do you feel about the One who has already laid down His life for you?"

Ramon's eyes widened. "*¿Jesús Cristo?* I was baptized into the Church."

Desi shook her head. "I didn't ask about your church status. How are things between you and Jesús Cristo?"

He took two steps into the froufrou room. "I am faithful to attend Mass. I light candles, give to the poor, say prayers, go to confession. That is my part. The priest makes things right with God on my behalf. That is his part."

"Now is not the time to send someone else to speak to God for you."

Ramon's brows drew together, and he stared at the carpet.

Had she offended him? She held her breath.

He lifted his head, gaze guarded, but not angry. "There is truth in what you say. I will think on it." He turned and left, brisk as a soldier.

Did I do it right, Lord? No answer except a calm acceptance that the matter of Ramon Sanchez was safe in God's hands.

Desi spotted the phone on the desk, an ornate object fashioned in the pole style of the early 1900s, but with buttons, not a dial. She pounced on it and rang the operator.

After giving the woman her credit card information and the number she wished to reach, Desi settled onto the desk chair for the call to go through to the FBI office. Might as well try there first. Fidgeting with a stray paper clip, she waited.

"Señorita Jacobs?" The operator came back on. "Telephone service is temporarily unavailable throughout much of Boston. You can try back later."

Disappointment weighted her stomach. "That's all right. Buenos días—no, wait. You said much of Boston. Not everywhere?"

"Sí. Some sectors are operational."

Desi rattled off the number for Tony's apartment. "Try that one."

A minute later, a ring tone sounded. Hope sparked. The phone continued to ring, and her expectation ebbed. Tony's voice came on the answering machine. She drank in the spiel until the beeps sounded. "Hey, hon. It's me. Just calling to let you know I miss you. I imagine you're either still socked in at the office or snuggled in bed, dead to the world. I'll call again later. Love you beyond reason. Bye."

Next, she tried the HJ Securities office and Max's house, but neither location had telephone service. Yikes! Could she get a flight to Boston? The operator put her through to the Mérida airport. A few minutes later, she hung up. No flights in the foreseeable future. The eastern seaboard of Massachusetts was buried in white, with more snow expected.

Heart leaden, she rested her elbows on the desk blotter and put her head in her hands. *God, I don't understand. Now that I'm ready to rush home, nature won't let me.*

She sat up, and the blotter shifted, jarring a flower vase. Desi grabbed it before it toppled. A familiar business card border peeped at her from the blotter's edge. She pulled the card out. Those Greybecks turned up everywhere. Maybe Señora Sanchez was considering an upgraded security system. Made sense in light of the Fraternidad threat. But why hide the card, and why was it dog-eared from use? She flipped the card over and found a U.S. phone number written in ink. Whoa! Pretty hinky if this was a personal number.

Curiosity drove her back to the operator. While she waited for the call to go through, Desi slipped the card under the blotter and straightened everything she'd disturbed.

"I'm sorry. The party you wish to reach is unavailable," said a recorded female voice with a Bronx accent. "Please leave a message after the tone."

Desi hung up. A generic answering service. Strange.

She left the office, shaking her head, and went upstairs. Her last thread of communication with Tony had better be intact. She snatched up her laptop, marched out of the bedroom, and nearly collided with Juanita.

The woman jumped back, mouth agape. Desi recoiled, swallowed, and took a deep breath. No wonder the housekeeper never spoke. The woman had no tongue. Was the problem congenital or something more sinister?

Desi worked up a smile. "Sorry for startling you. I appreciate all your kindness."

Juanita smiled, bobbed her head, and moved up the hall.

Desi wandered down to the living room. Would it be rude to ask Señor Sanchez what had happened to Juanita? She booted up her computer. The password screen appeared, and she logged in. A few keystrokes later she was reading her e-mail. *Tony, hon, I'd better see something from you.*

"Señorita Jacobs! Desiree!"

Desi looked up.

Ramon Sanchez stood at the top of the steps, face a pale mask. "Señor Corona's wife was murdered last night."

"Oh, dear heavens!" Desi lunged to her feet. "That nice man. Do they have any idea who might have—"

"A burglar, apparently. When Esteban arrived home last night he found his wife clubbed to death with a marble statuette and many of their valuables missing."

"How terrible for him. No wonder he didn't call you with my change of plans."

Ramon inclined his head, lips thin. "Excuse me, por favor. I must notify others."

"Of course."

The man hustled away, and Desi sank to the cushioned sofa, the taste of ashes on her tongue. She turned her attention to the laptop screen. More than ever, she needed to hear from… A subject line grabbed her attention. "Urgent! About Tony!" The sender was Max. Desi tapped the mouse button, and the message spread across the screen.

> Get home if you have to burrow under the earth like Bugs
> Bunny! Tony had an accident at work. He's in a coma. They
> don't know if he'll make it.

Nine

"I'm not much, God, but if You need a soul, You got a volunteer. Take me, leave him—straight-up swap."

The gravelly mutter dragged Tony from a dark, warm place—a place he wanted to stay. *Familiar voice. Who? Think... Too hard. Go away.*

The voice continued, as if carrying through layers of cotton. "I know the docs say his insides could be real messed up, but I'm not gonna believe it. Lucano's too tough. He wasn't supposed to make it this lo—ong..." The last word broke in the middle and trailed away.

Blessed quiet. Good. Tony drifted, sank...

The bed jiggled. "But he looks bad, Jesus. Like nobody's home."

The words carried, vague and distant, as if whispered into the far end of a long tube. He didn't have to go toward the voice. He could turn and walk away—never go back. Maybe he would.

Tony sank into welcome night.

—⁓—

Desi gnawed the nail on her right forefinger and stared out the window of a Mexican government jet. Ramon Sanchez had made arrangements, never mind the mess he was dealing with himself.

"We are over the United States now." The pilot's voice came from the intercom.

She'd asked to be notified when they left the Gulf of Mexico and zoomed over home soil headed for Albany, New York. That was as close as a plane could get to the blizzard's squall line. How would she cover the 160-plus miles between Albany and Boston? Desi bit down hard on the nail and left a drop of blood behind. Beg, borrow, or steal a tank.

I'm on my way, Tony. Don't leave me.

—⟶≈⟵—

"Wake up, Lucano. You're sleeping on the job."

The male voice bellowed down the tube again. He'd tell it to shut up, but he couldn't talk. Couldn't move. Someone stuff a sock in it for him.

"Quit your slacking. Wake u-up." The command descended into a thin plea.

Silence. Tony faded.

—⟶≈⟵—

Desi climbed out of the plane onto the tarmac in Albany. A wind blast reacquainted her with New England winter. She snuggled into Pilar's parka and boots left over from a vacation to Aspen.

She hurried toward the terminal, head ducked, stomach churning.

Tony had been submerged in ice water for almost seven minutes in this subzero weather. The frigid conditions slowed the death process, or she'd be returning to Boston for a funeral. For now, his heart was beating, and he was breathing, but he'd lost his spleen, and other vital organs weren't working properly. And who knew how much brain damage—

A whimper left Desi's throat as she flung open the door and stepped inside the building. She found the terminal hot spot and booted up. Another e-mail from Max. Tony appeared to be in stable condition, but his kidneys still didn't work, and no response to stimuli. They were worried about pneumonia. IVs dripped medicine into his veins. Tony's mom was on her way back from visiting relatives in California. Everyone was praying. God was in control. Keep the faith, blah, blah...

Pulse throbbing, Desi set the laptop aside and ducked her head to her knees.

Dear merciful, heavenly Father, help my unbelief. We need a miracle.

She straightened, spine stiff, thoughts on lockdown. She'd be no good to Tony if she melted into a hysterical puddle. Her hands shook as she pulled out her cell phone, fully recharged on the plane with the charger she bought just before dashing to the airport. She knew a few people who might be able to get her that tank.

—⁓—

Two feminine voices ran together like gnats buzzing in his ears. Not as annoying as that guy's gravelly rumble, but not welcome.

"Mrs. Webb. Mrs. Burke." A third female voice intruded. "I need to check Mr. Lucano's vital signs and line placement."

"Will the doctor look in on him again today?"

Such a familiar drawl. Tony groped for an identity.

"Not unless he takes a turn one way or another. We need those kidneys to start working, or he may need dialysis, but we can wait a few days for that. Rest is the best thing now."

Yeah. Let him sleep. Forever would be okay.

Someone touched his arm. "We'll be back in the mornin', Tony. You hang in there."

"My grandkids need their honorary uncle," the other familiar voice said.

Who were these people? He knew, but... Where was he? What was happening? Nothing made sense.

He hurt.

Feet approached in squeaky shoes. A person who smelled like antiseptic lifted his arm, and something twinged beneath the skin of his hand.

"IV site appears good. No redness. No swelling."

Leave me alone!

The covers left his body, and a chill rushed through him. *Hey, put those back.*

Hands messed with body parts he considered private. A palm strike to the sternum should handle the problem. *Come on, arm, do it!* Nothing. Nobody heard him. Nobody knew he was going crazy trapped inside this dead thing.

He could leave. He had only to choose. If he sank into the darkness, he'd come out on the other side, a place of eternal light and forever warmth. Don't ask how he knew. He just did.

"The catheter looks fine, Mr. Lucano." She tucked the covers around him again. *Thank You, Jesus.* "All sorts of people are counting on you to get well."

All sorts of people? Those voices that taunted his memory? They wanted him to hang around, but what about what he wanted? Better to be absent from the body and present with the Lord. Good words. Good thought. Good choice. Sleep and be with Jesus.

—∿∿—

Friends in high places were an excellent thing when a person had to get home in the teeth of a blizzard. A call to the director of the FBI, who called the governor of New York, who called the director of transportation for the state of New York, who called the transportation station in Albany, and here she was, strapped to a jump seat behind the driver of a snowplow.

Desi stared out the plow's window into the snarling white world. Earmuffs dulled the roar of the machine and the howl of the storm—a droning backdrop to the cries of her heart.

I'm close, Tony. Hang in there.

Her teeth ground together. But would twenty miles an hour be quick enough when she still had a hundred to go? What if she was too late? What if—?

Don't think like that!

God was with Tony. She had to hang on to hope. She'd concentrate on the wedding. That's it. Not the social nightmare the event had morphed into. Nope, she'd marry the man in his hospital room if he'd wake up and say, "I do."

—m—

Somebody blew his nose near Tony's ear. Loud.

"Don't let him die, God. Please. I don't beg nobody for nothing, but for him—" Strangled sound. "You're the only hope, God. 'Cuz I can't leave it to chance whether this guy lives or dies. He's my pard, and he's…like a son to me. Just don't ever tell him I said that." Long sniff. "Hey, by the way, this talking to You stuff isn't so hard. But don't tell him I said that either."

If you want to keep secrets, don't talk out loud. Had he said that? Couldn't have. He got no reaction. Besides, there was some kind of goofy hose down his throat. Someone must have beaten the living tar out of him to make every molecule throb like this. Funny, he had no memory of anything except…fiery cold. Like hell's deep freeze. A shudder wracked him.

A big hand wrapped around his and squeezed.

"Squeeze back if you've been eavesdropping on me yakking to God."

Could he do it? He hadn't been able to wring any cooperation out of his body yet. Did he want to try?

"Come on, pard. You've got Max and Lana going out of their skulls. And those kids of Max's are praying up a storm. Their Uncle Tony can't check out on them." The hand tightened. "Desi's on her way. You don't wanna be snoozing when she walks in."

Desiree! Something like an electrical charge zapped through his brain. He saw the face of a woman with hazel eyes, soft sable hair, and a saucy smile. Those full, firm lips—they tasted like everything he'd ever wanted. His Des. No way was he leaving her.

Tony gathered every atom of will and forced it down his arm. Was it enough? Did he ripple his fingers or only think he had?

"Wha-hoo!"

Tony winced on the inside.

"Good going, Lucano! You're not gonna die. I'll let everybody know. You wait here."

Like I'm going someplace, Stevo?

Heavy footsteps receded.

Steve Crane. Yep, that's the loudmouth—the friend who stuck like a burr in his side. Good thing too. *But don't tell him I thought that, God.*

Tendrils of black fog wrapped around him, and he didn't resist. He wasn't going to wake up all the way for anyone but Desi. Kidneys, get busy! He needed to bust out of this hospital bed and marry that woman.

—⁂—

In the wee hours of the morning, Desi opened the snowplow's door into a realm of cold silence. She clambered down the steps against the protest of cramped muscles. The hospital building towered above her.

White mounds glittered under the entrance light, blocking her access, and the plow couldn't get an inch closer without ripping off the canopy over the door. If her eyes were lasers, they'd burn a path.

"Stand aside, Ms. J." A cheerful voice spoke behind her. "I'll have you inside in a jiffy."

Desi looked up to find the driver climbing out of his cab, shovel in hand. Muscling down the freeway in a snowplow would never be her idea of fun, but her driver looked like Buddy Hackett and drove like John Wayne. Clamp the reins in his teeth, pull out his six-guns, and charge the enemy, grinning all the way.

"Have at it." Desi stepped aside.

Powder flew first one direction, then the other. The driver paused and leaned on his shovel. "Crazy how that blizzard shut down soon's we hit Boston. Like it just give up on stoppin' us. Big Bertha there." He jerked a nod at his plow. "She don't take no guff from Old Man Winter." He went back to scooping.

Did Desi hear him whistling under his breath? Her fingers clenched and unclenched in her pockets. *Hurry! You dear, sweet man, hurry!* Now that she stood outside the building that held her Tony, each moment of delay sank sharp claws into her heart. *I'm here, sweetheart. Can you feel me loving you?*

The snowplow driver finished his work, saluted Desi with his shovel, and stepped out of her way. With a hurried but heartfelt "Thank you," she dashed up the open path and yanked on the door. Locked. A small sign on the window of the lit vestibule said After Hours, Ring Bell. She found the button, slapped her palm over it, and leaned.

Two eternal minutes later, a black woman in a white pantsuit strode toward the door, frown puckering her face. Desi took her hand from the bell and stamped her chilled feet.

The woman pressed a button inside the entry. "This is not the emergency entrance." Her snarl came through a speaker above Desi's head.

She found her intercom button. "I'm Desiree Jacobs. My fiancé, Anthony Lucano, is a patient here, and I'm going to see him."

The nurse didn't bother to hide her eye roll. "Come back during visiting hours, ma'am. How did you get here, anyway?"

Desi pointed to the mammoth plow, and the driver flashed his lights, grinning fit to bust. "Shall I ride that over to the home of the man in charge of the Boston FBI office and have him tell you to let me in?"

Nurse Snark's mouth fell open. "Oh, you're here for the miracle man, that FBI agent."

The door buzzed, and Desi darted inside.

"Follow me." The nurse turned on her heel.

Desi peeled off her jacket as she hustled behind her guide. A third person fell in behind them—a security guard.

The nurse glared at him. "About time you showed up."

He shrugged. "Doing rounds."

"A smoke in the john is more like it," the nurse muttered as they crossed the lobby and reached an elevator. The guard waved them into the car and wandered off toward a desk.

The nurse punched in two floor numbers. "Your man's the talk of the hospital. Wish I could escort you to him, but call lights are crazy tonight. Got to get back to my duty station. You get off on the eighth floor." She wrinkled her nose. "Watch out for Claudia Stetler. She's an old-school RN and pinches hospital policies so hard they squeal."

"You saw that megaplow out there?"

"Yeah." The nurse looked at her with frank appraisal.

"I may be petite on the outside, but that's me on the inside."

The nurse chuckled. "Oh, honey, now I really wish I could go with you."

———ᴍᴍ———

"I don't care if your policy says only immediate family or next of kin in the patient's room after visiting hours."

Desi's voice pricked Tony's consciousness.

"I'm his fiancée," she went on, her voice closer, "and I—"

"Miss, I must uphold the regulations of this hospital." The squeaky shoes indicated the antiseptic-smelling nurse who kept bothering him. He should have decked her when he had the chance. "I don't see a ring on your finger. How do I know—?"

"In the past forty-eight hours, I've been robbed, knocked down, threatened at gunpoint, and nearly arrested in Mexico."

When had all that stuff happened to her? Why didn't he know about it?

"I've spent hours in an airplane and the cab of a snowplow." Desi's voice rang like iron on anvil. "And you think you're going to stand between me and my man?"

So close. Just outside his door. Tony's breathing quickened.

"Please keep your voice down." The nurse sounded like his second-grade teacher trying to restore order after recess. "You can stay in the waiting room with a pillow and blanket until after the doctor sees him in the morning. We mustn't disturb him now."

Lady, what do you think you've been doing all night long?

"Step—out—of—the—way." Desi's precise enunciation could have cut glass. "Or I'll raise such a ruckus every patient on this floor will wake up and press their call button. And then I'll contact the mayor, the chairman of the hospital board, and the head of the Boston FBI to join the party—and believe me, they'll show up."

If he could laugh, he would. His Desi, all right. A shushing noise and change in the atmosphere said the door had opened.

"Oh, Tony." Desi exhaled his name.

He had to see her—had to open his eyes.

"Just for a few seconds then, miss." The nurse sounded like she'd been weaned on prune juice. "Let me check his—"

Tony's eyes popped open. What do you know? He did it. But he wasn't looking at Desi. He was staring at the nurse, who stared back. The woman wasn't the enormous battle-ax he'd pictured. Not an inch over five feet tall, pearl-gray hair, and glasses perched on a small nose, she was as dainty as Desiree, but a few decades older. Just as feisty, though.

Out! He tried to say it aloud, but the tube in his throat made a gurgle of the word. He lifted his hand and pointed toward the door.

Her eyes lit. "Why, Mr. Lucano, you're awake and aware. That's wonderful. I'll go chart that while you spend time with your lovely fiancée." She turned on her heel, shoes squeaking.

"Oh, darling." Desi floated toward him, disheveled, beautiful.

His eyes drifted shut. *Open!* The inner command had no affect. He mentally called his rebellious body an angry name.

"Shhhh," she said, as if reading his thoughts. "Relax, sweetheart. I'm here." Her breath fanned his face, and her lips found his forehead. Warm contentment spread through him.

Her fingers sifted through his hair. "Rest, so you can get better, and we can make a date with the pastor."

Tony smiled, and not just on the inside.

The door shushed. "Ten minutes, miss." That nurse again. "The night duty ICU physician is on his way. As Mr. Lucano continues to regain consciousness, we can begin dialing down the oxygen and possibly extubate by morning. If all goes well, we should be able to move him to a step-down unit where you can be with him all the time. I assume you'll want a pillow and blanket in the waiting room so you can stay nearby during this process?"

"You assume correctly. Thank you. And my name is Desiree."

"Very good, Desiree. Mine is Claudia. Use the call button if you need anything."

"Claudia?"

"Yes, miss— Desiree."

"Thank you for taking good care of Tony."

"You're most welcome." The door shushed again.

Tony found a spark of energy, and his eyes popped open. Her face hovered inches from his. *What took you so long?* The words lay trapped in his throat, but comprehension flared in her tense smile.

Desi gave a tiny laugh, but the sound came out sad. "I've always been with you. In here." Her hand settled over his heart.

Tony forced his arm up and dropped his hand over hers.

The ten minutes passed too quickly, and the next few hours crawled by with doctor visits and the nurse tinkering with gadgets at his bedside. But at last that stupid hose came out of his throat, and he was wheeled to a room on a lower floor. Desi sat by his side. Clutching her pillow and blanket, she didn't look ready to move soon. That suited him just fine.

Exhaustion dragged his eyelids down. He faded into a fuzzy realm of sensory impressions—running feet, gunshots, cold, a figure slumped against a van, a body floating in gray water, the sound of his teeth chattering, a whiplash, then falling. And cold. Always cold. As if trapped in an ice cube. Tony groaned.

Someone touched his face, his hair, murmuring words of comfort. Desi?

"Co-o-old." The groan came again.

"I'll warm you, darling." A muted sob.

The mattress shifted, and a soft, warm body snuggled next to him. A fresh blanket covered them both, and Desi settled her head on his shoulder. Her breath caressed his neck. The familiar, exotic scent of her hair filled his nostrils. Heaven had met earth at last.

Normal, healthy sleep wrapped him in a silken cocoon.

"I never thought I'd walk in on my son in bed with a woman not his wife!" The breathless voice jolted Tony to awareness. *Mom?*

Ten

Tony turned his head toward the door. His tall, sturdy mother stood there, smiling at him, but moisture shimmered in her dark eyes. The corners of his mouth lifted. "Yeah, you taught me better than that. Guess I'll have to marry her now." His words came out hoarse, but at least they didn't sputter like a backfiring jalopy.

His mother sniffed and stepped toward the bed. "You've got that much sense, anyway, Anthony Lucano. Maybe she can keep you from fool stunts like taking a dip in ice water." She took his hand. For a woman, she had a mechanic's grip. *"Mio figlio caro."*

Her murmur of "My beloved son" barely carried to his ears, but her love held him as if he were a babe in her arms again.

Desi stirred and lifted her head. "Mrs. Lucano?"

"You need to get used to calling me Mom, *cara.*"

Desi sat up, the seam of Tony's hospital gown imprinted on her cheek. She ran a hand across her bed-head. Her gaze stopped on the window where light seeped through the blinds. "Oh, my. It's got to be midmorning. I only meant to warm you up, not sleep with you."

He grinned and waggled his eyebrows. Man, it felt good to do something normal without concentrating for five minutes to make it happen. "We were perfect together."

She glanced at her future mother-in-law and went fire red. His mom laughed.

Desi hopped off the bed and stuck her hands on her hips. "Tony Lucano, you're awful. If you weren't half dead, I'd smack you."

His mom laughed harder. "That's the second scolding this young man has gotten this morning."

Tony shifted and groaned. "I'd rather get beat up by you two than whatever worked me over to land me here."

"You don't remember what happened?" Desi laid a hand on his arm.

"Bits and pieces. I mean, I know I was on a shipboard bust, but things get fuzzy after I chase some trigger-happy woman onto the deck. Something about gunshots, then falling and trying to swim my way out of the devil's fish tank. Am I shot?"

"No, caro." His mother smoothed the hair on his brow. "They had to take out your spleen. How did the water bruise you so badly? The side of your face is black and blue."

"I'm bruised all over. No wonder I feel like day-old road kill."

"I'd say you have more reason than that." The masculine voice came from the doorway. A big-boned man dressed in green scrubs walked in fingering the stethoscope around his neck.

He nodded at the women, then fixed his gaze on Tony. "I'm Dr. Braniff, your attending physician when they brought you in. To be honest, I didn't think I'd come back to find you still breathing, much less awake and lucid. You are one lucky man."

Luck? Tony glanced at his mom. Wrong word to use around her.

"Nothing chancy about it, Doctor Braniff," she said. "And not entirely to do with your skill either, though I thank you from the bottom of my heart."

The doctor grinned. "You're welcome. I think." He scratched the side of his nearly bald head. The lines on his face and veins showing in his hands placed him in his sixties. "I've been doctoring long enough to know Someone other than me ultimately calls the shots."

"Sensible man." She stuck out her hand. "Gina Lucano, the miracle boy's mother."

"Pleased to meet you, Gina Lucano."

Tony narrowed his eyes. Did that handshake last a shade too long? And did his mother have extra color in her cheeks? Maybe he should go back to sleep and start this day over. Or maybe the week. Everything felt...weird.

Brisk footsteps brought a nurse through the door. Not Nurse Claudia. The newcomer was young and pudgy and the color of cocoa. She carried a cloth-covered metal tray.

"We need to do another round of blood work," Dr. Braniff said, "and see where we're at with kidney function, among other things. And I need to take a listen to those lungs. We suctioned a little ocean out of you, young man." He glanced toward the women. "If you would excuse us, ladies?"

"Of course." Gina nodded. "Desi and I will wait down the hall."

"I'll stop there before I go on with my rounds."

Tony turned his head in time to catch with his mouth the kiss Desi had aimed for his cheek. He grinned at her. She grinned back. Yep, he still had his reflexes, even though it hurt to use them. He'd be out of here in no time, back to work, or better yet, standing at the altar with the most fabulous female on the planet.

The women left, and Tony turned his attention toward the doctor, who was staring at the chart with the name Lucano on the tab. He'd seen that kind of frown before and never liked what was said afterward. Unease bit his gut.

—⁃⁃⁃⁃—

Desiree sat on a sofa in the waiting room, hugging herself. Why wasn't she jumping up and down that Tony seemed to be doing so well? But then, he looked about how he said he felt. The doctor hadn't said so, but there could be a million complications from what had happened.

Where's my faith, God?

Sturdy arms came around her. *"Mia figlia."* Desi buried her face in Gina's shoulder. Her future mother-in-law rubbed circles on her back. "Our Tony is strong and so are we."

"I'm not strong. Not today." She met eyes the same rich shade of brown as Tony's. "It's not just Tony. There's something wrong with me-e." The last word ended in a gasping hiccup. She pressed her lips together, throat pulled tight, but couldn't stop a pair of tears from escaping her eyes. "I don't know what to do—my wedding, my job. Nothing's working. I've failed at everything. And why am I even thinking about these things with Tony in there?"

Flushing hot, Desi jumped up and paced to the far end of the guest area. If she didn't want to be anywhere near herself, Gina must be doubly disgusted.

"Look at me, *donna giovane*." Gina's voice sounded right behind her.

Desi scrunched into herself. Young lady. Daddy used that phrase when she was about to receive correction. But he'd gone to be with the mother Desi couldn't remember because she died when Desi was a baby. Her parents were happy together now, but death had left Desi with no one except Tony. And Max, of course, but she had kids to think about, as well as a husband in prison. And Tony's mother wanted Desi to call her "Mom," something she hadn't been able to do. Why? She adored the grand lady who had raised her fiancé.

Desi turned. Gina's expression radiated calm acceptance. Desi flung herself into the woman's arms and clung, tears pouring over the dam. Gina rocked her, cooing, "Shhh. Shhh. Shhh." Not telling her to stop crying, but that age-old sound of mother comforting child.

"Oh no! Tony's not—"

The gasped words drew Desi away from Gina's embrace. A pale-faced Max stood in the entrance. Desi scrubbed at her tears. A burly figure came up behind Max and wrapped an arm around her shoulder. Steve Crane's other arm was already around the shoulder of a woman who appeared like a decades-older mirror image of Max.

"My son is awake and talking," Gina said.

Desi nodded. "I'm just having a bit of a meltdown."

Max's freckles faded as normal color returned to her cheeks. "I don't blame you." She held out her arms.

Desi went into them and got a king-sized squeeze, then was passed to the next person. Oh, good grief, she was hugging Crane, the man who annoyed her like vinegar to the teeth, and he was hugging back. It felt okay, actually. She moved on to Lana Burke, Max's mother, and got more of that mom-cooing. She'd have to learn how to make that sound when she started having Tony's babies. A small laugh came out. Hope sprang eternal, and she wasn't letting it go.

"My star patient has quite a fan club." Doctor Braniff stepped in. His gaze stopped on Crane. "I hear you sat with Tony and talked to him."

The big man shifted his feet. "Yeah. Talked."

Desi stared at him. Why did that statement turn Tony's ex-partner the color of beet juice?

The doctor nodded. "Good job. We find interaction with friends and loved ones can help pull comatose patients back from the brink."

Desi's heart fluttered. Nasty word—*brink*.

"Mrs. Lucano." The doctor turned to Tony's mother.

"Gina, please."

"Gina, your son has given me permission to share his medical information with you and with his fiancée, Desiree Jacobs. I assume that's you." He smiled toward Desi.

"Call me Desi, and yes, that's me."

"I should finish rounds by three o'clock." He glanced at his watch. "Come to my office then, and we can talk. The results from this morning's blood draw should be back."

"We'll be there, Doctor." Gina nodded, a regal tilt to her head.

Admiration flashed in the doctor's gray eyes, and Desi didn't blame him. Tony's mom commanded a room without half trying, and not because her stature dwarfed most women. For a female with nothing dainty about her and more silver than black in her hair, she exuded timeless elegance. Desi wanted to be her when she grew up.

"Good." Braniff tore his attention from Gina and looked around the room. "Feel free to visit Tony in small groups, but don't be surprised if he dozes off on you. He's recovering from extreme trauma, and his body will demand sleep. He was fading when I left him. On the other hand, no one can get too much support." He strode away.

Desi watched Gina's gaze follow him. Then the woman turned thoughtful eyes on Desi. "Our Tony is blessed to have such a one supervising his care."

"No argument there." A grin crept over her face.

Gina's chin came up. "What are you smiling at, cara?"

Desi shrugged. "Just…blessings."

Gina let out a soft humph.

"We're going to see Tony." Max broke in.

"I'll go with you." Desi stepped forward.

Gina clucked her tongue. "I don't know about you, mia figlia, but I could use a shower and a good breakfast after spending a day and a night in airports and airplanes from Los Angeles to Minneapolis to New York to Boston. My luggage sits in the lobby with the receptionist."

A fatigue headache throbbed behind Desi's eyes. "And I'm pretty sure my morning breath could be deployed as a weapon of mass destruction. My place is closest. Let's go make ourselves presentable."

"Me, I will make presentable." She jerked a thumb at herself. "You are always beautiful."

Lana walked up to Desi. "We'll stay until you get back." Her high, sweet tone was the polar opposite of Steve Crane's gravel bass. "Right, dear?" She beamed up at Crane, who had lumbered on her heels like a love-struck bear.

"Sure thing, honey."

Did that grizzly just say *honey*? Desi glanced at Max, who grinned and shrugged.

"Get on home." The redhead waved her away. "We'll chew the fat later, girlfriend."

Judging by the look that accompanied that statement, it could be a long chew. More problems at HJ Securities? Desi thrust the worry away. First, they had to find out what kind of battle lay ahead for Tony. For all of them.

—␣␣—

Desi blow-dried her hair and fluffed it around her shoulders. A hot shower usually did wonders for her outlook, but ugly memories crowded her. The eerie wheeze of Albon Guererra. The smell of jalapeño sweat. The drugged eyes of young men waving homemade weapons. A gunshot and the gasps of a wounded woman. Merciless fingers pinching her face. She touched the bruises on her chin. Then to come home and see her tower of strength leveled in a hospital bed…

She swallowed a whimper as she went into the living room and sank into an easy chair. Below, water hummed in pipes from the shower running in the first-floor bathroom. Daddy's ground-floor apartment was empty—not of furniture—but of his presence.

Would Tony want to live here with her? They could reconvert the house into a single-family dwelling. Dad had made it into upstairs and downstairs apartments when Desi returned home from college a single woman, ready to partner with him in business. On the other hand, she and Tony would be starting a family. This was a nice neighborhood, but it was mostly empty nesters.

Whoa! She was getting ahead of herself. Tony's recovery came first. This big unknown was like teetering on a ledge, unsure whether they'd tumble a few feet to solid ground or off a cliff.

You're borrowing trouble, Des. Get on with what you know to do.

She got her Palm Pilot from her laptop case and found Ramon Sanchez's cell number, then punched it in on her cordless phone. Cell towers were down over a big area, but her house still had landline service. Sanchez's phone rang until the voice mail kicked in.

"Ramon, I've reached Boston, and my fiancé has come out of the coma. We're not sure what lies ahead. Please let me know what you found out about Zapopa and her grandson. Thank you so much for everything. My prayers are with you and your family."

Desi ended the call and went back to the bathroom where she applied makeup, careful to conceal the bruises. No need to explain those to Tony right now. She checked the time on the bedside alarm clock. Over two hours until their meeting with the doctor. She'd give Gina twenty minutes before whipping up scrambled eggs and toast. Her bed beckoned, but she turned away. If she lay down, she probably wouldn't wake up until tomorrow.

She went to the kitchen and brewed tea. What was tomorrow? Monday. That made today Sunday. Hands curled around the warm tea mug, she wandered to the living room and peered out at the street from a dormer window. A plow had opened a single lane for traffic. The taxi driver had taken creative routes to get them here. No doubt church had been canceled this morning.

Desi sat down and dialed her pastor's number—Tony's pastor too. But his phone was out of service, which meant he probably didn't know about Tony's accident. Sighing, she cradled the phone and sank back against the sofa. She should e-mail Pastor Grange, just as soon as she worked up the energy to move.

Hopefully, Tony was resting well, not plagued by doubts and fears. He didn't need anything to distract him from getting better. Not her business struggles, and no harrowing tales from south of the border. How she'd keep her missing engagement ring a secret, she had no idea, but she'd think of something. And no wedding hassles either. They needed a quiet service, immediate family and close friends. She pictured the two of them at the front of their church, the soloist softly singing their love as they adored each other with their eyes…

A heavenly scent of cinnamon and dough drew her from sleep. She sat up with a start. She'd dozed off, but for how long? A robust voice began to belt out a praise chorus from the kitchen. Gina…Tony's mom…Mom. So now the guest was cooking for the hostess. Desi's mouth watered. Evidently her appetite didn't care.

She stretched, then went to the kitchen and found Gina scraping bits of dough from the counter. The woman wore brown slacks and a rib-knit sweater covered by an apron Desi had forgotten she owned. The enticing cinnamon scent came from the oven, complemented by the smell of fresh coffee.

Gina smiled. "I'm so pleased you got a nap. You must be exhausted."

"I am, but I didn't intend to make you cook."

"It felt good to be useful."

Desi laughed. "Useful? More like a miracle worker, given my bare cupboards."

Gina shrugged. "I got creative with a tube of biscuit dough."

"I bought that before I left for Pakistan. It must have been near its expiration date."

"A day away." Gina finished wiping the counter.

"Have a seat and let me wait on you." Desi went to the coffee maker and filled two mugs. "Nondairy creamer and nonsugar sweetener, right?"

Tony's mom sank into a chair with a sigh Desi doubted she meant to release. "Thick and black would do me well right now."

Desi set the mug and a spoon in front of her guest. On impulse, she bent and wrapped her arms around the woman's sturdy shoulders.

Gina patted one of Desi's hands. "My son is blessed beyond measure."

Desi sat across from her. "From birth, I'd say."

Gina's dark eyes twinkled as she brought the mug to her lips. Desi sipped her own coffee, and comfortable silence settled. If not for the looming appointment with the doctor, this would be a cozy morning after the storm—a time to bask in warmth, indulge in comfort food, and enjoy the company of a person she'd like whether she'd ever met Tony. But they didn't have that luxury, might not have any such thing in the foreseeable future.

Desi gulped her coffee, and the liquid scalded her tongue. With a soft growl, she set the mug away from her.

Gina touched her arm. "Your worries are written on your forehead, mia figlia."

"I had—" she started, and then cleared her throat. "I had an unsettling time in Mexico, which has left me ill prepared to deal with a crisis at home."

"Tell me."

The simple invitation and the soulful eyes drew her like a compass to the North Pole. Desi spilled the whole sorry tale from the time she boarded the airplane from Mexico City to Mérida until she arrived at Tony's hospital room. While she spoke, Gina took the rolls from the oven and served them hot with butter—sorry, no icing—and poured them more coffee. Desi dug in as she continued her saga.

"And now I have no engagement ring," Desi finished, pushing away her empty plate. "No medallion. I failed my assignment for the Mexican government. The Greybecks are doing their best to ensure that I lose my business, and I almost lost Tony too. I don't overwhelm easily, but I'm about ready to check myself into the funny farm. Except I can't. Somehow, I have to pull myself together." Desi inhaled a ragged breath.

Gina nodded. "Good. Good."

"Good?" Desi glared. She'd talked like a house afire for twenty minutes, but had her listener heard a word she said?

"Yes, very good. With such strong attacks, one can only assume something wonderful is about to happen, and the devil is trying to stop it. We will not let him. I will alert my prayer team without revealing what must remain confidential." She spoke as if that answer settled everything.

Maybe it did.

Gina wiped her mouth on a paper napkin. "Now it is time to speak of something else. If we hear things about our Tony that we would rather not, we ladies must be in one accord. My son is a stubborn one and has a few old-school notions."

Desi's stomach muscles clenched. Gina was hinting at a fear Desi hadn't even let herself name. "You mean like he shouldn't burden a wife with a less-than-healthy specimen of masculinity."

"Ah, you know him. But the two of us, we are more than a match, eh? I want a daughter officially my own, and my son will oblige his mother *molto rapidamente*. I warn you, cara, he will be a bad patient, but an excellent husband." She winked.

Desi laughed, and her heart lightened. "Thank you."

The woman's dark brows arched. "For what?"

"For listening to my problems…and for not insulting me by asking whether I'd still want Tony if he came with medical issues."

"When dealing with a woman of character, one need not question such matters."

Desi rose and kissed Gina's cheek. "I'll call for a taxi. I'm afraid my car is trapped in a garage half-buried under white stuff."

While they put their coats on in the first-floor foyer, Desi's gaze fell on Gina's suitcase sitting against the wall. "Here I laid my burdens on you and forgot to ask about your visit with the Lucano clan in California. I know you hoped to build a bridge for Tony's sake."

The older woman's eyes flashed. "I begin to think my son is right. The relatives on the law-abiding branch are not worth the effort. They are too law-abiding…in the religious sense. I might find more open minds among the mafioso Lucanos. I received a proper Sicilian welcome as the widow of a Lucano, but they are offended at Tony."

"Why?" Desi jerked on her gloves. "Tony's three generations removed from mob connections."

"Ah, but he has taken his own path in matters of faith." Gina wagged a finger.

"Because he's not Roman Catholic?" Desi's insides did a slow burn. How could people call themselves Christians if they rejected others in the family of God because they didn't wear the same label? She opened her mouth to spew hot words, but reined her temper back. Cliquish behavior happened among Protestants and Catholics alike.

That didn't mean she had to accept it.

Gina shook her head. "In a small way I can understand how they feel. When Tony at last took Jesus as his Lord and Savior, I thought, 'Ah, now he will go to Mass with me as he did when he was a boy.' But he is too much his father's son." She laughed, and tension faded from her posture. "He must forge a new path."

Desi chuckled. "That's our Tony, all right. Always challenging the status quo. Part of what makes him a successful FBI agent, but as he says, an occasional irritant to his superiors."

"And an interesting challenge to his mother and fiancée." They both laughed.

Desi glanced out the diamond of beveled glass in the front door. "Our cab is here." She opened the door for her future mother-in-law.

As the cold hit their faces, the woman touched Desi's shoulder. "Thank you for encouraging this old lady. I think we will need all the cheer we can get in the coming days."

Inside the warm taxi, humor faded and uncertainty grew as Desi watched traffic inch along. Major issues loomed like the mountains of snow restricting the road and obstructing the view. Only none of their problems would be so easy to move.

Eleven

*D*esi walked into the hospital waiting room and found Max sitting alone, reading a magazine.

She lifted her head and smiled. "Hey there, girl. You look good enough to knock Tony's socks off, if he was wearin' any."

Desi's laugh was weaker than she liked. Time to seriously buck up. "Did Lana and Steve go home to take care of the grandkids?"

"Nope." Max shook her red mop. "The kiddos are havin' a snow-day heyday at the neighbors' house. They've got a brood right around Luke and Emily's ages. Anything that involves cookies, hot chocolate, and playmates puts us adults out of sight, out of mind."

"That's a load off your shoulders."

"You got it." Max glanced up the hall. "My mother should be back any minute. She scooted down to the little girls' room, and we left Steve snoozin' in Tony's room." She laughed. "It was so cute. Here we are chattin' away—well, Mom and I are—and pretty soon a snore comes from the hospital bed. No surprise there, except it's got an echo from the galoot slouched on the chair in the corner. Mom and I shut off the light and tiptoed out, pinchin' our lips shut so we didn't bust a gut before we made our escape."

Desi's laugh came out lighter this time. "Another mother-daughter pair that knows how to enjoy each other."

Max put an arm around Desi. "I'm glad the Lord sent a great parent into your life."

"It's not like having Dad back, but it's more than I ever expected."

"Where is the mom-in-law-to-be?"

"She stopped at the nurses' station to ask directions to Dr. Braniff's office while I checked to see how you people were holding up."

"We're dandy, so you go get the scoop on Tony." Max waved toward the elevators.

Desi turned to see Gina approaching.

The woman wore a tight smile. "The practitioners' offices are on the second floor."

Desi raised a hand toward Max. "Keep up the prayers."

"You got it." Anxious hope glowed from her green eyes.

On the way down to the second floor, Desi's stomach rode in her throat as if the bottom had dropped out of the elevator. They found the doctor's office by two minutes to three, but waited another fifteen minutes for him to show up.

He ushered them into his carpeted domain with a smile and an apology. "Things always take longer than you think. Have a seat." He waved toward a pair of guest chairs. Braniff's desk was crowded with medical journals and office paraphernalia. He jiggled his computer mouse. "Give me a minute to check the results from the blood draw."

Gina settled into her chair; Desi perched on the edge of hers. The doctor's lips pursed as he clicked his mouse and scanned pages. Desi dragged her gaze away and studied cherry-wood bookshelves stuffed with medical tomes. She knew better than to stare at someone as if she could will an outcome. Dozens of boardroom drills while administrators considered the merits of HJ Securities had taught her that manifest anxiety was counterproductive.

Good grief, if she could keep her cool in a Mexican museum surrounded by hostile board members and a pair of Greybeck scoundrels, she could control herself now. Maybe. Desi's fingers dug into her legs. She would not leap across the desk to throttle answers out of the doctor.

Braniff unwound his stethoscope from his neck and set it on the desk. "You've probably heard wondrous tales about children resuscitated after as much as an hour under water in hypothermic conditions. With adults, the opportunity for resuscitation and recovery is much shorter."

Gina nodded. Desi sat stiff.

"We used extreme measures to restore Tony's body temperature. Every drop of his blood was removed, warmed, and then fed back into his body. A patient can go into shock and die during the process. And then we were forced to perform an emergency splenectomy. Tony's superior physical condition contributed to his ability to withstand the trauma of medical intervention, on top of the other traumas. Now that he's conscious, apparently with all his mental faculties, a number of hurdles remain."

The doctor leaned forward and folded his hands. "The body's natural defense mechanisms during hypothermia ensure that blood flow to vital organs is the last to be disrupted. But his body temperature fell so low, and he was without oxygen for so long—" He frowned.

"Cut to the chase, Doctor." Gina's tone was well modulated but scalpel sharp.

Desi suppressed an urge to cheer. The next best thing to a leap across the desk—a lionhearted mom.

Dr. Braniff consulted his computer screen. "His lab results aren't what we'd like to see in regard to liver function, but with medication, proper diet, and time, livers regenerate. His kidneys are the main concern. He appears to have acute tubular necrosis, a rare complication of severe hypothermia. The breakdown of muscle tissue has overwhelmed the kidneys with protein. In most cases, given time, the organs clear up and recover fully, but…" He fiddled with his stethoscope.

Desi gripped the arms of her chair. "Not always." Was that her voice so firm and clear?

Braniff's expression remained clinically stoic. "I think we can be confident that his kidneys will recover to a degree, but to what degree is unknown at this point. He could require periodic dialysis for the rest of his life. But that is the least likely scenario."

"However, you want us to be aware of the possibility." Gina clasped her hands together on her lap.

The doctor's face softened. "Yes. I would do you no favors to with-hold the complete picture."

Desi laid her hand on top of Gina's. "Does Tony—" Her throat filled, and she cleared it. "Does Tony know?"

The doctor nodded. "In general terms."

Tony's mother puffed out a long breath. "We appreciate your frankness, Dr. Braniff."

"Actually, my name is Frank. You can call me that if you like."

"Very well, Dr. Frank." Gina canted her head. "No, that doesn't work. Sounds like a character from a Shelley novel."

The doctor laughed. "I'm glad my last name is Braniff."

"Then I shall continue calling you Dr. Braniff. That works best in the context where you are my son's doctor. And now I have a few questions."

"Fire away." His gaze took on a fresh level of respect and admiration.

"What about Tony's lungs and his heart?"

"His lungs sounded clear this morning, but we've been pumping antibiotic into him to stave off pneumonia. His heart sounded good too, but the tale won't be told until we give him a stress test a few weeks down the road. For the moment, getting his strength back will be chal-lenge enough. As an athletic man, he's going to be appalled at how weak he is."

Desi could vouch for that. Not being able to do for himself would irk Tony to no end. Gina had pegged her son spot-on. He'd be a baaad patient. "How long will he be in the hospital?"

"Until either he receives his first dialysis, or we see his kidneys start to work." He fiddled with his stethoscope between thumb and fore-finger. "We're doing all we can to facilitate the latter by regulating his diet and fluid intake. He's receiving an IV diuretic and something to reduce potassium levels in the blood. Also, we'll get him up in a chair today, perhaps even allow a short walk, which may stimulate his func-tions. He'll be weak from trauma and woozy from pain meds, so order-lies will support him."

Gina nodded. "Yes, I've heard that activity can be a good internal stimulant. But why on earth is the poor boy bruised from top to bot-tom? And how did his spleen get ruptured? Can a fall into the water do that?"

"I understand that when he was found, the swells were slamming his body into the quay. We're luck—" He stopped. "We can be thank-ful we're not dealing with broken bones."

Desi mustered her thoughts, and one item stood out. "The first thing Tony's going to worry about is his job."

"You are wrong, mia figlia." Gina touched her cheek. "The first thing he will think about is you."

"But what if he can't return to the FBI? Losing his career will destroy him!"

—⁓—

Enough lying around. Tony yawned, and his jaw creaked. He rubbed it and two-day-old whiskers rasped his palm. He must look as bad as he felt, but at least he didn't feel as bad as he had a few hours ago. His nap had done some good. Chased away all the company too.

With no one here to cluck over him, he might even make it out of bed. A man needed to jump to his feet after life knocked him down. His dad drilled that advice into Tony before the senior Lucano left his family to keep them off the radar of a mobster with a vendetta. After Dad walked out—well, Tony hung on to that standard through all the anger and confusion, and he hadn't regretted it.

He lifted one arm over his head, then the other. A groan left his lips. His muscles hadn't complained this bad since he was a kid newly enrolled in martial arts class.

Work through the pain. You can do it, Lucano.

He fumbled until he located the button that raised the head of the bed and pressed it until the mattress stopped moving. Whoops! A little dizzy there. He waited for the room to right itself.

With the light off and the blinds mostly closed, shadows striated the walls. In one dark corner crouched an armchair with a big blob draped over it. Some kind of medical equipment? On the opposite wall, a closet stood at attention near an open doorway that must lead to a bathroom—which he didn't need to use right now. Unfortunately.

He shoved away the doctor's unvarnished words about renal failure. Find a short-term goal and go for it. A stroll across the room to open the blinds made a good excuse for a walk.

Tony tossed the covers away and flopped his legs off the bed. Breath hissed between his teeth. Man, it hurt to move.

He glanced down at himself. Why couldn't they have given him some decent pajamas? He felt ridiculous in this hospital gown, and the open back chilled his spine. Good thing no one was here to see, particularly since that stupid catheter led to a bag—still all but empty—on a low hook of his IV pole.

He stared at the few feet between him and the window. Every inch stretched a mile. Oh, well, he ran many miles a day. He couldn't let a few baby steps intimidate him. Maybe he could use the IV pole as a mobile support. Smart idea. Nothing wrong with the old noggin anyway. He wrapped the hand with the IV line in it around the pole. Cold!

He jerked the hand away. Since when did a little cold bother him? He let out a long breath.

Since someone, probably McCluskey's guys, fished him out of the big drink in the middle of winter. Mental note—thank McCluskey.

Tony grabbed the pole. *Fish or cut bait, Lucano.* He eased off the bed and yelped as his bare feet hit the linoleum. Tremors shot up his body, invading his brain and edging his vision with black. He wobbled a step forward, and his toe connected with the base of the pole. The pole teetered toward him, bag wagging, and his knees buckled.

Someone shouted as he hit the floor, IV apparatus crashing around him. Sharp pains in his hand and shoulder competed with shrieks of abused bruises. He lay on his side, not daring to move. Groans escaped between clenched teeth.

The light flipped on, and Tony clamped his eyes shut. A familiar voice fried the air with choice words. Someone touched him, and Tony squinted up at Stevo kneeling beside him. Ah, the dark blob from the chair in the corner.

Tony shot him a jaw-clenched grin. "Sorry...to disturb...your beauty rest."

Hand on the call button, Stevo scowled back. Typical expression, except for the fear in his ice-blue eyes. "You trying to kill yourself, Lucano? Pull a fool stunt like this again, and I'll do it for you." He vented another colorful thought. "Your hand is bleeding like a stuck pig."

"That may be...the least...of our problems... I think I broke—"

Tony spiraled into blackness.

—⁓—

Dr. Braniff leaned his elbows on his desk and folded his hands in front of him. "The verdict isn't in about his career. His health information waiver with the FBI allows me to share medical information with his immediate supervisor. I plan to recommend a medical leave of absence of at least twelve weeks. We should know in that amount of time if Tony will still be suited for work as an agent."

Desi's heart clunked into her toes. How could she bear the look in Tony's eyes if he was disqualified from the work he loved? But she needed to be there for him if that moment came. They could still have a life together. *Please God, let him see that.* Besides, didn't a leave of absence offer a great opportunity for a wedding and honeymoon?

Desi met Gina's gaze and read in the older woman's eyes the same determination to share the pain and make something good happen in spite of it. "Let me be the one to tell him, okay? I'll choose the time and—"

"He knows, cara. If the doctor has given Tony even a little of this information, he understands that his job is at stake."

"I need to go to him. I—"

The ring of the desk telephone sent her nerves skittering.

The doctor picked up. "Braniff." His nostrils flared, and then he rose. "I'll be right there." He cradled the handset. "It seems our star patient has overexerted himself and taken a tumble. We may have a broken bone after all."

Twelve

'm a blockhead." With his hospital bed raised to sitting position, Tony gazed at the pair of stern-faced women. The ache in his cracked collarbone added a wordless scold. "I confess and repent. My hop out of bed yesterday was temporary insanity. It won't happen again."

His mother sniffed. "So you will ask for help?"

"Sure. When I need it."

Desi snorted and crossed her arms. "And who determines when you need help?"

"Um. Let me guess. My two favorite ladies?" He grinned.

Desi lifted an eyebrow, no smile. Mom glared. Guess his charm fell short on this subject.

His mother tapped his good shoulder. "And the doctor. You will follow his instructions?"

Tony clamped his lips shut. Better not answer that loaded question too hastily. He shifted, and the brace on his collarbone pulled. Okay, they win. Lifting a hand, he made the Boy Scout symbol. "No reasonable instruction shall be ignored."

The women shared one of those looks that told a guy his goose was already sliced, diced, and sautéed. Fat chance he'd have any say over what was reasonable—at least as long as he was under their watchful eyes. Sounded like that might be a long time. A sigh heaved from his chest.

Desi's face softened. She pressed her lips to his. "Darling, will it really be so awful to have your two favorite ladies waiting on you hand and foot?"

Her touch spread warmth better than a blanket. "Not if I can have as many of those as I want."

Desi's cheeks went pink. "My pleasure."

His mom took his hand—the one that wasn't swathed in a bandage that covered the spot where he'd ripped the IV line out. He'd refused to let them poke the other hand now that he could eat, drink, and take medications by mouth, but no way would he mention that bit of rebellion to his faithful guardians.

"Caro, our plan is for the best."

He knew that cajoling coo and narrowed his eyes.

She laughed. "Desi has the perfect setup for us in her first-floor apartment. I can move in with you there. The couch is very comfortable for me, and she will be upstairs. The proprieties are served, and we will both be your devoted slaves."

More like taskmasters—er, untaskmasters. "But what kind of a son makes his mother sleep on the couch while he takes the bed?"

"The kind of son who wishes to recover from an accident, marry the woman of his dreams, and present his mother with grandchildren."

Grinning, Tony shook his head. "You both look way too smug, but okay, I surrender. Anything to get me out of here."

The door swished open. "Now, Mr. Lucano, don't tell me you're not having a special time in this fine facility." It was the cocoa-colored nurse who had helped the doctor the day before. She carried a covered tray.

He scowled. "Torture chamber, you mean. What diabolical instruments do you have there?"

The nurse giggled. His mother muttered, "Oh, you!" Desi just grinned.

The nurse lifted the cover from the tray, but not so much that he could see what was on it. The smell of food teased his nostrils.

"If you don't want your lunch," she said, "I can always take it back."

"Oh, no you don't. Bring it right here." He tapped the overbed table. "I hope there's more substance to it than the mush and toast I had for breakfast. Not even a piece of bacon! How's a man supposed to survive without meat?"

"Complain, complain." The nurse deposited the tray. Her badge said Olivia.

Tony curled a lip. "Half a baked potato, a slice of dark bread, some funky-colored liquid—"

"Vegetable broth," Olivia announced as if she were presenting a treat.

"—peaches, and a cup of tea. Still no meat?"

"Sorry." The nurse sashayed toward the door. "A bland, low-protein, high-carb diet until those innards start working."

The innards in question curdled as Tony stared at the unappealing meal tray. No kidney action yet. Unless that changed today— Nope! Not thinking about dialysis or other dumb things that weren't going to happen.

"If you want, we can feed you." Desi batted her eyelashes.

Tony picked up his fork. *When did they start making these things so heavy?* He stabbed at a peach, and it slid around the dish. He set his fork down. "Here's a thought. Since you two are determined to watch after me, how about one of you runs down to the deli and sneaks me back a ham sandwich? It'll help me regain my strength." He glanced from one stone-faced woman to the other. "No?" He shrugged and wished he hadn't. "Worth a try, anyway."

Desi cut him a neat slice of peach with the side of the fork and handed the utensil to him. He grimaced and ate like a good little boy.

The ladies better enjoy this while they can, because Anthony Marco Lucano is coming off this bed sooner rather than later.

If he was so convinced of that, why did his gut feel like somebody had dumped a load of gravel into him?

—⁓—

Whispering voices brought Tony awake.

"At least he doesn't resemble a beached codfish anymore."

"Real sensitive, Haj." Polanski sounded ready to take a poke at the stocky Japanese.

"Well, you gotta admit he looked pretty terrible when they hauled him off."

Slight humph. "True. I didn't think I'd be standing here three days later—"

"Talking about your supervisor like he can't hear every word." Tony opened his eyes and stared at the visitors surrounding him.

Hajimoto and Polanski and even the ever-sober Slidell grinned wide enough to break their faces. Tony hit the button to sit up.

"Glad you decided to stick around, boss," Haj said.

"Couldn't leave you yahoos to fend for yourselves, could I?"

Everyone laughed. Well, not Dell, but for him the grin was a breakthrough.

Tony waved toward the guest chairs that seemed to multiply like rabbits in the corner of his room. "Pull up seats, team. If I don't get an update on our case, I'm going to bust."

Polanski's brows drew together. "Should you be thinking about work? I mean—"

"Don't any of you start treating me like an invalid." Tony glared. "I get plenty of that from people who shall remain nameless, as adorable as they are."

Haj snickered while they dragged chairs closer to the bed. "Yeah, the poor guy's got a corner on the market for female attention, and we're supposed to feel sorry for him."

"I don't." Dell's square face showed not a flicker of humor. "You had a marginal chance of survival, and less than that of waking up with all your faculties."

Tony stretched one arm and flexed the other one, mindful of his damaged collarbone. "I'm a breathing testimony to the mercy of God." His squad stared at him. They didn't voice agreement, but they didn't disagree either. "On with the update. What did we bag in the hold of that ship?"

"Jackpot!" Polanski said. "But man, conditions in that hold were beyond gross." She wrinkled her nose. "We liberated around fifty young women and teenage girls from various South American countries. They would have ended up in brothels up and down the East Coast. No casualties there. A few among the smugglers—who are all incarcerated or dead, by the way."

"Five arrested and three in the morgue." Dell pursed his lips.

"Several of the women required hospitalization." Polanski went on as if she hadn't been interrupted. "Most were malnourished and dehydrated but are doing fine. Unfortunately, most of them will be deported back to whatever poverty they came from." She sighed.

"I hear you." Tony shook his head.

"You're not going to believe what else we found," Haj jumped in. "And it wasn't drugs."

"Don't steal my thunder." Polanski socked her partner in the shoulder. "She cried in my arms when we unlocked her cage."

"Yeah, but I interviewed her."

"I know, but—"

"Who?" Tony's bark drew their attention.

Polanski opened her mouth. Haj opened his.

Dell cleared his throat. "Rosa Garza. She's a—"

"Native of Boston," Tony said. "A U.S. citizen. Okay, you surprised me."

"How did you know about her?" The question came in unison from Haj and Polanski.

"The night of the bust, I was in the break room and read a newspaper article about the missing sisters. Does Ms. Garza say what happened to the other one? Martina something?"

"Martina López." Haj nodded. "Rosa doesn't know what happened to her younger sister. They were separated after Fraternidad gang members snatched them at a rural bus station."

"Rosa?" Tony lifted a brow.

The stocky Japanese flushed. "Doesn't mean anything, boss. Me and a female immigration agent interviewed her yesterday. She was more comfortable with us calling her 'Rosa' than 'Mrs. Garza.' She's divorced from an abusive husband, and now she's been through…" He scowled. "Well, stuff that should never happen."

"That's graphic enough. I'll read the full report later. Not that I'm looking forward to it. Did we bag anybody important from the Fraternidad de la Garra?"

"Important, yes. Talking, no," Polanski said. "We got one of the top lieutenants from the Yucatán Fraternidad. He lawyered up right away with one of those smart suits that specialize in getting members of organized crime out on the streets again. Only the judge wouldn't consider bail due to flight risk, so we've still got the guy in the slammer."

"The rest of them were hired hands," Haj said. "The only Anglo was a clerk from Jagre Shipping who was driving the transport truck. He fingered the manager of the Boston office as the one giving orders. We swooped in to make the arrest, but he'd already skipped. We've got an APB out. Nab him, and he should lead us to the next person up the food chain."

"Okay, stay with it. So who was the Calamity Jane taking potshots at us?"

"She was identified as Angelina Hernández," Slidell said, "suspected companion of the Mexican Fraternidad gang leader who calls himself El Jaguar. The Mexican government is less than happy she's dead. They hoped she'd one day lead them to El Jaguar's jungle headquarters."

"Why was Hernández on the ship?"

Haj shrugged. "We've asked our suspects that question, but we get blank stares."

Tony shifted position. Maybe that pressure in the pit of his belly was just frustration with inactivity. "Did we recover what Hernández was trying to escape with?"

"Negative." Polanski shook her head. "Fishing you out was top priority."

"Probably a package of heroin." Haj stretched and yawned. "Sorry, long day. If it was drugs, the ocean took care of keeping it off the street."

Tony nodded. Guess Cooke wouldn't get his one-up on the DEA with this bust. "If any of you sees McCluskey, tell him thanks for making sure I didn't become part of the Atlantic."

"Sure thing." Polanski pressed her lips together.

Haj looked away. Dell didn't change expression, but he patted his comb-over, a sure sign of upset.

"All right. What did I say?"

Polanski poked Haj. "Lay it on the line. We'll back you up."

"Uh-oh." Tony glanced from one to the next. "I'm in as much trouble with my squad as I was with my favorite women over my walking episode. Spit it out, and don't pull punches."

Haj grimaced. "See, boss, we miss Erickson too, and Bergstrom has a way to go to measure up, but we figure it'd be nice if you'd cut the kid a break."

"Whew! That one came out of left field." Had he been so out of line with the latest addition to the squad that the others had noticed? It was pretty normal to assign the newbie scut jobs like tallying everybody's expense accounts. Did they think he'd ordered Bergstrom to help fix that broken floor scrubber? The kid did that on his own.

Haj shuffled his feet under Tony's steady gaze. "I mean, he's got a pretty nice pat on the back coming, you know. After all, he... Aw, nuts!"

Polanski glared at her partner and then turned toward Tony. "What Haj can't seem to spit out is a reminder that you owe Bergstrom big-time."

He owed Bergstrom? Tony sorted through the images from the last moments before his accident. Oh, yes. Now he remembered. "Because he shot the woman who was shooting at me? Yeah, that was good work. No more than we're trained to do, but I was on my way down to dish out that pat on the back when I met with an unexpected detour. Don't worry. I'll give Bergstrom good press in my report. Has the in-house shrink cleared him since the shooting?"

"Not that!" Polanski pulled a prune face. "Didn't anyone tell you?"

"Tell me what?"

"Bergstrom found you." Dell dropped the bomb without inflection. Tony's lungs went hollow. Found him? After he fell in?

Haj leaned forward. "Who did you think witnessed the accident and radioed for McCluskey's divers?"

"Well, sure, but—"

"Then he dove in and located you. By then, he was too frozen to pull you to the surface, but he pointed McCluskey's boys in the right direction, and they hauled you out."

Polanski jerked a nod. "He spent a night in the hospital."

Tony melted against the mattress. "Honest, guys, I didn't know. Is he okay?"

Haj flashed a smile. "Sure. The kid was pretty cold, but not near the Popsicle you were. Remember, he was sitting in that warm truck cab the whole time we were enjoying the sea breezes on deck with our coats off."

"So where is he today? Did he think the big bad boss wouldn't want to shake his hand? Even I know better than to bite the hand that saves me."

Haj and Polanski chuckled. Dell offered a minismile.

"Nah." Polanski shook her head, still grinning. "He's not scared of you, just in love with his wife. He'd rather be with her, especially right now."

"Huh? Oh, yes, they're expecting a baby. When's it due?"

"Overdue. So he didn't mind collecting a few days of sick leave to be at home."

"Tell him… Never mind, I'll tell him." A familiar sensation came over Tony in his lower abdomen. Familiar, but scary different. He glanced at the catheter bag on the side of the bed away from his visitors, and his mouth went dry. "Would you tell someone at the nurses' station that their favorite patient needs urgent attention?" He steeled himself against waves of woozy sensation. "I'd push the button, but sometimes it takes a little while for them to answer."

Haj glanced at Polanski. "That beached fish look is back."

"Get going, you clod." She shoved him, and he hustled out. Then she turned toward Tony. "We'll stay till someone comes. Are you in pain?"

"No…yes…sort of. I can't tell. I just feel…"

"Weird?"

"That's as good a description as any."

Trotting feet sounded in the hallway. A moment later, Nurse Olivia, a male orderly, and Hajimoto burst through the door.

"I'll have to ask you all to leave," the nurse said.

"Sure. See you later, boss." Polanski stood and waved. Dell did the same. They scooted for the door, Haj herded along in front of them.

"My kidneys appear to be processing something," Tony gritted at his helpers, black edging his vision. "But I don't think red's the right color."

Thirteen

At Tony's town house in the gated community ten blocks from her house, Desi stood in front of his closet and browsed through his wardrobe. Her hunk of a fiancé had good taste, but then, she already knew that. He was also organized. She could have guessed that too. She picked out a few casual outfits, took the clothes off the hangers, and laid them on the bed beside a suitcase.

Humming came from the direction of the bathroom—Gina stocking Tony's shaving kit. Desi smiled. Wouldn't it be wonderful if they were packing for a honeymoon?

She folded a polo shirt and laid it in the case. The last time she did this with a man's clothes, she was preparing her father's belongings for donation to Goodwill. The remembered scent of Hiram Jacobs's woodsy cologne teased her. The backs of her eyelids prickled, but she blinked them, slamming the door on the reminder. With everything going on in the here and now, she didn't need to wander down a rabbit trail into the past.

A rather tinny melody of "Agnus Dei" sounded from the living room.

"What's that, cara?"

"My cell phone." Desi strode into the living room, took the phone from her purse, and checked the caller ID. HJ Securities' local office. Phone service must be back up. "Desi here."

"Hey, girlfriend."

"Hi, Max. Good to hear from you. I appreciate you holding down the fort on this postblizzard Monday. How's everything on the battle front?"

Max groaned. "You had to ask! The Greybecks are spreadin' stink again."

"Oh, you mean that deceptive information about events at the Museo de Arte Mejicana?"

"That and more juicy gossip masquerading as news."

"More!"

"With the Greybecks there's always more."

Spider feet scurried up Desi's spine. "Lay it on me. What now?"

"Check today's paper. I called so you wouldn't get blindsided."

"It's that bad?"

"Let's just say we've had one Boston-area client drop their contract today."

Desi's heart stalled, then jump-started. Losing a client far from home base was tough, but to start losing them in one's own backyard? "Boiling in oil is too good for the Greybecks."

"Fine by me to reinstate drawing and quartering."

"I'll grab Tony's newspaper from the doorway."

"Front page of the business section, and hang on to your blood pressure. We'll weather this like everything else those lowlifes have pulled."

"I'm done with grin and bear it, Max. Whatever this new attack involves, it's not going unpunished." She slapped her phone closed and marched for the front door.

Cold rushed her as she pulled it open and several newspapers flopped inside from between the outer and inner doors. She scooped them up and retreated into the warm living room. A little leafing brought her to the current issue. She scanned the headlines in the business section. Nothing applicable above the fold. At least whatever it was didn't rate top billing. She flipped to the bottom portion.

In the right-hand corner, a moderate-sized headline above a short article proclaimed, "National Treasures Go Missing Under Care of Security Expert." Desi forced herself to read from the beginning. Ah, yes, it was the same blather the Mexican president had shown her—at least through the first third of the article, and then—she let out a shriek.

> After the recovery of the crown of Pakal, Greybeck and Sons
> were told that the theft was staged by HJ Securities headquar-
> tered in Boston and carried out by the CEO of the corporation,
> Desiree Jacobs. Damage was noted on one of the leaf tips.
> Examination showed the crown to be a fake made of lead and
> gold paint. The Mexican authorities did not question Ms.
> Jacobs, claiming the real crown was safe, but they refused to
> produce the artifact for inspection.

President Montoya and Señor Corona would be livid. Maybe the Greybecks hoped the article wouldn't come to the attention of the Mexican government. No, the Greybecks were sneaky and underhanded, but not naive. It cost them nothing to expose secrets after they lost the museum contract. Of course, the article didn't name the Greybecks as the source. Pretty slim cover-up for a smoking gun of edited facts designed to cause trouble south of the border.

"What is it, cara?" Gina came into the room. "Are you all right?"

"Let me finish reading, and then you can take a look while I plan murder and mayhem."

Gina's eyes widened.

Desi returned to the article.

Following this series of "questionable events," Greybeck and Sons
terminated their relationship with the Museo de Arte Mejicana.

Desi shook her head. "That's not how it happened. The skunks
were fired."

Had Señor Corona issued the announcement that the Greybecks
were dismissed by the Museo de Arte Mejicana and a native firm re-
tained? Desi had been too preoccupied to check. But the truth wouldn't
trump this statement in a Boston daily newspaper. People would believe
what they wanted. The Greybecks saved face by muddying the water.
Too typical. Utterly sickening.

Desi's mouth tasted like paste as the final paragraph unfolded.

According to an inside source, Ms. Jacobs of HJ Securities left
Mexico City without a contract from the Museo de Arte Mejicana and flew to Mérida on the Yucatán Peninsula. She was in
possession of an artifact of value to the Mexican people, which
was later reported stolen from the security expert and has not
been recovered. Ms. Jacobs has returned to Boston but was
unavailable for comment.

"That's right, you yellow journalist. I've been busy with my fiancé.
And the medallion belonged to me, not the Mexican people."

Gina's brow wrinkled. "The journalist is a coward?"

"Yellow journalism twists facts to stir people up. This article works
the angles to make smoke and mirrors seem like the real thing." She
thrust the paper at Tony's mom.

Then she stalked into the bedroom and folded clothes like she'd
rather rip them in pieces. How had the Greybecks found out her medallion was stolen? Were they behind the theft? They were capable of anything to discredit her and destroy her company. Maybe her assumption

that Sir Jalapeño grabbed the necklace for resale to a gang leader was off base. Then again, she'd reported the theft to Ramon Sanchez. Word could have gotten around the law enforcement community in Mérida, filtering down to antiquities dealers and possibly reaching Clayton's ears.

Bother! She'd rather think those back stabbers were thieves, not mere rumormongers. There was no jail sentence for gossip, unless she could prove slander, and so far they were playing it too smart to make a good case against them.

Desi jammed socks into the suitcase. What was she doing? Señor Corona needed to know about the article. Had he returned to his duties since his wife's murder? Oh, dear! She'd been too caught up in crisis to send him a condolence card. Maybe she should contact President Montoya.

"Agnus Dei" sounded again. She charged for the living room and snatched the phone. The prefix on the caller number was Mexico. She took a deep breath. "Desiree Jacobs speaking."

"Ms. Jacobs, Ramon Sanchez here. How is your fiancé?"

Not Señor Corona. A less explosive call. Tension eased from Desi's shoulders. "Tony's improving. His mother and I will look after him while he recovers."

"Excellent. I have a similar report in regard to Zapopa and her grandson. She has been discharged from the hospital with some one-sided paralysis from the head wound, but she and Manuel have relocated to a safer neighborhood. She will receive therapy, and Manuel will get a stipend from the government until his grandmother can care for herself. Then a job will be found for him. If he proves ambitious, a scholarship program could send him to vocational training."

"Excellent! Many thanks, Ramon. Have you referred the hospital bills to HJ Securities?"

"Unnecessary, Ms. Jacobs."

"Desiree."

"Since these unfortunate events occurred while you were on assignment for the Mexican government, Desiree, we will, as you Americans say, pick up the tab." Ramon chuckled.

"You've lifted a burden from my mind. Now I'd like to do something for you. Considering the threat you're under, the security on your home should be enhanced. May I send a team down to help make you and your family safer? HJ Securities will pick up the tab."

An intake of breath. "You would do this even though you encountered danger in my country?"

"I also received great kindness. Not only did you provide an emergency airplane ride, but you've shouldered the burdens I left behind."

"These actions were no more than correct."

"As is my offer. During my flight home, I made a personal vow to return your kindness."

Gina stepped into Desi's line of vision, nodded approval, and returned to the back rooms.

Ramon laughed. "Then I must graciously accept, eh?"

"I think you must."

"When shall I expect the HJ Securities team?"

"I'll tap the Dallas office. The team leader will call you early tomorrow."

"Pilar will be relieved. She has been quite nervous of late."

Pilar! Desi went still inside. Of course! She knew the Greybecks. But how could she tactfully ask Ramon if he had told his wife about the medallion theft? *Please, give me wisdom, God.* "One more thing. Is there anything to report about my missing items?"

"Nothing favorable, unfortunately. Your carry-on was recovered, ripped and empty. I'm sure your ring was sold for whatever the little urchin could get. I have the word out among the pawnshops. As to your medallion, this Preston Standish, Esquire, seems to have dropped off the face of the earth. There is no record of him after his arrival in Mérida. I'm so sorry."

"You have nothing to apologize for. I'm sorry to have brought my difficulties into your household. I'm sure Pilar didn't need to hear about more crime in her city."

"Pilar? I didn't mention— *Ay, caramba*, she might have overheard me on the phone with the *capitán* of the policía. My apologies if you did not wish your privacy invaded that way."

Desi groaned on the inside. At least she had a good idea who leaked information about the medallion. But why was Pilar Sanchez chummy with the Greybecks? Maybe Ramon knew. "I'm not sure what it means, and there's probably an innocent explanation." Her words rushed out. *Good going, girl, make it sound like the darkest secret since David seduced Bathsheba.*

"I beg your pardon," Ramon said. "What are you trying to say?"

"Are you familiar with Greybeck and Sons, the security firm that was let go by the Museo de Arte Mejicana?"

"I have heard the name." His words trailed out slowly.

"When I used Pilar's phone, I accidentally found their business card under her blotter. The card was well-used, and there was a personal answering service number written on the back. A New York number." She clamped her mouth shut. She'd said enough.

"How…interesting." Ramon sounded puzzled but not shocked. "I will ask her. My wife makes many contacts at social functions. Perhaps she was considering engaging their services to install security devices as you have offered to do."

Desi forced a laugh. She'd eat her left shoe if the explanation were that simple. "Guess we beat the Greybecks to it this time. My people will be in touch soon."

"Bueno. And I will call if I hear anything about your stolen property."

"That's all I can ask. Buenos dí— Aack! I almost forgot. Unforgivable! Have they caught Señora Corona's killer?"

Heavy silence. Shouldn't she have asked?

A deep sigh floated through the connection. "The incident has gained international media attention, but you have been out of touch. Señor Corona has been arrested for the crime."

"What?" Desi's breath snagged.

"I am not free to speak of the details. The matter pains my heart."

"Mine too." She cleared her throat. "Stay safe, Ramon—you and your family."

"Safety, sí. A priceless commodity. Almost as rare as some of the antiquities you protect." Ramon released a brief chuckle, lacking in humor.

"There is One who holds us in the palm of His hand, no matter what."

"In the midst of your troubles, you remind me of this. Your Tony is a lucky man."

Desi laughed, heart lighter. "I needed to remind myself of that. Buenos días, Ramon."

An unfamiliar ringtone sounded as Desi put her phone into her purse. Had Tony left his cell at home?

"It's mine this time," Gina called.

Desi picked up the newspaper from the easy chair and tore out the offensive article. She stuffed that into her purse too, then headed toward the bedroom. The tone of Gina's voice prickled the hairs on Desi's neck, though she couldn't make out the words. She rushed forward. The expression on the woman's face halted her in the doorway.

Gina closed her phone. "That was the hospital. They are taking Tony into surgery. He's bleeding internally. Maybe his tumble yesterday tore something inside from his splenectomy."

Desi made a beeline for her coat draped over the sofa, Gina's footsteps close behind.

"Cara, wait! We must do one thing first."

Desi whirled. "What could be more important than getting to Tony?"

Gina held out her hands. "We need to pray."

Desi put her small hands into those big ones. Gina was right. A dear friend died a few years back from internal bleeding detected too late—and Tony's body had been through so much trauma already... She gulped. His window for survival had just slammed down on all their fingers. Only the mercy of God could lift it again.

Fourteen

*D*esi paced the OR waiting room.

"You're going to wear a hole and fall through." Max threw an arm around her shoulder.

Desi leaned into the support. "What would I do without my friends?" She gazed around the room at Steve and Lana and Gina.

Lana had brought Special K bars, and Steve was sprawled in an armchair, nibbling at one. He must be beside himself. The galoot never nibbled; he gobbled. Lana sat on the edge of a love seat and knitted, cute and composed as ever. Her needle fumbled, and a word left her lips that Desi had never heard from Max's mother before. Well, maybe not so composed, after all.

Gina occupied a seat near a window that provided a view of the Boston snowscape. With her elbow on the windowsill and her chin resting on the back of her hand, her profile radiated serenity. The pose was worthy of a classic painting. "Madonna of the Waiting Room"?

"See her?" Desi nudged Max. "She's a rock, and I'm a wreck."

"Check your eyeballs, girlfriend. Where are they pointed? On outer reality or inner? Gina's a rock because she's focused on her Rock. She's not seeing outside. She's seeing inside. Watch close. Her lips are moving. You do like that, and you'll get the same result."

A wry chuckle left Desi's throat. "No wonder I pay you such big money to work for me." She planted a quick smooch on Max's cheek. "I'm going to grab myself by the scruff and imitate Gina—er, Mom."

Desi sighed. "I need to get my emotions around having a new parent too."

"Don't push yourself faster than you're ready to go. When the time is right, calling her Mom will come naturally."

Desi subsided into a cushioned chair. She closed her eyes and willed her body to relax, but her mind proved a stubborn customer. Turmoil persisted like static hiss in the background.

Lord, You know I'm struggling here. Forgive me for lack of trust. I know You love Tony more than I do, though that's hard for me to fathom. Help me to release him to Your care and stand in faith for the victory that Your Word promises.

"Pastor Grange!"

Max's voice brought Desi's eyes open. Their pastor, a light-haired man of medium height, walked toward them. Max stepped forward, and his smile bloomed.

"How are the kids these days?"

"Better than last time we spoke. They're happier now that they can count on seeing their daddy every Thursday. I never fuss at them about bedtime when we go to the prison. I'll take a little crankiness the next day. Spendin' time with their father is too important."

"Wonderful." The pastor nodded. "And Dean?"

Max beamed. "He's getting more like the godly man who waltzed me up the aisle. He appreciates your visits and counsel."

"I enjoy our conversations. He's found the joy and humility that can only come from a deep revelation of God's forgiveness. Don't be too surprised if the Lord intervenes and Dean is released before anyone anticipates." He tapped Max's arm, then turned toward Desi.

She extended her hand. The pastor squeezed it, and she battled a rush of tears. Good thing they could talk about something besides Tony for a moment. "Thanks for your efforts with Dean. It took me a while to get over his involvement with a bunch of crooks who meant to kill me, but I think I can finally say I'm getting a revelation of forgiveness too."

"Forgiveness is as vital for the one who needs to do the forgiving as for the one who needs to be forgiven." He released her hand. "Any word on Tony?"

"It's too early yet, but the wait is shredding me into itsy-bitsy pieces."

"Sounds like we'd better apply a little glue."

"Glue?"

The pastor glanced around the room. "Good to see so many familiar faces. Lana...Steve."

Desi stared at the couple now holding each other's hands. Lana was a regular in church with her family, but when had Pastor Grange met Steve Crane? Some private encounter? Uh-oh! Did she hear wedding bells not her own?

"And this must be Tony's mother." The pastor held out his hand to the tall woman.

"You know Gina too?" Desi blinked at her minister.

Pastor Grange shook hands with Gina. "We've never met, just spoken on the phone a time or two when I called Tony about deacon duties, and she was at his town house." He turned his attention back to Gina. "Your son resembles you."

The woman laughed. "I've never thought so. He's his father's son."

"Oh, no." Desi folded her arms across her chest. "He's a lot like you in appearance and personality. Maybe that's why I'm so tickled to get you as a mother-in-law."

"Thank you, cara." Gina touched Desi's cheek.

Desi bit her lip, tears surging toward the surface again. She couldn't lose Tony now that she was so close to getting both a husband and a mom. She lowered her head. What a selfish thought, but isn't that what fears were made of?

Gina fixed the pastor with a stern gaze. "Let's do the glue."

He nodded. "Anyone willing to engage their faith, please, join us." He took Desi's hand, then Gina's, and closed his eyes. Max clasped hands with Desi on her other side. Then came Lana. The circle was complete.

Not quite.

Steve inserted his bulk between Lana and Gina. A flush rose from his neck, but gentleness softened his craggy features in a way Desi had never seen before. Had something more wonderful than an engagement happened for the Man with the Iron Heart?

The pastor began his petition to the Almighty. "Lord, we seek You as the source of all healing and place our loved one, Tony, in Your capable hands. Guide the medical staff and give them wisdom and understanding as they work with You to preserve his life."

Simple, direct words—full of faith. The prayer echoed the cry in Desi's heart, only magnified by the unity of Christ's love surrounding her. The true glue that held the universe together. More than enough to put one man's battered body back together. As Pastor Grange continued to speak to God as to a treasured friend, confidence rose in Desi's spirit, hope sang to her emotions, and peace settled the turmoil in her mind.

The little group unlinked hands and smiled at one another. Desi flopped her arms against her sides and laughed. "I feel like I'm the one who just got healed."

Gina hugged her. "We all need times of refreshing."

Pastor Grange consulted his watch. "I've got another critical hospital visit, or I'd stay to hear the good report. You have my number." He nodded toward Desi and strode away.

Another half hour ticked by in small talk and coffee slurping. Desi took the opportunity to update Max on the conversation with Ramon Sanchez.

"I'll research the Corona murder as soon as I get home," Max said. "And don't worry about lining up a team for Mérida. Your all-purpose employee's got that covered. You keep your focus on Tony." Her head swiveled toward the hallway. "O-o-okay."

Desi turned, pulse throbbing in her neck. Dr. Braniff walked toward them, shoulders slumped, eyes weary, no smile.

He stopped in the entrance. "I see everyone here is on my patient's approved list to share results. We found the minor bleed, repaired it, and Tony's in recovery."

Desi smiled and smacked her palms together.

The doctor frowned. "However, we got some irregular heartbeats during the procedure. This could have been a reaction to the anesthesia, or it might indicate deeper problems that have gone undetected until now."

Steve groaned deep and long.

Braniff held up a hand. "We'll do a battery of tests over the next few weeks to rule out chronic conditions. As I said, there may be nothing to worry about."

"Thank you, Doctor," Gina breathed.

Desi struggled for a clear thought. What did a potential heart condition mean to Tony's career—to their lives together?

"Even if we discover a problem," the doctor said, "chances are it will be manageable." He smiled. "A little nod from heaven, and Tony should recover to lead a normal life."

"Normal in whose book?" Steve grated. "He's an FBI agent. That's not just what he is, that's who he is."

"The fate of his career lies with the bureau."

The Steve Crane that Desi knew from adversarial days turned ice-block eyes on the group. "Bureau agents practically need superpowers. If he can't meet the physical requirements—"

Lana wrapped her fingers around his arm. The big man visibly sagged. She led him off toward a corner of the room, murmuring words Desi couldn't make out.

She shook the doctor's hand. "Thank you so much. You've been instrumental in saving Tony's life. Whatever—" she swallowed a lump—"issues might occur, we'll weather them. The most important goal has been accomplished. That nod from heaven? We've got it."

"Amen!" Gina came up beside Desi.

Braniff looked from one to the other. "I see a lot of family reactions in my line of work, but you impress me with the strength of your convictions. Whatever you're doing, keep it up. It's working." He nodded to Desi, smiled at Gina, then headed toward the nurses' desk.

Gina humphed. "Pity he seems content to remain on the sidelines of faith. He'd enter a new dimension as a doctor if he became a player, not just a spectator."

"I suspect he thinks active faith would distract him from his work rather than enhance it."

"I suspect you're right, mia figlia. No wonder Tony admires your powers of observation."

A spurt of mischief shot through Desi. Probably a symptom of relief that Tony was on the road to recovery. "Too bad. I suppose lack of spiritual depth shoots down any hopes Dr. Frank might entertain about seeing you socially."

Gina's eyes widened. "The doctor? Interested in me? Wherever did you get such a notion? Besides—" she lifted her chin—"I'm too old to consider dating. Now if you'll excuse me, I need to visit the powder room."

Max let out a husky chuckle as Tony's mother disappeared up the hall, spine stiff, cheeks rosy. "Methinks the lady doth protest too much."

Desi laughed. "I should check my mouth at the desk sometimes. But it actually felt good to get my first scolding from a parent in too many months."

Max's gaze was assessing. "You know what felt good to me? Seein' your sassiness perk up. It's been droopin' for a while."

"How soon do you think they'll let me see Tony?"

"Shouldn't be long, but we'll leave you to it." Max waved Steve and Lana over. "My babysitter needs to get home. Call if anything comes up."

After hugs between the women and a pat on the shoulder from a grim-faced Steve Crane, Desi watched the threesome head for the elevator. When they were gone, she flopped onto a sofa and laid her head back. "Just call me limp dishrag," she said to the ceiling.

Honestly, she'd been wrung out and twisted every which way in less than a week's time.

Lord, please give me strength, because if You don't, I'm going to mess up on something, and that will hurt more people than just me.

—⁓⁓—

A gentle hand smoothed Tony's brow, then soft lips met his. The familiar exotic scent of Desi's hair pleased his nostrils. He breathed deep and willed his eyelids to lift. They managed a slit. The love of his life smiled at him. So beautiful, but man, she looked ready to wilt on her feet. He'd been pretty hard on her these past days, and if things didn't turn around pronto, she'd be smart to walk away. They hadn't exchanged vows yet. She was a vibrant woman, and she could…

Forget that thought. Desi wasn't the kind to leave when the road got rough. *Thank You, Jesus!* This guy didn't mind admitting he needed his woman. But did she need him in the shape he was in? Pain of a non-physical sort shot through him.

Desi traced a finger across his mouth. "Why the frown? Do you hurt?"

Something was missing from her hand. His eyes came fully open. "Your ring? Where?" His voice sounded like he hadn't used it in the last century.

"Not to worry." Her lips smiled, but her eyes didn't. "I'm surprised Mr. Observant didn't notice sooner. A pint-sized suitcase snatcher purloined it in Mexico. An insurance claim will replace it, but you haven't given me much time to think about anything so mundane."

"I remember now." He licked dry lips. "You told the nurse who was trying to stop you from coming into my room. More trouble than a stolen ring."

Desi laughed. "I know you're on the mend when you get your Grand Inquisitor look. It's a long story, but we can save it for later." Her voice broke, and her lips quivered. "Oh, Tony. I was so scared! I need you." A tear traveled down her cheek.

"Hey, sweetheart, I'm here." He lifted an arm, and she rested her head on his shoulder. He laced his fingers in her hair. "I seem to recall you sentencing me to ancient age with you. Do you think I'd dare change the plan? Just a couple of old codgers rocking on the porch."

"Yeah." Her soft body relaxed against him.

Well worth a twinge in the incision if his beat-up self could offer her a shoulder to cry on. Just went to prove he could still be her man when the codger days came, because he couldn't be much more of a wreck then than now. A chuckle left his throat.

She drew away and wiped wetness from her cheeks. "Good to hear you laugh, hon. We'll need plenty of that to carry us through all the days of our lives." Her attempt at a smile wavered.

"What aren't we talking about, babe?" A yawn sneaked past Tony's guard. Blasted anesthesia hadn't quite worn off. "And don't say we'll save it for later."

Desi stared into his face as if searching for something. The green and gold flecks that made her eyes so unique glinted down at him. "I love you, Tony, no matter what. You know that. It won't matter to me what you choose to do in life, I'll be there supporting you."

So that was the problem. She was worried about his career with the bureau. "Yeah, as I was waking up, I overheard yakking between the medical staff about possible heart issues, but I'm not buying it. Just watch me come back better than ever."

A grin snuck over her features. "You're the kind of man who'll make good on that promise, and I'll cheer you on. But first—" she tapped the tip of his nose—"you need a good night's sleep, and so do I. I'll see you in the morning, and we'll start making it happen."

She leaned down, and he made sure to collect more than a mere peck on the lips. After she left, Tony closed his eyes, but they wouldn't stay that way. He watched shadows creep along the wall and listened to hospital rustles and squeaks and beeps.

In a little while, a nurse he'd never met before came in and checked his vital signs and the postsurgical IV. "Do you need me to increase the drip on the pain medication, Mr. Lucano?"

"It's Tony, and no, thanks. You wouldn't happen to have any instant healing pills, would you? I need to be up and doing. I haven't loitered in bed this much since I was a newborn."

The nurse chuckled. "Rest and time are the best healing pills for you right now, Tony. Don't get ahead of yourself."

Ahead of himself? He'd been sent back to preschool. He talked big, and Desi had faith in him, but what would he do if he couldn't meet the physical standards for his job? Become an insurance investigator? Or better yet, he could hang out a shingle and turn gumshoe.

What was that 1940s flick Desi and he watched the last time they were together? *The Maltese Falcon*? Sure, he'd make a perfect Sam Spade if he could learn to talk out of one side of his mouth like Humphrey Bogart.

Not going to happen! He was an FBI agent first, last, and always. Could he do something else if he had to? Of course. But he wasn't going to change jobs without an epic battle. And a man who meant to take a wife and start a family needed to have his career nailed down. Desi would pitch a fit, but the wedding would have to wait until he had his life back.

Fifteen

*T*ony looked out the window of Hiram Jacobs's bedroom toward Desi's white-capped garage. The crystals on the surface of the snowbanks glistened in the sunlight. Tony shivered—subzero out there yet. He turned away, enticed by breakfast smells from the kitchen. Various body aches set up a minor objection to the movement, but better than yesterday.

Ten days since his tumble into the harbor and five blessed days out of the hospital. So far, so good on his cardiac tests, but there were more to come. For now he stood on his own two feet, even if they were encased in slippers because it hurt to bend and put on socks. Best of all, he had his feminine wardens' permission to move around the apartment without someone trailing on his heels. Of course, he'd better not abuse his privileges, or Mom and Desi'd be on him like a pair of security guards on a shoplifter.

Tony stopped beside Hiram's dresser and picked up a photograph in a gilded frame. The woman smiling back at him had Desi's sable hair, strong features, and full mouth, but her eyes were blue. Des got her hazel eyes from her dad, but this must be the mother Desi never knew—the one killed in a car accident when she was a baby. Hiram never remarried, and that spoke volumes of devotion. Of course, if mother was anything like daughter, a man could search the world over and not find a pale imitation.

So why was he thinking about putting off his wedding to this matchless treasure? Had his accident addled his good sense? No. Tony squared his shoulders, and his collarbone brace pulled. Desiree deserved his best, and that's what she was going to get.

He headed for the kitchen. Oops! He halted and put a hand on the wall. A little too brisk. The wobbly feeling faded, and he started again at a slower pace, that bacon smell drawing him by the taste buds. Good old protein—one of the joys of working kidneys.

Standing at the stove, Desi glanced over her shoulder and smiled. She wore jeans and a sweater and looked as delicious as anything on the menu. He slipped his arms around her waist and nuzzled her neck.

"Good morning to you too. Have a seat. Breakfast is served." She went back to lining crispy strips on a paper towel–covered plate. The breakfast counter was set for two, complete with glasses full of orange juice and a thermal pot of coffee.

Tony eased onto a stool. "Where's Mom?"

Desi set the plate of bacon on the counter. "She went out to pick up a few household items, but I ordered her not to come back until after her ladies' Bible study this morning."

"You ordered her?" Tony laughed.

Desi pulled a pan from the oven. "Cajoled is more like it." She took the cover from the pan and revealed a stack of pancakes. "We need to return to doing normal things."

"Amen to that." Tony transferred three slices of bacon to his plate and speared a pair of cakes with his fork almost before she set the pan down.

"Yikes! Good thing I got my hand out of the way." She kissed his cheek. "I see where your attention is this morning. You didn't try to turn your head and catch me on the mouth."

"Later, babe, and we'll make it worth waiting for."

Flushed but smiling, she joined him at the counter and filled her plate as full as his. No dainty eater here, the kind that made a guy edgy with her picking. They both dug in, talking between bites about the weather forecast, the basketball game on TV this afternoon—well, that was mostly his contribution—and a Charlie Chaplin retrospective showing downtown next month—her contribution.

She cleaned her plate and snagged another pancake. "We're really blessed, aren't we?"

Her tone was matter-of-fact, but he caught a note of wistfulness, like she was trying to convince herself.

Tony canted his head. "I'm still living and breathing and 'lookin' at you, kid.'" His Bogart needed work, but she laughed anyway.

"Your survival isn't a blessing. It's a miracle that I'll thank God for every day forever."

"I'm with you on that one. So what's got you weighing blessings versus trials?" He popped the last of his bacon into his mouth. No seconds. His appetite wasn't all there yet.

She shook her head and buttered her pancake.

"Nothing doing, babe." Tony tapped his fork on his empty plate. "I've been patient, but it's time you filled me in on Mexico. And what about those tense phone calls between you and Max? The ones you think I don't hear? No whitewashing. I want the straight story."

She wrinkled her nose. Tony fought the urge to kiss the cute little beak, but now was serious talk time. Serious kissing could come later…if she wasn't too mad at him if they ended up discussing wedding postponement, a chat he'd gladly put off. He reached for the coffeepot.

Desi's hand closed around his on the handle. "Let's take our coffee into the living room. You can sit in Dad's recliner. I'll let you carry your empty cup, but I get to carry this." She hefted the carafe. "No lifting, remember?" With a saucy look, she left the kitchen.

Tony followed, frowning. She must be keeping some tough stuff under wraps if she forgot to eat her pancake and walked away from dirty dishes. He settled into his spot in the living room but didn't raise the recliner foot. Hiram had picked out a quality chair that Tony didn't mind adopting as his own, only he couldn't let himself get too comfortable right now. He fell asleep at the droop of an eyelid.

Desi poured their coffee, grace personified, but her lips were pencil slashes and her brows drawn together. At last she sat on the end of the sofa nearest him and folded her hands in her lap. "I'll start with the craziness in Mexico. We go downhill from there." She sighed and gave him a blow-by-blow of events after her phone call to him from the taxi in Mexico City.

Insides seething, Tony let her talk, mentally marking down names like Esteban Corona, Albon Guerrera, and Preston Standish. The Greybecks—Randolph, Clayton, and Wilson—were already on his personal most-wanted list. Nothing they did surprised him. Not even Clayton showing up in Mérida. If dead fish stank, these guys were dirty. Maybe he'd do the private-eye thing after all and look into his hunch during his convalescence.

Then Desi got to the part about losing her engagement ring. "One minute, I'm walking along minding my own business, and the next I'm on my rear watching a kid not much bigger than Max's Luke run off with my carry-on." She said the words in a light tone and tried to smile, but her face crumpled as she stared at her empty ring finger.

Tony got up and eased beside her on the sofa. She came into his arms without a scold or a protest. "First off—" he stroked her hair— "none of this is your fault. Well, except the part about stopping to see that ex-con Guerrera."

"I knew you'd hate that." Her voice sounded muffled against his sweatshirt.

"Secondly, we're going to get your ring back. I can't stand not seeing it on your finger. We'll call the insurance adjuster today and get the ball rolling."

"Already did that." She snuggled closer. So what if his shoulder twinged a bit.

"Then I'm going to have Haj dig into Preston Standish, Esquire. Haj is a bulldog about finding people who don't want to be located—and on ferreting out who they really are."

Desi lifted her head. "But the crime happened in Mexico."

Tony kissed the tip of her nose. "The FBI has a bigger international presence than you know, darlin'. Besides, you're an American citizen. Depending on what we turn up, this case could turn out to be our bailiwick."

"Go for it." She stood. "But you're likely to find out Standish is just a background shade in the bigger picture." She ran stiff fingers through her hair. "There's this drug lord who collects antique jewelry. He goes by this cheesy name, El Jaguar—"

"Say what?" Tony sat forward, ignoring the screech from his incision.

Her eyes widened. "You know about the guy?"

"You've just connected your series of unfortunate events to an ongoing interagency and international investigation, and that's already more than I should spill."

She glared down at him. "Don't tell me the Jaguar had something to do with why you were down at that pier in the middle of a blizzard."

"Okay, I won't tell you, but I always say you're sharper than Excalibur."

Desi groaned. "You'd better let me finish the story. You are sooo not going to like it."

She was right. By the time she got to her encounter with a gangster in Ramon Sanchez's limo, he was up and pacing. "I need to wring a few necks," he muttered.

"No, you need to sit down." Desi took his arm and guided him to the recliner.

He scowled but lowered himself into the chair. If he weren't so blasted weak, he'd... What? How could he throttle crooks he couldn't identify or catch?

Identify and catch them, that's how.

Gentle fingers touched his cheek. "Your glare could peel paint." She smoothed the rebellious hair on his brow. "Let me dump out this cold coffee and pour us fresh."

She made the trip to the kitchen while Tony stewed. Trails were growing colder than the sidewalk outside. How many times would he realize he hated being out of commission?

Desi breezed back into the room, refilled their cups from the carafe on the coffee table, handed him a steaming mug, and resumed her seat on the sofa.

Tony took a sip, then set the cup on the lamp table. "You're going to see action on this, Des. I promise you."

"I believe you, sweetheart." She reached across the small space that separated them and took his hand. "The rest of my time in Mexico was fairly pleasant until I got word about the murder of Señor Corona's wife and then your accident."

She outlined her experience in the Sanchez household, including speculations about Pilar Sanchez and the Greybecks.

"So now, I've sent a team down to Mérida to set up security for Ramon's home, but I don't know what to think about Señor Corona. He's been arrested for the murder of his wife. It turns out her frequent illnesses were a cover-up for alcoholism, and the two of them fought constantly. Worse, they found his fingerprints in the blood on the murder weapon and spatter on his clothes. Supposedly, he bludgeoned her with a marble statuette." She sat back and huffed. "I can't see him doing such a thing. To me, he was the soul of honor in a very awkward situation."

Tony shook his head. "In the heat of the moment, honor doesn't always speak very loud. Besides, he may not be as upright as you think. You said he seemed disturbed about your medallion. Maybe he knew something he didn't want to share."

"I think a presidential aide knows many things he can't share. Much like an FBI agent."

Tony chuckled. "Low blow, Des."

She smiled, but the gesture was feeble. "Not as low as those Grey-becks. They've been spreading manure hot and heavy, and it's germinating bad seed about HJ Securities."

Tony sat at attention.

"Those conversations you've overheard between Max and me, that's us beating our heads against a wall to find a solution." Her gaze darted away and came back shuttered. "We'll come up with something. You know the dynamic duo. We don't know how to quit."

She got up and collected the coffee cups. Tony grabbed her wrist. She didn't look at him.

"Tell me, Des. It'll bother me more not to know than to have the cards on the table."

She set the cups on the fireplace mantel and crossed her arms, as if holding herself together. "If we don't come up with something soon, I could lose my business."

The words came out in a whisper, but they hammered Tony like a club.

Desi lifted her head, and her wounded look pierced him. "But like I said—we're blessed. We've got each other. Each morning I tell myself I'm one day closer to marrying you, and the thought keeps me going. Let's do it, Tony." She knelt in front of him and took his hands. "No more waiting. No more nightmare guest list. Forget pomp and circumstance. Just you, me, the minister, and the people we love. We could do it tomorrow. Next week. Soon!"

Tony's mouth opened, but no words came out. Every molecule ached to sweep her into his arms and carry her to the altar that second, but his body said no, his good sense said no, and finally his voice said no.

Then he died as he watched the life fade from her eyes.

Desi pulled her hands from Tony's, stood, and wiped them on her jeans. She tottered toward the foyer and access to her apartment. *Go home.* The most sensible thought she could muster.

Now, when she cast aside inconsequentials like seating arrangements and demanding schedules and offered herself without reservation, he turned her down. What did that mean?

"Des!" His voice came from right behind her.

A hand gripped her shoulder, and she stopped but didn't turn around. Her hands clenched. She couldn't even slug him, hurt as he was.

"Sweetheart, listen to me." His breath caressed her ear. "Becoming your husband is my top priority. You have no idea how much I think about it every day. But your desperation and my dependency are not good foundations for starting a marriage."

The hand left her shoulder, and she felt him back away.

"Look at me, Des."

She shook her head, and stupid tears fell hot on her cheeks. Seemed like every other minute her eyes sprang a leak. "I hate it, but you're right. I'm in no shape to be a wife."

Tony gave a thready chuckle. "Hon, you're great. It's me who needs an overhaul."

Desi forced her feet to turn her body around. Let him see her at her blotchy-faced, bawl-baby worst. If she couldn't do that, they'd better cancel the whole thing…permanently. She stared into his eyes. They radiated love, and her tears became a fountain dripping onto her sweater. "You need to heal on the outside, and you'll do that. I know you. Just like you said, you'll come back better than ever." She drew in a stuttering breath. "But I'm a mess on the inside. It's getting worse, and not because of business problems or your accident. I don't know what's wrong with me-e." A sob squeezed her rib cage.

Then Tony's arms wrapped around her. He was still plenty strong, and she was too weak to pull away. She buried her face in his sweatshirt and inhaled his spicy masculine cologne. Different from her dad's, but she loved it just as much—loved Tony just as much.

But, oh, she still missed Daddy!

Dumb, big baby thinking. She was a grown woman. She should be past this. She…

Tony drew her across the room. He sat in the recliner and patted his lap.

"I can't." Her words sounded like she was talking through water. "You're not—"

"Shush and sit. My legs aren't hurt, and this shoulder's good." He patted his left one.

Desi shook her head. She was not going to…but she melted into the comfort anyway. And the tears rolled on.

Tony had never been so glad to be uncomfortable in his life. Desi was a featherweight, but his gut was tender, and her head on one shoulder pulled the injured one. Yet he'd let her sit here all day and not utter a complaint. He'd known something was eating her. Something that drove her to bury herself in work these past months.

Maybe she didn't even know what it was. Or maybe she did and couldn't admit the problem. Probably the latter. Des had this habit of trying to be strong for everyone around her—to the point of refusing to lean on someone when she was hurting. Okay, so he had to plead guilty to the same. Just meant he understood her.

He kissed the top of her head and rubbed her shaking back. Man, those sobs hurt his heart worse than the rest of him. He'd let her get the waterworks out of her system, and then maybe they could figure out the cause. That might take some doing, because he'd have to turn in his badge on this one. He hadn't a clue.

Gradually, her trembling eased, and the sobs became little hiccups. Her body relaxed against him. Warmth spread through Tony as his own muscles unwound and discomfort faded.

"Des?" He looked down past his nose to the dainty head resting on his shoulder. Dark lashes fanned against her damp cheek. Her full lips were slightly parted. Babe in slumber land. Probably just what she needed. All right, discussion could wait. And was that the cutest mini-snore in the universe? He could sleep next to this for the rest of his life, no problem.

Tony smiled and laid his head back. His eyes drifted shut.

—☍—

"Good heavens! I can't leave you two alone for a minute."

Gina's voice drew Desi from a warm, welcoming place. She stirred, and a groan sounded from the chest beneath her ear. Tony! With a gasp, she sat up straight, staring into his startled face only inches from hers.

He hissed in a breath. "Gently, sweetheart."

"Oh, Tony, I'm so sorry." She slipped off his lap. "What was I thinking?"

"I don't think thinking was involved." He grinned up at her, then shifted into a different position and grimaced.

Gina laughed, and heat crawled up Desi's neck. She rubbed her eyes and found her cheeks crusty from tears. "I'm a menace as a nurse-maid. I should be fired."

"Sorry, babe." Tony chuckled. "I'm afraid you're stuck with the job. I won't allow anyone else to do my close personal therapy."

Gina set her purse and Bible on the coffee table. "I should certainly hope not, *giovanotto*. Have you two managed to set a date yet? I bought my mother-of-the-bride-and-groom dress a month ago, and every day it begs to be worn."

Desi stared at her feet. How did she explain to this adorable mom-in-law-to-be that some mysterious emotional malady was plaguing the woman who wanted to marry her son?

"You'd better hang that dress in the back of the closet for a while," Tony said. "I've got a ways to go before I'm husband material. Weeks, probably months, of physical training to regain my fitness levels, and then—"

"*Idiota!*" Gina flash-fried her son with a glare, then wagged a finger in his face. "Of all the ridiculous statements I've heard from your mouth. The standards of the FBI do not dictate your family life. Many women are happily married to men who couldn't pass a single bureau training test."

"But—"

"There is no 'but,' except in your head."

Desi clapped her hands. "*Brava, mia madre*. But the problem isn't so much with Tony as with me."

Gina's eyes widened. "You! All of a sudden you do not wish to marry—"

"Of course I wish. The sooner the better, if I could get past some stupid hang-up I can't even figure out myself."

"Hmm." The woman leveled an assessing gaze. "Come." She motioned toward the upstairs. "You and I will have *il discorso franco*—the heart-to-heart talk." She swept toward the foyer, sucking Desi in her wake.

"But Tony—"

"Is a big boy who knows how to use the remote control."

The bell rang as they passed the front door. Desi peeked out the diamond of beveled glass. Steve Crane stood there, cheeks bitten red with the cold. Someone to sit with Tony, anyway. She opened the door, and Crane entered with a rush of frigid air.

"Brrrr!" A shiver shook his big body. "Here." He thrust a box toward Desi. "Lana made cookies and insisted I bring some over for our prize patient. Never mind it's twenty below with the windchill."

Desi pointed to the living room. "Take them in to him. There's hot coffee in the pot. Pig out, you two. Gina—er, Mom and I are going to have a discorso franco."

"A what?"

She left him staring after them as she followed a chuckling Gina up the stairs. Tony's mom went straight to the kitchen and filled the teakettle. She pointed Desi toward the table. "So you are a watering pot these days, eh?"

Desi sat and shoved a stray toast crumb around on the tabletop. "Must be hormones or something, but I can't be PMSing all the time, and I'm too young for menopause."

"Praise the Lord for that. I expect grandbabies before I'm too old to enjoy them."

"We're on the same page about children. Tony and I won't wait long after we're married. We're seasoned adults, not a couple of kids just starting out, and we're not getting any younger."

"Very sensible." Gina pulled mugs from the cupboard and plunked tea bags into them.

"If we can just get those 'I do's' said. But things keep cropping up to put on the brakes."

"I am not surprised. The enemy of our souls cannot favor such a powerful union." Gina leaned a hip against the counter. "But I also think you both have baggage best dealt with. Tony must see himself as more than his job, and you must give yourself permission to grieve."

"About Daddy, you mean? But I've cried a bucket, and I'm tired of it."

"You never talk about him."

"But I think about him."

"Not the same thing."

Desi swallowed against the tightness in her throat. "I'm afraid if I talk, I'll cry."

"You're crying anyway."

A laugh loosened Desi's vocal cords. "Ouch! Direct hit."

The teakettle sang, and Gina poured hot water into the mugs. She set the steeping tea on the table and sat down.

An orange tang wafted to Desi's nostrils. Staring into the darkening water, she rubbed the handle of her mug. "I don't want to burden people with my emotional outbursts."

"People, no. Your friends, yes. If you don't, you deny the ones who love you and Hiram the right to grieve with you...and to celebrate the life that was here and now continues on the other side. You might surprise yourself with laughter more than tears if you open up. You have many good memories, no?"

"I have many great memories. Yes!" She chewed her bottom lip. "There's just one thing I can't get past."

"What is it, mia figlia?"

Desi carried her mug to the counter and tossed the wet tea bag into the sink. "I have this perfect wedding pictured in my mind. A gossamer veil mists my vision as I await my entrance gowned in satin. The church is scented with bouquets of enormous stargazer lilies and bright red roses. Traditional, but I love it. All our friends beam for joy. Tony, too handsome for words in his black tux, watches for me, drawing me with his eyes. The majestic strains of 'The Wedding March' reach my ears. And then…" Her breath caught. "I can't finish the fantasy." Her shoulders slumped. "I don't know if I can walk up that aisle alone. Not without bursting into tears, and I can't do that to Tony on our special day."

She stared out the kitchen window into the glittering cold. "Maybe that's why I shop the boutiques and browse the Internet and can't settle on a wedding dress. We should put the ceremony off indefinitely. I could get into counseling and—"

Strong hands pulled her around. Gina's brown gaze probed deep. "Is that what you really want? To wait?"

Mutely, Desi shook her head.

"Then maybe it's better if you make plans and move ahead despite your fears. Do you think perhaps this is what your father would approve?"

"I have no doubt. But this time you and Daddy may be putting too much confidence in a woman who has reached the end of her strength."

Gina patted Desi's cheek. "Then you are in the best position possible to receive all the grace you will need."

Grace. She'd appreciate a truckload of it. But it would probably take a smack with a two-by-four to convince Tony he didn't need to be Superman to be her man.

Sixteen

*T*ony chomped a bite out of another chocolate-chip cookie. He waved the remainder at Stevo. "You are going to get fat, my friend. Lana can bake up a storm."

The guy polished off his third cookie. "Poor me." He grinned. "She does all kinds of Susie-homemaker stuff. She knitted me that scarf." He pointed toward the length of blue wool draped over his coat on the back of an empty chair. "So, you about ready to start training?"

Tony scowled. "The doctor says another four weeks before I can even jog again."

Stevo shook his head. "You're gonna go stir-crazy."

"Tell me about it. I do a stress test in three weeks. If the old ticker checks out okay, I can start walking on the treadmill. No weightlifting, though, until further notice."

"Not to worry, pard. As soon as you get the go-ahead, I'll take over your training. Rocky had Mickey, and you've got the evil Stevo to whip you into shape."

Tony snorted a laugh. "I can hardly wait."

"It's a dirty job, and probably thankless as all get-out, but just call me a sucker. I'm volunteering." The burly man snitched another cookie out of the box. "A little advance fortification." He took a bite. "We've got to get you strong enough," he said with his mouth full, "to stand in front of a preacher and live through a honeymoon."

Tony groaned. "I suppose Max and Lana told you there'll be a wedding soon. Take advantage of my leave of absence and all that."

Stevo shrugged. "Sounds reasonable to me."

"I can't believe you said that." Tony's spine stiffened. "Of all people, I figured you'd get it. I need to know my job's secure first."

"Sure. A guy's got to support his family. Or at least contribute to the support."

"Finally, someone who understands." His back muscles loosened.

"Sure." Steve polished off the cookie. "But what's that got to do with grabbing a great girl like Desi while the grabbing is good? Unless you think God's gonna bring you this far and then leave you high and dry on the career part."

Tony opened his mouth, but his mind drew a blank. Breath stalled in his lungs as he stared into the other man's blocky face. The guy expected an answer. What could he say? *Yeah, Stevo, God's done wonders so far, but there's a limit to what He can do.* Stupid statement, and false too. But wasn't he thinking and acting like he was on his own to save his job?

He sank back in his seat, laughing. "I just got my faith chops busted by a guy who didn't want God's name mentioned around him a few months ago."

Stevo turned the color of rare steak, but he grinned. "Hey, I dig in my heels about some stuff, but once I let loose of the brakes, watch out!"

"Does that mean you and the Big Guy are on speaking terms now?"

Tony's ex-partner sat forward, elbows on his knees. "Better than that, I'd say."

Tony whooped and pumped a fist.

"Keep it down, would ya?" Stevo's mouth scowled, but his eyes didn't. "Now are you going to quit being a knot-head and get married already?"

"Seems you and your new Best Friend don't give me much choice." A warm awareness settled deep in Tony's gut. He'd missed the trail on the marriage thing for staring at the forest. "You're looking at a reformed knot-head."

A thrill exploded in his chest. He was going to make Desiree his wife as soon as possible. He'd have the right to wake up beside her every morning, slip between the sheets with her at night, help her anytime with pesky zippers or buttons... Chill, *ragazzo*! Better not follow that thought any further right now, but if the role of husband didn't give him motivation to regain his strength, nothing would—not even his career with the FBI.

Steve grinned like he was reading Tony's mind. Not a tough puzzle for any card-carrying member of the male gender.

Tony glared. "So what about you and Lana?"

Stevo stretched his arms wide and yawned. "I'll get around to it, but I need to rest up first. Maybe now I can sleep all night without spending half of it talking to God about you."

"Thanks. I mean that, and not for just now. You helped pull me through in a lot of ways you probably don't know."

"You did it for me not that long ago. I figure a little turnabout's fair play, so don't go around thinking you owe me something."

Tony laughed. Now that was the growly ex-partner he knew. "Then I guess I might as well make you mad and warn you a tux rental's in your immediate future."

"What?" The guy snorted. "You've got me down as usher?"

"Nothing that easy. You'll have my back as guardian of the wedding ring. Think you can handle the assignment?"

Stevo's mouth flopped open, and his eyes blinked like camera shutters. "But what about the guys on your active squad? I figured—"

"Don't try to wiggle out of it, Crane. I'll find something for the others to do. Can't have them slacking off like they're retired or something."

Stevo's brows snapped together in a glower that didn't quite work because of his eye blinks. "You're skating on thin ice, Lucano." The guy sounded like something had pinched his windpipe. "I'd better give Lana and Max the news." He leaped up and grabbed his coat and scarf.

"I'll call you with the date." Tony stifled the laugh that was aching to pop out.

"You do that." Stevo gave a backward wave on his way to the foyer.

Tony scooted to the edge of the recliner and stood. He couldn't let the guy get out the door that easily. This was too much fun. "Tell Lana thanks for the cookies." He caught up to Steve as he shrugged into his coat by the front door.

Footsteps sounded on the stairs that led to Desi's apartment. She appeared on the bottom landing, cheeks flushed, lips parted. His mother hovered behind her, expression stern.

He answered with a slow smile fixed on Desiree. "You two been praying up there?"

Des shook her head. "More like hoping. We'd—I'd like to talk to you."

"Back at ya." He took a step toward her. "How does eight weeks from Saturday sound?"

Desi shrieked. His mother mouthed, "Finally!" Tony opened his arms, and softness came into them. He captured the only pair of lips he needed to taste.

"I gotta get out of here." Stevo's voice came out half an octave too high.

The door opened and closed, and a wave of chill entered the hall, but Tony didn't even shiver. Too much warmth radiated from the inside out.

—⁓—

Late that night, after much discussion and umpteen phone calls, Desi fell asleep with the memory of Tony's lips on hers and wishing she could hear him breathing beside her now. When she awoke, sunlight trickled into her bedroom around the edges of the blinds. Her mind was alert, but she lay still beneath the thick quilt. What was different about today?

The wedding was on. That knowledge edged her awareness with anticipation. But another positive change clamored to be recognized. What? She unwound her body from a sleep curl with a luxurious stretch from the tips of her fingers to her ends of her toes. Today would be a good day. Ideas bubbled beneath the surface, eager for action.

Desi sat up. That was the difference! The heaviness that had hung on her like a leaden mantle had eased. The feeling hadn't disappeared, but it had faded to more of an unpleasant memory than an immediate presence. She got out of bed. The first order of business was—

Deal with the Greybecks.

She halted her trek toward the bathroom. Where had that thought come from? She must have been busy on the inside while she slept. A hot shower might draw specifics to the surface.

The shower helped, but she continued to mull details while she fixed herself tea and toast. Gina was planning to give Tony breakfast. In fact, Gina'd have to keep Tony company today. Time for the boss to sweep into HJ Securities headquarters and call a council of war.

Two hours later, Desi stood at the head of the table in the HJ Securities conference room. Ten faces stared back at her, including Max's freckled one. The redhead wore a grin the size of her home state of Texas.

Desi laid a folder on the table. "I know Max thinks I've called you together to announce my wedding scheduled for eight weeks from Saturday, and she's right. You're all invited."

Applause erupted amid laughter and calls of "It's about time."

Desi basked in the excitement, then motioned for quiet. "My real purpose in calling you together is to outline a change in course for HJ Securities." All faces sobered. "We've been taking a hit from skewed media reports and the rumor mill." People nodded amid scattered grumbles of "rotten Greybecks." Desi smiled. "That's about to come to a screeching halt.

"Scott." She nodded at the grizzled public relations veteran seated across from Max. "Traditionally, we've confined our advertising to trade publications that reach the kinds of clients we serve. But in today's business climate, we need to expand publicity efforts to touch a more universal market. Let's position ourselves as the people-friendly security company—not just for the rich, but concerned about Joe Citizen and his safety in his own home."

Glances were exchanged around the table.

Regan, the CFO, frowned and scratched her ear. "You're talking considerable expenditure and an addition of manpower if we're going to start installing security systems in private middle-class homes."

Desi shook her head. "I'm not talking about changing our service demographic, just elevating public perception. I want us to take out one week of ads for HJ Securities in every newspaper and any other media that have published or broadcast negative reports, and I want to include some of the great statistics we've kept in-house so far."

She tapped the folder on the table. "The material is in here. For instance, a few months ago, I told the administrator of a robbed museum that in the last decade no institution we've served has suffered loss due to HJ Securities' systems or operations failure. One hundred percent of the time, losses have occurred because of human error or dishonesty. He didn't want to hear that and fired us. Later, when his own secretary was arrested as an accomplice, he resigned, and the new administrator rehired us with the unanimous support of the board of directors."

Scott and Regan exchanged glances. "The ads are doable," he said. "I'll finesse the wording to keep client identities confidential."

Regan leaned forward. "And a one-week blitz shouldn't cut into our budget too badly."

Max waggled a hand. "I'm not sure such a short round of ads is going to do much good. People need to hear things consistently over a long period of time before the message sinks in."

"Excellent point." Desi took her seat at the head of the table. "The ads are just the icing to entice people to try the cake we're going to feed them on a regular basis." Blank stares focused on her. "I want us to offer a free column or sound bite to print and radio media, containing tips on household security for the average person." She glanced at Scott. "I know that's placing more responsibility on your plate, but if we offer a valuable service to their customers, the media will look closer at their sources before running tripe about us. Input, anyone?"

For a half hour the group discussed the nuts and bolts of the project. Excitement ran high. Desi's blood pumped with a ferocity she hadn't felt in a long time. People smiled and joked, and that, too, had been in short supply for a while. Everybody had ideas for column content.

"Sounds like you've got plenty of help, Scott," she said. "But tap the other offices too. This needs to be a global team effort."

The PR man threw a salute above his grin.

Desi folded her hands on the table. "You realize this little end run won't solve all our issues with Greybeck and Sons, but it's a proactive step and one they won't anticipate."

Max rubbed her hands together like a villainous conspirator. "The beauty of this plan is that we're not out to fight fire with fire. We douse flames of doubt and suspicion in the public mind with a blast of somethin' new and refreshin'."

Cheers and claps met the comment.

Then Max stood, grinned wickedly, and winked at Desi. "Enough business. How about we get down to the important stuff." She nodded toward the field representative at the opposite end of the table, and he opened the door. The receptionist wheeled a cart inside, laden with cake, punch, and coffee. A bouquet of helium-filled balloons bobbed from the handle.

Scott laughed. "Talk about feeding people cake."

Blue letters on the frosting said, "Congratulations, Boss-Lady." Desi clapped a hand over her mouth as everyone pulled packages wrapped in wedding shower paper from under the table.

Max grabbed Desi in a hug. "This little shindig's been planned since you announced your engagement, just waitin' to spring it as soon as you set a date. It's a good thing you haven't been around much, or one of us probably would have let the polecat out of the sack."

Desi laughed and wiped at her cheeks. "I'll be here more from now on. An old married woman can't go gallivanting around the world at a moment's notice."

"We're all for that." Regan began to cut the cake. One of the others passed the plates, and someone else poured punch and coffee.

Time passed with more hilarity. Torn gift-wrap strewed the floor, and used paper plates littered the table.

Desi glanced at her watch. "Max, we've got to go. Sorry, people." She stood up. "I'll be back later this afternoon. And I promise to put in a full day at this sweatshop tomorrow, but the bride, the matron of honor, and the groom's mom have an appointment at a bridal boutique."

"Get out of here." Scott waved them away.

Regan grinned. "And don't come back until you have a dress, Ms. Bride." She licked frosting from her finger.

Desi and Max hustled out of the office into the cold. They picked up Gina and headed downtown. Seated next to Desi in the front passenger seat, Tony's mother tugged at the buttons on her coat and crossed and uncrossed her ankles. Every now and then, a sigh escaped her lips.

Was Gina worried they wouldn't get this wedding put together in time? Or maybe Tony...of course. "Tony'll be all right for a couple of hours on his own."

Gina blinked like she'd said something off the wall. "I know, cara." She went back to twisting her coat buttons.

Desi frowned.

"Your father would've been proud of you this mornin'," Max said from the rear seat.

Desi's heart lifted. "I hope so."

Max laughed. "Not long ago, mention of your dad wouldn't have brought a smile. What happened?"

"An epiphany of sorts yesterday, aided by this great lady." Desi touched Gina's arm.

"Glad I could help." The woman stared out the side window.

Something was up. But what?

"I've set one more thing in motion about the Greybecks," Desi said. "Steve's been hired to poke into their business dealings and personal backgrounds. More than business rivalry is going on. I think they're trying to hide dirty laundry by airing—or inventing—ours."

Max whistled between her teeth. "I think you've clobbered the nail on the head."

"The thought occurred to me in Mexico during a conversation with the president, but other things shoved it from my mind."

"Yeah, like we haven't had anything going on."

Desi turned onto a street of specialty shops and boutiques. "Now, where is this place?"

"There." Gina pointed toward a bay window displaying a gowned mannequin draped in jewelry. Tony's mother seemed to shrink in her seat as they drifted past the storefront.

Desi slipped into a parking spot about half a block away. As they got out, a brisk wind ruffled Desi's hair and sent a shiver through her middle. They quick-footed toward the boutique.

"High-end place." Desi nodded toward the gown and accessories in the window.

"Nothin' but the best for you, girl." Max opened the door.

A smiling, model-thin sales attendant greeted them and took their coats. "I'm Victoria, and I'll assist you today. Follow me, please."

Desi hid a smile. Victoria? Naturally, no one who called herself Vicky could work in a place that smelled like wads of old money. They entered a separate room with no windows, just tastefully placed velvet-covered chairs and a tri-paneled mirror in front of a round stage.

Victoria beamed at Gina. "Wonderful to see you again, Mrs. Lucano. And which of these beautiful young women is your prospective daughter-in-law?"

Gina had been here? "I'm the bride." Those words tasted great coming out of her mouth, but what was with the pale face and pinched nostrils on Tony's mom?

"Marvelous." Victoria looked Desi up and down. "Alterations should be minimal."

Gina let out a high-pitched laugh. "Let us see your collection to start with."

Victoria's brows shot up. "If that's what you'd like."

Desi glanced from one woman to the other. What was going on here?

Gina grasped Desi's hands. "Humor an old lady. Try on anything you like, and no peeking at price tags."

Questions and protests gave way to a steady succession of gowns pulled from racks and held out for inspection. Desi selected three she knew were beyond her budget, but Gina urged her on, and Max matched the woman's enthusiasm. Too bad she'd have to hustle them out of here and head for a more modestly priced store as soon as she indulged their insanity and tried on the gowns. Dutifully, she modeled them to nods and smiles. Lovely gowns, yes. The right one for her? She hadn't seen it yet.

As Desi removed the third dress in the changing room, Victoria came in, carrying another plastic-covered gown. "Mrs. Lucano believes you may like this one. A one-of-a-kind Vera Wang. I'm eager to see it on you." The saleswoman unzipped the bag as if she were handling a fragile antiquity. Desi glimpsed gossamer lace on the skirt. At last, the woman freed the dress from its cocoon and stepped back.

Desi's mouth flopped open. If anyone had asked her to describe the perfect bridal gown, she couldn't have come up with anything close to this knockout Elizabeth-Taylor-meets-Jennifer-Lopez creation. Shimmering seed pearls embellished the embroidered, fitted bodice. Delicate lace sleeves joined ribbon straps at the shoulders, and the hip-hugging satin skirt flared at the knees into a lace-tiered sweep with the mere suggestion of a train. Desi gulped. She already wanted this dress like she craved oxygen, but how could she justify the expense?

"Let's get you into this." Victoria offered a perky smile.

Desi couldn't muster a return smile. Why should she torment herself by trying the gown on? The reckless moment might taint the day of her wedding when she walked down the aisle in a more reasonably priced dress. "I'm sorry. My time is short, and—"

"Don't worry, Ms. Jacobs. We'll have you out of here *tout de suite*."

Since when did Desiree Jacobs pass up a good chance when it was offered? At least she could see herself once in this matchless creation. She stepped into the gown and let Victoria button her in. Sweeping from the dressing room, she didn't waste a second checking for approval from Max and Gina. Max's squeal and Gina's gasp said it all. Desi flowed onto the stage and stared into the trifold mirror.

"Oh, my! Oh, dear!" She fanned a hand in front of her face. "I think I love this dress as much as I do Tony." She let out a shaky laugh.

Gina burst into tears.

Desi rushed to her future mother-in-law. "I was joking."

Tears streamed down the older woman's face, but a smile blossomed. "Maybe now you will forgive me."

"Forgive you?" Alarm and puzzlement battled in Desi's mind. Gina Lucano never beat around the bush. The problem must be catastrophic.

Max joined them, glancing from one to the other.

Gina drew in a breath. "Now that the wedding is set I could no longer put off this moment of truth. I confessed my transgression to my son this morning, and he was certain you would be furious at your meddling mother-in-law." Her gaze fell, and so did her voice. "And I would not blame you—even though you love the dress."

"Gina!" Max pressed her hands to her cheeks. "Don't tell me you bought the gown."

Desi shot her friend a scornful look. "That's a bit off the deep end, Max."

Gina drew herself up to her stately height. "It is so. At least—" She flushed, and her posture loosened. "I have made the nonrefundable deposit. I consider it an investment well made to give you the chance to wear this dress."

Heat flared inside Desi, then ebbed into chill calm. "You reserved the gown? But when? Why?" Should she be angry or shout for joy?

"Please, sit down with me, cara." She gestured toward the chairs.

"No way am I going to put a wrinkle in this fabric."

"Very well, then I shall sit." She perched on the velvet seat. "Last month I was out on the town with the ladies from my Red Hat Society, and we came here on a lark. To browse, not buy. But I found the most divine mother-of-the-bride-and-groom dress."

"That's right. You said you'd bought one already."

"Don't interrupt, cara. This is difficult enough." She brushed a nonexistent speck from her pants. "My dress was on the sale rack for last year's line, a steal if you consider full price."

"This one was on the sale rack too?" Desi gazed down at the amazing confection that adorned her body.

Gina shook her head. "As soon as I saw the gown, I knew it was perfect for you, mia figlia, but a poor waif of a debutante was trying it on and simply hadn't the figure for it." She tutted. "Her mother quite rightly insisted the gown was unsuitable, and the spoiled little *monella* threw a tantrum. I whispered a few words in Victoria's ear. And, voilà, the gown was no longer for sale." Gina and Victoria exchanged satisfied glances in the visual equivalent of a high-five.

"Mrs. Lucano saved my day." The saleswoman grinned. "I swept into the midst of the mother-daughter scene and said, 'Oh, dear, I'm so sorry. I showed you a dress that's been sold. Let me show you what else we have.' And that was the end of the drama. They didn't buy here, but they didn't chase away any more customers with the shouting and the language, either. We were glad when they left," Victoria declared with a sharp nod.

How like Gina to assess a situation and move in with a solution. Tony was so much her son. But the woman couldn't be serious that this dress was for her?

Gina rose. "I humbly beg your pardon for presuming, but I knew in here—" she pressed her hands to her heart—"that you were meant to marry my son in this gown. And please, by way of atonement, if you truly love it, let the dress be my wedding gift to you."

Desi's mouth went dry. Presumptuous to the nth degree didn't begin to describe a mother-in-law-to-be who picked out the bride's dress. But this gift didn't smack of manipulation or control. It spoke of a heart to serve someone else's happiness regardless of cost. The volumes of love that poured from Gina's eyes could not be withstood.

"Oh, Mama Gina!" She threw her arms around the older woman, this gift from God to her. "Thank you so much. I'll wear this dress with extra pride because it came from your heart." She stepped back and fingered the lace on the sleeves.

The woman smacked her hands together. "Mama Gina. Yes, you must call me that."

Victoria handed tissues around and took one herself as they all dabbed at their faces. A brief fitting later, Desi emerged from the dressing room in her business clothes. "Max and I need to head back to the office, and I suppose you need to get back to Tony. No telling what that bad boy's been up to unsupervised."

Mama Gina chuckled. "You know him well. I'll call for a cab to take me home."

"In a pig's eye!" Max's contribution.

"I couldn't have said it better." Desi nodded. "We'll drop you off."

Mama Gina looked from one to the other. "But it's out of your way."

"Not out of the way when I need to step inside and deliver a scolding for upsetting you about my reaction to the dress."

"His warning was justified. You must admit that."

"I could have been angry, but I'm not, so there. The man is wrong once in a while."

The edges of Mama Gina's eyes crinkled. "We'll let that be our little secret. I doubt he'd believe us anyway."

They left the shop laughing, and the drive home passed in discussion of wedding details. Desi turned onto her street, and a late-model blue sedan passed her going the other direction. At first the face of the driver didn't register, and then his identity exploded in her brain.

"Preston Standish!"

Desi slammed on the brakes, pulse skittering, and her car slid to a halt on the snow-packed road. Her passengers let out little shrieks. "Hang on!" She pressed the accelerator and cranked the wheel. Her car lurched into a U-turn. She stepped on the gas, and the vehicle shot forward in pursuit of the sedan fast fading in the distance.

"Oh, my goodness." Mama Gina gripped the edge of the seat. "Is that the man who took your medallion in Mexico?"

"No two schnozzolas like that in the world." Homes streamed past her accelerating vehicle, but blessedly few pedestrians on this bitter cold middle of the workday. Standish was not getting out of her sight. "Call 9-1-1 and ask for backup."

"Backup?" Max squeaked. "We're not cops."

"Tell them we're on the trail of an international criminal. Give them Tony's name."

"They'll ask for location, make, and model, and say to let the professionals handle this."

"Good advice, cara." Mama Gina's voice quavered as the car fishtailed on a strip of ice.

Desi leaned forward, lips peeled back, a stranglehold on the wheel. Good. They'd narrowed the sedan's lead, and a stop sign loomed. Surprise, surprise, Sir Schnoz ran the sign.

"Desi, please!" Mama Gina's fingers dug into her arm. "What about Tony? That man came from the direction of your house."

Desi hit the brakes, her heart tripping over itself. The car screeched to a stop sideways in the road with the hood only feet from the stop-sign pole. What was the matter with her? Tony should have been her first consideration. Yanking the wheel, she turned the car and sped toward home. A single prayer throbbed in her soul.

Dear God, please let Tony be all right.

Seventeen

*D*esi's heart rate matched her choppy quick-step up the sidewalk toward her front door. Max and Mama Gina's feet pattered behind her. Desi leaped onto the porch and grabbed the door handle—locked, as it should be. A good sign? Maybe. But what if Tony had let Standish in, not knowing who he was? With Tony so weak, the beanpole British thief could have done whatever he wanted and then turned the door lock before he pulled it shut on the way out.

Desi fumbled through her key ring. How stupid not to have singled out her house key while she hustled up the walk. Something wasn't right, but what? Knowledge nipped at the edges of her thoughts. Oh, yes, that idiot delivery man left her package of printer supplies on the porch again when he was supposed to leave it in the drop box by the garage—*Never mind!*

A soft whimper sounded behind her. Mama Gina? Max? "Hurry!" That was Mama Gina.

Desi isolated the right key, jammed it into the lock, and turned it. Bodies crowded her from behind, and the three of them all but tumbled through the door.

"Tony?" Desi's voice held a sandpaper rasp.

No answer. The house lay wrapped in silence. A vise squeezed Desi's chest.

"Anthony Marco Lucano!" Mama Gina's bellow could rattle the windowpanes.

"What?" a groggy voice responded from the living room.

Desi sagged against the wall. Max and Mama Gina surged ahead, and Desi wobbled after.

Tony sat in the recliner with his slipper-clad feet up and his laptop computer open in front of him. He blinked at them, scowling. "What kind of trouble am I in now?"

"No trouble." Mama Gina beamed. "We're just happy to see you, mio figlio."

"You could have fooled me." Tony yawned. "Fell asleep reading e-mail. You three all right? You look like you've been—"

"Run hard and put up wet?" A laugh trickled between Max's lips.

"Exactly. Des, I know Mom got carried away on that dress thing, but—"

"Mama Gina is a brilliant dress buyer." Desi finally found her voice.

Tony frowned. "So where's the crisis?"

Desi collapsed onto the sofa. "We saw Preston Standish in a car coming from the direction of this house."

Tony flipped a lever on the chair. His feet popped down, and he sat forward, expression cop flat. "Details, ladies. Make, model, tag number."

"Dark blue."

"Four-door sedan."

Desi's color description overlapped Mama Gina's contribution. "That's the best we've got." Her heart sank. Some eyewitnesses they were. "We weren't paying attention at first, and then there was too much adrenaline pumping during the car chase."

Tony went fire red. "Car chase!"

Desi winced. Yep, he was his mother's son in lung power. *Great going, Des, you needed to mention your harebrained road race.*

Tony struggled to his feet. "We've been through this before, Des. You can't take off after a criminal like you're playing tag with a ten-year-old.

We have no idea how dangerous this Standish might be, especially if he's involved with some south-of-the-border gang."

"I'm not stupid, Tony." She stood, hands on hips. Here she'd been scared out of her wits for him, and now he had the gall to scold her.

"But you are impulsive and impatient and—"

"Dense as a doorknob, obviously." If her blood pressure rose any higher, it would blow the top off her head. "We have no proof Standish is anything more than a sneak thief. And not a clever one, since a foolish female like me caught on to his method of stealing my medallion."

Tony's jaw jutted. "And what did you plan to do when you caught this harmless crook?"

A shrill whistle cut the air. Desi's scathing retort stuck in her throat. Max lowered two fingers from her mouth.

"Grazie." Mama Gina nodded to the redhead, then turned toward Desi. "It was very silly of you to give chase, cara, but no one was hurt." She raised a brow at Tony. "And you, giovanotto, are wasting time when you should be reporting that this man is loose in Boston."

Tony snatched the phone from the side table. "A blue sedan isn't much to go on."

Desi crossed her arms, still steamed enough to bake clams with her breath. "If we had gotten closer to Standish, we could have seen the license number."

Tony scowled, phone to his ear.

Grinning, Max waved both hands. "I got it when the vehicle passed us."

Everyone stared at her like she'd grown a third eye.

She shrugged. "Numbers stick in my head."

"Haj," Tony said into the receiver, "more information on Standish. You won't believe it, but he's in Boston." Tony rattled off the description of the car, and then the license number as Max fed it to him. He cradled the phone. "Haj was already checking into Standish, but that lit a fire under him. There'll be an APB out within minutes."

"Now we have progress." Mama Gina nodded. "All this excitement has made me hungry." She headed for the kitchen.

Max glanced at Desi under her lashes. "Um, I'll lend a hand with lunch." She hustled out.

Desi's stomach churned. Sweat trickled beneath her blouse, and not just because she still was wearing her coat. Why was she fighting with Tony when she'd almost lost him days ago? Besides, he was right. She was impulsive and impatient, always charging ahead in the heat of the moment.

"Des." Tony's fingers swept one side of her hair behind an ear. "You've got guts, but honestly, you give me gray hair sometimes." He offered a lopsided smile. "On the other hand, not many guys have a woman who'd ride a snowplow into the teeth of a blizzard to get to him, so don't turn wimp on me, just—"

"Grow some good sense with my guts?" A small laugh spilled out.

"You've got sense, but it flies out the window when you feel the need to save the world. Now me—" he jabbed a thumb at himself— "I'd like to quit acting compulsively overprotective."

Desi shook her head. "You're not overprotective exactly. You just love me a lot."

"Guilty." He reached for her.

She sighed as Tony's arms encircled her. They'd probably always have a tug of war over safety versus necessary risk, but God had answered her prayer today. Tony was safe. Standish could drop off the end of the earth, medallion and all, as long as he left them alone.

A picture formed before her mind's eye—a box on the porch. A chill trickled down Desi's spine. She'd known something wasn't right, but she hadn't realized what she saw—or hadn't seen. Desi pulled from Tony's embrace.

"What?"

"No labels!" She gripped his arms. "There's a package on the porch about the size and shape of a toaster. It's wrapped in brown paper, and there's nothing written on the outside, which means no delivery person left the box. It had to be—"

"Standish!" Tony's face turned to granite. "We need to get Mom and Max and walk out the back door. We'll go to the neighbor's house to call this in."

"The back walk isn't shoveled. You could tear your stitches."

"No matter. We'll have to wade through the drifts, because none of us is going near that package until it's been examined by trained experts."

"That's extreme, isn't it? I mean, the guy never threatened me. Why would he—?"

Tony's forefinger pressed her lips. "Standish was in Mérida when that explosion and fire happened. And now he was here in your neighborhood."

Desi nodded, suddenly without breath to answer.

"We're going to err on the side of caution."

She turned toward the hall.

"Where are you going?"

She halted. "To get your jacket from the foyer closet."

His long-suffering sigh spoke a volume of exasperation. "We're leaving. Now! I won't die from a chilly walk to the neighbor's house."

Desi clamped her teeth together. She could remind him the cold had nearly killed him once, but she wouldn't, because he was right. Again. She snatched her purse from the sofa and headed for the kitchen, Tony on her heels with his laptop under his arm.

"Get your coats on, ladies, and grab your lives." She pointed to the purses and outerwear deposited on kitchen chairs. "We're outta here pronto."

Max quit shredding lettuce into a bowl and gaped. Mama Gina stopped stirring hamburger in a skillet and stared like Desi was from another planet.

"Don't argue, and don't ask questions." Tony grabbed the coats and held them out. "There's a mystery package on the porch, and we're not going to open it to see what's inside."

Max dropped the lettuce. "I noticed a box but assumed it was a normal delivery."

"Not without routing labels. Shut off the stove, Mom, and let's move."

"All right." Face a mask of calm, Gina flicked the knob on the stove and took her wrap.

Max whipped her coat on and opened the door, freckles standing out on pale cheeks. A gust of arctic air laden with snow particles swirled through the room.

"Go, Max. Go, Mama Gina." Desi waved them on. "We'll be right behind. You can help break the wind for Tony, and I'll share as much warmth with him as I can."

In a cluster, the group moved through the door and down ice-patched steps into a knee-high drift. Desi wrapped her arms around Tony, and his shiver flowed into her body. Max and Mama Gina blazed a path toward the side gate in the privacy fence. Tony's shivers increased.

Enough of the noble, self-sacrificing male malarkey. Desi stripped off her coat and wrapped it around Tony, ignoring the icy wind that sliced through her blouse. "Don't argue."

Tony's mute nod spoke volumes.

Max undid the gate latch and rammed against the panel until the drift on the other side gave way enough to let a body slip through. At everyone's urging, Mama Gina went first, followed by Max. Desi pressed Tony ahead of her, and Max and his mom helped steady him as he waded into the drift. Desi winced at the sound of his pained grunts.

Standing in the open gateway, she looked back at her house. So peaceful. So normal. This was silly. Standish, that jalapeño-sweating scarecrow, a bomber? The only bombs that guy had set off were his jokes, and those were fizzles. Tony should be snoozing in the recliner, not straining his incision slogging through ice and snow.

"C'mon, girl," Max said.

Desi turned. "I'm all for getting out of this icebox."

A fist of heat slammed her in the back as a roar blasted her eardrums.

Eighteen

*D*esi lay on the ground, staring up at the overcast sky. Nice to have snow against her smarting back. Where was she? Why did the world smell of smoke? Somebody better turn those sirens off before she screamed. The shrill wails faded. About time. What was that crackling noise? And why did the snow reflect pink shadows? Impressions kaleidoscoped.

Flames licking toward a bulbous moon.

Cries of "¡Fuego! ¡Fuego!"

A woman wailing for her baby.

"This is the work of the Fraternidad…"

A man with an insignia on his cap bent over her. Not an impression. Real. He reached for her, and she swung her fist. He dodged the blow and pressed her flat.

"Easy, miss. We're going to help you."

Her head swam. Help her. Should she believe him? "No!" She lunged upward, but firm hands held her down. Her breath came in pants. "Tony! Where is he? I have to—"

"I'm right here, darlin'." His face swam into her vision. "Let the paramedic do his job. I'll be with you." His hand found hers and latched on.

"You're okay?"

"I'm fine." He smiled, but the edges of his mouth showed white.

Or maybe not. If only his features would stop squiggling around.

Another paramedic knelt beside her. She carried some kind of harness thingy, and they started strapping it around her head and neck.

"Tony-y-y-y!"

"Relax, honey." He squeezed her hand.

If Tony said relax, she could. She would. Take deep breaths. In through the nose, out through the mouth, just as she had practiced for the Museo de Arte Mejicana job.

They slipped a board under her and picked her up. Tony never released her hand. Then she was in the ambulance—Tony too. How did that happen so fast? She must have blacked out.

Tony hovered close, just as he promised. Good man. Reliable. "Max? Mama Gina?"

"They're fine too," he mouthed, or maybe she couldn't hear him above the siren that started as the vehicle moved out. Why couldn't they turn the stupid thing off? Her head pounded as if she had a crew of carpenters in there.

Jabbering medical lingo, the paramedics worked over her, putting an IV needle in her hand, hanging a bag, yada yada.

She kept her eyes on Tony. "Why are you wearing my coat?"

He leaned close. "What?"

"My coat. You're going to pop the seams, and you look ridiculous in lavender."

He smoothed hair from her brow. "Some stubborn dame insisted I keep warm. Take it easy now, hon. Everything's going to be all right."

Desi's eyes drifted shut. Then a jolt of comprehension shot through her, and her lids popped open. "Did my home blow up?"

Tony didn't answer, but his face told the truth. Desi closed her eyes again. Tony had lied to her. Nothing was going to be all right.

—⁓—

Tony eased through the teeming bull pen in the FBI office. He didn't exactly blend in, wearing a sweat suit and an old army pea jacket from his condo closet. Showing up here in Desi's lavender coat hadn't been an option. Plus, he'd had to insist over his mother's protests to get her to put socks and tennis shoes on him and let him take off for downtown in a taxi.

Grins and smart remarks greeted him, along with too many back pats that weren't exactly the remedy for sore muscles and a tender incision. But a guy didn't ignore his co-workers when they wanted to let off steam after almost losing one of their own. Not even if he was in a hurry and hot to take a chunk out of the scum that tried to kill his fiancée.

The door to his office stood open, and Polanski was seated behind his desk, dark head bent over a sheaf of papers. He tapped on the jamb. Odd, knocking on his own door.

Polanski's head lifted, her eyes widened, and she jumped up and strode toward him. "What's the latest on Desiree?"

"Concussion. Minor burns. She's sedated, and they're keeping her overnight, but she's going to be fine. That's more than I can say for her home."

"We're on it, you know. No stone unturned. Are you sure you should be out and about?"

"I couldn't just take it easy after an attack like this."

Polanski offered a grim smile. "I hear you."

"Hey, it's the boss-man!"

Haj's voice brought Tony's head around. "Progress?"

The agent shook his head, frowning.

"We'll get him, though." Dell came to stand beside Haj.

"I found something you should see." Bergstrom's head popped over a partition.

Tony took a deep breath and snail-shuffled around the corner of the work station. He stuck out his hand. Bergstrom stared at it, blinked, and then shook it.

"You've got the makings of a good agent, Berg." Tony squeezed the man's hand and released it. "But don't let it go to your head. And thanks. A lot."

The younger agent beamed back at Tony's half grin. "No problem, sir."

"That's boss-man to you."

"Gotcha. And Berg's good. Yep."

"I second all that," Haj said.

"Me too." Polanski joined them, Dell nodding beside her.

Tony looked from one smile to the next. "Enough old-home week. What've you got, Berg?"

The younger agent pointed to words on his computer screen written in short lines like poetry. "I think that changes our perspective on the bomber's target."

"Not Des?" Tony bent toward the screen, ignoring a protest from his incision. "It's in Spanish. I take it you read the language. What's it say?" He straightened, hand on his stomach.

"It's a *narcocorrido*—a song Mexican *bandidos* write to taunt enemies or celebrate victories. These days, smugglers splash them all over the Internet. This one's a vow by a gang leader, El Jaguar, to take revenge on the man who killed his ladylove."

"But that would be you." Tony nodded toward Berg.

"Nuh-uh, boss-man," Polanski said. "Yours was the only agent's name reported in connection with the shipboard bust that ended in the demise of Angelina, and that was only because of your oceanic acrobatics. El Jaguar would have no idea who else was involved."

"Exactly." Dell's head bobbed. "And it wouldn't have been hard to find out where you went after your hospital discharge."

Tony let out a long groan. His fault Des almost died. Her childhood home and heritage gone, and he was to blame. His knees wobbled.

"Hey!" Haj's cry sounded distant.

Several pairs of hands helped Tony into a chair.

"You need to go home and rest." Polanski leaned close. "Every law enforcement agency in the city is on the case. We'll find the creep. Trust us."

Tony scrubbed at his face. "Apparently, I don't have much choice. I'm just holding you up, hanging out here." Frustration twisted his insides.

———

"We got him, Des." Tony looked down at her lying on her side in bed. A night in the hospital hadn't put color in her skin or driven the shadows from her eyes. If only he could scoop her into his arms, but her back was sore. Besides, he'd probably drop her.

"Got who?" Her voice was a thread.

"Standish. He's in custody." Her expression remained dull. Too bad his Christian faith and his oath as a lawman wouldn't allow him to blow up the louse's condo on the Riviera—with him in it. "He's an ex-MI5 demolitions expert turned mercenary and making a mint at it. His name's not Standish. It's Myles—Heyden Myles. He chose Standish for his American travels as a play on—"

"Miles Standish. I get it, Tony. I have a concussion, but I haven't lost all my marbles."

Tony cheered mentally over the cranky rebuke. Irritation rated as emotional reaction. "Boston law enforcement blew a gasket tracking him down. Nobody's comfortable having a bomber in the area. He must've ditched his rental car right after you gave up the chase. They found the vehicle fast, then nothing all night long. But a couple of uniforms spotted him coming out of a sleazy motel around dawn. He was unarmed and didn't resist arrest."

Desi snorted. "Can't shoot his way out of a paper bag, just blows up other people's lives."

Tony squeezed her hand. Losing her childhood home and personal belongings—the mementos of her parents—was like losing a life. Later, she'd figure out how blessed they were to be breathing. But how much later? Her gaze stayed empty.

She tugged at her sheet. "The doc says I can leave if this morning's CT scan comes back negative for brain hemorrhage. Max wants me to move in with her. Mama Gina says I can rattle around in her house while she bunks with you at your town house."

"What do you want to do?"

"Turn back time and throttle a jolly Brit with my medallion chain. Or better yet, refuse President Montoya's assignment and race back to Boston. This whole mess started because I grasped at straws to fight the Greybecks." She sat up on one elbow. "But why my home? What did anybody have to gain?"

"It wasn't your fault, Des. This probably would have happened even if you had turned down the assignment in Mexico. You weren't the target."

"You?" Her eyes widened, and she sank against the mattress.

"Standish's—er, Myles's employer is the faceless El Jaguar. The gang leader sent his pet bomber after me in retaliation for the death of his girlfriend during that raid on the pier."

"Standish told the FBI all this?"

"Most crooks clam up when they're caught, but a few won't shut up. Standish is the latter kind. Polanski says he's having a ball recounting his exploits. Seems to think he's impressive."

"Did he say what he did with my medallion?"

"He took it as a gift for his employer, thoughtful soul that he is."

Desi sighed. "I could have figured that out if my brain were firing on all cylinders. Say—" she stiffened—"if he's such a jabber box, why hasn't he given you the identity of the Jaguar?"

"Standish has never met him, only dealt with him through senior underlings. Now, I've strained the limit of what I can tell you without trespassing on case confidentiality."

Desi grimaced.

"Are you in pain?"

A great weariness of soul gazed at him. "No...Yes! But I don't want to talk about what hurts. And I don't want to move in with Max or take over Mama Gina's house. I want to be your wife and live with you." She gripped the sleeve of his sweatshirt. "Pastor Grange was here before you came. He'd perform the ceremony in a heartbeat."

"After what happened, don't you want to postpone—?"

"Tony, you're the only one I've got left." She buried her face in the pillow.

"Hey, hey, hey." He stroked her hair, the sable strands soft except for singed and brittle ends. "Max, my mother, and a few other people might object to that statement."

She lifted her head and scowled. "Don't nitpick. You know what I meant."

"You deserve a beautiful church wedding. We can't allow a criminal act to steal that."

She balled her fist around the sheet. "Sometimes I wish you weren't so blasted sensible."

"At the moment, I'm at a loss."

"You are? What about?"

Tony stuffed his hands in the pockets of his sweatpants. "Right before you ladies burst in on me yesterday, I was going through my e-mail and found a message from one of those California Lucanos— that bunch Mom went to visit."

Desi's brows went up. "What did the person want?"

Tony grinned on the inside. A little distraction—just what the doctor ordered. "He's ten years old, and his parents would 'kill him' if they found out he was e-mailing a non-Catholic Lucano, but he's determined to be an FBI agent. He wants me to tell him how to go about it."

"What's the problem? You can give him the inside scoop. The kid's gutsy and smart to grab on to a connection with a real agent."

Tony frowned. "I wish it were that simple. Jason's in a wheelchair. There's no way he can pass the physical fitness requirements, but I don't know how to tell him."

"Poor guy. Aren't there ancillary services he could apply for?"

"Jason wants to be a special agent. Nothing else will do." He rubbed a hand through his hair. "I understand the focus."

"Is there any chance Jason will walk again?"

"Mom says he's in the chair from a head injury. He's making progress in therapy, but the doctors say it'll be a miracle if he graduates beyond crutches. But Mom said, 'What do doctors know?' and put Jason on her prayer chain. They're believing for total healing." Tony stared at his tennis shoes. "I'm all for that, but I don't want to feed the kid false hope either."

"You do have a dilemma." She reached for his hand.

The door whooshed open, and Max, Lana, and Tony's mother trooped through. Tony'd seen that look on women's faces before. They were on a mission—a strong cue that the lone male should leave before he got roped into something. He rose.

"Not so fast, giovanotto." His mother poked a finger in his direction.

Tony groaned out loud. When Mom called him "young man," that meant either a scolding or an assignment that he was pretty sure not to like. She grinned. No doubt reading him like he was still Jason's age and trying to wiggle out of his chores.

"We have the perfect solution." She spread her arms. "Steve Crane will move in with you. While he helps you train for your fitness tests, you can mentor him in the faith. And Desiree and I will live in my house until the wedding so she will not be alone. Is this not brilliant?"

"Not!"

The three women glared at him as if he'd just rammed his fist through a work of art.

A gurgle sounded, followed by a giggle. Everyone stared at Desi.

"Priceless! The look on your face." She flapped a hand at Tony. "Get out of here. Run!"

He fled. Oh, great! Steve Crane strode toward him up the hall.

"Don't go in there, Stevo."

"What's up?"

"Max, Lana, and my mom are plotting."

Crane grunted. "That's clear as mud."

"Let's go grab some java and I'll explain."

"No time. I'm here to get last-minute instructions from Desi before I leave. If Lana's here too, I won't need to make an extra stop to say good-bye."

"Leave?"

"Desi didn't tell you? I'm HJ Securities' new part-time private eye. First assignment, check into the Greybecks. Their headquarters is in New York." He glanced at his watch. "My plane leaves in two and a half hours."

"Whew! That short-circuits plans to turn you and me into roommates."

"They want you to move in with me?"

"No, you're supposed to move in with me. It's part of this big scheme where everyone's got appropriate supervision. My mother's fingerprints are all over the deal."

Crane chuckled. "Quite a lady."

"She means well."

"When I get back, we can work something out."

"Over my dead body!"

Crane put his face in Tony's. "That could become a true statement. You may be in the clear for a while until this gangsta figures out a new approach, but you shouldn't go it alone in your condition. And you sure don't want the women in harm's way."

"Keep those thoughts between us, Stevo. Desi wanted to get married right away. I stalled her back to the original plan, but that only gives us eight weeks to bust this gang wide open, or there may be no wedding. I hate that I'm starting to know firsthand why my father walked out on us when a gangster made a target out of him." Tony gusted a breath. "We'll talk again when you get back from New York."

"You're on, roommate."

"Don't push it, Stevo."

Nineteen

Desi snuggled against Tony on the sofa. Two days home from the hospital. Or not home. Tony's town house. She swallowed a lump down into the heaviness that lived in the pit of her stomach.

Tony's warm breath fanned her scalp. He claimed he loved her new short hairdo. Maybe he was telling the truth. Soon she'd have the right to stay with him instead of heading back to Mama Gina's when the woman returned from her evening out with her Red Hat ladies.

The news had started on television. "Wars and rumors of wars," Tony murmured. "Sometimes I wonder why I watch this stuff. Nothing changes."

"It'll get worse...until the right Person returns to take charge."

Tony chuckled. "I wonder what the top stories will be when Jesus calls the shots?"

"Mobs Rejoice in the Streets. World Leaders Make Peace Pact. Hunger Eliminated."

"Law Enforcement Becomes Benevolence Administration." Tony laughed. "I like this game. It's—"

He hissed in a breath. Desi followed his gaze toward the television set.

"We're not there yet, babe. That's gang work. No question."

A black Mercedes riddled with bullet holes, windows shattered, filled center screen behind a line of yellow crime scene tape. The vehicle's front end sat up on the curb, and splotches of red marked dirty snow in the gutter. Knots of onlookers dotted the perimeter of the camera shot that must have been filmed hours ago when it was still daylight.

A commentator stood to one side, microphone to his lips. "Dead at the scene this afternoon on New York's Madison Avenue are Randolph and Wilson Greybeck, two of the three owners of the well-known security company Greybeck and Sons."

Desi sat bolt upright, tender skin on her back stinging. Randolph and Wilson dead? But why? And where was Clayton?

"…but the identity of the third fatality turned this local tragedy into an international incident. Ramon Sanchez, cultural affairs director for the Mexican state of Yucatán, was driving this rental car when five men tattooed with insignias of the violent Fraternidad de la Garra gang rushed the car at a stoplight and sprayed it with bullets. The gunmen escaped in the panic, but witnesses are being interviewed by the FBI."

Desi sagged, and her bandages pulled tight. "Oh, no, not Ramon! It's my fault."

"Des." Tony gripped her shoulders. "What are you talking about?"

"I told Ramon about a connection between his wife, Pilar, and the Greybecks. He must have discovered something disturbing. Why else would he have sought them out in New York?"

"You don't know that's what happened, hon." He frowned. "Wonder where Stevo was when this went down? He was supposed to be on the Greybecks' trail. And why hasn't he called? He'd better have a great excuse for not cluing us in before we heard it on the—"

Tony's house phone rang. Neither of them moved. The tape from New York ended, and the commentator in the studio came back on.

"Authorities are seeking Clayton Greybeck, the remaining owner of Greybeck and Sons, but he has yet to return from a business trip to Mexico. His exact whereabouts are unknown."

The phone rang a second time, and Steve's cell phone number popped up on the caller ID routed through the television. Tony eased off the couch and went for the kitchen extension.

Desi followed on his heels but could make little sense of the conversation from Tony's end. "Give it to me straight... You all right?... Why'd you do that?... Well, that's interesting... Got it... See you soon."

He cradled the phone and stared with that light-years-distant agent look.

"What?"

"That was Steve. He was close enough to the action to get winged by a stray bullet."

Desi gasped. "Is he okay?"

"He's got a new crease in his side, but they sewed him up in the ER. Since then, he's been under the bright lights explaining his interest in the Greybecks and why he happened to be carrying a gun purchased under the table at a New York pawnshop—the dumb cluck. If he weren't ex-FBI, he'd be facing more than confiscation and a chewing out. They released him a little while ago, and he's on his way to the airport to catch a red-eye flight home."

"Why buy a gun? Doesn't he have one?"

"Sure, but it's registered in Massachusetts. Major hassle to take a weapon on a plane if you're not active law enforcement. Stevo probably figured he wouldn't need one for a few days of snooping in the Big Apple."

Desi leaned against the kitchen peninsula. "So what happened to change his mind?"

"He noticed someone else paying attention to the Greybecks' movements, and the other guy was packing. Stevo didn't figure he had six months to wait for a license to buy one legally."

"Why didn't he report the man to the police?"

"One tail reporting the other tail? Explanations didn't seem worth the hassle until he figured out what the guy was up to."

"Who else was watching the Greybecks? The Fraternidad?"

"Steve doesn't know, but he was Hispanic and had unusual hands."

Desi's breath caught. "As in the index fingers longer than the middle fingers?"

Tony crossed his arms. "You knew this how?"

"Guess that's a detail I left out of my adventures in Mexico." She plunked down on a stool and told him about the thug from the street chase and about Albon Guerrera's hands.

Tony's brows drew together. "The elder Guerrera could be the brains with a younger relative to do the dirty work. The bureau's going to need cooperation from Mexico on this. I'll get your information to Polanski so she can take it to Cooke and get the ball rolling." He snatched the phone.

"Let me call President Montoya. He just lost a member of his government. He'll open doors fast."

"Go for it." Tony handed her the phone.

Desi looked up the number in her Palm Pilot and punched it in.

"Buenas tardes, residencia Montoya," a crisp female voice answered.

"This is Desiree Jacobs calling from the United States. I need to speak with President Montoya, por favor."

"I'm sorry." The tone was cold. "El Presidente is unavailable."

"Tell him Desiree Jacobs has important information about the Sanchez murder."

A breath sucked in. "*Un momento*, por favor."

Tony poured them glasses of water. She took hers and swallowed gratefully.

"What have you got for me, Ms. Jacobs?" Montoya's voice came on in English.

She launched into her story.

"Guerrera? ¡Ay, caramba!" Montoya added more angry words in his native tongue. "Why did you not share this information sooner?"

Extreme reaction from the dignified president. Desi's pulse fluttered. "I had no reason to believe these details had anything to do with my assignment for your government or with Señor Sanchez's struggles with the Fraternidad."

"Sí, sí, my apologies, señorita. Your encounters have greater significance than you could have known. New evidence has come to light in the murder of Esteban's wife."

"Esteban? Oh, yes, Señor Corona. But what—?"

"I, along with others inside the investigation, believe he was—how do you put it in America? Ah, yes, *framed* for his wife's murder, but what were we to do with the evidence against him except arrest him? Then today forensic results came back indicating the presence of another person at the scene of the tragedy—a blood relation to a convicted felon."

"Albon Guerrera."

"You were aware that Guerrera had been in prison? My sources say he kept this a secret."

"My father was instrumental in his capture and conviction for fencing stolen antiquities."

"Ha! Then perhaps the leopard has not changed his spots. Indeed, this Albon Guerrera and his unknown male relative are of great interest to us…if we could find them. The elder Guerrera has not been seen for days at his home or shop."

Tony paced, face cop-tight. He'd probably trade a limb to enter the conversation.

"Señor Presidente, could Tony, my FBI fiancé, join us on another extension?"

"He is there? By all means, put him on."

She nodded at Tony. He grinned and half-loped, half-limped toward the bedroom.

Desi tugged fingers through hair much shorter than it should be. Did she have the bombing attack to blame on the Guerreras too? The antiquities dealer would take pleasure in hurting the daughter of Hiram Jacobs, and if he could kill Tony at the same time... "Albon's disappearance supports Tony's theory that the senior Guerrera could be the man in charge. But in charge of what? Antiquities theft? That would be Albon's specialty. The Fraternidad? The mystery Guerrera was present when Señor Corona's wife was murdered and at the attack in New York. What could be the connection between antiquities theft and the drug and slave trade in the United States? And why kill Señor Corona's wife?"

A soft click. "Hello, Mr. President, Tony Lucano here."

"Good evening, Señor Lucano. Your fiancée has asked pertinent questions. I am about to answer them with information that your bureau may find valuable."

"I'm all ears."

Montoya chuckled. "Another Americanism I must remember." He cleared his throat. "My aide Esteban was in charge of a confidential investigation into the disappearance of our national treasures. With him in jail, that investigation is effectively stopped. I am certain this was the motive behind his wife's murder. In the case of Ramon Sanchez, he was a target, certainly, but I ask myself, why wait to carry out an attack until he was in New York?"

"The Greybecks were targets too," Tony said.

"A logical conclusion."

Desi pinched the bridge of her nose. How did she get her mind around that development? "Then we have to wonder if the Greybecks played a role in the antiquities thefts and were eliminated as loose ends. They would have made fabulous consultants on how to get around safeguards on cultural property."

"You are sharp indeed, señorita." The president laughed without humor. "Art for drugs. Have you heard this phrase?"

"Certainly. It's the theory that stolen art and antiquities are used as collateral in deals for drugs and other contraband."

"I believe we have fact, not theory. El Jaguar is a middleman for heroin producers in Colombia and slave traffickers in Brazil. The antiquities save him cash outlay up front if he can use them as collateral until he collects his money from the distributors in the United States."

"With due respect, Señor Presidente, if you knew a deadly gang was involved in stealing your national treasures, why did you hire me to find them?"

"You almost got her killed." Tony's snarl would have put a maneating tiger to shame.

"Unwittingly, I assure you. I did not have this insight until after your unfortunate incidents in Mérida, Señorita Jacobs. Ramon and I began to communicate and compare notes. We came to the conclusion I just shared, and now he is dead."

Sorrow squeezed Desi's heart. "Yes, and the world is the poorer."

"Agreed."

"But what sent him to New York to meet with the Greybecks?"

Montoya sighed. "Unfortunately, Ramon did not inform me. This is the mystery that perhaps our odd-fingered man can solve for us. We must find him."

"The bureau is on the hunt at this end," Tony said.

"And we will watch return routes on our end."

Desi rested her forehead in the palm of her hand. A headache nagged. Better not tell Tony. He fussed about residual effects from her concussion. "Mr. President, you might want to question Ramon's wife, Pilar. She was acquainted with the Greybecks, perhaps well acquainted, and the missing youngest Greybeck was last seen in Mexico."

The president let out a sour exclamation. "The involvement of Pilar is unwelcome information, but it suggests a personal motive for

Ramon to leave the country. We will speak to her and begin a search for Clayton Greybeck."

"Mr. President," Tony said, "in my opinion, we can best solve these related crimes by keeping each other informed."

"I disagree."

Desi's head throbbed. Here came problems.

"We can best catch these criminals by active cooperation," Montoya said. "We have two federales in Boston participating in the interrogation of the Fraternidad de la Garra members you captured in your harbor. I place them at the disposal of your bureau in this wider investigation. Please send us two of yours to be included in our efforts in Mexico."

"I'll submit the request." The pleasure in Tony's voice was as palpable as the pulse in Desi's brain. "I only wish one of them could be me, but I don't have medical clearance yet."

"Ah, yes. Congratulations on your recovery, Señor Lucano."

"I'm one thankful man."

"As you should be, especially when you are engaged to be married." Desi's headache receded a bit. "I'm counting the days."

"Days, is it?" Montoya laughed.

"Well, March twenty-third. That's around eight weeks, actually."

"Congratulations again to you both. We'll be in touch."

They ended the call, and Desi laid her aching head against the cool counter. Her burns itched. They'd put together major puzzle pieces, so why did she feel let down?

Because when the subject of the wedding came up, Tony said nothing. He'd been closemouthed about their nuptials since she left the hospital. What was going on in his head? Something big, something bad, and she couldn't pry it out of him with a crowbar.

—⚏—

Seventeen eternal days later, Tony sat down at his kitchen table while his mom fussed over something she was cooking. In a few minutes, she plunked a plate in front of him.

"Are you going to marry that girl?" She planted her fists on her hips.

"I'm going to marry her." He picked up the sandwich. Toasted bread crunched between his teeth as warm cheese and ham flooded his taste buds. Not long ago he would have taken enjoyment of a meal for granted. No more.

His mother leaned toward him. "Every time we talk about the ceremony you make yourself scarce. Desi is worried."

"There's a madman on the loose who nearly killed us all. We've had agents on the hunt in Mexico for weeks. I need to hear they've nabbed El Jaguar."

"Aha! You are your father's son, but that does not mean you must repeat his mistakes."

Tony paced to the refrigerator with his half-empty milk glass. "A mistake. Is that what you really thought about Dad's decision to protect us by leaving? You always defended him when I bad-mouthed him." He filled his glass and went back to the table.

"Because a son should respect his father. But a husband should include the wife in such a decision. He did not. He announced one day that he feared a gangster would hurt us in order to get to him. Then he was gone, and the child support he sent could not replace him. You were a handful to raise alone, but a good boy, basically." She patted his cheek.

"Mom, I know you want Desi and me to be married and get going on a family, but—"

"Tell me, caro, what are you going to do next time a criminal makes a threat? Or when someone you put in prison is released? Turn your back on life, love, and family?"

His mom sure knew how to prod a guy where it hurt. "I've wrestled with those questions since that bomb nearly took Desi from me."

"Have you asked her what she thinks about the risks?"

"I know what she'd say. She'd want us to be together for as much time as we have."

"Then why don't you respect her choice?"

"Because I can't live in a world without her in it!" Had he just shouted at his mother? Her stricken face said he had. "Whether I'm with her or not," he continued softly, "I have to know she's somewhere, breathing the same air. That must have been the way Dad felt about you."

Mom's hand fell on his shoulder. "Ah, mio figlio, it comes down to this then. Are you the sort of man who thinks he will keep his loved ones safe by his own efforts, or can you walk forward with Desi, knowing that the only certainty is the safe harbor of heaven at the end?"

"I'm the sort of man who needs to weigh the options and choose based on—"

"Logic? Ha! For this sort of thing, the intellect works only if you are omniscient."

"No, not logic." He looked up at her. "God's voice of wisdom in my heart."

"Then you will come to the right decision." Mom kissed his forehead. "Now eat your sandwich so we can leave for the clinic, and you can pass your stress test. After we hear the wonderful results, I will take my busybody self home and give you space to hear from God."

—◆◆◆—

Stress test completed and passed, Tony walked into his town house alone, the first time he'd been without a chaperon since his accident. He'd even driven himself home. Another first in a long time.

He tossed his keys on the counter, tired from the stress test, yet wired from the results that showed a healthy heart and gave him the green light to start limited fitness training. The bureau had allotted him three months to return to partial duty and five to get up to full speed. A future was possible.

Maybe. He had no guarantee that his accident hadn't impaired his abilities in ways that would only be noticed when he exerted himself toward the physical fitness levels of a special agent. And he sure had no guarantee that a gang leader wouldn't blow him up or shoot him at any given moment, as well as anyone else he was with. Stevo was still pushing to become a temporary roommate slash bodyguard, not just a physical trainer. Nothing doing.

Tony grabbed a protein shake from the refrigerator and settled into his recliner. This one fitted his body better than Hiram's, but he missed the other one because of what the loss meant to Desi. A failed attempt on his life had cost Desi her childhood home, something he could never replace. What kind of selfish jerk would he be to expect her to take the ultimate risk as his wife? How could he not? Was it better to protect her physical life and rip her heart out…and his own?

He crushed his empty can in his fist, then stared at what he'd done. His strength was returning all right. But it said a bunch that he considered such an ordinary act a milestone.

His phone rang, and he jerked. Too deep in thought. He grabbed the cordless in the kitchen. Caller ID was all zeros, which meant the office was on the line. His heart slammed his ribs. Had they caught the slime balls with the funny fingers?

"Lucano here."

"Congratulations, boss-man." Polanski laughed. "The ASAC came by to crow that you passed your stress test."

Tony headed back to his chair with the handset. So the clinic had already informed Bernard Cooke of the results. The office was keeping close tabs on him, and that could work for or against his chances of returning to the active roster. "News travels fast around that place, except when you're trying to get an urgent memo through."

She snickered. "Well, I've got a few reports for you. Which do you want first, the—"

"Good stuff or the bad stuff?"

"No, the ambivalent or the more ambivalent."

Tony groaned. Too often that was the best it got. "Throw me whatever's available."

"Still no sign of Albon Guerrera or his counterpart, but word from snitches both stateside and south of the border say El Jaguar has packed up and fled to Brazil. Haj and Berg are returning from Mexico City, and the Mexican federales are leaving Boston to go home."

"So the hunt's called off?"

"No, just cooling down to the methodical work that drives us all loopy."

"I hear you."

"This guy'll slip up one day, and we'll be ready. The investigation's netted good results in other areas. The crackdown on the Fraternidad de la Garra has put a lot of hard cases behind bars on both sides of the border. New York has three of the five gunmen in custody, but the shooters don't know why they made Swiss cheese of that vehicle, only that they were following orders. On the Yucatán Peninsula, a sweep by federales and judiciales has disrupted Fraternidad activity, and they figure it's only a matter of time until they find their jungle headquarters."

Tony drummed his fingers on the arm of his chair. "Yeah, you'd think somebody they netted in the roundup would know where it is. Any word on what Pilar Sanchez said about her husband's motive for running off to the States?"

"Nope. President Montoya has classified that information. Insists it has nothing to do with our investigation."

Tony snorted. "Now, that's a stretch, when so many of the same people are involved. Sounds like El Presidente thinks the truth may be an embarrassment."

"No doubt in my mind." Papers rustled. "Oh, there *is* a bit of non-ambivalent information on the Greybecks. Dell says their balance sheet shows Greybeck and Sons leveraged almost to the point of bankruptcy, yet all three stinkers have offshore accounts worth millions. With Randolph and Wilson dead, Clayton could claim it all, but he has yet to surface."

"Let's hope he met a horrible end in Mexico."

"Bloodthirsty, are we? But justified, I'd say. Your hunch panned out. Our search of the Greybecks' private property uncovered records that link them to Jagre Shipping. And Berg was right about the name. Think about it—the first letters of jaguar and Greybeck joined together."

"Very clever." Tony let out a humorless laugh.

"Right. The Greybecks acted as the corporate organizers for a lawless gang. These were very bad people."

"They gave Desi and her business fits. She's still working to counteract the damage they did, but with them out of the picture, she'll recover nicely."

"That's a load off her mind before the wedding, eh? We're holding our breaths for those invitations. And you'd better send one to Cooke, . or you may end up stationed in Timbuktu."

Tony chuckled. "I'll put in a good word for him with Desi."

They ended the call, and Tony stared out his bay window into the deepening dusk.

Was the Jaguar really gone, or was he crouching around the next bend in the road? Any gangster determined enough to hire a mercenary bomber wouldn't give up easily.

And what about the pesky invitations? He'd never asked Desi when those needed to be sent. Probably soon, with the big event a scant five weeks away. Which meant he had less than no time to decide if there was going to be a wedding. And whatever he decided, he needed to know beyond a doubt that he'd heard from God, because only the Almighty could give them any hope of surviving either choice.

Tony put his head in his hands and prayed like his soul depended on it. Midnight loomed before he knew what he had to do. Tomorrow he would talk to Desi. No more putting off the moment of truth.

Twenty

*D*esi addressed an envelope, stuffed an invitation inside, and sealed it. Where was the joy she should feel with this activity? She pushed her chair away from Mama Gina's kitchen table and went to the sink with her empty coffee cup.

Mama Gina had spent a lot of time in her bedroom since they had returned yesterday from Tony's clinic appointment. She could be praying or taking an afternoon nap, but Desi doubted she was snoozing. Tony was home alone. His phone call this morning said he had business to handle today, but was he all right by himself?

Cut it out! Why wouldn't he be?

The destruction of her home had turned her paranoid. Like at the clinic. A man in the waiting room smiled at her, and she gripped the chair arms to keep from rushing out of the room. Strangers were suddenly the enemy.

A vision of the frozen, blackened shell of her home rose in her mind's eye. She'd only gone once to see the damage after her release from the hospital, and the image haunted her. Tony had made a phone call and arranged for the hazardous scar on the neighborhood to be covered and fenced in until spring when a crew could carry the devastation away. She probably wouldn't go near the place until then...and maybe not even then. A shiver wracked her.

Maybe she should make an appointment with the reputable counselor who attended her church. *Yeah, right!* When would she get around to that? Besides, the source of her raw emotions was no secret from herself. She grieved not only her father's absence from her life, but the loss of the tangible bits of himself he'd left behind in the home they'd shared.

Desi shook herself, rinsed her cup, and deposited it in the dishwasher. Mama Gina's little brick house was too quiet. The tick of a clock sent mouse feet scurrying across her skin. *Stop giving yourself the willies, woman!*

She returned to the table and picked up the small stack of simple embossed invitation cards they'd chosen—she and Mama Gina, not Tony. The man acted like marriage no longer interested him. Her bare ring finger mocked her.

The doorbell rang, and Desi jerked, marring the envelope she'd just started to address. Was it her place to answer the door in Mama Gina's home? The doorbell rang again, but no sound came from the direction of the master bedroom. Couldn't hurt to see who was there. She strode through the living room, but stopped with her hand on the doorknob.

Why was she sweating? She was just answering a bell. She could do this. Desi twisted the lock and flung open the door. It banged the inner wall.

Tony blinked. "Whoa!"

Desi released the breath she hadn't known she was holding. "Sorry about that. I'm stronger than I thought." Her giggle rated about ten and a half on the goof-o-meter. "You must feel pretty chipper to brave the tundra."

Unsmiling, Tony shed his winter things. Underneath he wore a suit and tie and looked good enough to model for *GQ*.

"Sit down, sweetheart." He motioned toward the big easy chair. "Things have gotten complicated, and we have to figure out where we're going from here."

"Sounds scary. Should I fasten a seat belt?"

"We're both adults, so I hope we can make this a smooth ride."

Desi plopped onto the cushion and pressed her hands together in her lap. Tony loomed over her. She stared into his chiseled face. How often she'd seen that unreadable granite expression in the days before the two of them had moved from loathing to love.

He knelt in front of her, and her heart flipped. Then he cleared his throat and glanced down. Desi's gaze followed. A scream welled in her throat, but only a squeak escaped. The ring he offered eclipsed the first one like the Hope diamond outshone a common rock.

"Was that a 'yes,' darlin'? Will you still say 'I do' with this block-head?"

She held out her hand and didn't care that it shook. Tony slid on the ring, and the platinum band fit. Not like the first one in gold that they'd had to resize. A marquis-cut diamond, at least a full carat, sparkled up at her, set off by smaller diamonds embedded in the band.

She studied Tony through tear-glazed eyes. "What did you do? Sell your car?"

"My town house too." He laughed. "Just kidding. The insurance check came in the mail today, and I cashed in a small CD to go with it. I wanted to show you how much you're worth to me, and this—" he touched her ring—"doesn't even begin to tell the tale."

"If you don't kiss me, I *am* going to call you a blockhead."

"Never let it be said this man needs that invitation twice."

And that was the end of conversation for a good long while.

A clatter from the kitchen drew them apart, flushed and breathing raggedly. Then Mama Gina's voice burst out singing something robust in Italian.

Tony gave a husky chuckle. "Our chaperon is happy but deter-mined to let us know this isn't our wedding night yet."

Desi rested her forehead against his. "I'm grateful for her."

"Me too. I think we're going to need her services a lot these next few weeks." He stood and smiled. "But this evening I want to take you out to eat. We haven't done that since before you left for your international assignments."

Desi rose and looked at him from beneath lowered lashes. "I don't know, Mr. Lucano, do you think we're safe out on the town by ourselves?"

Tony pressed his lips together and stuffed his hands in his pockets. "What did I say?"

"Nothing. I get what you mean."

Desi blew out through her nose. "We're not reaffirming our engagement on the right foot if there are secrets."

"I don't want to throw a damper on our evening."

"By mentioning that we could still be the target of some crazy gangster? And I do mean 'we.' Whatever we're into, we're in it together, and if Albon Guerrera is the Jaguar, he's got no love for me either."

Tension faded from Tony's face. "I *am* a blockhead for not knowing you'd have this figured out already."

"Is that the shoe that's been pinching your toes? Why didn't you say so? We could have had this conversation already and put it behind us."

"I think this was something the Lord and I had to work out between us before I was ready to take it up with you."

Desi tugged on his tie. "Well, you just settle it, buster. We know what each other does for a living, and we're not safe people, but we sure are surrounded by the favor of the Lord." She laughed. "Hey, I needed that pep talk for myself. I feel about a bazillion pounds lighter." She waggled her ring finger. "Except for right here."

Tony chuckled and swept her close.

"Why don't you two lovebirds stay in for supper? I'll make linguine."

They turned toward Mama Gina, standing in the kitchen doorway.

"Sorry, Mom. I'm taking my best girl out. The reservations are made. Their linguine isn't as good as yours, but the atmosphere is just what the doctor ordered."

Mama Gina sniffed. "Go on, then. I was tired of being your best girl anyway."

Tony strode over and planted a kiss on his mother's cheek. "You'll always be my other best girl."

"Get out of here." She swatted his arm.

Desi's shoulders sagged. "We can't go."

"Why ever not, *cara?*"

"Are you worried about me?" Tony asked. "I'm fine. We'll make it a short date."

"This is not a cliché when I say I have nothing to wear."

"You look dressed to me."

"Tony-y-y! You're in a suit and tie, and I'm wearing jeans and a sweatshirt. Other than this and a couple of outfits for work, I'm a little short in the wardrobe department."

"So am I. I've got a closet full of suits and almost nothing casual to lounge around in."

Desi shook her head. "Guess we'll have to take Mama Gina up on her offer to feed us. Her kitchen doesn't have a dress code."

"Nonsense, *bambini.*" The older woman smacked her hands together. "Mama Gina to the rescue." She cocked a brow at Desi. "Did you forget I picked up your dry cleaning yesterday? The clothes that have been there so long they were about to donate them to Goodwill? It seems to me I saw a snappy black sheath that cries out to be worn on an occasion such as this."

Forty-five minutes later Desi sat opposite Tony at a candlelit table for two beneath the low-beamed rafters of a private alcove. Divine, spicy aromas wafted around them. Conversations were low-voiced, the clink of silverware and glasses muted. A single red rose floated in a bowl in the center of the linen tablecloth. Desi slipped off her work pump— dress shoes weren't in fairy godmother Gina's power—and ran a nylon-clad toe up the calf of Tony's leg.

A lazy smile spread across his face. "You *are* a dangerous woman."

"You have no idea, Mr. Lucano."

His eyes flared hot, and he reached across the table and twined their fingers.

Desi leaned toward him, then stopped on a gasp. "Is that Steve Crane and Lana Burke at a table across the room?"

"No doubt." Tony didn't turn his head.

"You knew they'd be here?"

"Not really, but this is one of their favorite places. Stevo's the one who told me about it."

"He's got better taste than I imagined. But you'd better not tell him I said that."

"No worries, babe. And we're not going over to greet them either. This evening is for you and me."

"*Convenuto.*"

Tony chuckled. "My mom is rubbing off on you."

"Italian mama, Italian restaurant, Italian fiancé. A girl's got to go with the flow."

Tony's hearty laugh turned heads at nearby tables. "The day you go with the flow, my darlin', I'll turn in my badge, because we'll both be ready for retirement."

She lifted her glass. "To a long and feisty life together."

He clinked his against hers. "Convenuto."

———— ⁄⁄⁄ ————

Unable to eat another bite, Tony laid his fork across his half-empty dessert plate. He watched Desi place a spoonful of tiramisu on her tongue, then close her eyes, tilt back her head, and smile. Good thing they were getting married soon if just watching her eat turned him teenage hormonal.

Desi dabbed her napkin to her mouth. "I need to visit the ladies' room before we leave. A guy with a fatigue crease between his eyebrows needs to get home and grab some beauty sleep." She sashayed toward the back of the restaurant, leaving him with his mouth open.

He shut it as Stevo's bulk overshadowed the table.

"Lana headed for the little girls' room, too. Swanky place, huh?"

"Excellent recommendation, pal o' mine."

Stevo chuckled, then sobered. "Lana and I are gonna follow you home."

"I'm not tired enough to be dangerous on the road."

"Not thinking about *you* being dangerous."

"What are you planning to do, Stevo? Follow me around for the rest of my life?"

"Just until you tie the knot and leave town for parts unknown— except to your faithful ex-pard. Or until you're operating at top capacity for yourself. Or until somebody catches up with a certain bad a—er, guy. Whichever comes first. Smile, here come the women."

Tony stood and adjusted his suit jacket. "The Lord's got you cleaning up your language."

"The Lord and Lana," Stevo answered out of the corner of his mouth.

"Good influences."

"You got that right."

The ladies joined them, laughing. Lana held up Desi's ring hand. "Isn't it gorgeous?" She twinkled at Tony. "You have excellent taste."

Tony caught a black scowl from Stevo. Now what was eating the guy?

They headed for the door with Desi and Lana in the lead, chatting like family.

Lana stopped suddenly. "I'm sorry, everyone. I left my lipstick in the ladies' room. Wait for me by the maître d's desk, would you?"

"I'll go with you," Desi said.

"Nonsense, dear." She hustled off.

Tony placed a hand in the small of Desi's back. She stepped ahead of him, and Stevo brought up the rear. Beyond the maître d's desk, a group of customers departed, inviting a brief rush of cool air that flickered candle flames. Shadows wavered on the walls.

A lone man at a nearby table stood, lips peeled back. White teeth flashed in a dusky face. The man's arm rose, a bulky object in his fist.

A shout rasped from Tony's throat. He shoved Desi to the floor. A gun spoke and glass shattered. She screamed and wriggled, but he pinned her beneath his body. Steve's bellow melded with another blast. Something hit Tony in the back. Heart throbbing, he waited for the pain or for heaven's light to take him.

Twenty-One

*P*ain came, but only the complaint of his still-tender incision. And no
bright light or heavenly scent, only the bitter tang of gunpowder.

"To...ny." Desi's voice carried above the screams of patrons. "Are
you...all right?"

"I'm fine."

"Could you...get off me? I can't...breathe."

Women sobbed, and excited voices buzzed. Tony raised himself on
hands and knees. Salt and pepper shakers and silverware littered the floor.
One of those items must have struck him. A few feet away, the bottoms
of a man's shoes pointed toward the ceiling.

"You can get up now, pard." Stevo said. "Desi's safe. Everybody's
safe."

Tony gripped a table's edge and stood. Beyond an upended chair
lay a man's inert body. He looked to be in his midtwenties. Dark wetness stained his white shirt, and a thin trail crept across the floorboards.
One hand gripped a Glock pistol; the other lay across his chest as if he
were napping. The index finger was longer than the middle finger.

Stevo gestured with his snub-nosed Smith & Wesson. "This guy
won't give you any more trouble."

Tony reached down and helped Desi up. She clung to him, touch-
ing his face, running her hands over his chest, his arms. He chuckled.
"I'm really okay. You?"

"Bruised but wonderful."

"I need to ask if you recognize the shooter."

She turned as if fighting a strong current. Her expression hardened, but she shook her head. "Only the hands. I never saw his face."

A commotion started behind them, and they whirled to see Lana shove past bystanders, white face focused on Steve. The man stuffed his gun under his jacket. Lana buried her face in his shoulder, and he patted and cooed while she wept. Tony gaped. Now he'd seen everything. King Misogyny is dead. Long live Mr. Sensitivity.

Soon the place swarmed with city cops, and then FBI and evidence recovery technicians as the federals took over the investigation. Desi and Lana went to sit at a table and wait for their turn to give a statement.

Tony stuck out his hand to Stevo, and they shook. "Good thing you're legal to carry a concealed weapon in Massachusetts, buddy."

"You know it." He grimaced. "I hate packing when I'm with Lana. Makes her uncomfortable. Speaking of which, you showed me up with that rock on Desi's finger. How am I gonna propose with nothing but the dinky solitaire I can afford on my pension?"

"No wonder you were ready to punch me out." Tony glanced at the women. "From the way Lana's eyeing you, I figure you could hand her a pebble, and she'd say, 'Where's the preacher?'"

"Really? I was afraid she'd be disgusted because I killed a guy."

"Oh, yeah. That's why she would've decked anyone who stood between you two after it was over."

"Initial reaction." Stevo stared toward his shoes.

"I don't think she sees a shooter, Crane, but a man who risked his life for his friends."

"Yeah?" Stevo's head lifted. "I can handle hero." He swaggered toward the women.

Tony shook his head. Some things changed; some things didn't.

A few minutes later, statements given, Desi appeared at Tony's side. She curled her fingers around his. "Let's blow this joint. We've got a wedding caper to pull off."

—⁓—

Tony tugged the sleeves of his tux and rolled his shoulders. The mirror said he looked like a groom. Good thing, because that's what he'd be in a few days. Anticipation rippled through him. The salesman approached, smiling.

Tony nodded. "I don't think more alterations will be necessary."

"Excellent, sir."

Tony went to the dressing room. As he shrugged out of his jacket, his cell started to play "Take Me Out to the Ball Game." He flipped it open. "Lucano."

"It's Polanski. Breaking news. We ID'd the funny-fingered gunman from the restaurant."

Tony grinned. Nothing like the breakthrough. "Only took four weeks? Fast work, team."

"Oooh, I'm laughing, boss-man."

"I was serious. It's a bear to process and cross-match DNA and fingerprints internationally."

"Yes, well, lab evidence didn't do the trick. Our dead guy is the mystery man who was at the scene of the murder of Esteban Corona's wife. He wore one of Señor Corona's shirts when he clobbered the wife, hence the incriminating blood spatter on the husband's shirt. Plus Corona touched the murder weapon when he found his wife lying on the floor, unwittingly helping to frame himself. Corona's been released, by the way. Unfortunately, connecting funny-fingers to that murder didn't tell us who he was."

"So what did?" Tony settled on the chair in the dressing room.

"We traced this guy's movements from Boston back to New York, which was his point of entry into the United States. He used aliases to book flights, rent cars, et cetera. The authorities in Mexico picked up his trail in Mérida but lost it. We figure he originated from the jungle headquarters of El Jaguar."

"He's too young to be the Jaguar. The gang leader's been active since this guy was a snot-nosed kid."

"True, but he appears to be the Jaguar's finger man, not to overuse a term." She gave a dry snicker. "He directed the attack on the Grey-becks' Mercedes, then went to Boston to finish what bomber Myles started. Blam! End of the road for him in an upscale Italian restaurant."

"So who is he already?"

"His name's Fausto Guerrera, Albon Guerrera's great-nephew. We can thank old-fashioned legwork for that information. While we and the federales were banging our heads against a wall, the Mexico City police had the brainstorm to show his picture around the area where the old antiquities dealer lived. And bingo, we find out all kinds of nifty things! Orphaned Fausto stayed with his Uncle Albon for a couple of years as a boy. Nasty piece of work. Got hooked up with a bad crowd, disrespected his uncle, and finally ran off. No one saw him for years, and then about the time Esteban Corona's wife was killed, he showed up at Albon's apartment. The old man went missing shortly afterward."

Tony stood and started unbuttoning his dress shirt. "The senior Guerrera's too old to be the Jaguar, despite Desi's suspicions about him. Macho gangs like the Fraternidad wouldn't follow a twisted-up wreck. And I sure can't see him as lover to a thirty-year-old bombshell like Angelina Hernández. But he's a good fit to broker the exchange of antiquities as collateral for drugs and human contraband. When the Mexican authorities find El Jaguar's jungle hideout, they'll probably find Guerrera too."

"Right on all counts but one," Polanski said. "Guerrera's body was discovered in a Mexico City sewer last night. He's been dead for weeks. Just another loose end tied up for a gang boss getting ready to disappear."

Tony slapped the wall. "And another dead end for us. At least Desi'll be relieved Guerrera's no longer a threat, but I'd feel a lot better if we knew the identity of the animal still loose out there. Rumor says he's taken off for Brazil. Or maybe he's lying low in his jungle lair. If the Mexicans don't find that place, we haven't shut him down, just set him back."

Polanski sighed. "Sometimes that's the best deal we get."

—⚶—

Desi stared at herself in the mirror and adjusted the veiled hat to a rakish tilt over her sable curls. The white felt derby sported a curved brim and a hatband of seed pearls. The fine netting of the veil gathered at one side into a gauzy flower shape.

And the gown. What could she say? Every time she tried the creation on, she loved it more. But today was no mere fitting. She inhaled. Today was the real thing. She released the breath. Below the double-stranded rope of pearls that adorned her neck, the fitted bodice showed not a millimeter of cleavage, yet hugged every curve.

Watch out, Tony, here I come! The reflection in the mirror returned her sultry smile.

Bright voices and hurrying feet passed in the hallway outside the church dressing room. Time was short. She'd better get her makeup on.

A rap sounded on the door, then Mama Gina slipped into the room. The fitted cut of her emerald-green suit complemented her tall, buxom figure. "Am I too late?"

"Too late for what?"

"Oh, good, you haven't started with your makeup." The woman set a shoebox on the table beside the hat. "You look *fantastico*. The most beautiful bride in history."

Desi laughed. "Aren't we all?"

"Some are beautiful on the inside, some on the outside, but only a few inside *and* out. And you, mia figlia, are the fairest among the few. My son should fall on his knees every day and bless the Lord for you."

Desi hugged her almost mother-in-law. "I thank God for sending me someone special like *you* to stand in for my parents."

Mama Gina's lips took on a peculiar twist. "I think you will like what I brought."

Desi studied the scuffed shoebox that didn't bear the least resemblance to a wedding gift.

"Go ahead, cara. It won't bite. Sting a bit maybe. In a good way."

Desi lifted the lid with thumb and forefinger. A singed photo of her birth mother stared at her atop a stack of what appeared to be photos, papers, and small memorabilia—like her father's gold tie clasp, soot stained and slightly melted, but all the more precious.

"Oh, my goodness!" She flapped her hands so hard her fingers snapped together. "How? Who? When?"

"Tony hired a salvage expert to sift through the remains of your home. A few things survived beneath nonflammable debris."

Desi collapsed onto a stool. "I'm going to hug that man to within an inch of his life—right after I smack him. Here it's my wedding day, and he turns me into a puddle. How am I supposed to walk down the aisle?"

"With this." Gina held out a velvet-covered jewelry case. "From Tony also."

Desi flipped up the lid. A gold locket on a chain of white seed pearls shimmered at her. She lifted the locket and opened it. On the left, her birth mother smiled the sassy smile Desi knew from her own mirror. On the right, her father grinned back. Familiar mischief sparkled in his eyes. Clear as a bell, Desi heard him say, "The game's afoot, my dear."

Laughter bubbled up, then tears, and then a sweeping combination that scoured her heart free of fear and sorrow. For a long time, she sat on that stool and rocked and laughed and cried.

Someone tapped on the door, and Max hustled in. Her gown of midnight blue satin flowed in an elegant sweep to the floor. She stared at Desi, fists on hips. "Girlfriend, you are *not* goin' in lookin' like that."

Desi held up the open locket. "No, I'm going in escorted by *both* my parents."

Max clapped her palms to her cheeks. "No way! That's amazin'. Brilliant!" She whirled on Mama Gina. "Did Tony do this or you?"

"You must blame my son for everything—the locket, the box, and the bride's appearance, though I did warn him that the wedding day might not be the best time."

"We've got an emergency on our hands," Max fired back. "I'm going to get my mother."

Within fifteen minutes, Desi's puffy red eyes were iced into normalcy, her gown steamed free of wrinkles, and makeup deftly applied. Her head spun from three women bustling around her.

"And now," Mama Gina pronounced, "the crown." She set the veiled hat on Desi's head. Max and Lana clapped.

Desi smiled. "I'm ready." She touched the locket that replaced the double strand of pearls at her throat. "*We're* ready."

No one could tell her that her parents weren't smiling down on her from heaven, as real and as present as anyone seated in a pew. Her parents' hopes and dreams were as much a part of the flow of her existence as her own. She wouldn't be here if they hadn't made brave plans for a life together. Even though their marriage had been interrupted and their days cut short by tragedy, their hopes lived on in her—and now in this new union about to be consummated.

Desi closed her eyes. *Lord, no matter what comes, please make Tony and me worthy of their trust…and of Yours.*

—∿—

At the front of the church, Tony waited for his bride. The organ played on…and on…and on. The several dozen guests stirred and shuffled and stared. Could anyone see how his heart was thumping fit to burst from his chest?

And his stubborn mother seated in the front pew kept her eyes averted so he couldn't get so much as a clue as to how Desi had reacted to his surprise gifts. Had he made a big mistake? But he couldn't see doing it any other way. He needed to give her the locket and box today when the memory would forever be woven into "the mystery of covenant union between a man and a woman." Those were Pastor Grange's words during premarital counseling. And they were good words. The kind a man could chew on and live by.

Standing a few feet away with his Bible open, the pastor smiled at him. Tony couldn't muster one back. Was it okay for the groom to rush up the aisle and carry his bride to the altar? He could manage the feat now, and all the blame went to the guy standing behind him.

Steve Crane looked halfway civilized in his tux today, but that was deception. Evil Stevo had done everything in his power to make these past weeks of strength training rank right down there with the seventh pit of hell.

The music changed, and seven-year-old Luke Webb started down the aisle with his four-year-old sister, Emily. Luke placed one shiny-shoed foot in front of the other, tense gaze fixed on the lacy white pillow balanced across his hands. Tony hid a smile. If only he could assure the poor guy again that the bows tied on the rings would hold and that even if he dropped the whole thing, nothing would get away. Emily skipped around her brother—literally—smiling and waving. A basket swung at her side, spilling red silk rose petals on the runner. Well, that was one way to get them spread around. Amusement rippled through the gathering.

When the kids reached the front, Luke shoved the pillow at Stevo and scuttled to his seat between Max Webb's sister Jo and Jo's daughter, Karen. Tony winked at Luke, and the little guy finally cracked a smile as he wiped sweat from his forehead with his tux sleeve. Emily tugged at Tony's pants leg and lifted her arms. He picked her up, kissed her plump cheek, and deposited her on the other side of a chuckling Jo.

By the time he got back to his position, Max was gliding down the aisle. If Desi's best friend beamed any brighter, she could start a career as a lighthouse.

The organ crescendoed into "The Wedding March," and Tony's heart rate hit the moon.

Desiree!

Everyone rose at the bride's entrance. No more than this unearthly creature's due. Tony's world narrowed to one occupant, and she floated toward him. Pure. Seductive. Did her dainty feet even touch the floor? His own sure didn't feel connected to anything so ordinary.

One of her hands left the cascading floral arrangement she carried, and her fingertips touched the gold locket at her throat.

Desi reached the front of the church, gave her bouquet to Max, and turned to face him. Amazing that his hands didn't shake as he lifted the gauze veil. Her face glowed with beauty deeper than the smooth skin, fine features, and full, parted lips. *Thank you,* she mouthed. Sparklers ignited in Tony's belly. Could he kiss his bride *now?*

Their hands joined, her little ones swallowed in his big ones. The pastor spoke, but the words washed around Tony. Desi's expressive face, the sweep of her eyelashes, the ebb and flow of color on her cheeks captivated his attention. The vows sprang from the core of his being. Rings found the proper fingers, a candle was lit, more talking, some kneeling, then standing. The pace slowed as bride and groom shared Communion, a reminder of the third Party to their marriage. Finally the pastor said the words that cut Tony loose.

Husband and wife? Yes! And he *did* kiss his bride. Not a common kiss. Oh, no. He claimed her, and her soft lips gave as good as she got. Life with her would always be that way.

—⁂—

Standing beside Mama Gina in the reception hall, Desi watched Tony mingle with guests. He'd shed his tux jacket, and the white shirt stretched across broad shoulders with every smooth, controlled movement. Her Tony was almost back to his old self as he proved when the music started, and he turned out to be an expert at the Chicken Dance. *Thank You, Jesus.*

That new agent, Bergstrom, held his infant son toward Tony, and the suave groom took the baby like he was handling a dozen eggs minus the carton. Well, maybe not *every* movement smooth and controlled. Desi laughed out loud and Mama Gina with her.

The older woman shook her head. "When the time comes, he'll catch on."

"I've got as much to learn in the baby department as he does."

"Then you will learn together. It is the best way. Shoo, now. Go to him."

Desi kissed Mama Gina's cheek and walked toward her man as he passed the child to the infant's mother. Tony slapped the new father on the shoulder and waved as Bergstrom ushered his family toward the door.

She looped her arm in Tony's. "You ready to bask in the tropical sun?"

He brushed his lips against her ear. "The basking depends on whether we leave our suite."

She swatted his solid bicep, but a delicious tingle shivered through her.

"Mr. and Mrs. Lucano!"

Tony took Bernard Cooke's hand. Desi greeted the big black man and his stocky wife.

Mrs. Cooke wrinkled her nose. "Bernie'd win a best impression contest if there were a foghorn category."

Tony's boss frowned down at his wife, but his eyes smiled. "Keeps the troops in line, woman." He nodded toward Desi. "I just wanted to offer my condolences to the bride."

Everyone chuckled.

"Thank you for coming," Desi said. "Your support has meant a lot, and not just for today. Your hospital visit and granting extended leave— well, we appreciate everything."

"The bureau doesn't let go of a good agent lightly." He jabbed a finger at Tony. "We expect you back in top form, Lucano."

"I'm on it, sir."

"Don't cut yourself any slack." Then he looked at Desi. "You're the wind in his sails now, the starch in his backbone, the—"

"Power behind the throne." Mrs. Cooke laughed and gathered Desi in a rib-creaking hug. "Welcome to the bureau, dear."

Catching her breath, Desi watched the couple leave. "Wow! I think I just got inducted into the military."

"Pretty close." Tony's chin jutted.

She touched his arm. "Don't worry. You'll make it."

Tony pressed the back of her hand to his lips. "This is *our* time. Forget the bureau."

"I never thought I'd hear those words from you."

"You won't hear them often." His lopsided grin sent her blood racing.

"Hey, you two, it's about time you scoot out of here." Max rustled up to them, her sister in tow. The resemblance was clear in the freckles and flyaway red hair, but not so much in the eyes. Similar shades of green, but Max's radiated vigor and enthusiasm, while tired wariness lurked behind Jo's smile.

Desi hugged Jo. "I visited with your daughter, and she says Brent's almost finished his degree and has a job offer right there in Albuquerque."

Jo smiled. "I'm lucky they're stickin' around. Don't know what I'd do if I couldn't see little Adam as much as I want."

"Brent and Karen have found a great new church too." Max said.

"Wonderful." Desi looked at Jo. "Have you gone with them yet?"

"They keep tryin' to drag me along, but I'm not ready to listen to no new preacher."

Max flung an arm around Jo. "You know my sister. Born with a knot in her head."

"Hey!" Jo delivered an elbow to Max's middle.

The sisters wandered off, laughing.

Tony's arm circled Desi's waist. "I'm with Max's orders to vamoose."

"You won't hear an argument from me."

He laughed. "I'll savor the moment."

Hand in hand, they strolled toward the door, saying good-bye to guests. At last, they reached the coatrack. From across the room, Regan, the HJ Securities CFO, waved the bridal bouquet she'd caught. Desi waved back, while Tony helped her put on her coat. Then he grabbed her arm, and they threw politeness to the winds and charged out the door. Ignoring the nip of a March wind, they barreled for Tony's car, and he tucked her into the passenger seat, taking tender care of her dress. No wonder she loved this man.

When they reached his town house—*their* town house—Tony pulled the car into the garage. Desi grabbed the door handle, but Tony tugged her back and caught her lips with his. When they came up for air, the windows wore a coat of steam.

"Whew!" Her voice quavered.

"Don't move." Tony tapped her nose with a finger. He got out and came around to her door. Offering his hand, he helped her emerge.

Desi took a step, not sure her knees would hold her up. Tony fixed the problem by scooping her into his arms. She snuggled her head into the crook of his neck and inhaled his fragrance that reminded her of new leather and seasoned pine. The journey across the threshold and through the rooms to their private sanctum took forever, yet passed in a blink.

Tony let her legs unfold to the floor but held her against him. Eyes closed, she turned her face up for his kiss, but when his lips didn't meet hers, she peeped at him through her lashes. He wore the kind of smile she imagined came over a man when he was about to step onto the pinnacle of a mountain and see at last what lay on the other side.

He turned her away from him. "I've had a recurring daydream of helping you with your fastenings whenever I please, but my wildest imagination never conjured this nightmare of a thousand tiny buttons."

Desi cast him a heavy-lidded gaze over her shoulder. "Not quite *that* many, Mr. Lucano. But I'll always present a challenge. You can count on it."

"I can hardly wait, Mrs. Lucano." His fingers worked the first button.

—⁓—

Early the next morning, Desi tossed makeup into her kit and ran a brush through her hair at the same time. They'd hit *snooze* on the alarm one too many times, and all the extra kisses they grabbed while getting ready didn't speed the process. Good thing they'd packed most things *before* the wedding, or the cause would be hopeless.

"Taxi's here, hon." Tony's call came from the living room.

She dashed out of the bathroom with her makeup kit, grabbed the handle of her wheelie, and almost bumped into her handsome hunk of a husband. He snatched a kiss, grabbed her suitcase, and headed out the front door. Desi threw on her coat and took her purse from the credenza. She turned away, let out a squeak, and turned back.

"The tickets!" She scooped them up, along with President Montoya's letter.

"Don't forget those." Tony held open the front door. "They cost us enough."

"Very funny, buster." She tapped his chest with the papers as she went by.

Settled into the taxi, Desi leaned her head on Tony's shoulder and closed her eyes. *Cancún, here we come.* First class all the way, and not to some teeming tourist haven, but a private villa twenty miles from the city, courtesy of the Mexican government. Who could argue with a free deluxe honeymoon, especially when a president insisted? Even if El Jaguar was still hunting for them, he'd already proved he could get to them anywhere. She and Tony had discussed the situation into the ground, and they agreed: Mexico was the last place he'd look.

Twenty-Two

*D*esi stood on the veranda of their villa, sipping chai tea. The warm sea breeze fluttered her silk robe against bare legs. She breathed deep and gathered the scents of mimosa and ocean tang. The rays of the morning sun teased sparkles from white sand and danced with turquoise waves. A third gorgeous honeymoon day.

She stepped to the veranda rail and looked down the beach. A tall male figure dressed in shorts and a T-shirt raced along the edge of the water, long legs devouring the distance between them. His face came into focus, gaze fixed on her like a homing beacon. She smiled and waved. Tony's pace redoubled, arms pumping, muscles gleaming with sweat. All man, and all hers. Oops! And a huge distraction. Warmth seeped through her robe where she'd slopped tea down her front.

Tony's sneaker-clad feet smacked the stone steps that led to the veranda. He leaped up the last two and landed in front of her. His breath sawed in and out, and he bent over and gripped the tops of his knees. Then he popped upright and paced the length of the veranda rail.

Desi wiped at the wet spot on her robe. "How far did you go today?"

He lifted a hand, four fingers up.

Same as yesterday, but she smiled. "That's great."

"Not far…enough… Too slow."

"But you're getting faster, right?"

He continued his cool-down stride and didn't answer.

Tony's fierce words from last evening haunted Desi's ears. "It's like I've hit a wall." And before they went to sleep she'd caught him studying his fitness chart with a furrow in his brow.

"What's on for this morning?"

His question brought Desi back to the present. She checked her watch. "We've got reservations with a group on a snorkeling adventure boat in fifty minutes."

"A group? Then I'd better grab a shower." He stepped through the French doors into their bedroom suite and peeled off his T-shirt. "I'm pretty ripe." He disappeared into the bathroom.

Desi stood still, lower lip caught between her teeth. Tony or snorkeling? Snorkeling or Tony? Snorkeling could wait. She strode into the bathroom.

He looked over his shoulder from adjusting the spray of water and laughed. She shot him a wicked grin and shut the door.

—⁂—

Hip-deep in the ocean in front of their villa, Tony moved in a slow circle, studying the rolling surface of the water. Moonlight gleamed from the tips of the swells. *You can't hide below forever, Des.* A splash sounded, followed by her husky laugh. He whirled and lunged, snagging her waist, and they both went under. She struggled, but only until he caught her mouth in a salty kiss. They rose from the water, laughing.

"Had enough, babe?" He tickled her dripping chin.

"I'm ready for a little R and R under the stars." She caught his hand, and they waded to the beach.

After a quick towel-off, they stretched out on a blanket, Desi's head on his shoulder. The soft shush of waves meeting the crushed coral sand acted like heated oil on Tony's muscles. A gentle breeze dried his skin without chilling his bones. "I could get used to this climate."

"I could get used to honeymooning forever."

Tony chuckled. "I'd drive you out of your tree when I started organizing your jewelry case for something to do."

"You'll probably get around to that anyway. But you're right, we each need to keep doing what we do best. Only now—" she propped herself up on her elbow and gazed down at him—"I want to add *wife* to my expertise. You'll have to help me learn."

He ran his thumb over her cheekbone. "You're already my favorite wife."

"Oh, you. I was serious."

"So was I. Sometimes when I crack a joke, I mean it the most."

"I'll try to remember that instead of hauling off and socking you." She sat up. "Isn't the night sky beautiful? The stars seem so close we could reach out and touch them. Oh, I brought that southern constellation chart we got at the tourist information center." Desi rummaged in her beach bag and pulled out a folded brochure and a small reading light. She pointed into the sky near the horizon. "That's Sirius, the brightest star in the sky."

His gaze followed her finger, then he sat up and studied the chart under the light. "Sorry, babe, but I think you've found Canopus, the second-brightest star. Says here it's part of the Carina constellation. You can't see the whole formation unless you travel a good way south, but there's a diagram. The shape is supposed to represent the rudder of a ship." He handed her the brochure and reading light.

She tapped her upper lip with one finger. "Oh, my!" The tapping stopped.

"What—"

"So simple!" She leaped to her feet. "Albon Guerrera said to 'gaze upward in the darkness,' but he knew I couldn't see Carina from Boston and only in part from Mexico. The dirty rat!"

"What's Guerrera got to do with a constellation?" Tony rose, shoulders knotting.

"Don't you see? The emeralds in my medallion form Carina. Remember the big gem in the upper right? We thought it was so strange the best jewel was set off to the side. That one's Canopus." She paced up the beach. "I could strangle Standish or Myles or whoever he is. Now that I've found a clue about the medallion, it's in the grubby hands of some gang leader."

Tony caught up to her. "I hate that you were robbed, but thank goodness you weren't hurt. The medallion's a thing—an object. You showed it around, hoping to give an identity to the bones you found in New Mexico. With this constellation clue, you might still be able to do that."

"You, Mr. Lucano, are a genius." She flashed him a megawatt smile and took off in the direction of the villa, feet spraying sand.

Grinning, Tony shook his head. He'd signed on for never-a-dull-moment with Desiree Jacobs—nope, Lucano now. His wife sparkled brighter than Canopus when a project grabbed her. He picked up their beach things and followed her inside. She was seated at the dinette table, talking on the phone.

"No, we're fine. Great, in fact!"

Tony pulled up a chair beside her. "Max?" he whispered.

She nodded. "Sorry for calling so late, girlfriend, but this can't wait. Or more like I can't wait." She gave Max the constellation information. "In your spare time—and, yes, that was a joke—I'd like you to sniff around with all your techno-genius. Somewhere in history there must be a native Mexican or Spanish immigrant family that found the Carina constellation significant. I want to know if there are any living descendants. Think you can handle that?" She laughed. "And, yep, that was a joke too."

The ladies chitchatted another five minutes, then ended the call.

Tony stretched. "Can we hit the sack now?"

"I'm too excited to think about sleep."

"We could always think about something else." He waggled his brows.

"You mean like our visit to Chichén Itzá tomorrow?"

"Exactly. Should be as thrilling as our snorkeling adventure this morning."

She socked his arm. "No way are we missing the ruins, bub. And the only decent time to visit them is before the tour buses come in. We can't reschedule dawn like a snorkeling boat."

"Okay, okay." Tony raised his hands. "Let's get some shut-eye, wife. We're on the road at sunup tomorrow."

—⁓—

Tony woke up before the alarm clock shrilled. Predawn haze filtered through the blinds on the French doors. His wife slept on her side facing him, lips parted, and there was that cute little snore. Yep, he could wake up next to this every day. He kissed her nose, and she stirred, sighed, and rolled over. Shame to wake her just because he couldn't sleep anymore.

He slipped out of bed and went to the bathroom to put on his running shorts. It'd have to be a quick workout this morning. Oh, blast, was that his cell phone? That'd wake Desi for sure. He hustled into the bedroom. Too late. She was sitting up, scraping her hands through her hair.

She blinked at him owlishly while he grabbed his phone off the side table. "I'll go in the other room."

She waved him off and flopped back onto the pillow.

Checking his caller ID, Tony left the room. "Lucano here. And you'd better have a great excuse for bugging newlyweds before 5:00 a.m. on their honeymoon, Stevo."

"Yeah, well, it's about six here. Time to be up and at 'em. You two okay?"

"Sure, why wouldn't we be?"

"I don't know. You tell me. At least, you sound as ornery as ever."

"And you sound—I don't know—uncertain. Very un-Stevolike. I know you didn't call to exchange unpleasantries. Some emergency back there?" He perched on a kitchen stool.

"Nothing like that."

"No emergency. Then what? Do I have to fly home and choke it out of you?"

Long growl. "I'd tell you the problem if I could, but I don't know what it is."

"You're not on the juice again are you?"

"Okay, I'll confess. It happened again last night."

"It?" Tony pounded the counter with the side of his fist. "You broke up with Lana. That's the only thing that would get you drinking again. I—"

"Who said I was drinking? And I did *not* break up with Lana. What are *you* drinking?"

Tony held the phone away from his ear. Where did this conversation go wrong? "Stevo, it's too early in the morning for a mystery. Spit out what you called to say."

"I didn't call to *say* anything. I needed to find out how you two were doing."

"This is all about 'Hi, how are ya?'"

"If I explain any more, you're going to think I'm nuts."

"You've already got me half convinced, so try me."

Heavy sigh. "I woke up last night in the dinky hours with this feeling I needed to talk to the Big Guy about you—Desi too. Been pacing the floor ever since. Finally, I couldn't stand it anymore, so I call and find out the whole thing's bogus."

"Whoa!" Tony jumped up. "I can hardly believe it."

"Yeah, sorry for bothering you. I just—"

"This is…amazing."

"Does that mean I'm off my rocker?"

"Not at all," Tony said. "You haven't been a believer very long, and you're already getting assignments from heaven. Pretty awesome there, buddy."

"But why was I praying if there's nothing wrong?"

"Maybe God had you pray in order to prevent something from happening. Or maybe there's something up ahead none of us knows about, and we need prayer to see us through."

A beat of silence. "I've still got this wound-so-tight-I'm-gonna-bust feeling in my gut."

"Then keep praying. We'd appreciate it."

"You doing anything dangerous today?"

"A drive into the jungle to see some Mayan ruins." Tony checked the clock. Forget the run this morning. He'd have to make it up this evening, big time. If his endurance didn't improve soon, he'd have to admit— *Don't go there!*

"Well, keep your eyeballs peeled, pal."

"You got it." At least this broken-down agent could do that much.

"Call me if anything exciting happens." Steve cleared his throat. "It'd make me feel better to know I'm not out of my gourd."

"Stevo, intercessory prayer is a normal part of the Christian life. But it sounds like the Lord's tapping you for serious duty. It's an honor."

"I don't feel honored, just…heavy."

"Hang in there. You know I'll watch over Desi."

"Yeah, but who's gonna watch over *you*?"

"Guess that's up to you and God."

—⁓—

"Oh, look." Desi pointed into the jungle. "There's a spider monkey." She laughed. "No, don't turn your head. We've whizzed past it already, and I'd rather have your eyes on the road." She found him staring at her. "Hey, I said eyes on the road, buster."

"Hard to do when I'm distracted by the great view sitting next to me."

Would that just-for-her smile always turn her insides to warm taffy? Hah! When it didn't, she'd be ready to check into the morgue. "Oh, right. With my hair torn apart by the wind." She lifted her face to catch more of the tropical airstream. "I love this convertible."

"What about me? Whoo-hoo! I'm a thirty-six-year-old kid in a candy shop. Who would have thought the villa came with access to the Ferrari in the garage?"

"There are some advantages to doing favors for presidents."

"Good thing the honeymoon gift came for *you* and had nothing to do with me. Even so, it was iffy for the bureau to let us accept the trip. The fact that I'm on leave and not active tipped the scales in our favor."

"You never told me that before." Irritation ruffled the edges of her happiness.

Tony shrugged. "You had a lot on your plate, planning the wedding and everything. Since we got the go-ahead all right, I didn't want to bother you with the details."

Okay, he meant well. At least he had told her about Steve's troubled phone call. "Details, shmetails. This day is too beautiful to set up a fuss, but you'd better not make a habit of keeping things from me. Except work stuff, of course."

"That was work stuff."

"You know what I mean. Confidential case information."

"So I should've granted you the privilege of worrying about something you couldn't influence or change?"

"Right."

"Sounds like a waste of brain cells to me."

"At least I would have known there was a possibility we'd have to change our plans."

"But the problem never occurred."

"Not the point."

"I give up." He lifted his hands from the wheel.

"Good. Now drive, sweetheart. This rocket won't steer itself." She gazed at the jungle. "Did you know jaguars roam in there? The four-footed kind," she added quickly.

Tony snorted. "Probably less dangerous than the two-legged variety."

"Strange to think somewhere in the rain forest a human animal directed the destruction of so many lives. Smuggling drugs. Forcing young girls into prostitution. Robbing his country of its heritage. And the stupid young men he recruited. Agh!"

"You count the Fraternidad members as victims?"

"I'm not that naive. Some enjoy the evil they do. They'd sign on with whatever bunch offered them a way to make quick bucks. But then there are the others, the ones who join to find hope."

"Hope?" Tony's glance said he was convinced she'd finally lost her last marble.

"Society hasn't given them any. They can't get an education, a job, a decent home, or common respect. The gang offers them those things and a place to belong. I'm thinking about Zapopa's grandson. So close to grabbing the fool's gold the gang offers, all because he had nothing else to look forward to for himself or his children after him. Do you see what I mean?"

Tony downshifted as they neared their turnoff. "I know what drives people to join gangs, but I've never heard it boiled down to hope. If that's what they're after, here's the real tragedy." He guided the vehicle into the paved parking lot at Chichén Itzá. "Joining a gang steals whatever hope they had left. They're gun fodder for whoever's at the top. They never see the high life they craved, and the end of the road is prison or death. What a waste!"

He parked the Ferrari near booths where Mexican vendors were starting to set out homemade wares. Few other vehicles stood in the lot.

Desi consulted her watch. "Fifteen minutes until the gate opens. This place is amazing. I can hardly wait to show it to you without the crowds or a pesky tour guide."

They got out of the car, browsed the native crafts, and purchased a couple of souvenirs. Then they stowed the packages in the trunk in time to be the first people onto the grounds. An hour later, after exploring a tomb pyramid and the Plaza of a Thousand Columns, they left a Mayan dwelling. Desi laughed as Tony turned at an angle to get out the door.

"These people must have been no bigger than you," he groused.

She bumped him with her hip. "Not everybody's built like Arnold Schwarzenegger."

"I don't plan on bulking up that much, but I'd like to be fit again."

Desi stepped in front of him. "I don't want to hear one more negative comment about your physical abilities. Don't trainers teach positive self-talk with their exercises?" She planted her hands on her hips. "And doesn't faith rejoice over the desired outcome *before* it happens?"

"I'm not where I should be, and progress is nil. The clock's ticking, babe. We might have to face it—you won't be married to an FBI agent. And that's the facts, ma'am."

"I don't care if you're a dogcatcher. I exchanged vows with Tony Lucano, not a G-man. Besides, I've got Plan B in mind, but I wasn't going to mention it…yet." Desi gulped down a lump in her throat. By the look on his face, she shouldn't have brought it up now either.

He stepped back and folded his arms over his chest. "Real heart-warming. Faith Woman has an alternate plan for her struggling hubby. Let's hear it. Some cockamamie idea of hiring me as an HJ Securities investigator, I'll bet. What were you going to do—pair Stevo and me?"

Desi's cheeks warmed. No one ever said her husband wasn't sharp on the uptake. "We're on our honeymoon. Can't we save business talk until we get back to Boston?"

"You pushed the subject." He stepped around her. "But if you don't want to talk, by all means, let's continue the tour. Where's this Pyramid of Kukulcan you've been bragging up all morning?" His words were clipped, like he was addressing a suspect.

Heat boiled through Desi's veins. Of all the stubborn… "Fine. We came here to see ancient ruins, so let's see them. That way." She pointed up a wooded path.

He stepped in that direction. "You coming?"

They walked—correction, stalked up a tree-covered path side by side, but with enough distance between them to fit the Temple of the Warriors. The forest loomed low and thick. Insects buzzed in the dead air. With no structures in sight, if Desi didn't know better, she'd think they were lost in the jungle. Then they burst into a vast open expanse dominated by a mammoth pyramid that surged toward the sky. They stopped in one accord.

"Way impressive, isn't it?" Desi said.

"That's a major understatement." Tony headed across the field.

Desi trotted to catch up. Tony reached the base of the pyramid and stood, legs splayed, head swiveling from statues to stairs to the temple at the top. She came up beside him.

"The Mayans built this temple pyramid to worship the god-king

Kukulcan," she said, "but the Spanish call it El Castillo, the castle. See these stone snake heads at the corners?"

"Nasty-looking critters."

"During the spring and autumn equinoxes, the rising and setting sun casts shadows down the sides of the steps that appear exactly like writhing snake bodies attached to the heads."

Tony shook his head. "Figuring out that trick took genius-level math. Goes to show that an advanced civilization can exist without electricity or the Internet. Then here we are with all the whiz-bang conveniences, and we act like savages."

Desi snorted. "These guys were pretty savage for all their smarts. Lots of bloody war topped off by human sacrifice. I'll tell you more about that when we get to the sacred cenote."

"Cenote?"

"It's pretty much a big sinkhole with water in the bottom. An underground river makes it a natural well. But it's a spooky place, unearthly quiet, and the water's scary deep and still. Like it's biding time for more gold and jewels and pots and *people* to be thrown into it."

"Enough on that subject. You game?" He pointed upward.

Her gaze traveled the steep stone stairs. "Of course."

"Race you." He charged upward.

"No fair!" Desi followed. "Your legs are longer."

"Since when does that bother you when we're out jogging?"

Desi ducked her head and moved her feet faster. Faster. Her legs ached, and her lungs strained. She wasn't going to make it. Then she hit something.

Strong arms caught her. "Hold on, darlin'. We're at the top. Enjoy the view."

Sucking air like a bellows, she scanned the vista. "This is like…sitting at the top…of a giant Ferris wheel. You can see everything."

Beyond the ancient city, the deep green canopy of the rain forest spread toward the horizon. Within the grounds, temples, platforms, pillars, and tombs looked small, and clusters of tourists moved around like swarms of beetles. A glint of sunlight off glass near the Platform of the Skulls caught her eye. A lone figure studied the pyramid with a pair of binoculars. On a whim, she lifted a hand in greeting. The person lowered the binoculars and turned away.

"Who are you waving at?" Tony tugged a strand of her hair.

"Some guy scoping out the area with binoculars."

"Where?"

She pointed. "Oh, he's gone. Must have wandered off to the next attraction. I'm glad we came up here." She rested her head against his chest. Should she point out which one of them was the most out of breath? And it wasn't him.

"I'm glad too, and sorry for being touchy."

"No, I'm sorry. I was double minded without realizing it. I tell you to have faith and then I announce a secondary plan."

"Planning for eventualities is good."

"Not when I truly believe you're going to get your badge back."

"You do?" He stared like she'd handed him the Holy Grail. "I don't want to disappoint you." He put his hands in his pockets.

"That's what I keep trying to get across. You *can't* disappoint me."

"Oh, yes, I can. I'm a fallible man, Mrs. Lucano. I just hope you'll hang in there with me when I mess up. Your confidence helps, and maybe it'll put me over the top with a miracle, because that's what it's going to take to get my career back."

Desi wrapped her arms around his middle, her throat too full for words. What could she say? She'd already told him every way she knew how that he could make it, but he was the one who needed to believe. If he didn't...or couldn't... She drew in a shaky breath.

Tony nudged her. "I can't come all the way up here and not kiss my wife at the top of the world."

He lowered his head, and she lifted up on her toes. The kiss deepened, lengthened. Warmth and well-being sifted through her. What problem could stand before their union?

Clapping and cheering erupted from below. Desi gasped and pulled away. A large tour group was climbing the pyramid, applauding and waving.

Desi grinned. "Might as well play to the crowd."

Tony shrugged. They joined hands and flourished a bow.

Laughing, she tugged Tony into the temple at the top of the pyramid, and they browsed carvings of the Mayan rain god Chaac. Then they headed down the stairs at a leisurely pace.

"Well, that was fun," Tony said when they reached bottom. "What next?"

"There's a doorway on the north side of El Castillo that leads to a tunnel and a set of stairs up to a room where we could see King Kukulcan's jaguar throne, but I've done enough steps for now. So it's the ball court. If that doesn't inspire you, Mr. Athlete, nothing will."

They crossed the open field and approached a vast, high-walled structure. Sticking out from it was a platform with a short tower built on top of it. Desi pointed toward a series of carvings on the tower. "More jaguars. The Mayans revered them, even named a military order after them. This is the Temple of the Jaguars. Makes you wonder if our modern-day El Jaguar is of Mayan ancestry. Sure would explain his choice of *nom de guerre*."

Tony took her hand and moved on. "I guess I can tell you this, since you're brilliant as usual. The bureau and the Mexican federales share your conviction that we're dealing with a descendant of the Maya. Unfortunately, that narrows the suspect list down to a third of the population of the state of Yucatán, not to mention the other Maya scattered throughout the country."

"Never mind then. Here's the ball court, and it's much more interesting than some slime-ball gangster." Desi watched Tony's slack-jawed face as he took in the massive stadium.

"The Patriots could play here."

She laughed. "What do you mean? The Patriots and the Celtics could play at the same time and not even bump into each other."

"The walls are at least four times my height."

"See the two stone rings sticking out near the tops on either side? The Mayans played with an eight-pound rubber ball, and the object was to get it through one of the rings."

"The rings are high and the holes are small, but anybody with the Celtics should have no problem scoring."

"Using only their hips, elbows, or knees to control the ball?"

"Say what?"

"No hands or feet."

Tony let out a low whistle. "Now that would be an interesting game to play."

"Not bad to be a spectator either. You need to walk down to the other end of the stadium. I'll stay put."

"And leave you alone?"

"What do you think is going to happen to me in this hive of international tourism?"

Tony frowned. "I'm not budging until you tell me what this is about."

"Very well, Señor Kill-joy. The acoustics are an unexplained phenomenon. It's possible to hear a conversation taking place at one end of the stadium from the other end. Now you'll never know what sweet nothings I would have said to you from here when you were over there. I'm not in the mood anymore."

"Get back in the mood, because this I've got to try." He strode up the dirt field.

Desi waited until he was about twenty feet away. "Can you hear me now?"

He threw a backhanded wave, and she read his thought like she was in his head. *Smart-aleck wife.*

She was still laughing when a group of Japanese strolled past, snapping pictures of carvings. They were too polite to stare at her, but a couple of them glanced at the crazy, giggling woman out of the corners of their eyes. Maybe they thought she was touched by the heat. She wandered over to the wall and leaned against it.

The hairs at the base of her neck prickled. These ruins were fascinating, but they gave her the willies sometimes. In Chichén Itzá she sensed the brilliance and depravity of the biblical city of Babel. She didn't believe in ghosts, but in spirits most definitely. This place was loaded with them. Goose bumps rose on her arms, though the temperature had to be in the nineties. Now she was spooking herself. *Get a grip, girl.*

"Desiree Jacobs."

An icy fist squeezed her insides. Then she realized she'd heard the voice with her outer ears, which meant flesh and blood had spoken. "Tony?"

Was he talking to her from the other side of the field already? Nope, he was still trotting toward the end, his figure too far away for comfort. Who in Mexico would speak with an American accent and call her by her maiden name? She licked dry lips and looked up.

Atop the wall stood a bearded man staring down at her. He wore a pair of binoculars around his neck and a furious sneer. "The rings on your finger are sharp, Des, but that display on the pyramid was a little too much."

Twenty-Three

*T*ony neared the far end of the ball court. Pretty nice jog. Interesting in a twisted sort of way with all the carvings on the wall of gods and warriors and ball players—even one of a player getting his head lopped off. Did the winner or the loser end up as the sacrifice? As Desi had promised, he could hear any number of conversations going on, near and far away. The problem was sorting them out to make sense of what was said.

He turned and stared up the field. Where did Desi go? He stepped around a tour group and craned his neck. There. Near the jaguar temple, looking up at some guy on the ledge.

A word pierced the tourist jabber. "Clayton." Desi's voice. And the scum looming above had to be that missing link Greybeck.

"...wrong man. I told you..." The man's snarl reached Tony garbled and incomplete.

"Out of my way." Tony shoved through a knot of gawkers, ignoring angry protests. In the clear, he broke into a run. He couldn't see Desi. Was she hidden behind another tour group? Or did Greybeck grab her? Why did he let that woman talk him into dumb moves like splitting up? And why had he decided Mexico was safe in the first place? This was his fault. Nobody else's.

PleaseGodpleaseGod. The incoherent prayer kept pace with his pounding feet. But the harder he pushed himself, the slower he went. Or was that his imagination?

Someone holding a camera stepped into his path. Tony whirled in a complete three-sixty like a running back avoiding a tackle. He ignored a twinge in his middle and stepped up his pace.

His gaze searched the grounds. No Des. A tour group stood at the end of the field acting unconcerned, so there couldn't be unfolding drama in the area. Greybeck might have dragged her off, but why hadn't she screamed bloody murder? Seconds counted if he hoped to catch them. He raced around the corner of the wall, and—*oof!*

A petite body flew backward and sprawled on her hind end. Desi!

He grabbed her up. "I've got you. It's okay now." He spoke into her ear while he scanned the area outside the ball court. No Greybeck in sight.

Desi wriggled against him. "Ow! Ow! Ow!"

He held her away and looked her up and down. "Did he hurt you?"

"You're the one who knocked me halfway across the continent and then squeezed the stuffing out of me."

"Did you see where Greybeck went?"

Tony stared in the direction she pointed. Nothing but gaggles of grinning tourists.

"He went past the Platform of the Skulls," she said, "heading for the path to the cenote."

"Grab any security guards you can find. Tell them they have a fugitive on the grounds. I'm going after him." He took off.

"Tony, wait! You're not armed. What if he's got a gun?"

Her cry spurred him on. As long as that guy and his gangster crowd were on the loose, Desi was in danger. Unacceptable. She'd lost enough—too much!—and Tony was through letting it happen. Catch Greybeck, and they'd get the location of the jungle headquarters. He had enough agent inside him to tackle one computer geek, didn't he?

Carved skulls grinned at him as he swept past a tall platform. The chill of their mockery followed him into a forested path beyond.

Excited Australian-accented voices and the sound of crying drew Tony forward. A group of older men and women and a guide came up the path. An elderly woman clutched her arm to her chest as tears streamed down her cheeks. Greybeck's work?

Tony strode up to them. "What happened?"

A white-haired man pointed into the forest. "Some big bloke with a beard charged through. Tossed us aside like we were sticks. My wife fell down. I think she broke her wrist."

"I'll get him, ma'am." Tony nodded toward the injured woman.

The tour guide grabbed his sleeve. "Leave the matter to the authorities, señor. We do not need someone else to get hurt, and we cannot have tourists fighting on the grounds."

Tony pulled his arm away. "I'm an FBI agent." He ran on.

The path ahead was deserted. Deep into the trees, Tony slowed, then stopped and listened. A bird called, insects hummed, shadows flickered under the waving limbs.

Snap!

Something bigger than a bird moved up ahead, but not in a hurry. A straggling tourist? A jungle creature? Not necessarily Greybeck. If that lowlife had a grain of sense, he wouldn't slow down until he was in another country. Tony trotted on, gaze sweeping both sides of the path.

From above, a heavy object drove Tony to the ground face-first. Air whooshed from his lungs and pain speared his ribs. The weight on top of him grunted. Human predator. Tony surged onto his elbows, and an arm wrapped around his throat. He rolled, putting Greybeck on the bottom, and clawed at the forearm crushing his windpipe. Was this joker Popeye's twin brother?

Tony rammed an elbow into the attacker's gut, and the chokehold loosened. Wrenching free, he lunged to his feet in a crouch, but a leg sweep whumped him onto his back. His head bounced off a tree trunk, and the jungle canopy spun like a green Frisbee.

Greybeck landed on Tony's chest, knees pinning Tony's arms to the dirt. The guy must be part elephant. Ice-blue eyes bored into Tony as vise-grip hands closed around his throat.

"Desiree was supposed...to follow me...but you'll do."

Dark spots danced before Tony's eyes. He bucked, and Greybeck sat like a rock. The man's fingers tightened. Weakness flowed through Tony's limbs the way it had when he lay in that hospital bed hovering between death and life. Greybeck leaned closer, and coyote breath fanned Tony's face. He groped for something—a rock, a stick—anything. Blood roared through his head, and the pulse pounded in his temples. His hands found nothing but grass and dirt.

A twig snapped. A rush of air—*craaack!*

Greybeck toppled off him, limp as a wet towel. Tony sucked in a breath, and his vision cleared. Desi stood over him, a fat branch in her hands, a ferocious snarl etched on her face. She'd never looked more beautiful. He sat up, rubbing the back of his head where a knot was starting to form.

She dropped the stick and knelt beside him. "Are you all right?"

"Yeah. Thanks." He cleared his throat and tried to swallow, but saliva was in short supply. "You sure have a gift for clocking bad guys." His voice sounded buffed with sandpaper.

"I've been aching to take a stick to Clayton for a long time."

Tony struggled to his feet. He stared at the inert body sprawled on the ground faceup. Down for the count. "Whew! I'm weaker than I thought. Couldn't fight off one electronics nerd." He laughed, but a sour feeling settled in his stomach.

"Clayton's no mere nerd. He's the Mr. Atlas of Nerds. Raw physical strength? He would've overpowered you when you were at your best."

"That's supposed to make me feel better?"

"It's not about feeling better—it's about fact. But you're faster and smarter. Not Mensa-smart. People savvy. And that's a quality Clayton couldn't beg, borrow, or steal. If I were a betting woman, I'd put the whole wad on you any day of the week."

Tony shook his head. "Except today." The man on the ground moaned. "Let's get this guy wrapped up. We'll have to use his belt for handcuffs. You did let security know about the fugitive, right?" Tony bent over Greybeck and started loosening the belt. When Desi didn't answer, Tony glanced over his shoulder.

She was tracing an aimless pattern in the dirt with the toe of her sandal. "No way could I let you take on Clayton by yourself, so I told one of the other tourists to get help."

Tony went back to loosening the belt. "Des, you needed to—" Pain exploded in his solar plexus as a blow from a fist flung him into Desi, and they went down in a heap.

Greybeck rose like some groggy colossus, a trickle of blood snaking down one cheek from under his hairline. At the sound of approaching voices, his nostrils flared, and then he whirled and raced away.

"Stay here." Tony shoved to his feet and tore after the fleeing fugitive. Fat chance she'd do what he said, but maybe she'd bring a security guard with her this time.

He spotted his quarry racing up the trail. A wobble in the guy's run indicated continuing effects from Desi's blow. *Way to go, darlin'.*

The way opened into a dirt clearing with ruins to the left and a drop-off ahead. Greybeck stood at the edge. He glanced back, and their gazes locked. Greybeck telegraphed a potent mix of desperation and fury, and then jumped. A grunt followed, and the smack of feet on stone.

Tony reached the drop-off and halted. Greybeck had landed on a ledge about five feet below, the first tier in a pair leading toward a pool of green water surrounded by sheer rock walls and jungle foliage. No way out except where Tony stood. The musclebound geek glared at

Tony and goat-hopped onto the lower tier. The next hop would be into the water.

"Give it up, Greybeck." Tony wiped sweat from his eyes. "There's nowhere to go, and security is on the way."

The man spouted a string of obscenities, bared his teeth, and leaped. The splash overlapped a shout behind Tony.

"Policía Federal Preventiva! Put your hands in the air."

Tony stiffened. The federales? Didn't Desi explain the white hats from the black hats? He looked over his shoulder. A tall, wiry man in camo pointed the business end of a Walther P99 pistol at Tony's heart.

Tony lifted his arms. "A wanted fugitive jumped into the cenote. Catch him, and you'll be a hero."

The federal sneered. "You are the only *gringo* I see. A woman is injured, and someone will answer."

Desi appeared at the head of the trail, hands behind her back, another armed federal gripping her shoulder. "I'm trying to tell you—"

"No more talk." Her captor shook her. "We will sort this out our way."

Tony stepped forward, but the pistol cocked, and he froze. "My name is Anthony Lucano. I'm an agent for the U.S. Federal Bureau of Investigation. The man you need is in the cenote."

"There is no one in the water, *bribón*. You will come with us."

—⁂—

Three hours later, Desi sat beside Tony in front of the desk of the local *jefe* at Cancún police headquarters. The chief sorted through a sheaf of papers and paid them no attention. Tony flickered a smile at Desi.

She bit her lip. How had honeymoon turned to horror so suddenly? Cuffed and humiliated, she and Tony had been led out the gate at Chichén Itzá and shoved into a police cruiser. After a long, miserable ride, they ended up in stinking cells, followed by a nightmare interrogation. Tony wore a fresh bruise on his cheek, evidence that questioning methods in Mexico weren't required to meet U.S. standards. Desi had probably been lucky to get by with a slap from a testy jail matron.

The chief put the papers down, and his cold black gaze settled on Tony. "Your office in Boston confirms your identity as Special Agent Anthony Lucano. However, they are clear that you are not in Mexico in an official capacity. You should not have interfered in police business."

"Clayton Greybeck threatened my wife, and he's wanted on both sides of the border. What would you have done?"

A smile no warmer than his eyes widened the chief's lips. "Exactly what you did, and I would have been taken to an American jail. We are releasing you and your wife to continue your honeymoon. Kindly confine yourselves to tourist activities."

"What about Greybeck? You never found him. He could still be a threat."

"If you don't feel safe, go home." The jefe lifted his chin. "But be assured that if the man did not come out of the water, he is still in it. We are dragging the cenote for his body. Unfortunately, the pit is deep, and there are many nooks and crevices."

Desi gripped the arms of her chair. "The cenote is fed by an underground river. What if there's access to the river from the pool and a way out?"

The jefe stared at her like she'd just belched in public. "Señora, I tell you, the cenote has been scientifically explored, and no such escape route exists."

"The last thorough excavation took place decades ago. Maybe something's changed or something was missed before." The chief's face flushed, and Desi closed her mouth. Why was she acting so contrary about a wild theory?

Tony grabbed her hand and squeezed. Desi pressed her lips together. Hint taken.

"Can we go now?" he said. "We need to return to Chichén Itzá and pick up our car."

"Ah, the Ferrari. One of my men brought it to town, and I inspected it personally."

Took it for a test drive, you mean. Desi kept her gaze lowered and her thought to herself.

"You will find the car in the impound lot," the chief continued.

Tony sighed. "How much?"

El Jefe shrugged. "I do not concern myself with such things."

Sure, as long as you get your cut. Desi crossed her arms. "If you ran the license plate, you know that the Ferrari belongs to President Montoya."

"The vehicle is registered to the government, of which I am a servant."

If steam could blow out her ears, she'd be a locomotive. "Didn't you call his office to verify that we are his guests? He may have an opinion about our treatment in your jurisdiction."

Tony shot her a glare.

The chief lowered his head. "It was not possible to contact El Presidente's office, and we do not know when communication will be restored."

"What are you talking about?" Desi unwound her arms.

"Haven't you heard? This afternoon an earthquake hit Mexico City—worse than 1985. The damage, the loss of life, unknown as yet, but many of my men have been dispatched to help. So please, be on your way, and do not cause for us any more trouble."

Shock gusted through Desi, then sorrow. Families devastated, homes lost, businesses destroyed. And the primitive conditions that followed a natural catastrophe… "Can we help?" The words slipped out before she could give them a second thought.

Tony wrapped an arm around her shoulder and ushered her from the office. "Let's go back to the villa. We'll learn more on the television news."

Desi let him handle the business of retrieving the Ferrari. On the road at last, she bowed her head to her knees and prayed as if her heart were torn in two. Tony's hand rested on her shoulder, and he prayed with her.

Faces appeared before her mind's eye—President Montoya, Señor Corona, the smiling concierge at the hotel, the maid, the room service waiter. *God, help them!* People from the open market where she'd shopped for a few pleasant hours before the caper at the Museo de Arte Mejicana. The museum! Was the beautiful building still standing? And what of the treasures inside? Her mind reeled from visions of fire and looting. She pictured the boardroom, the men gathered there, the chairman twisting his heirloom ring. *God, protect them!* She hadn't liked the board members, but did personal feelings matter when tragedy struck? Tears washed down her face.

When they arrived at the villa, Tony helped her inside, settled her on the sofa, and brought her a cup of hot tea. By then, her grief had subsided to little hiccups.

She sipped the tea. "I'm sorry. That was a bit extreme. I don't know what came over me. My family and loved ones, except you, are safe in the United States. And yet it was like I felt the pain of those people in Mexico City as if it were my own."

Tony settled on the sofa and gathered her close. "Months ago you lost your father and weeks ago, your home. You prayed from your own suffering. It was beautiful. Don't apologize."

Desi snuggled her face into Tony's collar. "I'm not a complete basket case then?"

"You're the cutest basket case I've ever been married to."

She sat up. "Television on! We need to see what's happening."

"Are you sure? Maybe you should lie down awhile. You look wiped out."

"No more than you. Find a news station while I get a cold washcloth for my eyes and a couple aspirin for a headache."

Tony saluted. "Aye-aye, cap'n."

They watched an hour of heartrending devastation—collapsed buildings, electrical fires, dazed and bloody faces, sooty-faced emergency workers—before Tony insisted they go out for supper. Desi picked at her food, and she noticed Tony didn't finish his. Did he have the same nagging feeling that they needed to help?

Her cell phone rang as they stepped back into the villa. Desi checked the caller ID, then flipped the phone open. "Hi, Max. We're fine. Cancún isn't anywhere near Mexico City."

"With you, I never rule out the possibility that you could be in the thick of things."

Desi snorted. "Was that a compliment or an insult?"

"Generally, a compliment, though your darin' habits do sometimes give your friends palpitations. But that's not why I called. I've got a little juice on the Spanish Carina family."

"Wow, girl! You work at the speed of light." Desi took a seat at the kitchen counter, and Tony settled beside her.

A chuckle came from the Boston end. "Well, here goes. The Carinas were a Spanish family of wealthy world traders. In the late 1700s, they immigrated to Mexico and took up a sizable land grant on the Yucatán Peninsula."

"Where are they now?"

"They don't exist."

"They died out?" Disappointment washed over Desi.

"Not hardly," Max said. "Quite a few of their descendents live in Mexico."

"Ma-a-ax, you're driving me nuts here."

"Not hard to do when you keep interruptin' me."

"My lips are buttoned." She made a twisting motion with her fingers over her mouth. Tony's chest started to shake, and Desi scowled at him.

"Here's the punch line," Max said. "In the mid-1800s the sole heir to the Carina fortune sold his considerable holdings, moved to Mexico City, and changed his name to Corona."

Desi sucked in a breath. "No wonder Señor Corona seemed protective of the antique piece of jewelry. It's a family heirloom. Why didn't he tell me?"

"You'll have to ask him."

"That might be difficult since phone communication is cut off between here and there."

"Let me keep pokin' around then. Now, catch me up on honeymoon fun."

Desi filled her in, and Max moaned. "In the thick of things, all right."

"Evidently we won't have to keep watching over our shoulders for Clayton Greybeck." Desi sighed. "The Mexican authorities are certain he drowned."

"You don't sound happy."

"For the personal relief factor, I am. But for Clayton, I'm not. He didn't have much of an eternity in his future."

"I hear you."

"Tony and I are going to concentrate on enjoying our honeymoon. We'll fly back to Boston in ten days toasted to a golden brown. After an assault and a nearby earthquake, what more could happen?"

"You do *not* want an answer to that."

"I take back the question."

Desi hung up and wandered into the living room to watch more news while Tony went for his run. After he showered, they headed for bed. Snuggled against one another like a pair of spoons, Desi still couldn't make her muscles unknot.

Tony pulled her closer. "The Red Cross is on site, babe, and the U.S. is sending aid."

"We always do."

"We're givers."

"One of the reasons we're a blessed nation in spite of the depravity and God-bashing. But we can't always leave it to the government. Sometimes individuals, especially Christians, have to take action too."

Tony didn't answer. His even breathing and relaxed arm across her waist said he was drifting into slumber. Desi stared into the dark. He'd had a tough day. She didn't want to count the bruises on his body…or hers, for that matter.

What should they do tomorrow? Make up their snorkeling adventure? Might as well. But how much could she enjoy anything with the knowledge that masses of people were suffering and dying a few hundred miles away? She closed her eyes. Doubtful she'd get any sleep.

—〜〜—

A poke in the ribs jerked Desi out of deep slumber. She squinted at the clock—3:00 a.m. "What?" She rolled over.

"I have a contact in the Red Cross who can probably get us on a team."

Exhilaration pumped through Desi. She and her man were on the same wavelength. "But what about your training schedule?"

"Forget that. The Lord'll either give me the strength or point me in a new career direction. Can you see spending the rest of our honeymoon in a disaster area?"

"I can't see us doing anything else."

Tony chuckled. "It'll probably be safer than the Yucatán. The farther away from any remnant of El Jaguar's gang, the better."

"Maybe I'll find Señor Corona and ask him about the medallion."

"I don't know, babe. If he'd wanted to claim the thing, he would have done it when you showed it to him. Maybe he's got personal reasons."

Desi stuck out her lower lip. "You're saying I can be a nosy buttinski sometimes?"

"I'm saying your curiosity level could shame the proverbial cat. Your survival rate too."

"Very funny. But what about the remains of that poor woman stored in a temporary vault in New Mexico?"

"Let's see what Max comes up with. That way you can make an informed decision about approaching a government official regarding something that smacks of family scandal."

"I hate to admit it, but you have a point."

He pulled her into a head-spinning kiss, halting further conversation. She went happily into his arms. Surely, with the Lord sending them to Mexico City, He intended for her find out what was up with Esteban Corona.

Twenty-Four

*T*ony squatted opposite his construction partner, and together they
hefted a stack of half-inch pressboard slabs. In tandem, they headed
across the dirt yard toward a line of unfinished shacks. A youthful shout
sounded, and then a rubber ball smacked him in the side. Children
laughed. Tony sent a mock growl toward a cluster of barefoot kids. One
of the boys grabbed the ball, and they ran toward a weed-grown field,
spindly legs churning, giggles floating on the breeze.

Tony smiled, and Matt, the young man he teamed with, chuckled.
Precious little to be happy about in this neighborhood where the quake
had leveled every tin and cardboard shack. But kids meant a future. If
only Tony knew he was making a permanent difference in their lives.

Near a half-finished wall, he and Matt deposited their load on the
ground. Tony arched a kink out of his back.

"Worn out, old man?" his twenty-something co-worker said.

"I'll work rings around you yet, infant."

"You're on."

Tony grabbed his hammer, pulled a nail out of the pouch at his
waist, and got busy. The hammers of other workers pounded a staccato
rhythm. A few dozen feet away, a rust-bucket of a backhoe groaned as
it dug shallow trenches for temporary water and sewer lines.

Temporary? Tony stepped back and surveyed the line of two-room
shanties. He couldn't fool himself. For nine out of ten families, these
flimsy walls would be the best home they'd ever have. Some future.

Tony drove another nail home. But what was the alternative? Let them continue to sleep on bare ground in the open?

He got no answer to his grousing. Not that he expected one after asking the same kinds of questions every day for the past week as he cleared debris—mostly by hand—uncovered mangled bodies, and finally got assigned to this construction project.

By the end of another fourteen-hour workday, the shanty stood completed, and the workers helped a widow and her two small children move in with little more than the ragged clothes on their backs, a few sticks of makeshift furniture, and a small stash of Red Cross food. Tears rolled down the cheeks of the stoop-shouldered woman as she waved good-bye to them with many cries of "Gracias, gracias, *señores*."

Tony climbed onto the back of the workers' truck and settled on a bench next to Matt. The truck jolted off up the pitted road.

Matt leaned his elbows on his knees. "A shower, a good meal, and we'll be new men."

"Right now, I'll admit to old. Try going on eighty." Tony rolled his shoulders.

"No old dude ever put in a day like you did today. I'm on the worn-out side myself." The young man stretched his arms. "Man, I didn't even know I *had* some of the muscles that hurt tonight. You're the lucky one, pal, with a wife along to rub your back."

"Des won't be at camp tonight. Some bigwig got wind she was here and recruited her to help secure cultural property. She'll probably have a hot bath and a feather mattress, not a lukewarm shower and a cot in a tent."

"I didn't hear her complain about camping out."

"Not Desiree. She's as adaptable as they come." *I'd rather stay here with you,* she'd whispered in his ear this morning before she kissed him good-bye and climbed into the government car. Now, as he sat with a bunch of smelly men in the back of a slat-sided truck, Desi's absence ached worse than the fatigue in his muscles.

What was his darlin' doing this very minute?

―〰―

Seated at an office desk in the Museo de Arte Mejicana, Desi keyed the mic on a satellite-linked two-way radio. "Señor Corona, this is Desiree Lucano. Come in, por favor."

She released the mic button and waited, tapping a foot. Her gaze strayed out a cracked window onto the street outside. The pavement had buckled neatly down the middle, allowing traffic to pass on both sides of the road. Fine, if a driver never wanted to turn left. Across the street the facade of a building had collapsed, exposing the inner framework. The museum had been lucky to lose only a couple of columns in the front and a corner of the roof.

Desi tried again to raise Señor Corona. No answer. Why was the man who had urged her into service with the government now ignoring her? Maybe he was afraid she'd bring up the medallion. Or maybe the presidential aide just had the world on his shoulders.

Desi returned to the damage reports and inventories on the table. Burst water pipes and small electrical fires had made a mess of the interior, damaging a lot of priceless cultural property and endangering the rest. Until repairs could be made, secure storage must be arranged. As daylight waned—her only working light—she made notes and evaluated the capacities of available intact storage areas such as bank vaults and the vault at the palace.

Transportation would be the trickiest part. She'd hoped to run ideas by Señor Corona, but since he wouldn't answer the radio, she'd have to go ahead with whatever she could arrange. Armored cars? But they couldn't get through the streets any better than other trucks. Tanks might work. Riiight. She'd phone the armory, and they'd release a few. Sending those through the streets would add nicely to public hysteria. Besides, tanks didn't have storage space for bulky objects. She tapped her upper lip. Mule train? *Two Mules for Sister Desi?*

"Desiree Jacobs," a cold voice said. "I did not expect to see you in my museum again."

"Señor Vidal." Rising, Desi nodded to the chairman of the board, who stood stiff-shouldered in the doorway. "It's Mrs. Lucano now. I'm filling in at Señor Corona's request. Your security agency lost their building and half their staff, and the museum administrator is in the hospital."

"Of these things I was aware." He stepped into the room. "So Corona took advantage of my incapacitation and hired a gringa."

"You were injured?" Desi motioned toward a chair.

Vidal ignored the offered seat. A yellowed bruise surrounded a healing cut under the man's left eye. The stiff shoulders could indicate more pain than pride.

"I can help," the man said.

"You want to help?" Desi blinked at him.

"I have a cargo helicopter that I use for my import-export business."

"I thought you were in finance."

He skewered her with a glance. "You have no businessmen in the United States with diversified interests?"

"I'll take you up on your offer."

The chairman's mouth curved upward, but the flare of his nostrils and the cold spark in his gaze chilled Desi. She liked the look less than his scowl, but she could hardly turn away the perfect solution to her dilemma.

"My helicopter will land in the rear courtyard first thing in the morning. I like to make the most of my time."

"You're coming along?"

"I expect you to do the same. We are responsible for a nation's priceless artifacts. I believe that requires our personal attention."

Desi crossed her arms to keep from belting him. "I wouldn't dream of transferring cultural heritage without direct supervision. But since you don't trust me to handle the matter, I'll expect you."

"I'm pleased we understand each other. Buenos días, señora."

That night, Desi paced her hotel room, talking to Tony on the radio. "The man had the gall to imply that I'm incapable of handling the project without him breathing down my neck."

"Hey, you got your transportation. You'll survive a couple of days of unpleasant company. The question is—will he be able to keep up with you? I know what you're like when you sink your teeth into an assignment."

"Thanks for the pep talk, but have you ever wanted to kick a gift horse in the tail?"

Tony's chuckle warmed her to her toes. "Go ahead and kick, just so long as you finish this gig and get back to me pronto."

"Count on it, sweetheart. I miss you."

"I miss you more."

"How about we continue this debate in person?"

"Sounds like fun."

They ended communications, laughing. Desi went to bed but tossed and turned. Less than two weeks married, and a night without Tony amounted to a night on a bed of thorns. She'd trade this soft mattress for a Red Cross cot in a heartbeat.

Desi rolled out at sunup, scratchy eyed and cranky. Vidal had better not mess with her today.

Dressed in casual pants and a button-down shirt, Desi made the short walk to the museum over cracked sidewalks and past workers removing rubble. A pair of uniformed *policías* flanked her, assigned for her protection by Señor Corona. She pulled out her radio and tried the aide again. Still no answer. Something must be wrong with his set. Guess the transport today was up to her and Señor Congeniality.

After she arrived at the museum, she sent the professional movers scurrying to organize last-minute items for the first load. Walking through gutted rooms, she shook her head at the ruin of a gorgeous institution. After renovation, the building would be beautiful again, but it was hard to picture with water dripping, cracked floors, and sooty walls.

Twenty minutes later, the thump of rotors sounded outside. Desi went to a window, minus its glass. Around the courtyard's perimeter, a half-dozen armed *policías* stood vigilant against intruders. They stepped back as the bloated whirlybird touched down. Rotor wind ruffled Desi's hair, and she covered her ears against the whine. Gradually, the wind and noise faded with the dying of the motor. Silence deafened, and then the belly of the massive chopper cracked open. The rear cargo door lowered and became a ramp that touched the ground. The board chairman emerged from a passenger door.

Desi stepped into the courtyard, nodded to Señor Vidal, and took up a position at the base of the ramp. The chairman stood at her back, staring over her shoulder at the manifest on her clipboard. Item by item, the handlers moved the boxed and bubble-wrapped pieces into the hold of the helicopter while Desi checked them off. Vidal remained silent, but his hot breath stirred the hairs on the top of her head.

A weird sensation grew in her belly—like she was in the presence of a predator. Her feet tingled with the urge to run. How foolish would it seem for the contract security expert to bolt screaming from the courtyard because a pompous bureaucrat needed to flex his authority? She glanced over her shoulder at Señor Vidal who was, of all things, smiling.

"I appreciate your priorities, señora. The most valuable items in the first load. We will breathe easier when these treasures are secured. Are we ready to leave?" He offered his arm.

Where had this courtly don come from? And why would she rather chop off her hand than accept the escort? She overrode her revulsion and let him help her into the rear passenger seat.

"You'll like this ride." His rapt gaze traveled over the interior of the whirlybird. "It's a Eurocopter, quietest on the market. The royal family of Monaco has the luxury passenger version, but I had mine custom designed for a cargo chopper. We won't even need headphones."

What do you know? Underneath the Ice Man exterior, Vidal was a regular guy in love with his gadgets. "Nothing but the best for Mexico's heritage," Desi said.

"Indeed."

One of the policías took the seat next to Desi, laying his rifle across his lap. The Mexican policeman gave her one of those flat cop stares they'd perfected the world over. He smelled of bad cigars. Something familiar about that. Desi frowned as she turned to watch the liftoff. The muted drone of the rotors filled the passenger compartment. Vidal was right. No need for headsets. They might have to speak up, but conversation could be carried on. Not that she had anything to say to her companions.

Airborne, they skimmed the tops of buildings. Destruction glared at her from every angle. She closed her eyes and took a deep breath. *God, please help these people. There's so little Tony and I can do. You are the hope of the suffering. Help them look to You.*

When Desi opened her eyes, she fished her laptop out of her soft-sided briefcase, along with the bulky sat-phone unit, which got her a direct satellite feed to access her e-mail. She found a few messages from HJ Securities offices around the globe. One was from Max. Desi clicked on that one. She needed a touch from home. She read:

Hey, girlfriend. Have I got some dirt for you! Love triangle, greed, land-grabs, revenge, bandits. Ingredients for a great movie.

Here's the deal. When the Carinas went to the New World, another family traveled with them and took up a neighboring land grant. The two families were close friends. For a couple of generations, everything was hunky-dory, and then an impetuous young Vidal ran off with the beautiful bride of a Carina don.

Vidal? The top of a steel-gray head showed above the seat ahead of her. She read on.

I notice that members of both families are on the board of directors at the Museo de Arte Mejicana, but with so much water under the bridge, I doubt either of them gives a hoot.

Desi swallowed. No wonder she'd had the impression that the bad blood between Corona and Vidal went deeper than a disagreement about which security company to hire.

As to the medallion, the unfaithful wife took a cask of jewelry that included the medallion. The lovers fled to New Mexico Territory and were never heard from again. Given that the woman's skull was found at the bottom of a canyon, we can deduce the runaways met with tragedy.

The Carina don was a powerful man, far more influential than the Vidals, and notorious for adding to his holdings by hook or by crook. Because of friendship, the Vidals had been spared.

No more. The Carinas proceeded to strip the Vidals of every possession. Eventually, the Vidal family fled into the jungle and lived in stick huts among the Maya.

Desi stopped breathing. Jungle? Maya? *Okay, wild imagination, settle down.* No way was she sitting in a helicopter with El Jaguar because of some ancient family history.

Vidal didn't live anywhere near the Yucatán jungle, said the voice of reason.

But he had his own air transportation to get there, answered the voice of suspicion.

Max's e-mail went on:

The Vidals weren't licked. They became bandits and assassins. Over a few generations, they killed off the Carinas—except one, who sold out and moved to Mexico City. In a sense, you could say the Vidals routed the enemy and won the war. Eventually, they emerged from the jungle, bought property with their ill-gotten gains, and became respectable again.

Desi's head whirled. She should have listened to her urge to flee while her feet were still on terra firma. *Stay calm. You're probably making too much out of an ugly slice of history.* When they touched down at the bank, she could slip away. She could—

Below, the city slid out of sight and countryside opened up.

"Where are we going?" Her words came out in a hoarse yell.

Vidal poked his head around his seat and grinned. The more the guy smiled, the less she liked it. "Be patient. You will see."

Desi turned toward the policeman. "Do something. This man is a crook."

The cop trained his gun on her, his gaze a new level of don't-mess-with-me. She'd seen that look in those eyes before. For an instant, she was in the back of a limo, inhaling the smell of bad cigars, while merciless fingers squeezed her jaw. A tremor shook her. The gunman grabbed her laptop and passed it to his boss.

"Give me a moment, won't you?" Vidal turned away.

Desi opened her mouth, but Rat Fink Cop shot her a stare, and she fumed in silence.

Vidal tossed the laptop into the empty seat next to him. "Your Max is very resourceful."

"What are your plans? Leave the country with this priceless art? You can't stay in Mexico. Too many people saw you leave with this load. When it disappears, they'll realize—"

"How do they know that we were not hijacked by the resourceful El Jaguar?"

"You are El Jaguar."

The man's smile faded into an exaggerated frown. "Poor, courageous Fernando Vidal. He gave his life for his country."

"You're going to kill yourself? Some people might call that a service to humanity."

The hired gun snickered. Vidal glared at him, and the man shrugged and turned away.

The gang leader pinned Desi beneath an iron stare. "If I hadn't promised to deliver you, I would toss you out right now."

Desi swallowed a rush of bile at the picture of herself in free fall without a parachute.

"By tomorrow, I shall be a national hero, missing and presumed dead. Corona will be ruined, my enemies eliminated, and I will be on my way to Brazil with no one hunting for me."

An antarctic breeze blew through Desi. "And I'm numbered among the enemies."

"You are a nuisance, but Agent Lucano is the enemy. He took my

Angelina from me."

Desi's breath hitched. "What have you planned for Tony?"

Señor Vidal's grin sent horror pulsing through her veins.

—⁓—

Tony hefted a bag of cement powder off the back of the supply truck and followed the guy ahead of him to a pallet fifty feet away. Wiping sweat from his face, he headed back for another.

"Just a bunch of ants in a line." Matt laughed as he trailed Tony to the truck.

"Good for us ants this isn't the height of summer." He threw a bag onto his shoulder, and a grunt filtered between gritted teeth. "We're pretty rank as it is by the end of the day."

"Speak for yourself."

The growl of a motor drew Tony's attention. A large truck lumbered over the rutted road toward the work site. "Great. Now we can unload bricks too."

Matt laughed. "Not to worry. That truck's got an attached crane that lifts the pallets and sets them on the ground. Then we get to carry the bricks in handbaskets to the work areas."

"Sounds like fun." Tony walked off with his bag.

When he got back for another, the brick truck had pulled up. A crane fitted with block and tackle and a whale-sized hook jutted from the forward section of the cargo bed. Workers crawled across pallets securing chains and talking in rapid-fire Spanish. Tony hesitated, tempted to hang around and watch the show, but he grabbed a bag and walked away.

Several pallets of bricks had been lowered to the ground by the time Tony hefted the last of the cement bags.

"¡*Hola*, gringo!"

Tony turned. Was that shout for him? Lots of gringos around here.

The operator who stood at the control panel on the side of the truck motioned to him. Tony stepped in that direction. Did the native workers need help? Seemed like they were doing fine.

One released the chain from a grounded pallet and waved to the operator. Hook swinging, the crane moved toward the cargo bed—too fast for the safety of the man on top of the load. Tony called a warning.

The operator grinned and pressed another button. The crane reversed direction, and the hook lashed toward Tony.

Barely time for a last breath.

Zero time to duck.

Twenty-Five

*P*ain shot up Desi's arms where she'd wound her fingers into vise grips around each other. *Lord, I know You haven't toppled off Your throne. You've brought Tony and me through so much. Please, help us again. Protect Tony. Help me—*

"Señor, someone wishes to speak with you." The copilot stood bent over in the space between his seat and the pilot's. Removing his headset, he handed it to his boss.

Desi couldn't hear his end of the radio conversation. She needed to get away from these people to warn Tony. Desi sent a sidelong glance toward the armed guard. Was he really a turncoat cop or a gang member dressed in uniform? The patented stare said cop.

Vidal handed the headset back to his copilot and turned toward Desi, fierce triumph in his stare. "It is done. Lucano is eliminated."

A scream tore from Desi's throat, and she lunged against her seat belt, clawing for that hateful smile. The cop's forearm slammed her against the seat, and his gun jabbed her temple. She froze. "It's not true! I don't believe you!"

"My man at the scene confirmed the kill." Vidal's gaze swept her up and down. "In another generation, you would wear a black gown and veil. But I'm afraid you will have no time for mourning. Give me your rings. They offend someone I find useful." He extended his palm.

Desi covered her left hand with her right. "You'll have to slice them from my cold, dead finger."

"Not out of the question." He turned away.

Except for the muted drone of the rotors, the silence of the tomb encased the helicopter. Tears fell in a steady stream on the hand that protected Desi's wedding rings.

—⁂—

Hours later, the Eurocopter set down in a tiny clearing in the midst of dense forest. Tree foliage and thick grasses whipped in the wind of the rotors. Desi stared, dry-eyed and numb. The rotor storm calmed, and the pilot and Vidal exited the craft. Rat Fink Cop remained next to Desi.

Why did she always end up in an aircraft with some kind of creep-azoid from Jerksville? And why should she care who she was with if Tony no longer lived in the same world? Wait a minute. Maybe she could work bad company to her advantage. The tip of her tongue moistened dry lips. She could jump out and run—force him to shoot her. She could… *Don't go there, girl!*

These people were not going to snuff them both out and go on their merry way. They were going to pay. How, she had no idea, but it would come to her. Hate scalded her throat.

Her door opened, and Vidal stood there…smile on his face.

Desi ripped away her seat belt and lunged, screeching, at the mur-derous scum. Vidal's astonished expression barely registered as she slammed into his chest. He back-pedaled, windmilling. She clawed—she kicked—she punched. Yelping, Vidal went to his knees, arms over his head. She aimed a kick for his groin, but someone slammed into her from the side.

The ground hit her hard, and air wheezed from her lungs. Jungle grasses caught at her clothes and skin as rough hands yanked her upright. Her manhandler whirled her to face him. Rat Fink Cop. If she didn't know better, she'd think he was fighting a grin. But amusement at his boss's expense didn't make him any gentler as he bound her hands in front of her with twine.

A soft bray came from the tree line, and then a mule led by a Mayan handler emerged into the clearing. Then another and another and another—a whole pack train. Just like she'd wished for at the museum. Her captor threw her up on one of the beasts and wrapped a loose end of her binding around the saddle horn. Then he returned to the helicopter.

Desi pulled in a quivering breath, and a musky animal scent filled her nostrils.

A steady stream of workers went in and out of the belly of the helicopter as it regurgitated Mexico's cultural heritage. Such reckless handling. Desi bit her tongue. Strange how she cared about art when her whole world had been destroyed. *Must be in our genes, Daddy. We've always been nuts that way. Pal around with Tony until I get there, okay?*

Desi sniffled and cranked her neck at an awkward angle to wipe her nose on her shoulder. Bits of grass clung to her clothes, the sun cooked her back, and sweat glued her shirt to her body.

At last, the pack train was ready, and the first mules were led into the trees. Her handler turned the animal but waited as others passed them. Mounted on a tall mule, Vidal rode by. He glared. No smile. Desi met the look. Maybe that bloody scratch on his cheek would go septic with some kind of fatal jungle rot. One could always hope.

Desi swayed and jounced as her animal entered the trees, following a faint trail. In the shade, the air was cooler but close, muggy, and full of buzzing insects. She could do little to fend them off except toss her head like the patient beast she rode.

She gritted her teeth. As a Christian, she ought to be ashamed of wishing someone to get sick and die. But *ought to* didn't make a dent in her feelings. Okay, so maybe she could hope he made peace with God on his agonized deathbed.

Nope, she'd be lying to herself. She wanted the guy to burn in hell.

Time passed in a fog of discomfort and grief. The pack train entered a gully, and hooves clicked against moss-covered rocks. A steep grade loomed, and the lead mules struggled upward in little leaps. Desi winced at what must be happening to delicate antiquities. Her handler grunted as he climbed, back bent. Desi clamped aching legs against her mount's sides. Leaning over the animal's neck, she breathed in mule sweat and clung to the pommel of the saddle.

Finally, they clambered over the lip of the ravine. Under the lowering sun, the rain forest cast long shadows across a clearing. Desi's animal stopped, but the pack mules threaded on between thatched huts. A typical Mayan village…except for the long brick structure tucked under the canopy of the forest and a concrete-block building next to it. Aerial reconnaissance would see only the native huts. No wonder the lair of El Jaguar had remained a mystery.

The aging Jaguar dismounted and strode toward the brick building. A woman emerged from the front door, a vaguely familiar figure, but Desi couldn't make out her identity. The pair embraced. Desi sniffed. Hadn't taken the larcenous Lothario long to find a new ladylove after the passing of his dear Angelina.

A burly figure burst out the door of the concrete-block building and trotted toward her, blond hair flashing in patches of sunlight. Clayton Greybeck. Another creep she'd just as soon stake out over an anthill and let the buzzards peck out his eyeballs.

Clayton loped up. What was it with these bad guys wearing smiles? At least he'd shaved and didn't look like the crazed lunatic he had been at Chichén Itzá. Probably because he thought everything was going his way again.

"Easy now, Des." He stopped a few feet away. "I'm going to untie you, and then you're going to come with me quietly. I'll explain when we get where we can talk."

"I hold you responsible for Tony." She spat each word through gritted teeth.

Blood surged into his face. "Sure, I wanted him out of the way, and I got a little nuts when I saw you two at Chichén Itzá. But you're alive today because of me, and you'd better appreciate it. Now, shut up!" He pulled a knife from his pocket and popped out the blade.

Desi's heart kabumped, but he only sliced the itchy twine. He pulled her down from the mule, and she yanked free of his grip, but her knees buckled. Clayton scooped her up and carried her toward the brick building. Desi slapped him. He said a nasty word and dropped her. She landed with all the grace of a sack of potatoes. Pain sparks danced in her head.

Clayton stared down at her, hands on his hips. "Get up then and walk."

Resenting every fresh bruise and her saddle-sore legs, Desi struggled to her feet.

"That way." Clayton pointed, and she preceded him in an unsteady but chin-up walk toward the house where Vidal had disappeared with his lady friend.

Desi tromped up a pair of stone steps and stepped inside. The interior was cooler than the great outdoors but musty smelling and lit with gas lamps on the walls. A long table took up most of the room. Food smells floated through an open doorway to the left, and utensils clattered.

Clayton took her elbow and guided her down a hallway. They passed a closed door, and Desi heard Vidal and a familiar female voice. Pilar Sanchez? Processing the revelation, she let herself be tugged into another room filled by a four-poster bed, a chair, a bureau, and an armoire.

"This one's ours." Clayton spread his arms.

"Ours?" Desi back-pedaled, snagged a heel on the chair leg, and caught herself against the bureau. "Are you insane?"

"Vidal would've crushed and discarded you like a scrap of paper if I hadn't insisted he bring you to me."

"You don't love me, Clayton, so what's this obsession?"

He shrugged thick shoulders. "I want you, and Greybecks always get what they want."

"Oh, puh-lease, don't try to tell me you're overcome by lust at the mere thought of me."

Clayton stepped toward her, and Desi backed up against the wall, heart fluttering like a trapped bird. What chance did she have against this mountain of muscle? None whatsoever. But her fingers turned to claws. He'd pay dearly.

He cupped her chin. "You're the kind of woman who challenges a man, and I'm a sucker for a dare. You need a little time for widowhood to wear off? I can buy that." He stepped back. "Just don't let it take too long. Vidal will notice if you're not making me happy, and you don't want to know what he'd do to you."

Desi's throat tightened. She could believe that statement.

"I'll take you to the washhouse. You can clean up, and Juanita will bring you a change of clothes. I'll fix myself a bed on the floor since I take it we're not sharing one tonight."

"Not unless you want to wake up dead."

He chuckled. "See what I mean, Des? Challenge of a lifetime. We'll make great kids. You'll like Brazil too. Plenty of money to do whatever we want." He pulled open the door.

Desi swallowed a torrent of furious words and marched out, fists knotted. If only a punch from her would amount to more than a gnat bite to him.

Outside, they passed the concrete-block building. Rat Fink Cop stood on the porch, shirtless, with a tattooed arm around a scantily clad woman. He bared his teeth in a wolfish grin. The woman's shadowed gaze darted away, and Desi's breath caught. She knew that face from a newspaper clipping Tony had shown her. A missing woman from Boston, but she couldn't recall the name.

Clayton hustled Desi along with a hand on her shoulder. "That guy's Salvador. He's no danger to you as long as you're with me."

Desi kept her doubts to herself, along with her knowledge of the woman's identity. "His companion didn't look too happy."

He chuckled. "Maybe not, but she and the other girls keep El Jaguar's men happy."

Desi's stomach rolled. Those poor women. And that was the house Clayton had come out of when she'd arrived. Maybe she should be grateful he hadn't saved himself for her. But someone else had paid the price. Resolve ignited in her belly. *God, if You'll give me a way, I'll get out of here and take the women with me.* She eyed the edge of the rain forest.

"Don't even think about it." Clayton squeezed her shoulder. "You'd be lost in minutes and wouldn't last a day." They stopped in front of a hut set apart from the others. A cistern on stilt legs stood next to it. "But I know what you're like, Des. You'll try something dumb, so I'm going to post a guard outside the door." He motioned toward a man wearing a side arm.

Desi stalked into the washhouse and slammed the door. She glared at the ceramic tub that took up most of the room. Maybe if she stayed stinky, she'd have less appeal for Clayton. Then again, that woman at the cinder-block house hadn't been too clean. Desi turned the single faucet knob and felt the stream that poured into the tub. Lukewarm. Perfect for a bath in the tropics.

She disrobed and climbed in, letting the tub fill around her. A cake of white soap sat in a dish hooked to the side. She rubbed at herself as if she could scrub away the horror of the past hours. Darkness robed her mind, and sobs clogged her throat. She washed blindly, frantically.

A woman's hand closed over hers. Desi gazed up through a fog. Juanita, the maid from Pilar and Ramon's house, gazed down at her, dark eyes liquid and gentle. The woman took the soap and handed her a small vial of shampoo, then squatted by the tub while Desi washed her hair and the sobs calmed. Desi took a towel from Juanita. The woman motioned toward a pile of clothing on a bench by the door, and then left on silent feet.

Desi slowly dried herself off. A few minutes later, clad in native blouse, skirt, and flip-flops, she left the washhouse. Ignoring the guard who trailed on her heels, Desi returned to the long house. Several people sat around the dining table—Vidal, Pilar, Clayton, and Salvador.

Clayton stood and pulled back a chair. Desi plunked down and stared at her bone china plate and soup bowl, odd elegance in the crude surroundings.

"Now that we are all here," Pilar said, "let the serving commence." She rang a small bell, and Juanita rustled from the kitchen. Pilar inhaled audibly as the servant set a steaming bowl on the table. "Fish soup. Excellent." She smiled at Desi. "The Mayans call it Che Chak. Try some."

Clayton ladled a chunk of fish and some pale liquid into Desi's bowl. Scents of lime and garlic teased her nose. Her stomach clenched. Any other time, any other place, and the soup would have made her mouth water.

Pilar spooned soup into her mouth and then dabbed at her lips with a cloth napkin. "It will be good to have another woman along in Rio. The stores are fabulous."

Vidal chuckled and twisted the ring on his finger. "My sister lives to shop."

Desi's eyes widened. "Your sister? Ramon Sanchez was married to the sister of El Jaguar? Did he know?" Desi crushed her napkin. "Was he part of this?"

Vidal took a long pull from a glass filled with dark liquid. Not his first drink, judging from his flushed face and heavy lids. He opened his mouth, but Pilar jumped in.

"My husband did not know the identity of El Jaguar, and he could have been spared if he had taken the deals he was offered. But he would not give up his notions of good and evil. He might have been the richest, most influential man in all of the Yucatán if he had cooperated—"

"Nonsense, woman!" Vidal bellowed. "El Jaguar is the richest, most influential man in the Yucatán. Always has been, always will be. A pity no one can know it was me, but I pass the mantle of the Vidal dynasty to my son." He slapped Salvador's back.

The son leveled his dead stare on his father, then returned to his soup. So Salvador was less than enamored of his parent. And it couldn't have done filial respect any good to see dear old dad beaten up by a half-pint female today.

The elder Vidal drained his glass and wiped his mouth with the back of his hand.

"Always has been?" Desi said. "I thought El Jaguar was a modern invention."

Vidal shrugged. "A reinvention."

A fresh picture focused in her mind. "Your bandido ancestors. The leader called himself El Jaguar. Am I right?"

Pilar clapped her hands. "I told you the woman is clever. The Vidals have never given up their influence with the Maya. It was easy to organize angry youth. The gang soon grew to include all types of oppressed Hispanics."

Right. El Jaguar and his Fraternidad were misunderstood Robin Hoods—the cry of gang leaders everywhere. "But why marry an honest man like Ramon Sanchez? You must have known he would oppose your plans, and you could only ruin him."

Vidal let out a drunken heehaw. "All part of the grand scheme to at last avenge all wrongs. The unfaithful Carina bride who ran off with a Vidal? She was a Sanchez."

"Oh, come on! That extramarital intrigue took place centuries ago."

Vidal's face crimsoned. "And for generations my family lived like animals trapped in the jungle. When we stepped back into society, the taint of the bandito dogged our steps. And all the while the Corona and Sanchez families, the ones responsible for our downfall, enjoyed respect and position. Only in my generation have we Vidals been restored to our proper place."

"So you destroy your hard-won respectability by turning gangster?"

Vidal grinned. "It is in the blood. We do it well. Salvador is stationed in Mérida. He will continue the operation from within the policía and groom Pilar's son as his lieutenant."

Desi glared at Pilar. "You would leave your son to this sick life? Did Ramon get too close to the truth? Is that why he had to die? What sent him to New York?"

"I'd be interested in that answer," Clayton said.

Desi shot a sidelong glance at him. His chin dimple pulsed in a white face. So Clayton didn't know everything about this organization either? Not too comforting when he was her only buffer between the local godfather and son.

Pilar set her empty bowl and spoon away. "Certainly, I—"

"Pilar?" The word was a warning growl from the senior Vidal.

The woman glared at her brother. "It's time for him to know. The understanding can only further convince him that the deaths of Randolph and Wilson were unintentional. We did not know they were in the rental car with Ramon."

Vidal shook his head and downed the last of his drink.

Clayton stared into his empty bowl, lips thin.

Pilar's gaze on Clayton was warm as a long-lost aunt's. Desi shivered. This was one slick black widow. And if Clayton believed that hooey about them not knowing his family was in the car with Ramon Sanchez, he was dimmer about people than she'd thought.

Pilar wound her fingers together. "My son Carlos is your half brother."

"What?" Clayton leaped up.

"Sit down!" The command came from Salvador.

Those were the first words Desi'd heard from the man since their unpleasant chat in the back of the Sanchez limo, and the creepy-crawly sensation in the pit of Desi's stomach hadn't changed from then to now.

Clayton sank into his chair. She didn't blame him. Eyes wide, mouth hanging open, the man was as thunderstruck as a pole-axed steer, in Max's vernacular.

Pilar touched Clayton's hand. "Randolph and I had an affair years ago."

He moved his hand into his lap. "So that's how our family became involved with yours. Dad would never tell me how he got hooked into helping with a smuggling scheme."

"When Ramon came to me with something Desiree said, I told him the truth about Carlos's parentage. Then he went to New York." She turned toward Desi. "I was angry with you at first, but now I see you did the cause of El Jaguar a favor."

"Sorry to oblige."

Juanita whisked into the room with a steaming platter—seasoned pork steaks, from the aroma. Conversation fell silent. The servant set the platter down and began picking up bowls. When she got to Desi, she stopped and looked a question at the full bowl.

Desi nodded. "It smells delicious, but I have no appetite. Wait a second!" Her nostrils flared, and she pinned Pilar beneath a hard stare. "Can Juanita read and write?"

"What a silly question. Of course not."

"Has she been to this location before?"

"She accompanies me everywhere. A lady cannot travel without her servant."

Desi rose, and not even Salvador's glare inspired her to sit down. "Did you have her tongue cut out to keep her from telling about the lair of El Jaguar?"

"Be calm. It was of no more consequence than docking a dog's tail."

Desi picked up her soup bowl and flung the contents at El Jaguar's sister. Pilar's shriek, Vidal's howl of laughter, and Salvador's shout sounded as one. Clayton dragged Desi from the table. She caught Juanita's astonished gape as they entered the hallway. Tipsy chortles and Hispanic curses in a feminine voice followed them.

Clayton flung her into the bedroom and bolted the door. Then he doubled over, clutching his stomach. His face turned a vibrant purple, and tears leaked from the edges of his eyes. Squeaks filtered between his lips.

Poison in the soup? Good thing she hadn't taken a bite. Oh, good grief, he was laughing so hard he couldn't get his breath. Desi flopped into a chair.

"You really…got us…in the soup…now." Clayton gasped.

A snort came out through Desi's nose.

"Good thing," he continued, "…the broth…had cooled…or we'd be…in hot water."

A full-blown chuckle escaped Desi's lips. Too bad this guy hadn't shown a decent sense of humor before. She might have liked him a little. Her breath caught, and she clamped a hand over her mouth. How could she laugh when Tony was— *Oh, Lord, please forgive me.*

Desi rose and lay down on the bed, curled into a tight ball.

Little rustles sounded behind her, and the light went out. Desi stiffened, ready to do battle. More rustles, and then a masculine sigh.

"It's okay, Des. Get some rest. I'm not a rapist, and I sure didn't ask to be a part of this."

"Don't even try to tell me you're a victim. The reluctant smuggler. Hah! You love the money as much as that bunch out in the dining room."

"The money, yeah. But the way it's gotten? Well, let's just say dear old dad wanted it this way, and a Greybeck always gets what he wants."

"Did he want to get shot into Swiss cheese?"

Silence.

"I'm sorry. That was raw." Desi rolled over. "I know what it's like to lose people you love." Sobs quivered in her chest, but she bit her knuckles. Not in front of the man who thought he could take Tony's place in her bed as easily as musical pillows.

"I didn't love them." A lifetime of discouragement weighted Clayton's voice. "Wilson and I never got along, and Randolph Greybeck wasn't lovable, but he was my dad. You know?"

Desi didn't answer. There was nothing to say.

She had to plan an escape with not a single good idea. The only person she knew would track her to the ends of the earth was no longer in this world. Despair sucked at her, and the feeble flicker of faith winked out like a snuffed lantern.

Twenty-Six

I 'm in Cancún, Stevo." Tony spoke low and urgently into the public
telephone near the bus depot. The place was busy even this late at
night, a factor that could work for or against him. Lots of noise to cover
up his conversation, but hard to see someone coming for him.

"What're you doing back in the Yucatán? I thought you were working in Mexico City?"

"Don't talk, just listen." His gaze scanned the passersby for anyone
showing interest in an Anglo on the phone. "Desi's missing, and I'm on
the run."

Stevo hissed in a breath. "El Jaguar?"

"You got it…and the federales."

"The federales! How did you get into it with them?"

"If you'll stop asking questions, I'll tell you." He sketched out the
details of the attempt on his life. "The other workers jumped on the crane
operator when he tried to run away, and then radioed the federales. By
the time they arrived, I at least had my breath back. We made the operator contact his boss with news of my demise, and things got interesting
after that." Tony's mind relived the scene as he shared it.

He snatched the radio from the crane operator. "At least you handled reporting my
death better than killing me." Coughing up cement dust, he shoved the man toward
a pair of federales.

A third agent, their supervisor, who had introduced himself as José Peña, grabbed the crane operator by the collar. "Tell us who hired you to commit murder." Peña twisted the collar. "Or we can get it out of you the hard way."

The would-be killer went as ashen as the powder that coated Tony from head to foot. "I do not know, señor. A radio frequency. That is all I have. Please, you must believe me."

With a foul exclamation, Peña released the crane operator. The other federales hauled him off, blubbering and begging.

The supervisory agent turned toward Tony. "You look like a powdered *sopapilla*."

"Yeah, well, the cement bag over my shoulder burst when the hook hit it." Tony rubbed his chest near his heart. Being kicked by a mule might've felt better. "I'm only alive because the bag cushioned the worst of the impact."

One of the gathered workers let out a high laugh. "He flew ten feet in a cloud of white."

The federal narrowed his eyes. "Do you require medical attention, señor?"

"I require to know that my wife is safe. She's at the Museo de Arte Mejicana."

"An officer will check on her." He crooked a finger in Tony's direction. "Walk with me."

Tony fell in beside the agent's swagger. "What haven't you told me?"

The man pursed his lips. "What is your wife's relationship with Señor Esteban Corona?"

"He's Desi's contact for a job on behalf of your government."

Peña stopped beside his car. "Señor Corona has not been seen for a day and a half, but documents have been found in his home linking him to the gang leader El Jaguar. It does not look good for the señor...or for anyone associated with him."

"That's nuts! The guy takes off and leaves incriminating documents behind? Didn't you search his property when he was accused of murder? Why weren't those things found then?"

The agent flashed his teeth. "We are asking ourselves these questions. This attempt to incriminate a respected presidential aide appears clumsy. And he is missing. Was he taken or did circumstance force him to flee without time to hide evidence he concealed before?"

"My wife has nothing to do with his disappearance and no connection to El Jaguar."

"Perhaps." The man shrugged. "But for many weeks, everywhere she goes there is activity by the Fraternidad, and the Greybecks—her business enemies—die. There have been rumors about HJ Securities. Perhaps El Presidente was mistaken to disregard them."

What was the penalty in Mexico for hitting a federal agent? He'd find out if this joker made one more insinuation about Desi. "My wife was hired by President Montoya to investigate missing antiquities. The trail led her to the Fraternidad de la Garra, and the Greybecks were in bed with the Fraternidad, smuggling drugs and human beings. That's established fact."

Peña inclined his head. "But we are left with many unanswered questions, are we not?"

"You're fishing and not catching a thing. This expedition is over." Tony turned on his heel and strode toward the transport truck.

"Where are you going, señor?" the federal called after him.

"Downtown to get Desi." He didn't slow down or glance back. "Then we're going to pack up and leave Mexico." Behind him, a radio bleeped, and he heard Peña answer. Tony grabbed Matt's arm. "Drive me out of here so you can bring the truck back." They crawled into the cab, Tony on the passenger side, and the other man started the vehicle.

Tony closed his eyes and rubbed his aching shoulder. "Let's go!"

"I can't," Matt said. "He's in the way."

Peña stood in front of the truck, his face a beefy purple.

Tony got out and stalked up to him. "What now?"

"You will come with me to headquarters. We have much to discuss."

"I'm not wasting time—"

"Do not resist." The federal gripped the butt of his side arm. "I am placing you under arrest until this matter is sorted out."

"Take it easy." Tony spread his hands. "Arrest! I'm the one who was almost killed."

"You are the husband—perhaps the accomplice—of a thief. A transport helicopter full of Mexico's treasures has disappeared, along with one of this country's most prominent businessmen...and your wife."

"What?" Terror squeezed Tony's heart.

"El Jaguar has claimed responsibility with the help of one he calls 'the American.' Now will you tell me that your wife is not involved?" The gun whipped from its holster.

Tony swung and connected with Peña's jaw. The agent reeled backward, one arm flailing, the other bringing up his gun.

A kick to the wrist sent the weapon flying. Peña staggered away, gripping his hand.

Tony leaped, and they both hit the ground.

Peña struggled to his knees, but Tony rose up behind him and wrapped an arm around the federal's neck, applying pressure on the jugular.

The man yanked and twisted at Tony's arm, but Tony tightened his hold.

"I'm sorry, Agent Peña," he said into the man's ear, "but I cannot sit in jail until you tire of asking questions the Mexican way. By then, it will be too late for Desi."

The federal went limp. Tony dragged the unconscious man into the shade of stacked bricks. He plucked Peña's extra gun clip from his belt. Then he found the Beretta pistol and stuck it in his waistband. Matt stood by the idling vehicle, eyes huge as dinner plates.

"He'll be all right," Tony said. "Wake up with a headache, that's all."

Matt shook his head. "Oh, man, you are in deeeep doo-doo."

"I'm taking the truck." He headed for the driver's side, Matt on his heels. "If you could wait until I'm out of sight to report the assault on a federal officer and the vehicle theft, I'd appreciate it. But don't wait long, or you'll be accused of helping me." He opened the door.

"Tony, stop." Matt grabbed his arm.

"I have to go."

"Take something." The younger man pulled out his wallet.

"I've got money."

"Bet you don't have this." Matt handed him a dog-eared business card. "Go see this guy. He'll get you out of the country, no questions asked. But you'd better have a few bucks."

Tony took the card. "Does he have a plane?"

"Yep."

"Thanks." Tony stuck the card in his shirt pocket and climbed into the truck.

He drove off, watching Matt wave to him in his side-view mirror. *Adios, amigo.*

Tony zigged and zagged around rubble and through cracked streets. He probably had less than a quarter of an hour to lose himself in the mess that was Mexico City.

Ten minutes later, he parked the truck behind a half-crumpled wall in what used to be a commercial district. He got out and walked until he entered an area where the earthquake had done minimal damage and taxis ran. Climbing into a cab, he showed the driver the card Matt had given him.

"Sí, señor." The driver streaked through breakneck traffic, oblivious to stop signs.

Spine stiff, Tony eyed both sides of the street. Business as usual. No one stared. No one pointed at the man on the lam. Is this the way all fugitives felt?

Every throb of his pulse threatened to snap the facade of control and unleash panic. His Des in the hands of a man like El Jaguar. Tony shut down his imagination. He'd be no good to his wife if he broke. He spun the pilot's business card between his thumb and forefinger.

Leave the country? Not hardly. He had one destination. The Yucatán jungle. And Desi's wild hunch about the underground passage from the Chichén Itzá cenote had better be right. Because if he couldn't find El Jaguar's jungle lair, he might as well let the federales bury him in their deepest dungeon and throw away the key.

Tony ended the tale, and Stevo's long, low whistle sounded in his ear.

"You sure do trouble up good, pard." The man paused and cleared his throat. "But you know Desi is awfully good at taking care of herself, right?"

Tony took a deep breath laden with exhaust fumes and people smells. "What I know is she keeps her angels scrambling. I have to find my wife."

"Based on a thread of a lead?" Stevo snorted. "Why are you on the phone with me? You need to let the office know what's going on."

"No!" Tony's shout turned heads. "They'll tell me to turn myself in," he continued in a more moderate tone. "But I need someone in the States to know the story. Besides, you'll pray."

"You can count on me for that. But don't even suggest keeping this from your mom. You need her prayer group in on the act."

Tony sighed. "Agreed."

"And I'm gonna call Polanski anyway."

"I expected no less. I'm sure she'll notify Cooke, and he'll bellow the roof down for my scalp. But if I don't talk to him, I won't be forced to disobey a direct order."

"Just listen close for directions from the Big Guy. You'll need all the help you can get."

"Don't I know it." Tony hung up, rubbing his shoulder. Would he even be able to handle what he found if—no, *when* he located Desi?

Twenty-Seven

*T*ony swam deeper into the cenote at Chichén Itzá, shoulder throbbing with every stroke. Probably a good thing to stay active, or that king-sized beauty of a bruise would stiffen. Light from the lamp on his forehead played along crevices, but in the murky water everything seemed distorted and tinted with green.

There!

He stuck his hand into an opening, but his fingers met stone. Another false hope. He moved on, blood pounding in his ears, lungs craving air.

Panic welled and his chest muscles tightened. He knew this sensation. Trapped in a liquid nightmare. No way out. Drowning. Can't— *Don't think bad thoughts.* Tony headed upward toward dawn's light. He broke the surface and hauled in air.

He'd been diving since 3:00 a.m. when he snuck onto the property. He couldn't go down again. Wouldn't.

Had to.

Soon workers would arrive for their shifts, and he'd have to hide until evening. Too long for Desi to wait when she needed him yesterday.

"¡Hola, gringo!" The shout came from above.

A uniformed state cop stared down at him. The judicial pulled out his gun. Tony gasped in air and dived. His last chance. If he didn't find the passage, he might as well not come up.

Pain stung his arm, and the water went pink in the area of his bicep. The officer had good aim. Tony changed trajectory and rammed the wall before he could stop.

He went still. A mild current pulled at him near his flippers. He moved down, and an opening gaped before him. He would have shouted if he could.

Tony plunged through. Walls hugged him as he forged on...and on. His flipper strokes weakened. Blackness edged his vision. Lethargy stole his thoughts. Part of him acknowledged the tunnel had widened. He drifted upward, and his snorkel tugged. That meant something.

Oh, yeah. Surface.

Tony blew out the little carbon dioxide left in his lungs then chanced a breath—his last if water entered. Air gurgled through the poorly cleared snorkel and teased his lungs. Fighting the need to choke, Tony blew again then inhaled pure, blessed O_2. He lifted his head but hit rock.

Okay, he'd found a couple of inches of air at the top of the tunnel. Hopefully, it'd last until he found where the underground stream came out. Greybeck must be Hercules to swim this tunnel with no snorkel or flippers, but then the guy already knew where the opening was and hadn't wasted most of the oxygen in his lungs looking for it.

The stream level dropped, and his head came out of the water, but the light beam dimmed. Great time to lose the battery. The water went shallow, and he crawled. The light winked out, and he moved on in the dark, the sound of his breathing magnified by sightlessness.

Unh!

His head hit something solid. Tony sat back, rubbing his noggin. He reached upward and found ceiling. To one side he touched a wall. A wave in the other direction met open air. He crawled on dry rock at a gentle upward slope, and then reached a crest and started down.

A rushing sound came from up ahead. More water. An underground river must join this passage from another direction.

Tony stopped. Trusting himself to this new water source could be fatal. He might have missed a passage in the dark—one that Greybeck knew about but he didn't. That was a big maybe. He could waste a lot of time backtracking to find something that didn't exist.

Big breath and full speed ahead.

The rush became a roar, spray splashed in his face, and then the stream snatched him, tumbled him, threw him. He burst into open air, flipped, and rocketed downward.

Tony hit water headfirst. Pain stabbed his sinuses. He went deep, fought for control, and swam toward the light above. His head broke the surface.

Holy mackerel!

Water sparkled—a vast, underground lake that seemed to have no end. The walls glittered. What? How? The light must come from somewhere.

He looked up. A wide beam speared from an opening in the cave roof. He followed it to a patch of shore. An odd-shaped craft rested on the sand. Tony swam toward it.

He splashed out of the water and then stared at the gray tube as tall as he was and twice as long. Submersible—miniature submarine. The river probably flowed all the way to the Atlantic. This baby could move a lot of drugs, antiquities, or people. Intriguing, but the ladder built into the far wall interested him more right now. The rungs led up to the hole in the top of the cave. Dollars to donuts the opening wasn't far from El Jaguar's lair…and Desi.

He removed his flippers, then stripped off snorkel, mask, and wet suit pants. The dry pack at his waist contained the gun and clip taken from Peña, chinos, a shirt, and tennis shoes. He tore a strip from the bottom of his shirt and bound the wound on his bicep. He'd have another scar to add to his collection. Nice souvenir of his swim in the ancient cenote. He changed, slipped the Beretta into his waistband, stuck the clip in his pocket, and started up the ladder.

Scents of rotting undergrowth and exotic flowers carried to his nostrils. He poked his head above ground and scanned the forest. No guards in evidence. He'd have to chance it.

Tony scrambled out of the hole and sprinted to the tree line. A faint path caught his eye, and he moved at a slow trot over matted grasses. A large animal—horse or mule—had left dried droppings here and there.

The scent of cigarette smoke alerted him to human presence. Tony halted. No cry of alarm sounded. He slipped into the forest, placing each foot as if he trod on rotting boards. *Where are you, gangsta?* In the jungle, the red flare of an inhaled cigarette answered him.

Ten feet away, a man leaned against a tree, M16 rifle cradled in the crook of an arm. His gaze was on the path, but the slouched shoulders and bent knee screamed boredom.

Tony eased behind a tree trunk, stooped, and picked up a small rock. A quick toss and the stone thumped onto the path.

The guard jerked to attention and tossed away his cigarette. *"¿Quien está?"* A simple enough Spanish phrase that Tony understood. "Who is there?" He chucked another stone. The guard rushed forward in a crouch, teeth bared.

Tony rammed him from behind, and the guard sprawled to the ground. Knees buried in the man's back, Tony brought the butt of the Beretta down on the back of the guard's head. A melon-crunch sounded, and the man went limp, but still breathing. Using the guard's belt, Tony bound the man's hands behind his back, then pulled off his pants and secured his feet. A strip from the downed gang member's shirt provided a gag.

Tony grabbed the guard's rifle, slung the strap around his shoulder, and continued along the path. A mule's bray brought him up short. He crouched and hugged the tree line as he crept forward. The forest thinned and gave way to empty sky. Tony got down on his belly and army-crawled over rock to the edge of a cliff.

About thirty feet below, a corral held a dozen mules. A man forked hay from a stack outside the corral into a feed bin inside the enclosure. The mules crowded in. A second man stepped out of what must be a storage shed and called to the first in a tongue that was not Spanish. Mayan? The first guy jabbed his pitchfork into the haystack and followed the second one down a path past a wooden building with a moss-covered, sheet-metal roof. A tall antenna jabbed from the peak of the roof. Communications device? Tony's heart rate quickened.

The men disappeared into the forest. Tony backed away from the cliff's edge and stood. The stony ground didn't betray a path like the grass had. He'd have to guess which direction led to the way down. He turned right, but after a few paces his belly knotted like when God was telling him he'd taken a wrong turn. Okay, left then. Soon the slope pitched downward, and trampled grasses revealed he was on the right track. *Thank You, Lord.*

The ground leveled, and the path veered toward the drop-off where a winding track angled toward the ground below. Except for the mules, no sound or movement came from the area. He hustled down and loped to the rear of the metal-roofed building. The structure had no windows. No way to tell what or who was inside.

He peered around the corner. Insects buzzed and grass waved. Beretta held close to his chest, muzzle upward, Tony crept forward in the shade of the building. He hardly breathed as his ears strained for any human sound. A few more feet and he came to a door. Back pressed against the wall, he tried the knob. It turned. He let out a long, silent exhale.

Either someone was in there, or these gangsters had an open-door policy. This was the sort of building where they'd store valuables—

things or people. Maybe Desi was locked in some miserable crate. Blood burned through his veins.

He cracked open the door. No voices, but rustling, followed by a grunt, and then hammering. Tony slipped in the door under cover of the noise. Wooden crates varying from microwave to medium television size lined freestanding shelves. Doubtful if the boxes contained appliances, but neither could they contain human beings. Someone was packing for a trip.

The dim lighting and the shelves didn't allow him to see the source of the noise. Someone yelped, and the banging abruptly quit, followed by a curse in Spanish. One man. No evidence of other human presence, but no reason to think Desi couldn't be here.

Tony eased across the dirt floor. The hammering started again, and he moved boldly. The door banged open, and Tony darted behind a shelf, heart thumping.

"Luis," someone called, and the hammering ceased. The man at the door barked words.

Tony understood the words *El Jaguar* and "¡Ándale, apúrate!"— come on, hurry up. He swallowed frustration at his poor command of the language. A man, presumably Luis, moved into Tony's line of sight. Both men went out the door, and it slammed shut. A key rattled in the lock, then silence.

Moving on, Tony came to a half-constructed crate with a hammer and a can of nails on the floor beside it. A groan brought his head around.

His scalp prickled. Desi? But that was no feminine moan. Tony inched forward. His gaze passed over a ham radio on a table against the wall—the reason for the roof antenna—and then landed on a barred cage. A man knelt inside an area too small to stand in or stretch out.

Tony moved closer. The prisoner's face was a mass of bruises. One eye was swollen shut, and dried blood crusted a cheek. Around his neck hung Desi's medallion. "Esteban Corona?"

"Sí. And you are?" The man spoke in English thickened by his puffy mouth.

"Tony Lucano. Desiree's husband."

Corona gripped the bars. "Is she with you?"

"She's here, but not with me."

"You must get her away."

"That's the plan. I'll let you out first." Tony tugged the heavy padlock on the door.

"The key is over there." Corona pointed to a wall rack that held a set of keys.

Moments later, Tony helped the aide crawl out of the cage. The man swayed, and Tony supported him to the chair by the radio. "You know how to work one of these things?"

Corona smiled, or rather, the less swollen side of his mouth did. "I had a set as a boy."

"Technology's changed, but see if you can figure this out and call for help."

"Where are we?" Corona's one open eye blinked up at him.

"A few miles from Chichén Itzá. That's the best I know. They'll search by air. Tell them to watch for a corral full of mules, plus a couple of buildings in a clearing. I figure the rest of the camp is nearby and probably appears to be a primitive Mayan village."

"Sí. This I have seen. You will find the village a few hundred yards up the path." Corona flicked the On button. Lights blinked. "Battery powered. I can do this."

"Send your transmission and get out of here. Crawl if you have to, and hide in the forest."

The aide grabbed Tony's wrist. "El Jaguar is Fernando Vidal, a family enemy." Corona touched the medallion on his chest. "This is a symbol of our mutual shame, so I could not bring myself to claim it, intending to leave the past buried. Unfortunately, Vidal has chosen the course of vengeance. I heard him and his son Salvador talking. They plan to take most of these artifacts, but leave the rest to be found with my dead body. It is to seem like I was El Jaguar, and a power struggle within the gang led to my death. Salvador is an officer with the Mérida policía. He will make sure the investigation leads to such a conclusion."

Tony snorted. "Clever, but an intragang war leaves more than the outgoing leader dead."

"Vidal and his son, the turncoat officer, are going to shoot some, maybe all of the others in the village."

Tony's gut roiled. *Including Desi?* "I need to get my wife."

Corona inclined his head. *"Vaya con Dios."*

Tony jerked a nod and strode for the door. He turned the deadbolt latch and peered outside. The way was clear outside, and Tony hustled up the path the mule handlers had taken. *I'm close, Des. Can you feel me?*

—⁓—

Limbs heavy, mind sluggish, Desiree made herself take a bite of the eggs and ham Juanita set before her. Thankfully, she was the only one at the table. She didn't even want to know where everyone else was. Well, she did, but only so she could avoid them.

The food tasted good on the tongue but sat poorly in her stomach. She had to eat. She'd need the strength for—what? No escape plan had miraculously materialized in the sleepless hours of the night. But murderous fantasies galore? Those she could do.

Vidal could have used his influence to help the Maya, but he corrupted their youth instead. He preyed upon the poor, Mayan and Hispanic. He killed. He stole. He deceived. He lied. Desi went still with her fork stabbed into a piece of ham.

So why did she believe him when he claimed Tony was dead?

Tingles washed down her body. Didn't she have more faith in God's protection than that? She set the fork on the plate. Bad things happened to believers. She should know. Her father was murdered. Her home had been blown sky high. Tony lost a spleen and might lose his job.

But he beat the odds and lived through the accident. No way did he survive the worst nature could dish out, and then fall victim to the schemes of a dirt-sucking worm. Desi stuffed a bite into her mouth and chewed like she was taking a chunk out of Vidal's hide.

Tony, you're alive, and you're coming for me. I'm going to believe that until I see you or gasp my dying breath.

Ravenous, she gobbled the rest of her breakfast. Juanita beamed over the clean plate.

—m—

From his perch on a tree limb several yards up a hillside, Tony studied the village. Many huts and trees covered the grounds. Unlikely an aircraft could land here. Probably the reason for the mules. The inaccessibility made the village less suspect for anyone looking for El Jaguar. Who would guess the transport lay underground?

Men in jeans and T-shirts moved around, stowing gear in packs. Only a few were armed. One of the gunmen was a tall, lean man who sent people scurrying wherever he went. Salvador?

The lean, mean one stopped in front of a gray-haired man who wore a suit and stood with legs apart, hands clasped behind his back. Fernando Vidal? The younger one said something and pointed to a brick house under the far tree line. The older one waved him away. Salvador obeyed, but not without snarling something over his shoulder that made Vidal stiffen.

Interesting. Perhaps a younger jungle cat was making a play for authority. The intragang war scheme might be more real than put on.

Someone stepped out of a cinder-block building next to the brick one. Clayton Greybeck. No mistaking the beefy build and blond hair. Tony punched down the growl that rose in his throat.

No women in sight. Where was Des? Had he guessed wrong? Maybe she hadn't been brought here. His gut squeezed.

No, wait! A figure dressed in a skirt and blouse stepped out of the cinder-block building and watched Greybeck stroll toward the brick structure. He couldn't see her face, but she had long black hair and appeared unkempt. Not Desi. Tony's shoulders slumped.

A door opened in the brick house, and another woman stepped out. She also wore a skirt and blouse, but her hair was short and sleek, and she carried herself like a princess. Des!

If he had wings, he'd swoop over there, scoop her up, and be gone before anyone knew what happened. His heart did it anyway, even if the rest of him was stuck in a tree. *I'm here, darlin'. I won't let them—Hey!*

What did Greybeck think he was doing? The man backed Desi against the building, put a hand on her hip, and leaned his head toward hers. Kissing her? Sure seemed that way. A snarl popped out before he could bottle it.

And what was up with Desi? The woman he knew would rake Greybeck's face with her nails, but she stood there. Kissing him back? Sure looked that way. Fury reddened his vision.

———※———

Desi scrounged up every scrap of self-control and refrained from ramming her knee into Clayton's groin. He reeked of cheap perfume. Three guesses where he'd been, and the first two didn't count.

"Let's make this a good act, Des," he whispered in her ear. "The Jaguar is watching."

"And you're doing your part to fool him by paying a visit next door."

Clayton nuzzled her neck. "We'll just keep him guessing about how virile I am."

Desi pasted herself to the wall. "You're about to lose it if you don't back off."

His weight mashed her against the brick. "A frown from me, and Vidal will give you a room in the pleasure house. The men are very attentive to a new girl."

Desi shuddered, and Clayton smiled. "I'm your white knight, babe. Don't forget it." He pressed his mouth to hers and strolled away.

She stalked to the washhouse and scrubbed her lips with soap. So much for her little stab of sympathy toward him last night. Clayton Greybeck was the Heisman Trophy–winner of jerks.

Tony, where are you? Now would be the time to show up with a few hundred federales.

—⁂—

Tony dropped to the ground and leaned his forehead against the tree trunk. The bark bit his flesh. Clatters and indistinct voices carried from the village. The rain forest rustled in the warm breeze, and tropical birds sang like daylight would never have enough hours. Gradually, Tony's heart stopped careening around in his chest, and his mind cleared.

Was he some kind of jealous idiot to leap to the worst conclusion about the woman whose pedestal he'd happily polish for the rest of his life? *Get real, Lucano. Your wife was* not *kissing Clayton Greybeck.* However, what that lowlife was doing to *her* required a reckoning.

Tony took a step. Shouts came from the upper end of the village. If he were still up on the branch he could see what caused them, but he could guess. Someone had discovered Esteban Corona was loose and had maybe even found the guard he'd clobbered in the forest.

One all-important question: Did Corona get that SOS out on the radio?

—⁓—

Angry shouts drew Desi out of the washhouse. The camp had gone wild. Men threw things down and raced toward the center of the village.

A hand grabbed Desi's elbow. "Clayt—" She stopped on a gasp, staring into Salvador's cold eyes. He propelled her toward the center of the village where Vidal paced in a cursing rage. Desi's gaze swept past him to another man who sagged in the grip of a pair of gun-toting gang members. "Señor Corona." She hurried forward, but Salvador jerked her to a halt.

The old gentleman lifted his head and sent her a weak smile.

Desi took in his condition, then glared up at the younger Vidal. "Animals!"

Clayton stepped up. "What's going on here?"

Salvador's gaze fastened on his father. "You have wasted valuable men and resources to kill the U.S. agent, and still he finds us."

Vidal's chin jutted. "You do not know it is him."

Desi looked from one ruddy face to the other. Tony? Hope bubbled.

"I can find out." Salvador pulled her close and pressed his gun to Desi's temple. "Lucano! Come here, unarmed, or your wife dies. I will not ask twice. You have ten seconds."

"Lucano's dead." Clayton jerked his head toward Vidal. "Stop this insanity."

"Shut up." El Jaguar sneered. "Just because we need you to operate our escape transportation doesn't mean you couldn't do it with a few broken ribs."

Clayton went white, and his chin dimple flexed.

Salvador's gun barrel dug into Desi's skin. Her heart bumped and skittered as the countdown began. *Tony, please be out there. No, Tony, don't give yourself up.* She closed her eyes. *God, please don't let Salvador shoot me.* Sweat beaded on her upper lip.

"Eight…nine…t—"

"Wait! I'm on my way. Takes time to get down there."

"Tony-y-y." The word sighed from Desi's throat. She sagged like Señor Corona.

Tony emerged from the forest, hands clasped behind his head.

Desi drank him in with her eyes. Disheveled. Dirty. A bloody rag around his arm. And scruffy with beard shadow. If a guy could be gorgeous, he was. His gaze captured hers. Strength returned to her limbs, and she straightened, chin high.

He stopped ten paces away. All eyes were riveted on him, but he smiled for her alone. "Hey there, darlin', you didn't think I'd let you finish our honeymoon without me, did you?"

Twenty-Eight

*T*ony pulled his gaze from his wife and locked stares with the one who held her. A dirty cop. Nothing he despised worse. Tony's contempt was mirrored back at him in the other man's face. Cold certainty gripped him. One of them would not leave this jungle alive.

Vidal stepped forward. "You have a gift for survival, Señor Lucano, but I am afraid you have made a fatal mistake."

Tony met hostile stares from armed men—Mayans, Hispanics, mixed bloods—all twenties or younger, every eye without mercy, pity, or hope. The look was the same in the middle of a Mexican jungle as in the jungle that was New York or Los Angeles or Boston. "Yeah, I see. El Jaguar's lair, a poor Mayan village. Impressive."

The elder gang leader reddened. The young rival chuckled and shoved Desi toward Clayton Greybeck. He grabbed at her, but she smacked him across the cheek and danced away.

"Everyone kindly keep their paws off me. Except for my husband, of course."

Greybeck stepped toward Desi. Tony lowered his hands, fists forming. Salvador and others raised their guns.

"What is going on here?" A skinny, middle-aged woman in fine clothes marched up.

"Enough!" Vidal's roar halted movement.

The aging jungle cat had authority left in him after all. Tony put his hands back in the air. He stole a glance toward Señor Corona. A simple nod would let him know help was on the way. Corona shrugged. Not the answer Tony was looking for.

Vidal studied Tony, then nodded toward Salvador. "Shoot him. This time, I want to see it done with my own eyes."

Tony held his breath.

"No!" Desi screamed.

Salvador lowered his weapon. "Let Greybeck do it."

Anger, frustration, and despair flowed across Clayton's face, emotions Tony understood from any man who'd deceived himself into thinking he had Desi and then discovered he never would.

The man's shoulders squared. "No problem. But not with a gun. I'm going to break him in half." He flexed his arms. "It'll be a fair fight. Do you hear me, Des?"

She went pale under his stare. "Don't do this."

"His death is on you, woman."

"You miss the point, as usual. Tony'll wipe the ground with you."

Tony's sore body questioned the thought. She saw what happened last time he and Greybeck tangled and knew the poor shape he was in before the arm wound and bum shoulder.

Vidal waved a dismissive hand. "We do not have time for this. Lucano may have alerted the federales to our location. We shoot him and we leave. Now!"

Several of the men nodded, but Salvador fired several bullets toward the sky. "If Lucano had communicated with the federales, they would be here."

"But the radio—"

"Was all but dead, because someone packed many fine clothes, but forgot to bring the fresh battery." Salvador glared at the skinny woman, who flushed and backed away. "I say we have a fine fight to send us off." He raised a fist. *¡Lucha!*

"¡Lucha! Lucha!" The men picked up the cry of "Fight, fight!" as they formed a ring.

Hands shoved Tony into the center. Greybeck grinned, circling him and warming up his arms with hugging motions like a wrestler. Tony turned in place, watching for a tell that would signal a charge. Every ache in his body screamed weakness, even the surgical scar, but he couldn't listen. Didn't dare. *Lord, Your Word says You give strength to the weak. If ever that Scripture needed literal fulfillment, now would be a good time.*

Greybeck's shoulder dropped, and he came in fast and hard. Tony pivoted on one foot and the man missed him, but flung a stiff-arm as he went by. The blow caught Tony on the bruised shoulder and staggered him. Pain blurred his vision.

He righted himself in time to catch a head-butt in the stomach. His belly muscles spasmed, air whooshed from his lungs, and he slammed to the ground on his back. Men cheered. A huge shadow loomed. Tony rolled away, and Greybeck's pounce missed.

They hauled themselves to their feet, eying each other, panting. Or rather, Tony panted against waves of nausea. Greybeck seemed hardly fazed.

The man feinted left and then struck right. Tony dodged the blow, the wind of the fist singing in his ear, and then whirled into a side kick that caught Greybeck on the left kidney. The man reeled away, clutching his side. Onlookers hissed and catcalled. Desi cheered.

Greybeck roared and charged, grabbing for him with massive arms. Tony dropped to his knees and punched both fists upward. He struck the man's bladder, and Greybeck's feet left the ground. He flipped over the top of Tony's head. About like bench-pressing two hundred–plus pounds in a split second. Every molecule felt the strain.

Tony struggled upright. Greybeck lay whimpering and clutching his belly. He'd wet himself. Tony stared at his opponent, brow knotted.

Was that all the fight this guy had in him? Disappointing in a way, but not surprising in a man who was all flash and no backbone.

The crowd went silent, then erupted into a cheer—fickle as any mob.

Tony's gaze found Desi's. The love in her eyes seeped into his pores better than a hot-oil rub. He went to her, and nobody stopped him from giving her the kiss he'd been saving for the moment he found her. They weren't safe yet, might not leave the jungle, but they were together.

The sound of a single pair of clapping hands drew them apart.

Lips curled in a snarl, Vidal glared at them. "You remind me of what was stolen from me when Angelina died." He turned toward Salvador. "Shoot them both."

The young man grinned. "Yes, *mi papá*, now is the time for bullets." He fired a spray, and El Jaguar's chest fountained red.

Tony shoved Desi through the crowd, grabbed her hand, and ran for the nearest hut. Automatic fire burst out behind them. Tony pushed Desi ahead of him, expecting to take a hit at any moment. They made the cover of the hut, and Tony glanced back.

Unarmed men, mostly Mayans, fled in every direction. Bullets chopped them down. The skinny woman already lay in a pool of blood. A pair of gunmen herded Greybeck toward the path to the mule pens. Ah, yes, had to spare the submersible driver—for the moment.

Where was Corona? No opportunity to search for him. "Let's go."

They raced for the rain forest, zigzagging from the cover of one hut or tree to the next. A bullet zinged past Tony's ear. He ducked and pressed Desi into a crouch as they ran.

Behind a hut at the edge of the village, Tony pulled Desi up short. He pointed toward the forest. "We need to get to that tree with the crooked trunk." With someone spraying bullets at them, the chances of making the distance were nil. "You go first. I'll distract the shooter."

"No, Tony, I—"

"Señor and Señora Lucano, do not make me hunt you. There is no chance of escape."

Salvador. And close.

An open window beckoned. "I'm going inside and making noise to attract him. When I yell or you hear bullets, you run. A Beretta plus a clip and an M16 rifle are under that tree. Grab them and run as far and as fast as you can. Eventually you'll come to another village, an honest one. They'll help you get to safety."

Her lips trembled, but she nodded. Tony smiled into the beautiful face he would probably never see again this side of heaven, then climbed into the dark hut.

—◦◦◦—

"I am getting impatient."

Desi jerked at the lash of Salvador's voice.

"In here," Tony said. "Come and get us."

A rattle of gunfire answered. Desi ran, trying not to imagine bullets tearing through the walls of the hut, spattering furniture, ripping into Tony... Her legs churned faster. No time for zigging and zagging. If someone had her in his sights, she was dead anyway.

The tree loomed closer, closer. More automatic fire burst behind her, but farther away. The other side of the village.

She darted behind the trunk, and her foot kicked something hard that skimmed into the grass. She dove after it and came up with the Beretta. Then she grabbed the rifle. Forget looking for the clip. Salvador's men were wrapping up the last of the massacre. Bodies lay everywhere. Soon the gunmen would converge on Tony if he wasn't already dead.

A crash came from the hut, then a spurt of bullets and men's shouts. One of them Tony's.

Desi ran toward the hut. Her breath rasped. Blood pounded in her ears. *Please, God, let me be in time.* She tripped on a stone, stumbled, righted herself, and ran on, skirts flapping.

She reached the window to hear the smack of a fist connecting with flesh. *Thank You, Jesus.* Desi looked in the window but could make out little in the dimness.

Two tall figures grappled and grunted beside an upended table. A gun spurted bullets and flame toward the ceiling. Which one was Tony? Both men were dark haired and well muscled.

One of them spat a curse in Spanish. The one on the left.

Desi poked the Beretta through the window, but her body shook as she panted from the breakneck sprint. Who said she could shoot anyway? She never had. But she would. For Tony.

The men staggered apart. One fired the gun wildly, struggling for balance, while the other dove behind the table.

"Tony, catch!" Desi tossed the pistol.

Salvador aimed his rifle as Tony snagged the gun in midair, turned, and fired. El Jaguar's traitorous son slammed against the wall. The M16 dropped from nerveless fingers, and his limp body slid to the dirt floor.

Tony met her at the window. "Thank you, disobedient wife." He climbed out as shouts and hurrying feet drew close to the hut they hid behind.

"I don't care to end it trapped like a rat." Tony gave her the Beretta and took the rifle. "No point in running. Let's take a few with us." He winked at her.

She mouthed a kiss, and gripped her gun with both hands. Shoot? Oh, yes. A time to kill. A time to die. Eternity to embrace.

They stepped forward as armed men poured from the tree line.

Desi blinked. What kind of craziness? They wore wet suits, and swim goggles dangled around their necks.

Tony bumped her, and she noticed he'd dropped his weapon and put his hands in the air. She did the same. A goggled man stopped in front of them, gun trained, while the others raced into the village. Bedlam erupted. Shrill cries of "Don't shoot. I surrender," mingled with fleeing feet, a spatter of gunfire, and shrieks of the wounded and dying. Finally, silence.

Minutes passed in barked communication between federales combing the village. Then orders came for them to be taken to the brick house. Swallowing bile, Desi averted her eyes from the bloody bodies littering the ground. Great stuff for future nightmares.

Almost to their destination, Desi looked up to catch a glimpse of Juanita's skirts disappearing through the door of the women's building next door, where the sound of feminine weeping carried on the now-still air. Thank goodness, the kind woman was spared. She would comfort the frightened ladies.

Desi followed Tony inside El Jaguar's headquarters building. A man sat at the head of the table. He rose when they entered.

"Agent Peña," Tony said, a note of caution in his voice.

"Agent Lucano. You may both put your hands down." He crooked a finger for them to approach.

Tony preceded her, and the Mexican agent stepped forward and slugged him in the jaw. Tony staggered and hit the wall.

Desi shrieked and ran to him.

Rubbing his chin, Tony wrapped an arm around her. "It's okay, Des. I had that coming."

"You most certainly did not. He should be thanking you, not hitting you." She glared at Agent Peña. "I will report this to the highest authority in your country."

"Leave it alone. Please!"

"But—"

"He gives you good advice, señora. Señor Lucano and I must come to an understanding." He transferred his gaze to Tony. "I will receive the credit for discovering El Jaguar's lair, no?"

"Sounds like a good deal to me."

"Then you and I have no further problem. Sit, por favor." He pointed to a pair of chairs.

Tony pulled one out for her, and Desi folded herself into it, still more than half tempted to clobber a federal. Then Desi noted a bruise on Peña's jaw that would roughly match the one Tony would show pretty soon. She bit her lip and settled back as her husband sat beside her.

Agent Peña folded his hands in front of him. "I have decided you are not in league with El Jaguar, Señor Lucano. You left a trail that a child could follow. Using your credit card to rent the snorkeling equipment? Tsk, tsk." The man put his elbows on the table and steepled his fingers. "However, as to your wife's part in this business, I am unclear."

Desi opened her mouth. Tony's heel squashed her little toe. She swallowed a yelp.

"She is equally innocent," Tony said.

"Of course." Peña sat back and smiled.

Desi sent the Mexican agent a narrow-eyed glare, which he ignored. The man was enjoying himself, and she'd swear off orange soda for life if he didn't know more than he was letting on, or else he'd insist on interrogating them separately.

"Por favor." The federal nodded to Tony. "Give me your version of the story."

Tony explained, and Peña grew more and more sober. "So where is Señor Corona?"

"We don't know."

Peña arched an eyebrow at Desi.

"I hope Señor Corona is all right. I haven't seen him since the shooting started. Did you capture Clayton Greybeck?"

"The husky blond gringo?"

"Sí. *Un bandido americano muy malo.*" Desi bared her teeth.

Peña chuckled and glanced at Tony. "You have your hands full with this one, eh?"

Tony slipped his arm across her shoulder. "Consider me a fortunate man."

They exchanged a guy-grin.

Should she hug her husband or pay him back a toe-stomp? "Clayton can tell you a great deal about antiquities gone missing."

Peña's eyes widened. "We will question Señor Greybeck most closely."

"Clayton deserves your attention. And those poor women next door need to be restored to their families. One of them is American. Juanita, a staff member from the Sanchez household, should get a medal and a well-paid job. Tony and I crave food, clean clothes, baths, and rest—not necessarily in that order. Plus, my husband needs medical treatment. He's gone through an accident and major surgery, and now he's been shot and mauled...and punched."

Peña nodded and rose. "I will organize matters." He stepped outside.

Desi slumped. With adrenaline fading, a nap in her husband's arms sounded heavenly.

Tony ruffled her hair. "Actually, Des, I ache all over, could eat a cow and sleep for a year, but I feel good. Strong. Like something's changed on the inside that makes all the difference. Now I know I'll make it."

"Qualify with your bureau physicals?"

"Yes, but what I really know is that it doesn't matter. I can be Tony Lucano with or without 'Special Agent' in front of my name."

"*Supervisory* Special Agent. But the only thing that counts with me is that you're señor to my señora."

Tony's gaze meshed with hers. She read warmth, amusement, and the kind of love that could keep a girl in lifelong tingles. "That's a forever deal, darlin'. You can count on it."

EPILOGUE

*D*esi fitted tall candles into silver holders on the dining room table. She stepped back and took in the china place settings for two, the sterling silverware, the cloth napkins in silver filigree rings, and the long-stemmed goblets. All wedding and shower presents.

A rich, tomatoey aroma wafted from the kitchen. Desi smiled. She didn't cook like Tony's mother, but she was getting the hang of a few easy things—like macaroni casserole.

A firm tread came up the hall, and Tony walked in. "What's the occasion?"

"Can't a wife fix a candlelight dinner for her husband? Or has the honeymoon worn off in three months?"

He grinned. "Not hardly, babe. I'll get matches." He headed for the kitchen.

Desi watched him move. She could do that all day and be content as a stroked cat. Fresh from the shower after a long workout at the gym, he looked yummier than the dish in the oven. She sniffed the air where he'd passed by. Smelled good too.

Candles lit, food steaming on the table, they sat down to eat. Tony blessed the meal, and they filled their plates. Desi helped herself to extra carrot sticks but went easy on the salt.

"Healthy girl," Tony said.

"That's me." She spread her napkin on her lap. "The office any better today?"

"Four walls and a desk."

Desi laughed. "That bad, huh?"

"At least I'm in the door." He tucked a bite into his mouth. "This is good, babe."

"Glad to hear it."

"Another thing you'll be glad to hear. Today, I nailed down a few loose ends on the case against those guys we arrested in the hold of that smuggling ship, and I suddenly realized what El Jaguar's girlfriend, Angelina Hernández, was carrying down that gangplank."

"What?" Desi sipped mineral water from her goblet.

"What major item is unaccounted for among the antiquities taken by Clayton Greybeck?"

Desi sucked in a breath. "The crown of Pakal? But why bring it to Boston?"

"That's what I asked myself. I had Dell do a little electronic trolling to find out who might have been in town at the time with an interest in such an item for collateral in a drug deal. Turns out one of the big we-know-it-but-can't-prove-it guys from a Brazilian cartel was here for a political conference on U.S.–South American relations, of all things. I took the findings to Bernard Cooke, and he authorized a dive operation. They start tomorrow."

"The crown is heavy. It would have sunk and stayed put. This is awesome. Great job, hon. The people of Mexico will be thrilled if we can return one of their best treasures."

"Yeah." Tony frowned.

"Oh, sweetheart. I know you'd love to be on site when they find it. I'm aching for you to get back out into the field too. Have they scheduled your fitness exams?"

"Three weeks."

Desi laid down her fork. "Already?"

Tony stared at his plate, lips compressed.

"Don't you think you'll pass?"

He quirked a smile. "I'll pass. I'm the one who asked for soonest possible."

"Then why the 'I don't know how to tell Desi this' look?"

"I'll be tested at Quantico, and then they want me to stay there."

"In Virginia? But what about your supervisor position here?"

"Polanski does an all-star job. It's not fair the way she's had to step up, then step down."

Desi crunched a carrot between her teeth. "So we're moving. I get that, but that's not what bugs me."

"It's not? I thought—"

"Don't assume, buster. First rule of marriage. Well, one of the first rules. I'm about ready to march into the ASAC's office and set him straight. You deserve a promotion, not a demotion."

Tony tilted his head back and laughed. "It's not a demotion, Des. Though I'd like to be a fly on the wall when you give the assistant special agent in charge a piece of your mind." He leaned forward. "They want me to teach martial arts and organized crime classes for a year. Then the hint is I'll be transferred a few miles north."

Desi screamed and clapped a hand over her mouth.

He nodded. "D.C. office. A supervisor is retiring from the Art Crime Team. I might fit pretty well there, eh? Especially with my own private art consultant wearing my wedding band."

She leaped up and threw her arms around his neck. He drew her onto his lap. "Congratulations, Mr. Capital-of-the-U.S. Agent. And while you teach all those eager young recruits at Quantico, I'll transform the Washington HJ Securities office into the headquarters."

"Is that going to cause a problem for you and Max?"

She kissed him and smiled. "Maxine Webb is my dearest friend, and she'll have the option to work out of the Boston office, which will remain open, or out of Washington. Of course, I want her close to me, but she has her husband to think about in a Massachusetts prison. I suspect she'll choose Boston, and she and I will keep on being as close as sisters."

"Speaking of relatives," Tony said, "do you remember what I told you about the Lucano kid in California who wants to be an agent?"

"The young man in a wheelchair?"

"I took your advice and e-mailed him the facts about qualifying as an agent. Didn't deter him a bit. In fact, an amazing thing happened. His mom called me today. Her son has improved markedly, and she thinks it's because he has a concrete goal."

"Like you do with your physical training?"

"Right. They want to bring him out here for a tour of the bureau office. I told them to come ahead. Is that all right?"

"That's wonderful."

"For my fractured family, it's a huge step. For the first time I've got a little hope that my mom's dream of reconciliation will happen."

"Believe it." Desi hopped off his lap. "But you're not the only one with news." From the counter, she picked up a small box stamped "Mexico City."

Brow furrowed, Tony lifted the lid. "Your medallion."

"A replica. The Corona family is keeping the original, and they're burying the woman's remains found in New Mexico, even though she's actually a Sanchez and not a blood relative."

"Good." Tony set the box on the table, and the faux emeralds twinkled in the candlelight.

Desi sighed. "I still think about Señor Corona."

"I'm glad they found his body."

"Injured as he was…to try to ride through the jungle on a mule to get help." Desi swallowed a lump. "He reminds me of you."

"Why? I don't have a mustache."

"Oh, you!" She swatted his arm. "And they haven't declared you a national hero either, though they should. Pretty ironic, huh?"

"That I haven't got a medal?"

"That Señor Corona gets the honor Vidal schemed and murdered to get for himself."

"Pretty sharp there, darlin'. Must be why I married you."

"One of many reasons. Besides, you kinda like me."

"There's that." Tony pulled her close. "How about we leave the dishes?"

She wiggled out of his arms and sashayed toward the living room. "One more surprise, sweetheart. You'll like it."

"Lead on, babe."

She took a DVD case from the coffee table and handed it to him.

"A classic movie? That's no surprise, coming from you."

"Not just any classic movie. *It's a Wonderful Life*."

Tony laughed. "That's a Christmas show. It's June."

"So? I don't intend for us to watch the whole thing. Just a teensy part." Desi clicked on the television, and then settled on the sofa. Tony draped an arm around her and drew her head to his shoulder. She found the scene she wanted and pushed Play.

Jimmy Stewart as George Bailey walks into the bedroom of his home in Bedford Falls. His wife, Mary, played by Donna Reed, is in bed, apparently asleep. Shoulders slumped, George removes his tie as he looks at a picture drawn by Mary before they were husband and wife. The caption says "George Lassos the Moon" and shows a man holding a rope tied around the moon. Frowning, George starts unbuttoning his shirt. Mary sits up, too perky to have been asleep. The couple exchanges a few words, and then Mary puts her face close to her husband and announces, "George lassos stork." Flummoxed, Stewart delivers his classic stammering, and then—

Desi stopped the movie with George's mouth hanging open. "Do you remember what he says next?"

"Sorry. You'll have to let me hear it."

Desi pushed the button.

George's big-eyed amazement continues with an exclamation. "Mary, are you on the nest?" She bobs her head like a regal bird. "Mm-hmm."

Desi froze the picture. Next to her, Tony had ceased to breathe. She snuck a peek at his face. His mouth had flopped open big enough to fit an ostrich egg.

A slow smile grew. "Desi, are you on the nest?"

She bobbed her head. "Won't Mama Gina be thrilled? With a grand-baby coming, I know she'll want to relocate to whatever city we—" Tony's whoop about cracked her eardrums. "Help!" she squeaked as he scooped her off the sofa and whirled her around.

Much later, snuggled in bed, Desi rubbed Tony's arm that lay across her waist. "I can hardly wait to have a little boy just like his daddy."

Tony propped himself up on his elbow and patted her flat tummy. "Sorry, darlin'. We're having a girl."

Desi laughed. "You sound so definite, Mr. Know-It-All."

"Only because I need another gorgeous female to wrap me around her tiny pinky."

"But what about me? I need a miniature magnificent male to bring me bugs and snakes and track dirt through the house and enchant me with sticky kisses."

Tony nuzzled her neck. "Then, Mrs. Lucano, I guess we'll have to take whichever God gives us as the perfect gift."

"Hopes and dreams, Mr. Lucano, bundled in a toothless smile and trusting eyes."

"We'll have to work hard to be worthy of that trust."

"Work? Oh, yes. But worthy? Only by grace, sweetheart."

DISCUSSION QUESTIONS

1. At the beginning of the story, Desiree is using work to cover her grief over her dad's death, rather than dealing with her emotions. What avoidance mechanisms do we sometimes use to keep from confronting the real issues in our lives?

2. President Montoya compliments Desiree's perceptiveness to see the deeper motives behind Greybeck and Sons' smear campaign, rather than being swept away by emotions that could blind her to the real root of the attack. Often we are tempted to become caught up in battling flesh and blood. What Scriptures admonish us to look beyond the person to the dark forces working through them? What methods can we use to combat those forces while walking in love toward those who behave badly toward us?

3. Tony runs into a sticky situation with his ex-partner's prayer request about the woman Steve wants to marry. Tony strives to convey the truth without giving offense. Did he succeed? Could he or should he have responded differently? Have you run into similar difficult situations with people who seek your prayers but not your Lord? How did you handle those situations?

4. Culture and environment can be huge factors in the choices we make. Zapopa's grandson must choose between honoring his grandmother, as his culture dictates, or giving in to the

hopelessness of his environment and staying with the gang. In this instance, the former path happens to line up with Scripture, and the latter leads to destruction. There are times when both culture and environment can steer us wrong, and we must rise above those factors in order to follow God's Word. Name ways for good or ill that your culture or environment has molded you and influenced your choices. Name ways that you have defied those influences in obedience to Christ. Name ways that you need to change in order to resist culture and environment and live a life pleasing to God.

5. When Tony is in a coma, he faces a grave choice—continue physical life or go on to be with the Lord. How much of a factor is our will in these matters of life or death? Later in the story, what nonphysical battle must Tony win in order to assure his full recovery? How important are our attitudes about ourselves in determining outcomes in the issues of life? Give examples from the Bible that illustrate this concept.

6. Why do you think Desi had so much trouble calling Tony's mother "Mom"? Was Max's advice good in telling Desi to be patient until that right moment came? Do we sometimes trip up our relationships with others by trying to force things, or conversely, by resisting a call to deepen a relationship? What finally broke through the barrier in Desi's heart and cemented her mother-daughter relationship with Gina?

7. How did you feel about Tony's gift to Desi on their wedding day? What healing revelation did that gift inspire in her heart? Share a time when a gift in season changed your life.

8. Tony and Desi have a deep conversation about the gang mentality. Do you agree with Desi's assessment that hopelessness is a prime factor influencing young people to form and join gangs? Why or why not? How important is a sense of hope to any person, group, culture, or race? What does the Bible say about hope and the human spirit?

9. El Jaguar does evil because he likes it. Clayton Greybeck appears to be a victim of upbringing and circumstance. For which person do you feel the most compassion? Why? Is that a purely human assessment? How does God evaluate evil?

10. At the end of the story, Tony states that he and Desi must work hard to be worthy of a child's trust. Desi counters that work is involved, but worthiness is only by grace. What does she mean by that? How do we walk out that balance of work and grace—especially in our attempts to influence children for good?

Jill loves to hear from readers. Please e-mail her at
jnelson@jillelizabethnelson.com or visit her online at
www.jillelizabethnelson.com for an opportunity
to sign up for her newsletter.

—⁂—

Other Novels in the To Catch a Thief Series
Reluctant Burglar
Reluctant Runaway

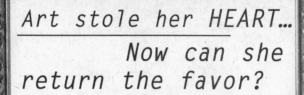

Art stole her HEART...
Now can she return the favor?

When Hiram Jacobs is murdered, the responsibility for his internationally renowned security company falls upon his daughter, Desiree. But a container full of stolen paintings screams the ugly truth—that her father was a thief. Can she trust God to guide her down the right path when no option seems right...let alone safe?

STOLEN Indian artifacts...
A *MURDERED* museum guard...
A *MISSING* woman...
A baby in *DANGER*...

Only Desiree can unearth the horrifying secret that links them all.
From the streets of Desi's beloved Boston to the mountain desert of
New Mexico, Desi and Tony must rely on God to thwart unseen
forces—and save a young woman and her baby from a villain more
evil than any of them can imagine.